D1339805

BY JEFF GRUBB

Star Wars: Scourge

STAR WARS™
SCOURGE

JEFF GRUBB

arrow books

Published by Arrow 2012

4 6 8 10 9 7 5 3

Copyright © 2012 by Lucasfilm Ltd. & ™ where indicated.
All rights reserved. Used under authorisation.

Excerpt from *Star Wars: X-Wing: Mercy Kill* copyright © 2012 by Lucasfilm
Ltd. & ™ where indicated. All rights reserved. Used under authorisation.

Jeff Grubb has asserted his rights under the Copyright, Designs and
Patents Act 1988 to be identified as the author of this work

This novel is a work of fiction. Names and characters are the product of
the author's imagination and any resemblance to actual persons,
living or dead, is entirely coincidental

This book is sold subject to the condition that it shall not,
by way of trade or otherwise, be lent, resold, hired out,
or otherwise circulated without the publisher's prior
consent in any form of binding or cover other than that
in which it is published and without a similar condition,
including this condition, being imposed
on the subsequent purchaser

First published in Great Britain in 2012 by
Arrow
Random House, 20 Vauxhall Bridge Road,
London SW1V 2SA

www.starwars.com
www.randomhouse.co.uk

Addresses for companies within The Random House Group Limited can be
found at: www.randomhouse.co.uk

The Random House Group Limited Reg. No. 954009

A CIP catalogue record for this book
is available from the British Library

ISBN 9780099542667

Penguin Random House is committed to a sustainable future for
our business, our readers and our planet. This book is made from
Forest Stewardship Council® certified paper.

Printed and bound in Great Britain by Clays Ltd, St Ives plc

To Kate, my Lovely Bride, who is known
in the better parts of the galaxy as Dr. Bunny Pierce,
and who is legendary for hitting golf balls
off the flight deck of her Imperial Star Destroyer.

ACKNOWLEDGMENTS

The events in this book were first detailed in the *Tempest Feud* game product for the *Star Wars* Roleplaying Game, from Wizards of the Coast, written by Jeff Grubb and Owen K. C. Stephens and edited by Christopher Perkins and Duane Maxwell. They occur in 19 ABY, in the time period between the founding of the Jedi praxeum on Yavin 4 and the coming of the Yuuzhan Vong.

The author would also like to thank Olivia Luna and Scott Hungerford for additional feedback and comments.

Do not attempt Jedi mind tricks at home.

REBELLION
0–5 YEARS AFTER
STAR WARS: A New Hope

Death Star
Shadow Games

0

> **STAR WARS: EPISODE IV**
> **A NEW HOPE**

Tales from the Mos Eisley Cantina
Tales from the Empire
Tales from the New Republic
Allegiance
Choices of One
Galaxies: The Ruins of Dantooine
Splinter of the Mind's Eye

3 YEARS AFTER STAR WARS: A New Hope

> **STAR WARS: EPISODE V**
> **THE EMPIRE STRIKES BACK**

Tales of the Bounty Hunters
Shadows of the Empire

4 YEARS AFTER STAR WARS: A New Hope

> **STAR WARS: EPISODE VI**
> **THE RETURN OF THE JEDI**

Tales from Jabba's Palace

The Bounty Hunter Wars
    The Mandalorian Armor
    Slave Ship
    Hard Merchandise

The Truce at Bakura
Luke Skywalker and the Shadows of
    Mindor

NEW REPUBLIC
5–25 YEARS AFTER
STAR WARS: A New Hope

X-Wing
    Rogue Squadron
    Wedge's Gamble
    The Krytos Trap
    The Bacta War
    Wraith Squadron
    Iron Fist
    Solo Command

The Courtship of Princess Leia
A Forest Apart*
Tatooine Ghost

The Thrawn Trilogy
    Heir to the Empire
    Dark Force Rising
    The Last Command

X-Wing: Isard's Revenge

The Jedi Academy Trilogy
    Jedi Search
    Dark Apprentice
    Champions of the Force

I, Jedi
Children of the Jedi
Darksaber
Planet of Twilight
X-Wing: Starfighters of Adumar
The Crystal Star

The Black Fleet Crisis Trilogy
    Before the Storm
    Shield of Lies
    Tyrant's Test

The New Rebellion

The Corellian Trilogy
    Ambush at Corellia
    Assault at Selonia
    Showdown at Centerpoint

The Hand of Thrawn Duology
    Specter of the Past
    Vision of the Future

Scourge

Fool's Bargain*
Survivor's Quest

*An eBook novella
**Forthcoming

THE STAR WARS NOVELS TIMELINE

NEW JEDI ORDER
25–40 YEARS AFTER
STAR WARS: A New Hope

LEGACY
40+ YEARS AFTER
STAR WARS: A New Hope

*An eBook novella
**Forthcoming

DRAMATIS PERSONAE

Angela Krin; lieutenant commander, CSA, and captain,
  Resolute (human female)
Eddey Be'ray; spacer (Bothan male)
Hedu; matriarch of the Bomu clan (Rodian female)
Koax; aide to the Spice Lord (Klatooinian female)
Mander Zuma; Jedi Master and archivist (human male)
Mika Anjiliac; businessbeing (masculine Hutt)
Popara Anjiliac; Hutt lord (masculine Hutt)
Reen Irana; spacer (Pantoran female)
Toro Irana; Jedi Knight (Pantoran male)
Vago Gejalli; adviser to Popara Anjiliac (feminine Hutt)
Zonnos Anjiliac; businessbeing (masculine Hutt)

A long time ago in a galaxy far, far away. . . .

DEATH OF A JEDI

The Pantoran Jedi Toro Irana was angry. He had been waiting on this hellhole planet for weeks now, and as his former Master, Mander Zuma, was all too fond of telling him, Toro's patience was never his most admirable trait. Meetings had been set up, canceled, rescheduled, moved to new locations, and canceled once again. And now, on top of everything else, his contact was keeping him waiting, in this rooftop restaurant, forty stories up and overlooking a planetary graveyard. By this time, Toro's patience had worn thin.

Toro could feel his blue skin itch and his lips swell. He reached for the bottle of scentwine to pour himself another round.

Even at the best of times a late arrival, a delay from decision and action, would frustrate him. Now, on the world of Makem Te, it drove Toro to distraction. The air of this planet reeked of smelter dust and desiccated meat. The world itself was dominated by the Tract, a huge iron-shod necropolis that from space resembled an ice cap. The restaurant windows commanded a sweeping view of the crypts and mausoleums of the Tract, which to Toro resembled nothing less than rows of odd-shaped peg teeth rising from skeletal jaws. Even a setting sun, blue-green through the swirling dust, could do nothing to improve the view. And as for the planet's inhabitants . . .

Toro suppressed a shudder and looked over at the Swokes Swokes milling around their dining troughs. His first opinion upon making planetfall was that they were huge lumps of malformed flesh, and increased familiarity did nothing to change that opinion. They looked more melted than crafted by any environment, their pale, sagging flesh spilling from their horned heads directly to their bodies, with no visible sign of a neck. Their teeth looked like the necropolis outside, except the Swokes Swokes spent less time maintaining them, and their incisors canted outward at all angles. Their faces were otherwise flat, with a random number of nostril holes and bland white eyes set into shallow black sockets. It would give them a comical look were the species not, to the last member, bullies and thugs.

In short, they were the perfect species for this backrocket planet, the perfect caretakers of this tombstone world. And right now, every last one of them was getting on his nerves. The restaurant for this meeting catered primarily to the lumpy natives, and the tables were dominated by long troughs, into which the host poured a noxious concoction of spice-leavened boiled meats mixed with what looked like shed shinga scales and live sandbugs. There were smaller, more traditional tables around the perimeter of the room, near the windows, but he and a couple of Nikto traders two booths over were the only customers who used them—and the only customers who didn't look half melted. The temperature was set comfortable for the Swokes Swokes, which was too cold by half for Toro, and the sound of the creatures eating would frighten the old Emperor himself.

Toro downed the scentwine, since its aroma killed most of the rest of the smells in the room. He waved for the waiter, who shambled toward him.

"More of these beetle-things," said Toro, pointing to

the pile of now-empty black shells. "And some of the local swill as well."

"Timasho payen," burbled the waiter, and then shifted from Swoken to a slurred, sloppy Basic. "Pay now, blue-skin."

"I'm waiting for someone," said Toro. "Run me a tab."

The Swokes Swokes burbled something else in Swoken, then provided a rough translation. "Going off my shift, blue-skin. Pay now."

Toro swung in his iron chair and let his robe fall open, revealing the gleam of his lightsaber. His hand drifted down to touch it, but not to grasp it.

"I said," he growled, "that you should run me a tab. My contact will cover it."

The Swokes Swokes frowned, or at least tried to frown through its rolls of ash-gray fat, but it backed off and a short time later another plate of broiled beetles and a two-handled mug of the local alcohol—potent but, like everything else in this place, imbued with a mild flavor of dust and spice. Still, if he rationed out the remaining purplish scentwine, it could mask most of the stench.

Toro examined the bottle. A Rodian brought it, along with his patron's apologies. Unavoidably delayed and all that garbage. Toro was sure that it was only a gambit to establish power and control in this situation, but knowing that made the young Jedi even more irritated. Still, the wine was a rose in the junkyard, a bright floral smell among the rest of this iron-shod planet. Had to have come from offworld, he realized. Another symbol of power and control from his contact.

Across the room, two Swokes Swokes started howling at each other in high-pitched screeches. Religious argument, guessed Toro, since most of the arguments on this planet were about religion and death. Toro wondered if it would come to blows. Not that it mattered. Swokes Swokes could regenerate all but the most grievous of damage. It was one reason members of the species were prized as mercenaries, guards, and leg breakers.

Toro could feel his temples throb at the guttural shrieks across the room. Enough. Finish the drink and he would be done. His contact would have to learn that he was not the only one with power in this relationship.

Something heavy and soft slammed into Toro from behind, throwing him forward across the table. The last of the scentwine spilled from its glass, and the bottle toppled and rolled out of his grasp, falling to the floor on the far side of the table with a brittle thump, along with the double-handled swill mug.

Toro turned in his chair, to find that his assailant was another Swokes Swokes, its body bedecked in jewelry set over the vital spots. This one was higher caste, but still had the soggy, blank-faced look of the rest of its species.

The Swokes Swokes spat out something that could have been an apology, but was more likely a warning.

Toro stood up, and for a moment the room swayed beneath his feet. "Watch where you're going," the Jedi snarled.

The bejeweled alien snapped something sharp. Definitely an insult, from the way the other Swokes Swokes with it reacted. It drew itself up to its full height, about a head taller than Toro. The two stared at each other for a long moment. Then the Swokes Swokes raised a four-fingered hand to push Toro out of the way.

Drinking or not, angry or not, Toro's reflexes snapped into a set response. Half a step backward to put distance between them, his hand effortlessly unsheathing the lightsaber and bringing it up in a smooth, practiced move, thumbing the switch and deploying the blade in a single action. The Swokes Swokes had only a second to regret its action before Toro brought the blade up and cut through the creature's forearm.

The Swokes Swokes shuddered but did not cry out, instead looking at the cauterized stump of its arm with puzzlement. *Right,* thought Toro, *the species not only regenerates, but it also lacks local pain centers. Another reason they make good leg breakers.* The injured Swokes Swokes let out a howl, more from indignation than pain.

Everyone turned in their seats to see the blue-skinned Pantoran, wielding a lightsaber, and his injured opponent. As one, the aliens rose from their meals, some grabbing iron dining forks as they did so, others hefting the heavy iron stools. They converged on the pair.

The injured Swokes Swokes pushed forward, its good arm raised like a warty club. Toro danced backward, up over the iron chair and onto the table itself, bringing the lightsaber around in a smooth, level arc. The Swokes Swokes's head separated at the approximate intersection of its neck and body, spilling backward into the surging mob.

"Regenerate *that*!" Toro said. The death of the high-caste alien gave half the group pause, while it infuriated the other half. Toro noted that the two Niktos from the other table were already heading for the door—along with the waiter—but that was all he had time to notice before the mob was on top of him.

Toro spun with the lightsaber, cutting through flesh and iron with equal ease. One of the attackers had thought enough to duck beneath the sweeping blade, and grabbed Toro's sword-arm in a soft but unrelenting embrace. Toro tossed the lightsaber to his left hand and brought up a booted foot into the alien's face. The entire face gave in like soft putty, which did not seem to trouble the creature in the slightest, but the grasp on Toro's arm lessened. The Jedi drew his blade through the attacker's arm and the detached limb loosened its grip fully now, vanishing into the tumult.

Something heavy and dark flew toward him, and Toro reached up and split an iron-shod stool in two with his blade, the pieces caroming off the window supports behind him. Two more Swokes Swokes grabbed at Toro's feet on the table, but he leapt up, spinning and dragging his blade across the table's surface, separating hands from arms as he did so.

Now makeshift missiles showered Toro—stools, eating utensils, two-handled goblets and bits of food. The Jedi wove his blade through the air, cutting down the more dangerous, dodging the merely disgusting. The glass behind him spidered from the heavier missiles, but did not break. Assailants would try to get close, but he would spin and leave these missing a few appendages for their trouble. Where they wore embedded jewels, signs of status among their people, the Jedi treated them as targets, carving them from too-soft flesh.

Toro realized that he was cursing now, cursing at this planet and its people and his contact and the uncaring universe that would put him in this place at this particular time. His chin was wet, and when he wiped his sleeve against it, it came away with a bubbling, bloody froth on it. Had he been injured? Had one of these melted, horrible creatures gotten lucky against him? He snarled and his vision seemed coated in blood as well. They would all pay for attacking him.

There was movement behind him, and Toro spun and lashed out without thinking. The table, already weakened from his assaults, collapsed, pitching him forward. Toro leapt, slashing as he did, and only then realizing that he had mistaken his opponent. His foe was only his reflection in the window, caught by the dying sun.

But then it was too late and he was through the window itself, the fury of his blade sharding it into a thousand daggers from the blow. He twisted to catch the ledge but he had leapt too far, and he spun out into open, dust-strewn air, forty stories above the necropolis.

The entire way down, all Toro could feel was the anger.

A MYSTERY ON MAKEM TE

Mander Zuma pursed his lips as he moved through the back alleys of Makem Te. He was far from the Tract, far from the necropolis that dominated this world, far from the site of Toro Irana's death.

And far from satisfied with what he had discovered so far about the death of his former apprentice.

Word had reached Yavin 4 and the new Jedi Order in the form of a complaint from the Congress of Caliphs that ruled Makem Te, of a blue-skinned Jedi who had killed a Caliph's nephew. Apologies were made through the New Republic's diplomatic channels, but Mander was pulled from his regular duties in the Archives and dispatched to find out what had really happened.

His assignment made perfect sense to Mander. He had taught Toro in the ways of the Force, and had monitored the young Jedi's own reports back to the Order. His own skill set dovetailed nicely with Toro's assigned mission. Yet the older Jedi was still reluctant to leave behind the Archives, to leave Yavin 4 after years of diligent and productive research.

What Mander found on this planet surprised him. Not that Toro had gotten into a fight—the young man had been headstrong and easily riled even when he had been his apprentice, and the Swokes Swokes were by all reports a prickly species to deal with. But the idea that Toro had gotten into an argument so easily, or that he had made such a fatal mistake in combat, troubled Mander deeply as he made the long trip from Yavin to Makem Te. As he stepped off the shuttle and breathed the dusty air of this world, the questions swirled within him. What had gone wrong? Had it been his training that had been at fault? Had Mander prepared him insufficiently? Or were there other factors at work?

As a student, Toro had been a superb warrior—limber and smooth, a blue-fleshed blur in combat. More important, he bonded with his lightsaber, treating the blade as an extension of his self. Even in training, Mander was impressed with the young Pantoran's skill and confidence.

Mander himself had none of that easiness in combat. The Force was strong in the older Jedi, but it was directed elsewhere. He could feel the energy moving through him, but his own lightsaber often felt like an alien thing, a lump in his hand. He had come to the Force late in life, as did many in the later years of the Empire, and it showed.

Toro was better with a lightsaber, and Mander was sure that he would have become a fine Jedi Knight. A better Jedi Knight than he. But now Toro was dead and Mander was not sure why.

Mander's first stop was to claim the body and examine it, a rented medical droid at his side burbling commentary. The dried flecks of blood on his apprentice's lips and the broken bones along one side of his body spoke of a sudden, violent end. But there was also a darkening of the young man's veins and arteries—violet against the sea-blue of his flesh—that had not be present in life, and pointed to an external agent at work.

Further, purple crystals budded at the corners of Toro's eyes. Mander was not sure if this was natural to the Pantorans in death, but he assumed it was not, and took a sample of the material. It had a pungent aroma, more cloying than the acrid dust of Makem Te's air. There were similar crystals in the dead Jedi's darkened veins, now stilled of pulsing life. Something had been injected or ingested, he decided.

Toro was under the influence of something else before the fight, Mander thought, and possibly the two events were tied. The older Jedi double-checked his evaluation before consigning Toro's body to the funeral pyre. The Swokes Swokes, regardless of their official indignation, were extremely helpful with funeral arrangements. It was a point of pride for them.

Mander Zuma visited the scene of Toro's death, the restaurant. It had been closed for a period of mourning for the Caliph's nephew, but already the smashed furniture had been stacked to one side for recycling and a new sheet of plate glass installed, replacing the one shattered by Toro's exit. The wait staff was initially unhelpful, but Mander's modest knowledge of Swoken, the native language—combined with a bit of the Force in the voice—helped smooth out the questions. By the end of the interview the staff was positively chatty about the incident.

Yes, the blue-skinned Jedi had been there. He was waiting for someone, he had said. He had been drinking. A lot. Local stuff, but a Rodian came in with another bottle. A gift. The Jedi had insulted the staff. Insulted the other diners. He had gotten into an argument with Choka Chok, the Caliph's nephew. The Jedi pulled his lightsaber and killed Choka Chok. Killed five more regulars as well, and had left a dozen regenerating. Screaming in that weird, liquid-sounding, offworlder Basic. Not a proper language at all. Foaming at the mouth. Then he had smashed his way through the window. The wait staff thought he was trying to escape, but had forgotten he was forty floors up. The joke was on him. No, no one had found the Jedi's energy blade, or at least reported that they had found it. Yes, yes, they had the bottle the Rodian brought somewhere around. They were still cleaning up the mess.

The Swokes Swokes provided the bottle and Mander calibrated his medical datapad. A few simple tests on the dregs in the bottle confirmed his hunch—there was something unusual in the scentwine. Potent, unknown, and similar in composition to the crystalline tears at the corners of the corpse's eyes. Distilled out, it had the same cloying smell. The wine's bouquet covered the smell.

Poison, then. The Rodian brought the wine. Was the poison what clouded his judgment at the end?

The possibility left Mander concerned. Why was Toro unwary enough to drink the wine in the first place? A Jedi in the field had to be aware of his surroundings and potential attacks. Had he trusted the Rodian, or whoever the Rodian represented? And what, if anything, did this have to do with his assigned task, to acquire the navigation coordinates for the Indrexu Spiral? Was someone trying to stop the New Republic from gaining those codes? Or had Toro stumbled onto something else?

Indeed, scanning the last communications from Toro to the new Jedi Order had been troubling as well. They had been brief, even terse. He had made initial contacts. He had begun negotiations. He was pleased with the progress. Nothing to indicate that there was a problem. Even so, there was a brusqueness in his communiqués that now gave Mander pause. Details were missing.

Now the trail led to this warehouse, made of ancient wood, reinforced with the cold iron that was so much a part of Swokes Swokes architecture. There were few Rodians on Makem Te, and it was relatively easy to track Toro's deadly wine steward back here. A Rodian family cartel ran a small trade out of these warehouses, trafficking in ornate funeral plaques and reliquaries and other offworld items.

The darkness of the alley cloaked him more effectively than any mind trick, but the lock was old and stubborn, and at last Mander used the Force to snap the hasp. So much for getting in and getting out without leaving any trace, he thought. Carefully, he slid the door open, but was met only with a hollow echo of the sliding metal. He slipped inside, leaving enough of a gap that he could leave quickly if things went bad.

Mander moved quietly at first, but, it was quickly clear that no one seemed to be present. Moonlight from the frosted skylights overhead shone on a bare floor. Mander reached into a vest pocket and pulled out a set of magnaspecs—two pinkish lenses set in hexagonal frames. He unfolded the lenses and placed them on the bridge of his nose; magnets in the frame held them there, pinching his flesh slightly. When he tapped the side of the lenses they issued a soft, pale red glow, heightening the available light in the dim warehouse.

Large wooden racks stood in neat ordered rows from floor to ceiling along the length of the structure. Empty cargo containers were lined along one wall, and a trio of manual loadlifters—great walker engines with huge spatulate hands—along the other. These Rodians were too poor, or too cheap, for droid-operated versions. The shelves were heavily laden with blank epitaph plates and bolts of funeral shrouds, all covered in a thin coating of dust. Scraps and more dust were heaped in the corners as well. Whatever business was being done out of this warehouse had precious little to do with mortuary arrangements.

In the center of the room was a pile of broken crates, damaged and abandoned in a rush to clear out. Clear spots showed where other crates once stood, and the dust was disturbed by the broad feet of the loadlifters. Somewhere far off, in some connecting warehouse, there was a soft thunder of people moving crates, but this place was devoid of workers.

Mander frowned. Whoever poisoned Toro expected someone to come after them, and had probably decided to put a few planets between them and their pursuers. No doubt the warehouse was under an assumed name and behind three shell companies. Tracking them down would not be easy.

Mander poked through the trash with his toe—funeral robes and tapestries, metal plates with Swokes Swokes memorials—about three or four containers' worth that had been breached and abandoned. And there, glittering in the moonlight, something dark and crystalline.

The Jedi knelt down next to the pile and examined the crystals. They were purplish, dark almost to the point of being black. He sniffed it, and it gave off a rich, pungent aroma. Spice, but unlike any he had seen before. He pulled out a plasticlear envelope and scooped a handful of crystals into it.

That was when he knew he was not alone. It could have been a shadow against the moonlight or a footstep landing too heavily, but at once he knew that someone else was in the warehouse with him. He rose slowly from his examination, trying to move naturally, his hand fumbling with the strap of the lightsaber. Still, he engaged it and brought the ignited blade up, glowing green, before the first blaster bolt erupted.

Mander parried the energy discharge, trying to send it back to his attacker but succeeding only in deflecting it among the racks of epitaph markers. Inwardly he cursed at his lack of skill. Another shot unleashed, again from near the warehouse's entrance, and again Mander turned the energy pulse aside, but only just, and it scorched the wall behind him. Mander reminded himself that he was in a wooden building containing flammable funeral shrouds. Too many such stray shots would be a bad thing.

"I can do this all day," he lied to the darkness. "Why don't you come out and we can talk?"

There was a shadow against the doorway, and for a moment Mander was sure that his assailant would try to flee. Instead, a lone figure walked into a rectangular square of moonlight. Smoke swirled from the barrel of her DL-22 heavy blaster. She was almost Mander's height, and even in the pale radiance Mander could see that her flesh was a rich blue, marked with yellow swirls on each cheek. Long hair—a deeper blue in shade, almost to the color of night—was worn short in the front, woven in a thick braid down the back. A Pantoran, then, like Toro. Her lips were a thin, grim line and her eyes flashed with anger.

"Why are you shooting at me?" said Mander calmly, as if being shot at in a warehouse were a common occurrence for him.

"I'm here for justice," she said, and the barrel came up. Despite himself, Mander brought up his lightsaber in defense, but she did not fire.

"Justice is good," said Mander, trying to keep his voice casual. "I'm seeking justice as well. Perhaps you'd like to help me find some." He paused and added, "You know, I once trained a Pantoran in the ways of the Force."

This time she did shoot, and Mander almost toppled back onto the pile of trash bringing his blade up. Almost too late, and as it was he deflected the bolt upward instead of back. There was the distant crash of a shattered skylight.

"You're the one responsible for Toro's death, then," said the Pantoran, her words as sharp as a vibroblade's edge.

"Relative?" asked Mander, willing himself to be ready for another shot. It did not come.

"Sister."

Mander forced himself to relax, or at least give the impression of relaxing. He deactivated his lightsaber, even though he wasn't sure he could reignite it fast enough should she choose to fire. "You're Reen Irana, then," he said. "Toro spoke to me of you."

The blaster jerked toward him for a moment, but the Pantoran did not fire. Mander added quickly, "I was not here when Toro died. I was back at the academy on Yavin Four. I came here when we heard the news. To find out what happened. And to finish Toro's assignment."

The blaster wavered, just a bit, but at last she pointed it away from the Jedi. Even in the moonlight, he could see a wetness glistening at the corner of her eyes. "It's your fault," she managed at last, her voice throaty with grief. Mander waited, giving her time to gather her thoughts. When she spoke again, the iron had returned to her words. "Toro was a dreamer, and you took him to become a Jedi and now he's dead. You're responsible."

Mander held his palms out and said simply, "Yes."

Reen was startled at the admission. She had apparently expected the Jedi to say many things, but not this.

Mander looked hard at the young Pantoran—he could see the resemblance to Toro in her face. He continued, "Yes I am responsible. Every man's journey is his own, but I did train your brother, and he was here on Makem Te on Jedi business. So yes, we . . . I . . . put him in harm's way. And . . . I failed to prepare him for what he faced here. That is why I am here. I want to find out who poisoned your brother, to see justice brought against them."

For the first time, the Pantoran seemed confused. "Poison?" she managed.

"I believe so," said Mander. "I found something strange in his blood. And now there is this." He held up the clear envelope with the crystals. "I found it here in the warehouse."

The Pantoran kept her blaster aimed at the Jedi, but reached out with the other hand. Mander held the envelope out to her, and she took it, taking a few steps back immediately in case this was a trick.

Reen stared at the purplish crystals, then shook her head. She holstered her blaster, and Mander returned his now-inert lightsaber to his belt.

"I think it is the poison that was used," said Mander. "A Rodian administered it with some wine he brought to your brother in the restaurant. That was why Toro was unable to defend himself at his full abilities. Why he made such a mistake in combat and plunged out the window."

Another noise in the darkness around them. Mander's head came up. It was not from outside the warehouse this time. Inside. Someone familiar with the area, who knew where to step. "Hold on," he said. "Others are here."

Reen began to say, "Don't worry. That's just—" But her words were cut off as Mander grabbed her and pulled her down. Blaster bolts erupted from three sides, firing into the pile of abandoned crates.

Reen had her own blaster out in a flash, and for a wild moment Mander was afraid she was going to use it on him. But instead she returned fire against the assault, using the discarded shipping containers as cover.

Mander rose to a crouch, his lightsaber ignited and at the ready. The shots were heavy but not well placed, and he managed to bounce a few of them back. There was a shout of pain, and a string of curses in Swoken. Mander thought he must have gotten one of them.

"I'd say a dozen," shouted Reen. "Some of them up on the racks. Swokes Swokes. Some Rodians, too."

"Must be the Rodians that use the warehouse," responded Mander.

"I know the clan," said Reen, bringing down a pair. "Bomu family. I recognize the facial tattoos. We're pinned down!"

"Hang on," said Mander, "I'm going to level the playing field."

Reen may have said something but Mander didn't pay attention. Instead he leapt forward, somersaulting toward one of the racks the Rodians were using as a perch. Blaster bolts fell around him, but he didn't use his blade to block. Rather, he pulled it effortlessly through the rack's iron supports, slicing the metal easily. The entire set of racks shuddered, and then began to collapse in on itself, the shriek of the metal matched by the surprised shouts of the ambushers.

Reen was at his side. "What did you do?"

"I made a new pile of trash to hide behind," said Mander as one of the surviving Swokes Swokes rose from the debris, a thick-barreled blaster in his hand. One swipe with the blade cut the weapon in two, and then the Swokes Swokes fell backward as Reen discharged a bolt squarely into the attacker's face.

There was a short pause in the battle, and then the blasterfire started again, heavier than before. Looking back, Mander saw that their previous hiding place was on fire, and the flames were already spreading through the bolts of funeral cloth and to the room's supports. The Rodians had climbed down to the ground, trying to surround the pair. They were now clear in the firelight.

"They're trying to burn us out. Can you make it to the door?" asked Mander, but Reen just shook her head and brought down a Rodian from across the room.

Mander looked across the open floor between him

and the entrance. Alone, on his best day, he might be able to make it. Carrying the Pantoran, he doubted he could get halfway before the cross fire caught him. He was about to chance it anyway when something extremely large shifted in the background.

It was one of the manual loadlifters, wading into a squad of Swokes Swokes. The huge flat feet smashed one, while the others broke and ran as it spun and slammed into another set of racks, toppling them against their neighbors in a chain of collapsing shelves. The Rodians and Swokes Swokes started pulling back, firing behind them to deter pursuit. Perched in the control pit of the lifter, limned by sparking control screens, was a Bothan—long-faced and furry.

Reen put a hand on Mander's shoulder. "Don't worry. He's with me."

The Bothan was having trouble handling the load-lifter, and as he tried to get the walker under control it grazed one of the already-burning roof supports. The support groaned menacingly, and parts of the roof and skylight started to cascade down around them.

"About time you showed up!" bellowed Reen at the pilot of the stumbling walker. "Now get us out of here before this place comes down around us."

The Bothan got the loadlifter under something like control, and brought one of the large pallet-hands level to the floor. Reen grabbed on, and Mander leapt ahead of her, turning to help her up. Then the pair gripped the sides of the lifter as the Bothan maneuvered it toward the doors through a tunnel of the now-flaming ware-house. The large door was still almost completely shut, but at the last moment the Bothan spun the lifter around and slammed through it backward, smashing the door off its hinges.

Then they were outside, tromping through the alleys. The loadlifter got clear of the worst of the fire, and set the pair down. The Bothan himself slid down from the side of the now-smoking control pit. Whatever the Bothan had done to get it working had set its internal electronics on fire.

"I thought you Jedi were never supposed to be surprised," said Reen.

"I was distracted," said Mander, trying to keep the irritation within himself out of his voice. She was right. Despite her presence, he should have noticed their assailants creeping into their positions.

In the distance there were shouts and klaxons. The local authorities were responding to the fire, and the flames were clear along the roofline now.

"We need to be elsewhere," said Reen. "A pity we didn't get one of the Rodians alive."

"We found the poison that they used on your brother," said Mander. "And we know that they're willing to kill to cover their tracks. For the moment, that's enough."

Dejarro of the Bomu clan made his way through the Swokes Swokes bazaar, past the hucksters selling memorial mementos and purified ointments and funeral wreaths. Past the stalls of seers and spiritualists who, for a small fee, would contact the spirits of the recently interred and, for a slightly larger fee, confirm that they were resting comfortably and satisfied with their funeral arrangements. Dejarro squeezed his way among the lumbering forms of the Makem Te inhabitants, his own Rodian frame unlikely to win any shoving match. He kept one hand inside his jacket, tightly gripping his heavy prize, fearful that something else would go wrong.

The word had come down that afternoon: Koax, the one-eyed Klatooinian, had arrived on the planet, bearing with her both the goodwill of her master, the Spice Lord, and the lordship's demands that the assigned task had been completed.

Dejarro of the Bomu clan carried both good news and bad along with his package, and it was a good question which of the three was the heaviest weight.

At the fourth street, at the alchemical shop, he turned right and made for a singularly empty shop that displayed funeral wrappings but had never seemed to succeed in selling any of them. The Swokes Swokes behind the counter, scarred from many regenerations, just nodded to him as he passed through. Dejarro had been here before. The Rodian climbed the iron spiral staircase to a windowless upper storage room.

The room was lit by a single bulb, hanging from a noose-like cord. Koax was waiting for him, surrounded by racks of long-sleeved robes, used to dress the dead before interment or cremation. To Dejarro, it felt like they were surrounded by silent witnesses to hear his report. There was a low table between the two of them.

The Klatooinian herself was lean and muscular, thinner than most of her species. She was dressed in dark red spacer's slacks and a vest, and kept a set of ceremonial throwing knives on her belt alongside her blaster. Dejarro knew the Klatooinians were mostly traditionalists, favoring the old weapons and ways. Koax apparently kept the affectations of the past alongside the more effective present.

The Klatooinian's face was thin as well, but what took Dejarro aback was the crater where one eye had once been. Some would have worn a patch, or had a plate bolted to their skull to hide the deformity, but Koax set a glowing red gem deep into her empty socket. The Rodian wondered if the gem allowed the Spice Lord's agent to see into alien frequencies or tell if someone was lying. The idea chilled Dejarro to the bone.

"*Waajo koosoro?*" asked the Klatooinian in fluid Huttese. Have you brought it?

Dejarro nodded and pulled the prize from beneath his

jacket. It was a thin cylinder fitted with a worn, comfortable grip along one side. It was heavier than Dejarro had thought it would be, particularly since he had seen it used with fluid, almost effortless grace. Heavy enough to hold the soul of a man, he had thought at the time.

He placed the lightsaber on the table between them.

Koax looked down at the device with her good eye, but did not reach out for it. The red gem set deep into her skull kept a bead on Dejarro, who waited to be dismissed or questioned.

"Were there any problems?" asked the Klatooinian.

"We found it on the street," said Dejarro, his voice sounding a little strained in the dusty dead air. "Not too far from the body."

"Did anyone see you take it?" She was still examining the deactivated blade before her.

"I don't think . . ." And Koax looked up at him, her gemstone eye blazing for a moment. "No! No. No one saw it. It went better than we had planned. I had the wine delivered, and we were prepared to move in when he started a fight by himself. Once he went out the window, we were afraid we had lost him. That he had used some sort of *Jeedai* trick to escape us. That he could fly away. But when we got to the bottom of the building, there he was, dead, and the item was right beside him, just as you see it now."

Koax grunted an affirmation, then said, "We?"

"The other members in good standing of the Bomu clan," said Dejarro. "Trusted family all. We would have taken the body itself, but the local law was already coming down on us. As it was, I grabbed the lightsaber and kept it, until I heard from you. Kept it safe, like you ordered."

"Did you turn it on?" asked Koax, almost casually.

"No, no," Dejarro assured her. "I don't know if it still

works or not. I just followed your orders. Drug the *Jeedai*. Take his lightsaber. Bring it to you. Nothing about figuring out if it worked."

Koax gave a throaty chuckle and reached out to the lightsaber, grasping its short hilt and activating the blade. It sprang like a genie from the bottle, a bolt of brilliant blue-white, accompanied by a flash of radiant thunder. The empty robes that hung around them threw back deep shadows, doubling their number.

Koax moved the blade back and forth, and it looked to Dejarro as if the blade fought her, like it had its own inertia—its own spirit—resisting her control, fighting her grip. Koax seemed to feel it as well, and frowned, then thumbed off the blade. At once the upper storage room was plunged back into a dim light, which to the Rodian seemed even darker than before.

"Good," said Koax, and reached for her belt. Despite himself, Dejarro's hand twitched toward his own weapons belt, but the Klatooinian instead brought out a vial tucked between her belt and her dun-colored flesh. Koax smiled, and it was not a pleasant smile. She had made Dejarro flinch, and understood in an instant how much the Rodian trusted her.

How much he feared her.

Koax set the vial on the table. Even in the dim light Dejarro could see that it was tightly packed with purplish crystals, deeper in hue than any he had seen before.

"Pure," said Koax. "None of that diluted garbage that reaches the street. Cut it, share, use it, I don't care. We're done."

Dejarro looked at the vial, then up at the Klatooinian, then nodded, reached out, and snagged the vial. He tucked it into an inner pocket and said, "There's something else."

Koax's eyebrow, the one above the gem-set socket, jerked upward slightly. "Something else?"

"It took you a while to contact us," said Dejarro. "While we were waiting, there was another."

"Another?" Koax repeated, her voice careful, trying to draw the story out.

"Another *Jeedai*," said the Rodian. "Came to the restaurant. Talked to the staff. Tracked us back to the warehouse."

Koax held her hands out, palms outward. "Didn't you think to burn out the warehouse and move your supplies, just to prevent that possibility?"

"We were in the process . . . that is, we intended to. But we didn't think he would get here before you," managed Dejarro.

Koax frowned and looked at the empty table once more. "Tell me what happened."

"We ambushed him," said Dejarro quietly. "Ambushed the *Jeedai*."

"Did you kill him?" said Koax, and her intent was clear in the tone of her question: One dead Jedi on Makem Te was a casualty. Two would attract more attention than the Spice Lord would want.

"We lost a lot of people. The *Jeedai* . . . he had backup, and he . . ." Dejarro froze when Koax transfixed him with the ruby eye.

"*Did* you *kill* him?" she repeated.

"No," said Dejarro, looking away. "There was a firefight. The warehouse caught fire in the battle."

"Too little, too late," said Koax. "You should have torched the place the night the first *Jeedai* died."

Dejarro nodded. "We didn't want to lose the stock. We had a lot of funeral supplies there."

Then Koax did something that Dejarro did not expect. She laughed. It was a full-throated, hearty, honest laugh, the laugh of someone confronted by the basic stupidity of the galaxy. "You kill a *Jeedai,* then are surprised to find another one comes looking for him. You let this new *Jeedai* uncover your operation, resulting in a firefight and setting the warehouse ablaze, and you're worried about the *stock*?"

Dejarro himself managed a sickly chuckle and said, "We're tapped out now, except for . . ." He tapped the vial in his pocket with his palm.

"I see," said Koax, pulling her features back into a stern repose. "So you need . . ."

"More of the hard spice. More Tempest," said Dejarro. "We can make it up to you. Just a little advance. Enough to keep the regulars stocked up. We did what you asked for. We didn't expect the *Jeedai* to bring backup."

"I don't think the Spice Lord will be happy about this development. Do you think that's the case?" asked Koax.

"If you want, I can talk to the Spice Lord," said Dejarro. "Explain things."

"The Spice Lord has more important matters to deal with than talking to street-level dealers," said Koax. "That is why the Spice Lord has me." She skewered him with her good eye, and a silence grew between the two.

"So." Dejarro's throat was dry now. "Do you think you could do something about this?"

"Yes, I think I could," she said. "I think I could warn the Spice Lord that there is another *Jeedai*. One with allies. I could also find out who these allies are, and tell you. Is that what you would want?"

Dejarro nodded. "The *Jeedai* killed my clanbrothers and clansisters," he said. "We need vengeance on their behalf."

"Consider it done," said Koax. "You have my word— the Bomu clan will get its vengeance against this *Jeedai*. But I will warn you, if the *Jeedai* killed so many of your clan just at the outset, there will be more lives lost before you get your vengeance."

Dejarro nodded enthusiastically. "Yes, yes, we know.

It is the price you pay for vengeance." The Rodian turned to leave the Klatooinian with her prize.

"One last thing," said Koax, and Dejarro froze in his tracks, turning slightly.

"I will have to tell the Spice Lord that we have this problem because the Bomu clan neglected to cover its tracks sufficiently," said Koax. "And I will have to report that I have taken appropriate action." The Klatooinian's hand drifted to her weapons belt.

Dejarro pulled his blaster, and if Koax had been going for her own, he would have beaten her to the draw. Instead, the Klatooinian pulled one of her throwing blades, and in a graceful, almost casual flick of the wrist, planted it deeply in the Rodian's neck from five paces away. Dejarro went down, gurgling.

Koax liked to think that last noise was an attempt at an apology.

The Spice Lord's agent knelt over the dead Rodian and pulled the small vial—the last pure sample of Tempest on Makem Te—from Dejarro's inside pocket. Then she pulled one of the death robes from its hooks and draped it solemnly over the body.

"Another victim of this new *Jeedai*," said Koax. "But I am good to my word, and will gladly throw as many of your clan in his way as I need to." She let out a deep sigh.

"But first," continued the one-eyed Klatooinian, "I will have to send a message to the Spice Lord, presenting the bad news. And let me tell you, Rodian, that you got off easy in that you had to deal with me instead of the one I serve."

CHAPTER TWO

NEGOTIATIONS

They sat quietly at the table: Mander Zuma, Reen Irana, and the Bothan. The three had headed away from the sirens, and after half an hour they found themselves at a Swokes Swokes tapcaf that specialized in "outlander cuisine"—or at least the Swokes Swokes's best guess of it. The establishment was missing the traditional trench down the center of the room, but the tables were still massive and, Mander noted, bolted to the floor.

They sat across from one another, the clear envelope with the crystals between them. Reen Irana stared at it like it was a live snake, fascinated and horrified. Her Bothan companion, who had not spoken a word during their fight or their later flight, was looking around the tapcaf. He looked like an impatient, easily distracted puppy, but Mander realized that he was checking out all the exits and making sure that they had not been followed.

"This is what killed my brother," she said at last. She sounded defeated.

"Likely," said Mander. "There were strange crystals at the corners of your brother's eyes, as well as in his blood."

She ran her hand through her dark blue hair. In a soft voice she said, "His blood. How was the rest of him? What did you discover when you examined his body?"

Mander was surprised by her directness. "I don't know if you would really be comfortable knowing the details . . ."

"Tell me!" she snapped, and several heads in the tap-caf turned their way. The Bothan looked at her and frowned. She nodded agreement, then said, more quietly, "What else did you find in the body?"

"Purplish crystals at the corners of the eyes and mouth," Mander said quickly. "Darkening and expansion of the veins and arteries. In addition to the damage from such a fall. And there was a surprising rigidity in the muscles. He was angry when he died."

The Pantoran slumped in her seat and bowed her head.

Mander looked at the now-concerned face of the Bothan, and back at the Pantoran. "I committed the body to the flames, as is the custom of our Order. Had I known you were in the area, I would have waited." There was no response.

Mander tapped the envelope and said, "It is definitely a spice—it dissolves easily, and could be put into the scentwine the Rodian brought him. I think that is how the poison was administered."

Reen Irana's shoulders shook, and at first Mander thought she was sobbing. Instead, he realized that it was a sharp, mocking laugh. "Poison?" she said, and her jaw stiffened. "If only it was simply that."

At once Mander realized that he had been mistaken. Reen Irana knew something more than he. What had he missed? He decided to wait for the Pantoran to tell him, and the silence grew between them.

When she finally spoke, she fought to control her words. "Are you Jedi all this naïve? This isn't just a poison. This is a narcotic. A hard version of spice. It's called Tempest."

Mander looked at the packet. Now he regarded it like a serpent as well.

Reen leaned forward and continued, "Spacers have been seeing this spice throughout the spiral arms. Along the Perlemian Trade Route and Hydian Way—even in the Corporate Sector and Hutt space. It's used either mixed in drinks or as an aerosol. It's a spice, but a nasty one—addictive and destructive. Heavy users are marked by a darkening of the blood vessels—you can see them through the flesh. They also . . ." She paused for a moment, thinking of her brother, before continuing. "Addicts are also prone to fits of uncontrollable rage."

"Like that which Toro showed in the restaurant," Mander said quietly. "It still could have been used as a poison."

Reen shuddered and shook her head. "It wasn't a poisoning. It was an *overdose*."

Mander blinked. He could not imagine Toro using a dangerous drug.

But before he could say anything, Reen continued. "The rage is a symptom of long-term use, as is the darkening of the blood vessels. The last few holos I've received from Toro—he was angry, upset. He blamed the Jedi for sending him out to the middle of nowhere. Felt he was getting a runaround from his contacts. He sounded bitter, frustrated. It wasn't like him. I didn't think about it at the time, but ran into a mutual friend on Keyorin, another Pantoran. The friend said that Toro looked sick, and had gotten angry when asked about it."

"Sick," Mander said. A statement, not a question.

Reen looked away from Mander. "He said that Toro's veins were showing dark through his flesh."

"You think he was already addicted," said Mander. He felt the air go out of him. It was one thing for young Toro to give in to a momentary flash of anger. It was another if he had been using a drug all this time, without anyone knowing.

No, he corrected himself. Without Mander or the Jedi Council knowing about it. Toro's sister knew, or at least suspected.

"I came here to confront him, to find out if he was okay," she said, making a gesture of frustration. "We were not . . . close. I left for space before he left to join your Jedi. But he was family, and I was worried."

"And you came here and found that he was dead," said Mander, hoping his voice covered what he felt inside.

"And that *another* Jedi was here, asking after him," said Reen. "I didn't know if you had been working with him, or looking for him as well, or . . ." She let her voice trail off.

"You didn't know if I was the one giving him the Tempest," said Mander flatly. Reen nodded, her mouth a thin line.

Mander said, "Your brother was on Makem Te at the behest of the Jedi Order. That is true. But his assignment had nothing to do with spice in any form."

"He was supposed to meet someone in the restaurant," said the Pantoran.

"Probably someone to do with his mission," said Mander.

"Or perhaps his source for the drug," said Reen.

Mander sighed. "Any evidence that would be at the warehouse is gone now. We can probably track down the Bomu clan, though. There aren't many Rodians on Makem Te."

"The Bomu clan is strictly small-time," said Reen. "They are scattered across a dozen worlds like this. They hire out to just about anyone. They would be middlebeings at best."

Mander suggested, "Still, they're our best hope for finding out where this drug, this Tempest, is coming from."

Reen thought for moment. "It is a pretty large clan, and provides muscle throughout the quadrant. Their scams vary from planet to planet, and sometimes different parts of the clan work for rival crime lords. The one thing that pulls them all together is vengeance. Take out one of them, and you can have the entire clan on your back in no time."

"I will remember to add them to the list of the Jedi's enemies," said Mander wryly.

The conversation stopped as the waiter, a lumbering Swokes Swokes, came with their meals. The waiter also set three small iron cups on the table, bubbling with what Mander hoped was an infusion of Ansionian tea, or at least the Makem Te equivalent. Once the waiter left, Mander noticed that the bag containing the Tempest crystals was missing.

He looked up sharply at Reen, who was staring into her cup as if the future lay there. Then he looked at the Bothan, who returned his glance with a gangly grin and reached into his vest, producing the envelope, which he handed back to Mander.

Mander put the envelope back into his own robe pocket, "Yes, we shouldn't leave things like this out to be found. And thank you for your help in rescuing both of us, earlier."

The Bothan raised both hands in an expression of *What else could I have done?* Reen looked up and said, "Sorry, I didn't make introductions. Eddey Be'ray, here, is one of the best mechanics in this part of space. He can hot-wire just about everything, from a speeder to a battle cruiser."

"Or a manual loadlifter," added Mander. "Does he speak?"

"Only when I have to," replied the Bothan, in a deep voice with an educated, Core accent. Despite himself, Mander blinked in surprise. It was not the voice he expected to come out of the furry muzzle of a Bothan.

"Eddey believes that when you don't say much, people forget about you, and they let things slip," said Reen. "Once he comes to trust you, he's positively chatty."

Again, the Bothan retreated into mime, raising both hands in a comical shrug and dug into a krayt steak.

Mander nodded. The intelligence-gathering abilities of the Bothan people were legendary. He turned back to Reen. "What can you tell me about the Tempest drug itself?"

"Not a lot," said Reen. "It showed up less than a year ago, and suddenly it's all over the place. At first it was like any other type of spice—used for medicinal and, um, recreational purposes."

Mander nodded for her to continue.

"Tempest is one of the really bad ones," said Reen, lowering her voice now and leaning forward. "It's extremely addictive, and long-term users are clearly marked. Like a lot of spice, it makes the user feel good, but at a price." She paused a moment, then added, "I need to ask. The Jedi, in your studies, do you use . . . you know?"

The question surprised Mander Zuma. He pursed his lips and said, "No." Another silence stretched out between them, and he added, "Some types of spice provide boosts in telepathy or empathy, but always at a cost of control. No Jedi would seriously use spice when dealing with the Force." Another silence, and even Eddey had stopped eating. Reen's eyes were unfocused, and her mind was wrapped up in a now-distant memory. The Jedi could imagine what she was thinking about.

Mander added, "I am very sorry about your brother."

"Even before I came here," she said, "I knew I had

lost him. I had lost him to his dreams. I had lost him to the Jedi. And I had lost him to the spice."

"Toro's mission to Makem Te had nothing to do with spice," Mander repeated. "He was here to negotiate for a set of space coordinates. I don't know how or why he became involved in Tempest. Regardless, I *am* sorry."

She looked into the Jedi's unwavering eyes. "I believe you," said Reen after a moment, and went back to picking at her steak. Then she looked up. "I'm sorry for shooting at you."

"You would not be the first," Mander said. The three ate in silence.

After a few moments, Reen said, "Where does that leave us?"

Mander suppressed a shrug. "I don't know if it leaves us anywhere. The spice that he used has been destroyed, along with its local distributors. I want to find out where the spice came from, but I also must finish Toro's mission, and I don't know if one is tied to the other. But someone else may want those coordinates, and someone definitely knew about Toro's . . . addiction, and deliberately spiked the wine with an overdose. That means I have competition for what I need, and must act quickly."

Reen did not look up from her meal. Then, as if realizing something for the first time, she said, "You said he was looking for space coordinates? Doesn't seem like much of a mission for a Jedi."

"They are for the Indrexu Spiral," said Mander in a low voice.

Both Reen and Eddey looked up, and Reen let out a low whistle. "The Indrexu Spiral? That's a knotty bit of space. It's a swirling maelstrom of proto-stars and dark matter just looking for ships to blow up. Even spacers who make the Kessel Run know better than to try it. Who would have been foolhardy enough to have mapped it?"

"That I do not know," said Mander. "But I do know who has the coordinates, and that Toro was supposed to meet with them in orbit above Makem Te."

Reen looked at him thoughtfully. "Once you get the coordinates, you'll need someone who knows the space lanes to confirm them."

"I know my galactic navigation," said Mander. "I've studied the relevant texts on my way here."

"Meaning you've never programmed a navicomp, have you?" Reen's eyes lit up. "Probably had some droid do it. It's an art form, you know. You mess up the numbers and . . . well, it's not pretty, that's all."

"Are you volunteering to help?" asked Mander, and the Bothan made a coughing noise like the steak was going down a breathing tube.

"Not volunteering," said Reen, ignoring her companion. "If Toro was killed for Jedi business, then it makes it my business as well. If someone overdosed or poisoned him to keep him from these coordinates, I'd like to meet them."

"And if they decide to come after me, you'd like to be there," said Mander.

Reen gave a shrug, and stabbed at the last of her steak. "You're my best lead," she said.

"Do you have a ship?" asked the Jedi.

Reen hesitated with the large forkful of steak and set it down on the iron plate. The Bothan was grinning, but said nothing.

"Well," said the Pantoran, suddenly more circumspect, "yes and no."

"How much yes and how much no?" asked Mander.

Reen said, "There *is* a ship—the *Ambition*. But it's not what you would call . . . functional." The Bothan was making a chuffing noise that Mander could swear was chuckling.

It was Mander's turn to raise his eyebrows. "How nonfunctional is it?"

"Extremely nonfunctional," said the Bothan, and there was clear amusement in his voice.

"It is in a couple of pieces," started Reen.

"More than a dozen major ones," added Eddey. "Not counting the—"

"A *few* pieces," corrected Reen, staring daggers at the Bothan. "Just a few pieces. Back on a landing pad on Keyorin. *If*," she added quickly, cutting off Eddey Be'ray, "they haven't sold it off for scrap to pay for the berthing fee." The Bothan merely smiled and folded his furred hands in front of himself.

"Ah," said Mander. "So you are stranded here. But someone with the coordinates for the Indrexu Spiral . . ."

". . . and the ability to check them out . . . ," Reen put in.

". . . would be able to write their own ticket," finished Mander. "Sounds fair enough. Yes, I think an experienced pilot would be helpful. If I get the coordinates and they check out, you can have them as well. The Jedi don't have much in the way of material belongings, so consider it Toro's bequest."

"He's giving in too easily," said the Bothan. "There has to be a catch."

"There is," said Mander. "The catch is the people who have the coordinates, the ones who kept Toro jumping through hoops for weeks."

"So my brother was negotiating with tough customers," said Reen. "How bad can they be?"

Mander said, "Toro was negotiating with the Hutts."

Now it was the previously calm Bothan's turn to react, his eyes wide and his fur raised from the crown of his head back along his spine. "You can't be serious?" he managed.

"Completely," said Mander. "I know that the Bothans and the Hutts have bad blood, so if you want to back out at this point, I would understand."

Eddey opened his mouth to reply, but Reen beat him to the punch. "Bad blood isn't the problem. Bothans and Hutts are natural competitors. The problem is that you can't trust *any* Hutts. Period."

"I believe the one we are dealing with can be trusted," said Mander.

Reen stifled a laugh and said, "The only people who tolerate the Hutts are those who have to work for them, and even then they work very hard to keep them at an arm's length. Every single Hutt is a criminal and a thief. Their entire civilization is built upon the powerful stealing from the weak. They survived the destruction of their original homeworld, Varl, and proceeded to steal another one from a less powerful species. Now Nal Hutta is a haven for the crime lords, and its moon, Nar Shaddaa, is rife with corruption."

"Granted," said Mander. "But the Old Republic dealt with the Hutts when they had to, and in this case the benefits were considered worth it. And if all Hutts are untrustworthy, that means you can depend on what they will do."

"They are predictable," said the Eddey Be'ray. "That is a far cry from dependable."

"You're making a mistake dealing with them in the first place," said Reen. "If you want my professional opinion."

"And in your long experience," said Mander, "you've never dealt with Hutts?"

"That's the point," countered Reen. "I *have*. And it is a job best done through middlebeings and fixers with strong stomachs and weak morals. It is not a question of *if* a Hutt will betray you, but *when*."

"So you're saying no, then?" Mander asked with a sigh.

Eddey made to say something, but Reen overrode him again. "I'm *saying* that you had best be careful. They're not like most of the other sentients you encounter out here on the Rim. Their brains don't even work the same way as everyone else's," she said. "And they're resistant to your Jedi mind tricks,"

"I have reliable information to that effect," said Mander. "I believe that it is one reason they are willing to deal with the Order. They feel we are at a disadvantage in negotiations, both with our limited ability to affect them and our tendency to deal with people fairly."

"In other words, *you're* predictable," muttered Eddey.

Reen ignored him. "They will stab you in the back at the first hint of a profit. And Hutts deal in spice," she said firmly.

"They do," said Mander. "So the question is: Do *these* Hutts deal in *that* type of spice?"

Reen bit her lip, and the Bothan watched her as the wheels turned. At length she said, "Do you think that this is involved with my brother's death?"

Mander shook his head. "You said that, not me. I don't have enough information one way or another. A rival group may be after the coordinates, and they gave your brother the overdose. Or it may be for some other matter he was investigating. Toro's reports were brief, so it could be that he became involved in investigating this Tempest himself. In any event, I can use someone who understands the possible perils, and you seem to meet that requirement. Are you still interested?"

Reen looked at Eddey, and if the Bothan communicated anything to the Pantoran, it eluded Mander's senses. But after a moment, she nodded. "We're in. Tell us about this 'trustworthy' Hutt that you poor, naïve Jedi have been dealing with."

"These Hutts belong to the Anjiliac clan. Have you heard of them?" Both of them looked at him blankly. "They are not one of the ruling clans, but are on the next level down, socially. The patriarch is Popara Anjiliac, and he is the one who has the navigation codes."

"Any idea where he got these codes in the first place?" said Reen.

"No," said Mander, "although it's not hard to speculate. The Anjiliacs are a trading clan, and apparently spend a great deal of effort in discovering new items and markets. The idea that someone in his employ discovered . . ."

". . . or stole . . ."

". . . or otherwise acquired the codes is not beyond reason.

"Popara and the Anjiliacs have a good reputation," continued Mander, adding quickly, "*Good* obviously being relative when dealing with Hutts. He is ancient in Hutt terms, and has built a reputation for straightforward trade. From all our reports, he is sharp but honest in his dealings, and always gets what he wants. He pays his people well, and has a surprising amount of loyalty."

"Luxury," said Eddey Be'ray, and the other two looked at him. The Bothan finished the last of his meal and said, "Hutts would see loyalty—or treating one's workers well—as a luxury, as much a status symbol as a humanoid dance-slave or a storied piece of holo-art. If this trustworthy Hutt cannot own entire planets, the ability to engage in such extravagant actions would be a conspicuous display of power."

Mander nodded. "I hadn't considered that as a possibility."

Reen put in, "Keep this in mind—the Hutts have no words in their language for 'thank you.' The best they can manage is *Bargon u noa-a-uyat che tah guma*— Your services will be rewarded."

"I know enough Huttese to get by," said Mander. "Even taught a bit to your brother. That is one of the reasons why he was chosen for this particular mission." Despite himself, Mander frowned at the reminder of sending Toro off. He pressed on. "Regardless, Popara Anjiliac has a good reputation, and I think we can trust him."

Reen looked at Mander a long moment, her head tilted. At last she said, "What kind of Jedi are you?"

Mander blinked for a moment, confused by the question. "What do you mean?"

Reen's eyes narrowed. "You didn't know about the Tempest. And you're negotiating for a set of space coordinates. With a *Hutt*. A Hutt that you're willing to trust."

"Your brother was willing to trust this Hutt," said Mander calmly, his face a mask now, belying his irritation.

"And look where that got him," she retorted. Then she realized what she had said. A shocked look crossed her face and she turned away.

Mander was unsure what to say. He looked at Eddey Be'ray, and the Bothan nodded at him to continue.

"A Jedi goes where he is needed," said Mander. "Your brother, regardless of his fate, knew this. I taught him that, as I myself was taught. I will finish Toro's task and, if I can, bring those responsible for his death to justice. I would appreciate your help." He looked at the Bothan. "Both of you."

Reen looked up and pushed the night-blue hair back across her forehead. "You'll *need* our help, if you're going to survive out here in the real world. You have to drive a hard bargain with the Hutts. Anyone who would trust a Hutt needs someone to keep them from walking into walls or falling down a well. It might as well be us."

The Bothan nodded, and Mander said, "Very well, then. Welcome aboard."

Reen leaned forward on the table and templed her fingers together. She said, "So when do we meet this 'good Hutt' of yours."

"First thing tomorrow," said Mander. "Popara's yacht should pull into orbit this evening. I am supposed to meet his factotum at the starport at dawn. Berth Y-27. Meet me there and you'll get a chance to draw your own conclusions."

POPARA THE HUTT

"*Uba sanuba charra mon,*" said the Hutt factotum, looking at the trio over the top of a heavy set of data goggles. At the Hutt's side, a protocol droid made of greenish metal translated. "You said you would be coming alone," it said in a neutral voice, lacking inflection.

"Do the Hutts consider members of one's entourage as independent beings?" countered Mander, his face an unconcerned mask. He had reviewed the available volumes on Hutt customs and society before he had left Yavin 4. "Or are they merely extensions of one's own will?"

The factotum had a greenish cast to its flesh, and its long lashes batted at Reen, Mander, and Eddey. A female, realized Mander, or rather a Hutt in female state. The great slug-like creatures could be either gender, and manifested secondary sexual traits differently throughout their lives. The idea of calling one male or female was usually left to the observer. The Hutts themselves seemed to be unconcerned about whether they were male or female at any moment. Indeed, many of their titles such as *Lorda,* or "master," were considered gender-neutral.

This one's head seemed to be narrower and taller than most as well, looking more like a spear point than a flattened triangle. She continued, speaking in the sibilant tongue of Huttese.

"And you are the previous Jedi's replacement in the negotiations?" translated the droid, an H-series 3PO unit. The Hutt's lackadaisical manner indicated that she didn't care if he was or not.

"I was his teacher," said Mander. "And I came to finish the task he was assigned."

The factotum punched a few toggles on her pad, then adjusted her data goggles up over her eyes. The goggles' oversized lenses made her eyes look huge, even for a Hutt. Surprisingly, the next time she spoke, it was in Basic, albeit in a halting fashion that communicated nothing so much as distaste for doing so, as if the words were bitter in her mouth. "I am Vago Gejalli. I am mighty Popara's . . . chief adviser, majordomo, and factotum. Benevolent Popara is . . . very busy, so most of your dealing will be with me. Treat me with the respect . . . that wise Popara has earned."

"Of course," said Mander, and the Hutt turned and slithered toward the shuttle. Mander turned to the others, and was struck by the scowls they both wore.

"You can still stay behind," he suggested.

"I would not miss this for all the spice on Ryloth," said Reen.

"Just remember, let me do the talking," Mander said. "Later I will ask about your impressions."

They boarded the ship, and Mander watched the jade-green 3PO unit organizing the stowage of supplies: rant-weed clusters, pickled zog, norrick loaves, and many kegs of Kashyyyk ale. The last was interesting, even in the larder of a Hutt epicure.

The shuttle lifted off smoothly from the spaceport, the ship helmed by a team of Gluss'sa'Nikto. The Pale Nikto spoke to one another in a low, atonal language but reported to Vago in Huttese. Mander did not doubt for a moment that the factotum was fluent in Nikto as well as in Basic, and did not doubt that she would rather sprain her tongue than speak it. The Hutt settled herself onto a great cushion along the back wall of the ship and busied herself with her datapad and goggles. It was as if Mander Zuma and his entourage had ceased to exist, having no more importance than the ale kegs.

Mander watched the sprawl of the Tract, the unlimited graveyard of Maken Te, extend out to the horizon as the shuttle rose. To Vago he said, "We appreciate benevolent Popara's willingness to continue negotiations in this matter even after Toro Irana's passing."

Vago responded without looking up from her pad, the droid translating. "You may thank efficient and diligent Vago for that kindness. Most of the negotiations were through her offices. The previous Jedi was fairly effective, and the offer tendered through him remains sufficient, regardless of who offers it."

Reen looked at the Hutt. "Then you knew my . . . I mean, you knew the previous Jedi."

Vago looked up at Reen and blinked, her eyes magnified beneath the data goggles. She looked at Mander as if expecting him to cuff an insolent subordinate for speaking out of turn. When the older Jedi did not, she huffed and muttered a reply in Huttese, the droid translating.

"He dealt through our agents, and I believe he met both of Popara's spawn at one time or another. He never met gentle and wise Popara, if that is what you are getting at. He was fairly effective, as I said." She then returned to whatever she had on her datapad, the Pale Nikto crew droning in their native languages as the ground dropped away beneath them. Eddey remained quiet, taking everything in. Reen and Mander watched the sky darken beyond the viewports and the tomb-dotted horizon turn into a planetary curve.

There was a sparkle about the edge of the curve, which grew as they approached from a solitary pip of light into the dagger-shape of an Ubrikkian space yacht. The long, tapered bow cut like a knife blade among the stars, and the navigation spars bracketed the four rear engines. This was an air-breathing craft, and could land on a planet, should Popara Anjiliac ever deign to put common dirt beneath his belly. Even so, the ship was buffed to a reflective brilliance.

Mander did not doubt that there were at least half a dozen turbo-blasters concealed along the length of the bow, and that the shuttle was being tracked in the yacht's crosshairs as they approached.

Vago snapped off her datapad and readjusted her goggles. *"Imru Ootmian,"* she said, then translated in Basic: "The *Wandering Outlander*." Then she barked an order in Huttese and the shuttle nestled itself at the belly of the yacht. The hissing of seals confirmed the docking, and Vago led the group to the lift tube, the green droid fussing among the Pale Nikto behind them, readying the cargo for transfer.

The lift tube itself was opulent, with mirrored walls, mosaic crystal floors, and door irises made of muskwood. Vago seemed supremely disinterested in both her surroundings and her companions. The door hissed to a stop and spiraled open.

The hatch revealed the hulking form of a Wookiee, who pushed his way into the tube without waiting for the others to depart. Reen and Mander stepped back, but Eddey held his ground, and the Wookiee was brought up short, towering over the smaller Bothan. The two locked eyes, and for that long moment it looked like the Wookiee would attack. Mander could smell the alcohol on the Wookiee's breath, and realized that this was why they were bringing on more ale from Kashyyyk. Finally, the Bothan stepped away and let the Wookiee shamble in, away from the Hutt. For her part, Vago slipped past the drunken Wookiee and shepherded the others down the hall.

"One of young Zonnos's companions," she said, without further explanation, biting off the words in Huttese. "There will be others on board."

The end of the hallway was another great door of muskwood, this one with settings of silver. Another green 3PO unit, this one a bit more dented and battered, stood by the door. Apparently, thought Mander, it hadn't gotten out of the Wookiee's way in time.

"Announce us," Vago said in Huttese, and the protocol droid snapped to attention and hand-palmed the lock, the hatch irising silently outward. In Basic, the droid crackled, "His most mighty and powerful lord, his most wise and generous master, his most understanding and thoughtful leader, Popara Anjiliac, Popara the Hutt."

The room was dark in the manner that Hutts preferred, and wafted with the smells of smoke and slightly spoiled meat. The room itself was Hutt-sized, with three great alcoves along the other walls. All three were sumptuously furnished with rich tapestries and thick cushions. Mander noted briefly that the one on their left was empty, but the one on their right held a large young Hutt laughing with a trio of Wookiees. Empty kegs and used hokuum pipes were scattered about. But he had scant time to take that in, for Popara the Hutt occupied the central alcove.

Mander knew that Popara was old—nine centuries if the data disks had been correct—and had the wiliness of one who'd had to fight to survive every year. Hutts grew continuously throughout their entire lives, and Popara was enormous, his flesh marked with gray patches and old whitened scars of earlier conflicts. His eyes, though, were as brilliant as a morning on Yavin 4. Three green-hued Twi'lek females in long, diaphanous robes dabbed him with perfumed sponges, and one of them broke from her ministries as the massive Hutt let out a low, almost animal growl.

"Chowbaso, Jeedai," said the old Hutt, and the floor itself vibrated from the deepness of his voice.

"Wise Popara bids you welcome," said the Twi'lek, flashing sharpened teeth as she spoke.

"Dobra grandio Ma Lorda Popara Anjiliac," said Mander Zuma, wrapping his tongue around the difficult glottal stops of the Huttese. I am honored, my lord Popara Anjiliac.

The great Hutt made a deep rumbling comment, and the Twi'lek handmaidens giggled. The tallest one said, "He says that your accent is horrible. He understands your language, and it is apparent you understand his. Shall I continue to translate for you and spare you further embarrassment?"

"Please," said Mander, "for the sake of my companions, if not just clarity for me."

Another flash of sharpened teeth, and the Hutt made another deep comment. "Puissant Popara declares that the offer the new Jedi Order has made for the coordinates of the Indrexu Spiral is sufficient."

"I am pleased that it is so, and appreciate Popara's willingness to part with it." Mander nodded.

Another deep rumble, which the Twi'lek translated as "Knowledge is like water—hard to contain once it has been unleashed. Though he notes that if you have a Bothan in your party, such knowledge will not be kept secret long." She looked daggers at Eddey, who merely held up both palms in that *Who, me?* response that Mander had already become accustomed to.

Mander started to say that the coordinates would help many, but the ancient Hutt let out a string of belches. "Sage Popara would, however, like to expand the deal we have agreed to. Mighty Popara bids you serve his family."

"Here it comes," said Reen under her breath.

Mander ignored her. "Please continue."

A long string of Huttese followed, sounding like a hot spring covered with mud. The Twi'lek's forehead creased as she sought to remember it all. "Concerned Popara notes that there is a plague on the planet Endregaad, on the far side of the Indrexu Spiral. The world is close to the Corporate Sector Authority, and the CSA has placed it under quarantine, interdicting all ships in and out. The plight of the Endregaadi has touched beneficent Popara's heart, and he wishes to make a gift of medicinal spice to the world. The CSA will have nothing to do with dealing with Hutts, and Popara regrets that their lack of appreciation may cause greater suffering. You will be provided a ship carrying the spice with the coordinates already locked into the computer."

Mander shot Reen a look at the mention of spice, and the spacer's eyes were wide. She started to say something, but was drowned out by the return of the Wookiee from the lift tube, the huge creature bearing a keg of ale underneath each burly arm and shouting a welcoming cry. The other Wookiees in the smaller Hutt's alcove responded in kind, and Mander took the opportunity to touch Reen on the shoulder and shake his head. The factotum Vago might tolerate such an interruption, the shake said, but it would be unlikely that Popara would, despite his stated benevolence.

For his part, the older Hutt unleashed a caustic tirade of abusive gutturals at the Wookiees and the younger Hutt. While the Twi'lek did not translate any of the exchange, Mander did not need to know Huttese to understand a parent berating a misbehaving child. The younger Hutt looked wounded, and he and the Wookiees settled into muttering, the new returnee pointing at Eddey in particular.

Addressing the Twi'lek, Mander said, "On behalf of

the Jedi and all caring and concerned peoples of the galaxy, we thank Popara for his generosity, but question his
interest in but one planet, and inquire if there is not
something else he needs us to be aware of."

The Twi'lek took a short, insulted intake of breath,
but the ancient Hutt let out a deep sigh and spoke in a
low tone to his translator, who then addressed Mander.
"Mighty Popara has seen two of his spawn grow to ma-
turity. Zonnos, here, is the elder of the two." She made
an almost imperceptible head-nod toward the Hutt and
his Wookiee entourage. "His youngest child is Mika.
Mika Anjiliac was on Endregaad when the plague hit,
and the CSA interdicted the world. There has been no
word of him since then, and Popara, a caring parent, is
concerned. The child is . . . impetuous."

Mander nodded and said, "I understand his concern
for one of a younger generation. We will be glad to see
delivery of the medical supplies and determine what
happened to your son."

"We keep the ship," Reen interrupted.

Mander shot her a sudden, shocked look, but the older
Hutt merely chortled. "Of course," said the Twi'lek.
"When gracious Popara expanded the deal, he meant to
expand both the risk and the reward. The ship will be
more than sufficient payment for this favor."

Popara the Hutt shifted forward on his cushions, his
great girth hanging over the sides, towering over Mander and the others like an avalanche of flesh. His eyes
softened, and for a moment he looked very, very old and
alone. In a quiet voice, he said, in Basic, "Bring me back
my son." Then he settled back, and it was as if the moment had not happened. He was no longer a concerned
father, merely a Hutt employer. Two of the robed Twi'leks
dabbed at him with scented fluids, and the third asked,
"Are you amenable to this addendum?"

"We will do our best," said Mander.

"Vago Gejalli will see to your needs," said the Twi'lek, and the great Hutt closed his eyes to mere slits—a sign that the audience was at an end.

"*Bargon u noa-a-uyat,*" Popara said, by way of benediction: You will be rewarded.

"Your thanks, the coordinates, and the ship are reward enough," said Mander. He turned, leading the two others through the muskwood doors.

In the hallway, the H-3PO unit directed them down to a meeting room. Reen leaned in close to Mander and said, "I told you that you need to drive a hard bargain with the Hutts."

"And I told *you*," said Mander, "to let me do the talking."

The briefing room was better lit but equally sumptuous, with raised ramps along one wall and a table and chairs more suitable for hominids in the center. Tasteful but opulent statues stood in niches along one wall. Reen examined one made of a rose-colored mineral depicting an incongruous Hutt emerging from a sweeping fountain of water. Reen reached out to touch a finger to the delicately carved foam.

Vago, behind them, spat out a string of Huttese. The slightly dented green H-3PO unit trailed after her like a moon in the Hutt's tidal wake. The droid said, "That statue was presented to mighty Popara to commemorate the successful birth of his youngest child Mika. It is carved of a single emradite crystal. Such statuary would often be protected by virulent contact poisons, but that one has been detoxified." Despite the nontoxic assurance, Reen pulled back her hand.

Vago ignored her and moved over to the table, toggling a switch. A holodisplay illuminated the schematics of a ship in the center of the table. It was shaped like a blunted arrowhead.

"This vessel is waiting at landing pad X-13 on Makem Te," said Vago through the droid. "It is being loaded as we speak."

Reen's attention was on the ship at once, the statue now forgotten. "That's a Suwantek TL-1200 freighter," she said. "Dependable model, easily modded and customized. Can be handled solo, but flies better with a crew. Two quad laser turrets. No custom work that I can see. Bit dinged up. It will do." She nodded her approval to Mander.

"Better condition than our last ship," muttered Eddey, punching up a detailed schematic.

Vago ignored both of them and handed Mander a datapad. The droid translated. "The medicinal spice will be loaded into the aft compartments. We don't know the specific details of the plague itself, so the spice is a broadband antisporant and pain suppressor."

Reen's head popped up from checking the ship's stats. Mander saw her jaw tighten slightly as she asked, "Does All-Wise Popara do a lot of trade in spice?"

Vago looked over her data goggles at the Pantoran, then shrugged. The droid translated without comment. "Some. Mostly medicinal. This is not the first time Great Popara has directed spice to handle a crisis. He also ships glitterstim when he chooses to speculate on the market."

"Nothing . . . worse?" said Reen. She tried to keep the words light, but Mander could see the shadow of a disapproving frown.

The Hutt factotum's eyes narrowed, and the droid hesitated before translating. "No. Benevolent Popara chooses not to deal in slaves or in hard spices. He sees that there is enough misery in the galaxy without adding to it, and enough opportunity that he may gain wealth without contributing to that misery."

"Regardless," said Mander, "I think we should check

the cargo before we get to Endregaad. It would be embarrassing to be found running contraband. The CSA in particular takes a dim view of spice smugglers."

Vago made a chuffing noise. "Understood," said the droid, taking the datapad from the Jedi. It handed the 'pad to Vago, who punched a few more buttons and handed it back. "This clears you to access the crates, and allows you to determine that they are what we claim them to be."

"I am sorry if I sound untrusting," said Mander.

Vago's face was a blank, offering no more clue to her thoughts than the droid translator. "Not at all. Hutts have a . . . shall we say, reputation . . . in such things. One assumes that all Hutts are criminals, just as all Bothans are spies." Despite himself, Mander shot a glance at Eddey, who was poring over the ship schematics and paying no apparent attention to any of them. Reen had joined him in investigating the plans.

"Wise Popara is no fool," Vago continued through the droid. "He has survived clan wars and assassination attempts, and has found a position of strength in honesty. That is one reason to deal with the Jedi. Your Order does not leap to conclusions quite as rapidly as others."

"We try to keep open minds," said Mander.

Vago let out a snort and spoke in Huttese, holding up a hand to instruct the droid not to translate for the others. In Huttese she said, "Pity that the CSA does not follow your example. We have hit a wall dealing with them. Zonnos himself has taken over the negotiations, and hasn't gotten much farther. In the meantime, Popara is distracted by his missing son, and the business suffers. And that makes it my worry."

"Hmmm," said Mander in Basic. "You are not worried about Mika?"

"I worry about Popara and his lineage," said Vago, choosing her words carefully. To Mander it seemed that the Hutt wanted him to hear the words without going through a translator. "Benevolent Popara inspires loyalty, and hopes to make that loyalty his gift to his children. Zonnos is more typical of our species, but Mika has potential. I think that is why Popara is . . . concerned."

"You are not Anjiliac clan, are you?" asked Mander. He shot a glance at his two companions, but they were still looking at the schematics. He wondered idly if the Bothan understood Huttese.

"No, I was spawned of the Gejalli family," said Vago.

"I am not familiar with that clan," said Mander.

"Because I am the only one in it," said Vago, her face expressionless. "I said that Popara has survived numerous clan wars. The Gejallis were among the clans that confused openness for weakness and sought to defeat the Anjiliacs. I am the survivor."

Mander raised an eyebrow. "And yet you work for him?"

Vago let out a deep sigh, and for a moment the officious mask of the majordomo slipped. "I was but a child, and by rights and tradition Popara could have ended my life. Instead he brought me in and trained me as his own. I owe him much and I want to see his true child returned to him. It is difficult to explain to an outlander."

"We outlanders understand more than you think," said Mander. "One last question: Why was Mika on Endregaad in the first place?" From the corner of his eye Mander noticed the Bothan's head come up a bit. Eddey was definitely listening now.

Vago stiffened slightly and lowered her hand, allowing the droid to resume its translation, the air of familiarity gone once more. "Family business. One of our many holdings is Skydove Freight. The office is in Tel Bollin, the main colony on the planet. Mika was negotiating with geode miners. A small task, but Popara wants his children to understand the business. No one anticipated the plague . . . or the quarantine."

"Does the other son, Zonnos, do small tasks as well?" asked Mander.

"Sometimes," said Vago through the droid, and then allowed herself a deep chuckle. "If they are not too complicated."

"Will the CSA be expecting us?"

"No. We offered aid but they turned it down," said Vago. "They will not be expecting it this soon in any event, as a normal ship would have to go around the Spiral. They will probably have at least one ship in orbit, and knowing the CSA it's probably an old rust bucket with limited maneuverability, but enough ordnance to start a small war."

"That would be expected with the Corporate Sector," said Mander.

"The coordinates should bring you in on the far side of the system. Prescient Vago recommends you run the blockade," translated the H-3PO unit. "Use some of the medicine to bribe the local officials on the ground. If you need to, offer the remaining spice to the CSA by way of an apology later. The plague is truly secondary compared with the safety of an Anjiliac scion."

Mander nodded. Popara may be described as benevolent, wise, and kindly, but the fate of a world would not matter next to Mika.

"The Anjiliac family leaves such matters to your discretion," spoke the droid. "And you will need to be vaccinated, of course. Vago will summon a medical droid. If you need anything else, this unit will see to your needs." Not waiting for the droid to finish, Vago Gejalli slithered through the door.

"Do we have enough information?" asked Mander. Reen had been drawn into the schematics. The Bothan looked up, and saw Mander pointing to the walls and to the droid. The Bothan nodded. Both of them assumed listening devices in the walls, and droids had big receptors.

"A moment, Jedi," said the droid. "There is someone else who would speak with you."

"Vago will be back soon enough, but I think we are available," said Mander.

"Not the others, I'm afraid," said the droid, looking at the Bothan. "Just the Jedi. For a moment."

Mander looked at Eddey, and the Bothan shrugged. The Jedi left Eddey and Reen going over the manifest, and followed the droid across the hall.

The warm room was dimly lit, and stank worse than the grand meeting room. As soon as he entered, two Wookiees closed in behind him, blocking the door. Two more flanked the elder son, Zonnos, sprawled on a repulsorlift couch.

The hairs on the back of Mander's neck stood up in a way that they had not in the presence of the older Hutt. The younger creature was in better shape, and although smaller, he seemed more malignant than his parent. His flesh had a bluish sheen, and even in this light Mander could see that his eyes were red and rheumy. Too much of the hokuum.

"Mighty Zonnos, may his digestion always be sound," said the droid, and the Wookiees behind them gave a laugh.

Mander said nothing, and Zonnos spat out a string of guttural noises, rounded by drink and almost impossible for Mander to translate. The droid put in, "Kindly Zonnos wants to wish you good luck on your mission and tell you that he has no hard feelings over an outlander being chosen to aid the family. This is a dangerous situation, and Zonnos wants you to know you have the support of the clan."

"I appreciate kindly Zonnos's concern, and that of clan Anjiliac," said Mander.

Another slurred garble, and the droid hesitated. One of the Wookiees smacked it across the back of the head, and it spat out, "Mighty Zonnos wants you to know that even if you fail to find his brother or—Ardos forbid—are too late to save him, you will still have an ally among the Anjiliacs."

Zonnos waited for the droid to finish, then managed a lazy, single wink. It laughed, and for a moment Mander's blood ran cold. Then the Wookiees grabbed Mander by the shoulders and forcefully escorted both him and the droid back into the hallway.

"That went better than usual," said the droid, touching its head casing where the Wookiee had smacked it. "Let us get back to the others."

When they returned, both Reen and Eddey were rubbing their shoulders from the ball-shaped medical droid administering a vaccination with a wicked-looking needle. Vago had returned as well. "Where did you disappear to?" asked the Hutt in her native language.

"Zonnos wanted to talk to me," said Mander, not waiting for the droid to translate. He figured that direct honesty was the best approach. Vago would cross-examine the droid in any event.

The Hutt factotum harrumphed and said in rapid Huttese, "Then I should make this a double dose. Exposure to Zonnos is sometimes fatal. I have included information on Endregaad, Mika, the disease itself, and what we know about the quarantine blockade." Vago focused Mander's attention so that he did not notice the ball-droid swooping around and quickly injecting him with a vaccine.

"There should be no problems with the vaccine," Vago said. She looked at the Bothan and added, "If there are any odd symptoms, contact us at once. The Threepio unit will see you are returned to the spaceport." Eddey just growled at Vago's back as the Hutt left, the medical droid swept up behind her.

"What just happened?" said Reen.

"Let's talk about it later," said Mander. "Are you ready to go?"

"I've got a ship, I've got a cargo, and I've got a lot of questions to be answered," said Reen. "Ready as I'll ever be. I've even named the ship."

"Oh? What's that?"

"New Ambition," said Reen with a smile.

"Just ignore the fact," added Eddey, "that the old *Ambition* is now so much scrap. Otherwise it is not an auspicious name at all."

"The one you hunt is named Mander Zuma," said Koax to the ghostly image. "He is a *Jeedai* of middling years and equally middling ability. Unlike most of his breed, he is surprisingly light in legends of daring that seem to accrete to these monks. He is, in short, a nondescript. Hardly a challenge for one such as yourself."

Across from the Klatooinian hovered the image of Hedu, matriarch of the Bomu clan. She was a thin, wasp-like female, made even more ethereal by the holographic projection. Behind her lurked the flickering of others shifting just at the edges of the image field—relatives acting as bodyguards, in the Rodian fashion.

The Rodian matriarch let out a long, wheezing sigh. She contained more air than her phantom image suggested. Even so, she managed to exhale a question. "You are sure he is the one? The one who killed my clanchildren on Makem Te?"

"I have confirmed it," said Koax, politely. "He made little point in concealing his identity, as the *Jeedai* priests are wont to do. He apparently was the teacher of the other *Jeedai*—the one you poisoned."

"On your orders," said Hedu.

"On the orders of the Spice Lord," said Koax, pulling her authorization around her like a cloak.

The Rodian matriarch made a gurgling, chugging noise that Koax assumed was laughter. "Perhaps the *Jeedai* hunts for his own vengeance."

Koax considered the Rodian's worldview, one of continual revenge against slights real and imagined, and thought that in this case it had merit. "Perhaps," she said. "One of his companions, definitely so."

"You have learned of his companions?" said the Rodian, her trumpet-belled antennae practically quivering.

"A Pantoran spacer, Reen Irana," said Koax. "Sister to the *Jeedai* you . . . *we* had killed."

The matriarch let out a long angry hiss, and Koax wondered if the Rodian leader had been dipping into her own private spice supplies. "Yes, that makes sense. The *Jeedai* seeks vengeance, and brings along others of a similar mind."

From everything that Koax had learned, that seemed unlikely, but she said nothing to dissuade the Rodian. "And a Bothan. They were the ones who killed your clanchildren and burned your stocks."

"Bothan," said the Rodian, and let out a string of curses. "You can always find one of them wherever there is trouble. Where are they now?"

"They are guests of a Hutt clan lord, aboard his yacht, in orbit over Makem Te," said Koax.

The matriarch stroked a few long hairs on her chin. "A carefully timed shuttle, loaded with explosives, could bring down any yacht."

"No," said Koax. "That will not do."

The matriarch seethed through the holographic connection, "The *Jeedai* has killed my clanchildren! Nothing else should stand in the way of vengeance."

"They are on a Hutt ship," said Koax calmly. "Do

you think that the protection that my lord offers is sufficient to protect you from a Hutt patriarch? It is bad enough that we have to worry about the Jedi Order. I do not want a Hutt mercantile clan prying into our business."

The ancient Rodian rocked back, hissing in displeasure, and almost disappeared from the holographic view entirely. Koax wondered if the refusal to condone the bombing had given the old raptor an aneurism. The Rodian recovered herself, though. Measuring her words as carefully as if they were grains of Tempest itself, she said, "What would you have us do?"

"I want your vow that you will not act against the Hutts," said Koax.

"As long as we have a chance against the *Jeedai* and his allies," responded the matriarch.

"Fair enough," said the Klatooinian. Her long fingers danced over the keys of the display. "They are making for the Endregaad system, in a Suwantek freighter. I am giving you the coordinates where they should appear."

Matriarch Hedu's eyes lit up at the sight of the figures, and Koax remembered that the ancient bird had been a spacer as well. She probably could outfly most of her clan. "I know these coordinates. Who is this *Jeedai*, that he walks such secret paths?"

"One favored by a Hutt consortium," said Koax. "And for that reason, if for no other, you should tread carefully. Intercept their ship on the way in. Do not do anything that would bring the Hutts down on top of our profitable trade."

Hedu chugged a deep laugh again, "Because our Spice Lord does not want to share with the Hutts, I suppose?"

"You may suppose as you see fit," said Koax, covering her lies with a thin smile.

Someone to the right of the old woman handed her a datapad. "Endregaad," she said, scanning the information. "Corps are all over it. Quarantined. Interdicted. Bad business."

"All the more reason to catch their ship on the way in, and leave nothing but debris for the Corporate Sector to find." Koax glared at the matriarch with her good eye. "Are we agreed?"

Matriarch Hedu of the Bomu clan pulled her snout inward, trying to physically stave off her acquiescence as long as she could. At last she said, "We are agreed. I can have one of our raiders in that sector within the day. There will be no survivors."

"Good," said Koax, and reached to disengage the screen. Before she could do so, though, Hedu added quickly, "I have but one question."

"Yes?" said Koax, her own patience thin now. It was always the last question, the last bit of information that created new problems. Thinking of the late Dejarro, whose death was now laid at the feet of the *Jeedai,* Koax realized it must be a genetic tic of the clan, to ask one question too many.

But the matriarch just smiled. "How did you discover all this information? Names, ship ID, coordinates? You must have some contacts among their Hutt patrons to know all this."

"The Spice Lord is mighty," said Koax, "with a great reach and powerful allies. Keep that in mind if you choose to go beyond my orders." And with that she broke the connection and the horrid, reed-thin Rodian flashed out of existence.

Koax let out a deep sigh. Would that all of her problems could disappear so easily. Tempest was now extant on half a hundred worlds, and while the Spice Lord had proven capable of meeting that great demand, there were always small matters to deal with: The local authorities. Rival gangs. Nosy interlopers trying to create, or steal, their own supply. Half a hundred worlds, half a hundred tasks too small for the Spice Lord . . . but fit entirely for that most trusted servant, Koax the one-eyed Klatooinian.

She turned back to her guest in the small room. A deactivated 3PO unit, its metallic casing the color of the green evening sky on her homeworld, was partially collapsed in one chair. Hours before, she had "borrowed" it from its Anjiliac masters as it oversaw the loading of medical supplies for Endregaad. She had walked up to it, asked it for directions, and then spoke the override code that the Spice Lord had given her. The 3PO unit froze up for a moment, then entered into a fugue state. After that, it had easily allowed Koax to walk it to a quiet quarter and find out what was going on aboard Popara Anjiliac's ship. Then she let it collapse in the chair while she did business with Matriarch Hedu.

She spoke another series of words now, and the droid reactivated, its eyes lighting up and its body suddenly shocking itself out of its dormant state.

"I'm sorry," it said, then repeated itself as its diagnostics kicked in. "I'm sorry. One moment. Something has gone wrong. Was I offline?"

"I think so," said Koax. "I found you wandering near the landing bays about an hour ago. You seemed confused. Do you remember who you are?"

"I am an H-Threepio unit in service of the Anjiliac clan. I report to Vago Gejalli. I am charged with . . ." It paused for a moment, and looked at Koax. "Do I know you?"

"I don't think so," said Koax. "I brought you here, and was just about to crack your housing and see if anything had worked loose." She held up a pair of calipers as proof of her intentions. "Then you started up again on your own. You gave me a start."

"Oh," said the droid, adding that information to its

datafiles. "I need to return to my post. They will be missing me."

"I don't doubt they will," said Koax. "Should I take you back to where I found you?"

The droid tilted its head slightly, then shook it. "I need to return to my post. They will be missing me." Gently it rocked forward and rose, as if trying to regain its bearings. It waddled to the door in the shuffle that all protocol droids seemed cursed with. It turned at the last moment and said, "Thank you."

"Do not mention it," said Koax. "But do yourself a favor and have your master run a full scan on you. Some of your couplings may be loose."

The droid nodded and was gone; back to oversee the loading, its newly rebooted subroutines still trying to understand what had happened to it. Koax had no doubt that the droid would remember nothing—she had done this before, but the slightest glimmer of possible recognition made her uncomfortable.

She went to the door and watched the droid move through the crowds of Swokes Swokes and other aliens, its movements getting more sure as it went. No, there would be no problem.

One more of the half a hundred things that had to be handled on the behalf of Koax's lord. Perhaps there would be a day where it would all just move smoothly. The arrival of the pallets of pressed and cut drugs, the distribution, the credits trickling back up through a dozen false fronts. Perhaps the Spice Lord would not need a fixer—a repair woman—someone who had the ability and coldhearted resolve to do what needed to be done to keep everything moving smoothly.

It would be nice if it happened, even for one day, Koax realized. But it was an unlikely dream, and the Klatooinian returned to her half a hundred other tasks.

TO THE PLAGUE PLANET

That evening Mander Zuma had a familiar dream, one that returned to him again and again over the years.

He was on Coruscant, in the great Jedi library, situated near the flat-topped peak of the Jedi Temple. Here were the computer terminals, here the hallways leading to the holocron vaults, here the long shelves of holographic records, here the busts of the Lost Twenty—Jedi who had left the Order. Yet something was wrong. The great-vaulted rooms were empty, and somewhere in the distance a bell tolled in long, heavy peals.

In the dream he walked. Sometimes it was hours, sometimes it only *felt* like hours. He met no one. Was this when the library was shut down, during the time of the Galactic Empire, when only the Emperor had access to the stacks, corrupting its volumes to meet his infernal needs? Was it sometime later? Where were the other Jedi? Would he find Master Tionne here?

But there was nothing except his own footsteps and the sound of the bell.

And then he noticed that the glowing holorecords of the stacks were slowly going out. Darkness was overtaking them, their blue illumination swallowed by oblivion. Turning, he saw that the rooms behind him were consumed by darkness that had now caught up with him. Around him the holorecords were dying.

Mander in his dream reached for his lightsaber, and it

felt scaly and cold in his hand. Looking down, he saw that it had been replaced by a serpent, which now coiled around his wrist. The snake opened its mouth, and in the place of fangs there were twin lightsabers, glowing with a deep ruby light.

And then he awoke and he was on Makem Te again, the heavy sun just poking up over the horizon and flooding his room. He blinked and gathered himself. The dream was the same, and it left him with the same feeling each time—a feeling of sadness, or insufficiency. Was there something he could have done in the dream? Was there something that he *should* have done? It did not feel prophetic, but rather accusatory. That he had been judged and found, not guilty, but merely unsatisfactory.

The *Imru Ootmian* had left the previous night, its next port of call wherever Popara's business took him. The *New Ambition,* as Reen had christened it, was at berth X-13, and she and Eddey had already moved into it, running every diagnostic they could think of. Reen had insisted on taking a full day to sweep the ship, stem-to-stern, for any type of bug. She would have taken another day if Mander had not made clear that they needed to be on their way to Endregaad.

Mander dressed and slowly packed his few belongings into a shoulder satchel: a spare set of clothing and the more formal robes he had worn to meet with Popara. He hefted his lightsaber.

Once again he thought about how little affinity he had for the weapon. He had built it himself, harvesting the crystal at its heart and meditating over it, imbuing it with the Force. Yet he never felt he had the connection with the device, the extension of one's own self into it. It was not a serpent, yet it wasn't a part of himself, either. It was a thing, a tool that could be used.

Mander Zuma shook his head and attached the lightsaber to his belt. Reen and the Bothan would be waiting for him. He shoved the dream to the back of his mind, where it would wait for another night to haunt him. Hoisting his satchel, he went to join his crew on the *New Ambition*.

"The ship's clean," said Reen, coming back from the cargo hold. They had lifted off from pad X-13 at the Makem Te spaceport and were now heading to the initial jump point pre-programmed into the navigation system.

She threw herself into the copilot's chair in a frustrated tangle. Eddey was at the main controls, and Mander, his magnaspecs pinching his nose, was fussing with the jump calculations, trying to make sense of the program. He had spent much of the previous day at it, and realized that Reen was correct—despite his knowledge of space navigation in theory, the complexities of implementing a real-world example were a challenge. Reen said it looked okay. He would have to trust that the calculations were correct.

Reen continued, "I've checked the cargo, the holds, and everywhere I would think to put a secret compartment. There's nothing except what they claim to be there. The medicinal spice is standard issue, though I will admit that it is of a superior grade. Nothing illegal there. Went over the ship with a bug-buster, and no trackers or listening devices. Ditto the computers. Everything is just as it is supposed to be."

"I'm glad you're happy," said Mander. He removed the magnaspecs, folded them in on themselves, and placed them in his robe pocket, over his heart.

"I'm not," replied the Pantoran, pushing an errant dark hair out of her eyes. "These are Hutts. There has to be something going on here that they are not telling us."

"There is probably much they didn't tell us," said Mander, "as well as all the things they did not tell us until the last moment."

Reen looked over at Mander. "And maybe there's more."

"Maybe," said Eddey, "no one has ever tried these coordinates before."

Mander blinked and looked at Reen. She shrugged and walked over to the Jedi's station, pointing at the unspooling code. "I'm not so sure. Most of this stuff looks like it was improvised. Pure seat-of-the-pants flying, nothing you could normally get a droid or a navbot to do. Droids are too linear in their thoughts. This is much more like the recording of a spacer who got herself into trouble and was shocked and surprised to find that she lived through the experience. But I checked the figures three times. It *should* work."

"And it would be a fairly elaborate effort just to test if the coordinates are correct. They have their own ships and pilots, and indeed, they gave us this one," Mander said. "Let's assume that what we've been told is true, and that these coordinates will take us to Endregaad."

Reen rubbed her arm where the vaccination needle had bit deep. "Speaking of trust, what do we know about this plague?"

Mander motioned toward Vago's datapad. "The Endregaad plague is so far confined primarily to Endregaad, thanks to the efforts of the Corporate Sector Authority. A smuggler's ship from the planet showed up in Rudrig, in the Tion Cluster, about three weeks ago. Its crew was too weak to land, and the ship was boarded and impounded. The CSA quickly slapped a lid down on Endregaad itself, and have one of their Dreadnoughts in orbit."

"No other cases offplanet?" asked Reen.

"Not according to this report, but the symptoms are

similar to a couple of other known diseases that come from blasted, irradiated worlds," Mander noted. "Symptoms include fever, dehydration, crusting around the mouth and ears, general weakness, and a thickening of the fingers and tongue. Repeated exposures can kill."

Reen rubbed her arm again. "I've never been to Endregaad. Is it a blasted, irradiated world?"

Mander noticed her action. "No, but it's no surprise you haven't visited it. It's hardly a tourist spot. Most of the planet is buttes, mesas, and dry washes. It is a pretty arid place, with the open bottomlands plagued by windstorms. One major city—Tel Bollin. Major product is the geode trade—crystals found within hollow rocks."

"Which is why Mika Anjiliac was there," noted Reen.

Mander nodded. "Again, from the report, it looks like it was purely routine business dealings. Then, a couple of days after he arrived, everything went blasters-up."

"And we have to find him," Reen said. "A single Hutt on a big world."

"He'll definitely stand out in a crowd," said Mander. "What do you think of his family?"

"Can't say I like any of them," said Reen. "Popara is fat, Zonnos is slovenly, and Vago acts like she owns us. That's the Hutt trifecta right there."

"Popara is honest," said Eddey. Mander and Reen both looked at him.

"I can tell," said Eddey. "It's not a Bothan ability or anything, but I can tell. Even when his words were translated through a droid. He didn't lie to you."

"But he may not have told the truth in all things," said Reen.

Eddey raised his hands, palms up.

"You had asked if Popara's clan ran spice," said Mander. "Did you get the response you expected?"

"No," said Reen, "I expected a stronger condemnation of it, if they were involved in trading hard spice. So it was a good answer, as far as they were concerned."

"A good answer," repeated Mander Zuma. Then added, "While you were sweeping the ship, I did take the opportunity of checking on the Bomu clan. No one had seen any of them on Makem Te since the night of the attack. They are all hiding, dead, or gone."

The Pantoran smuggler and the Bothan exchanged a glance—just a quick one, but enough to confirm to Mander that they had done some of their own checking when they were supposed to be readying the ship.

"Gone but not forgotten," said Reen. "Each Rodian clan spans at least a dozen planets. The survivors of our little set are likely on other worlds getting their aunts and uncles all indignant about us shooting up their place."

Mander nodded and returned to the business at hand. "Thoughts on Zonnos?"

"Reen's right," said Eddey. "Typical Hutt."

"You look up *Hutt* in a lexicon and you'll see Zonnos's picture," said Reen. "It appears he spends his time drinking his father's fortune with his Wookiee friends."

"They didn't seem to like you much," said Mander to Eddey.

Another shrug from the Bothan. "I rub some people the wrong way. Some Wookiees are brave and dedicated, some are bullies. The ones with Zonnos are the latter."

"And as you say, you can just tell," said Mander, and once again Eddey raised his palms in his *What can I do?* attitude.

"What did Zonnos want with you?" asked Reen, confident now that they were out of earshot of listening devices. "Back on the ship, when that droid pulled you away."

"Zonnos Anjiliac wanted to assure me that he had no

problem if we failed to find his brother—or failed to bring him back alive," said Mander.

"Sibling affection," said Reen. "Rivals for their father's attention."

"Zonnos fits the basic assumptions about Hutts well," Mander said, nodding. "He probably wouldn't do the deed himself, but he definitely won't be too heartbroken if something happened to Mika."

"Do Hutts even have hearts?" said Reen.

"Vago," said Mander, ignoring her and bringing up the next topic.

"Bureaucrat," replied Reen. "Petty functionary. Keeps the wheels going, and is afraid to step out of line."

"I don't think so," said Mander.

"What were you talking about in Huttese, back on the *Outlander*?" asked Eddey, clearly curious. "She didn't seem too offended by your horrible accent, by the way."

Mander looked at Eddey. It was an honest question, one he would not have asked if he already had the answer. *No,* Mander decided, *he doesn't know the language.* "She told me that Popara wiped out her family in one of their clan wars, but adopted her instead of killing her. I don't think she's just a bureaucrat. She's devoted to him, probably much more than those Twi'lek handmaidens. Vago is not afraid. But Reen is correct in one thing: she does keep the wheels spinning."

Reen counted the Hutts off on her fingers. "You think Popara is truly concerned about his son. Zonnos wouldn't mind being an only child . . ."

"And Vago wants things to run smoothly," said Mander. "She wants Popara to be looking at the balance sheets as opposed to fretting about his boy."

"So that means we go ahead," concluded Reen.

"That means we go ahead," said Mander. "Unless Zonnos and his Wookiees had the brains to sabotage the coordinates, the flight plan that Popara gave us should work."

A small chime sounded in the cabin. "We're ready to go," said Eddey. "We're clear of the gravitational well. Final coordinates locked in for the first jump."

"Let's get started, then," said Mander. He wanted to add, *And if the Hutts were lying to us, I apologize for getting us all killed.*

Eddey took a deep breath and threw the hyperdrive engage switch. The stars began to lengthen before them, and Mander found he was holding his breath.

The coordinates provided showed six jumps to navigate through the Indrexu Spiral. The first jump took them deep into the Spiral itself, such that the arcs of stars and cometary dust wheeled along the starboard side of the ship. The second put them uncomfortably close to an asteroid cluster—a moon that had either failed to form or been smashed millennia ago and left for dead. They had to wait half an hour before proceeding to the next point, dodging debris. The third point was in orbit around a ruined comet, its last icy blasts echoing in all directions. The fourth was nothing, or rather something dark and malignant that blotted out a quarter of the starfield behind them. Mander was particularly glad to leave that behind.

The penultimate link came out at the tipping point between two gargantuan suns, blue and orange. Flaming plumes from their dappled surfaces reached out and combined in an incandescent rainbow. Dark spots roiled along these liquid rivers like mountains, and for a moment Mander thought them immense living things that migrated along the fiery bridges between the suns, driven by unknowable internal clocks.

And then one last jump and the streaks of hyperdrive-molted light shrank back to the friendly, familiar stars. Reen punched in the local navigation coordinates. "I've got a fix on the local astronomical markers. We are where we are supposed to be. You were right. Nothing to worry about."

Mander said nothing, but allowed himself an embarrassed grin. Eddey started to run a post-jump analysis, but even Mander could see that all of the telltales were a comfortable green.

Reen said, "I have Endregaad. Far side of its orbit, so it is unlikely that we've been spotted by the CSA. We take a high arc and come down over the poles, and, depending on how many ships they have in system, see them before they see—"

She was cut off by twin streaks of ionic energy laced out across the nose of the vessel. The cockpit transceiver let out a bell-like tone and sparked to life.

"Attention, freighter!" said a voice in heavily accented Basic. "You are privileged to be under the guns of the illustrious Bomu clan. Dump your cargo, or be prepared to be boarded." The message was punctuated by another blast of the cannons.

"Light freighter off the port," said Eddey, "heavily modded. I see half a dozen hard points. Has us bracketed."

"Gone but not forgotten?" said Mander.

"Yeah," said Reen. "Get us out of here, Eddey."

The Bothan's furred hands swept over the control toggles, rerouting power to the engines. "Hang on," he said.

The ship was almost immediately rocked to one side, and energy sparked in the cockpit.

"Hit," said Eddey, scanning the telltales, a line of them flashing red. "There go our port weapons."

"Flip us," said Reen, already heading for the starboard turret.

Mander Zuma barely had time to shout as the stars

spun before him, bringing the still-functioning ion blaster turret to bear against their attacker. The deck did not shift, but the swirl of the stars in the viewport caused him to grip the arm of the chair. Even so, the sudden vertigo caused the Jedi to drop to one knee.

Eddey didn't ask about Mander's condition. Instead his long fingers were dancing over the controls. The ship leapt forward as Reen fired off a salvo. The beams of ionic energy danced over the hull of the attacking ship but did not leave so much as a scorch.

"Underpowered piece of standard equipment," muttered the Bothan, and then shouted aloud for Reen to hear him. "Going to keep the spin but shift our deflectors to aft. You'll have to shoot on the fly." Reen made a strangled noise that Mander assumed was agreement, and the ship shuddered again as the Bomu's freighter struck them from behind.

Mander felt helpless. The Bothan was better at the controls, and the Pantoran could handle the guns. He was deadweight at the moment, without a life-or-death task at hand. Instead, his fate was in the hands of the others—and there was nothing he could do.

No, Mander thought. He had the luxury of being able to think. He settled himself back into the jump seat, folded his hands over his chest, and closed his eyes against the spinning stars.

The ship shuddered again, and the Bothan cursed. "I would appreciate any good suggestions now, Jedi," he snapped. "I say we void the cargo hold and hope they stop to pick up the supplies." His fingers reached up to touch a toggle overhead.

"No," said Mander, reaching out and grabbing Eddey's wrist. "Head in that direction." He indicated a nondescript piece of space two points off the bow.

The Bothan looked panic-stricken now. "What's over there?"

"Help," said the Jedi. "But we won't reach it unless we get fancy."

The Bothan muttered something about his opinions of "getting fancy," but he brought the ship around, the yellow sphere of Endregaad's sun shifting into view. Behind them Reen shouted out a surprised retort, and a blast of ionic fire raked along the side of the ship. Sparks flew, and the Bothan said, "I hope you know what you're doing. We should dump the spice."

"If they're really the Bomu, they won't stop for the spice," said Mander. "That's just an excuse. I'm going to count to ten. On ten, you kill the engines and throw in the landing retros. Bring us to a stop."

"A full stop? Are you mad?" Eddey's face was twisted in fear.

"Completely mad," said Jedi, "One, two, three, four . . ."

"Hang on," snarled the Bothan, "I don't want to flood the ion chambers."

". . . five, six, seven . . ."

"Hold on to something, Reen!" shouted Eddey. "We're getting fancy! Be ready to fire!"

". . . eight, nine, *ten*!" Mander thumped the Bothan on the shoulder, and Eddey mashed one hand against a series of buttons, fingers spread like a jizz performer playing on a nalargon. The other hand pulled back fully on the retrojet lever, which fought the pilot for every millimeter. The ship shuddered as the stern engines sought to keep plunging forward. Behind him, Mander could hear the hull strain and hoped that the engine brackets would hold.

And suddenly they were stopped, still spinning, as the Bomu freighter sailed over them. Mander had timed the order perfectly, so that Reen's guns were locked on as they shot past. She strafed the lower hull, leaving long furrows along the ship's belly, from which billowed gases, frozen in an instant into a crystalline mist. Mander nodded. Their attacker had put all deflectors up front in anticipation of the chase.

Mander was going to tell Eddey to do the same thing, but the Bothan was already reconfiguring the shields, swinging them as the enemy ship came around for a head-on assault. Reen fired a few more rounds, but the Rodians had recovered and had their shields up as well.

Double ionic beams lanced forward and the ship shuddered again.

"I hope you have another plan," said Eddey. "Because we're dead in space and the deflectors won't take another hit like that."

"Wait for it," said Mander.

"Wait for what?" the Bothan started to say, but his answer crested over the stern of the Bomu freighter.

There were two of them: CSA starfighters. They were Intercept/Reconnaissance/Defense craft, IRDs for short, and consisted of full-vision cockpit, a pilot's seat, and an engine. And two forward-mounted blaster cannons, supported by concussion missiles. All of which they brought to bear against the now-unshielded stern of the Bomu raider.

The explosions began in the rear of the ship, cascading forward as the raider was unable to respond in time. There was a fireball, and the *New Ambition* flinched as the shock wave passed. Parts of their assailant drifted past their ship like small asteroids, some of them still on fire.

"You knew they were there," said the Bothan, looking at the scattered debris.

"I could feel a ripple in the Force," said Mander. "But I knew they'd be too late if we simply sent a distress signal. Better to meet them halfway, attract their attention with a display of firepower, and let them come to the rescue."

Reen appeared at the hatch of the cockpit. Blood oozed at the corner of her mouth, and she had a nasty darkening around one eye. "What do you call that maneuver?"

"Getting fancy," said Eddey, shaking his head at the amber and crimson lights that now covered one side of his display. The comlink burbled again.

"Attention unidentified freighter," said the voice— clipped, precise, and no-nonsense. "You have entered a quarantine system, by orders of the Corporate Sector Authority. No landings are permitted on Endregaad. Repeat, no landings are permitted. Either jump out of the system, or we will escort you to the *Resolute*. Please respond."

"We could turn tail and try to jump to hyperspace," said the Bothan, "but after what we put this ship through, I don't know about our chances."

Mander flicked open the comlink. "*New Ambition* to the *Resolute* fighters. We have been damaged and appreciate the offer of aid. We will follow you." He closed the transceiver and said "There is a time to sneak about, and a time to talk. This is a time to talk."

"For all our sakes," muttered Reen, "I hope you're right."

PLANETFALL

The CSA never threw away anything that it could use, and even though faster and better ships had come along since the *Resolute*'s hull was laid down, it was kept in service, gaining weapons upgrades and durasteel plating like barnacles. Even so, the ancient patchwork Dreadnought was a frightening thing to behold up close, bristling with turbolasers, missile tubes, and tractor beam projectors, a swarm of IRDs in patrol along its flanks. Parked in orbit over the dull, rusty surface of Endregaad, it was more impressive than the planet.

And, Mander thought as their ship limped into one of the stern landing bays, it was probably the jewel of its commander's eye.

They were met by a squad of CSA security, headed up by a young IRD pilot with sharp features and a stern expression. His uniform, visible beneath his flight suit, was pressed to perfection. Even before he opened his mouth, Mander knew that this was the owner of the voice they had heard on the transceiver. They were this pilot's trophy, and he would only hand them over in the presence of a superior officer.

"Lieutenant Orrell Lockerbee, Corporate Sector Authority ship *Resolute*," he said, and if he had clicked his heels Mander would not have been surprised.

"Mander Zuma of the new Jedi Order," said Mander.

"My companions Reen Irana and Eddey Be'ray. We appreciate your help back there."

The young flight officer scowled in the textbook-approved imitation of displeasure. "Your ship should not have been present in the system. We are under quarantine interdict."

"We are aware of the situation and are on a mercy mission," said Mander. He felt tempted to put a bit of the Force into the words, but resisted. "I presume you will present us to your commanding officer."

The flight officer stammered for a moment, the Jedi taking the next line of his carefully crafted speech away from him. Then his frown deepened and he said, "This way, please."

"A moment," said Reen. "The ship's taken some hard knocks, and Eddey and I should start repairs immediately."

Mander looked at her and raised an eyebrow. She had practically insisted on meeting with the Hutts back on Makem Te, but was now passing on meeting with the Corporate Authority. "Very well," he said, but the Bothan was already examining the long gouges in the side of the *New Ambition,* shaking his maned head. Mander motioned for the pilot to proceed. Two security officers fell in behind the Jedi, while the others stationed themselves at the dock exits. As he walked, the flight officer punched information into his wrist datapad. Mander knew there would be little small talk.

The interior of the CSA ship was spotless, of course, the halls patrolled by mouse droids searching for any speck of dust or hint of the untidy. There was no doubt that this was a warship, though—distant klaxons sounded for drills, speakers belched out muddled Basic, and the personnel—all neatly uniformed and used to sudden inspections—moved about with purpose. No one gave

a robed Jedi following an officer fresh off the flight deck
a second look.

Three long hallways and a turbolift later, Mander was
ushered into the command conference deck. The room
was spacious but neatly appointed, with only a few personal items hanging on the wall. A holo-chess set, one of
the few additions that showed a personal touch, idled
along one wall, its creatures repeating themselves in
looping animations. An impressive readout desk was
parked in front of the viewport, three chairs set up in
front of it. The commanding officer faced away from
them, staring out the viewport at the planet below. The
planet was a swirl of reddish brown clouds, but a major
storm blazed like a white scar across its northern hemi-
sphere.

"Lieutenant Orrel Lockerbee reporting, Commander,"
said the flight officer, saluting, and Mander was sure this
time his heels clicked. "I've brought the Jedi from the
surviving vessel."

"Thank you, Lieutenant," said the commanding officer, and turned to regard them both. She was a tall
young woman, her blood-red hair pulled back in a stern
bun. Her uniform was regulation issue, but its creases
were pressed to vibroknife-edge sharpness. This one had
risen far and fast in the meritocracy of the Corporate
Sector, Mander thought, and wondered if this was a first
command for a capital ship. She pressed the glowing
symbols on the translucent desktop and said, "The other
vessel?"

"A Ghtroc Seven-twenty light freighter, retrofitted as
a raider," responded the flight officer. "It was destroyed
in the engagement."

"It belonged to the Bomu clan, if that helps," said
Mander. "Rodians. I don't suppose there were any survivors to question?"

The commanding officer gave Mander a stern look,

then said, "Good job, Lieutenant. That will be all." Lockerbee saluted again and retreated. Mander wondered if they had done a time study to calculate how much profitable work was lost due to saluting, and if the commensurate increase in better discipline merited it. Knowing the CSA, someone probably had.

"Lieutenant Commander Angela Krin," said the officer, "in command of the CSA ship *Resolute,* and overseeing the quarantine on Endregaad."

"Mander Zuma of the new Jedi Order," responded Mander, hands folded patiently in front of him. "My companions are currently checking out the damage to our ship. We would like to thank you and your pilots for the timely rescue out there."

"You were lucky," said the commander. "We don't run as many deep patrols as I would like."

"Fortune favors the prepared," said the Jedi. "We were aware of the situation on Endregaad, and trusted that if we had difficulty, your well-organized and well-equipped forces would be able to come to our aid."

The corner of Commander Krin's mouth tugged slightly in what Mander could only ascribe to bemusement. She motioned for the Jedi to take one of the seats, and settled herself down across the table from him. "If you are aware of the situation on the planet, then you know that the CSA is not allowing anything on or off that rock until the disease is under control."

"Have you had any problems?" asked the Jedi.

"Early on, there were a number of attempts to get off the planet. Fortunately, there weren't a lot of vessels present at the time. Ships were intercepted, disabled, and impounded. There were a few spacers with pressing business, too, but as word spread of the interdict, that trailed off as well."

"And raiders like the Bomu clan trying to pick off

ships coming in-system." Mander let his voice trail off. "Endregaad is more dangerous than I had presumed."

"Yet you came here in any event."

Mander nodded. "A mission of mercy, as I told your officer."

Angela Krin pushed a few glowing squares on her desk. Their arrangement made Mander think of the holo-chess board. "We don't have your ship on any of our registries," she said.

"It is new," said Mander. "Maiden voyage. More of a trial by fire, it turned out."

Again, the tug at the corner of her lips. Mander could imagine, in another circumstance, she would have a pretty laugh. "Indeed. You are far from Yavin Four, Jedi. Why is the Order interested in Endregaad?"

"They aren't," said Mander, and Angela Krin's neat eyebrows rose in surprise. "Or rather, they are not any more or less interested in Endregaad than in any other planet. I am here on behalf of Popara of the Anjiliac clan of the Hutts. They provided the ship. I hired the crew."

Lieutenant Commander Krin's jawline tightened and her brow furrowed at the mention of Popara's name. "The Hutts, then. That's a surprise. You're working for them?"

"With them," said Mander. "And you know why Popara is interested in Endregaad. His son is somewhere on the surface."

"I know," said the commander, and she slumped a bit in her chair. "I have received *numerous* requests as to his status, ranging from the demanding to the insulting. I will tell you what I told them: I have no information of this Hutt, and no spare resources to find him. Not with a planet already weakened by the plague. I am afraid you came all this way for nothing. The Hutts wasted your time—and mine."

"It was not something I could turn away from, regardless of its likely outcome," said Mander.

"Now, about your cargo . . . ," began the commander, leaning forward and tapping a few symbols on her desk.

"It is yours," said Mander, simply.

Again, Krin was surprised, but tried not to show it. "We have to confiscate it."

"No you don't, since I just gave it to you," said the Jedi. "You and your organization are better established to distribute the medicinal spice than three people in a damaged freighter. I assume you can add it to your own supplies."

Angela Krin smiled now, a sad smile of someone who has been dealing with her own bureaucracy. Mander saw it at once: there were no additional supplies, at least not yet. "Help is on the way," she said.

"And some of it is here, now," said Mander. "With the heartfelt wishes of Popara Anjiliac, and with the hope of creating a lasting trust in these trying times."

The commanding officer ran a slender finger over the glyph-dotted desktop. After a moment, she said simply, "I can't let you land on Endregaad."

"I understand. We will conduct what investigations we can from here." Mander tilted his head slightly and smiled.

"We can provide some support, in particular in repairing your ship. Payment in kind for your . . . donated spice."

"That is greatly appreciated," said Mander. "If we are fortunate, perhaps we can find Mika Anjiliac before we have to return."

Angela Krin smiled now in agreement. "We will do what we can. Would you and your crew be interested in joining me for mess this evening?"

"I would love to," said Mander, "but I will have to ask the others."

* * *

"You did *what*?" said Reen, her face flushing to a richer blue, her bruised eye taking on a violet hue. They were standing in the crew lounge of the *New Ambition*. Eddey had one of the gyros disassembled on the table and was going over it with a fine-tipped vibro-pick, pulling away the worst of the scorched metal.

"I gave her the spice," said Mander. "After all, that is one of the reasons we came here—to help relieve the plague."

"That was our only bargaining chip!" said Reen, "And you gave it away at the very start!"

"It was not as if they would let us keep it," noted Mander. He had returned to the docking bay to find that Reen Irana was already in a tense standoff with Lieutenant Lockerbee and the security squad. She was adamant about not letting the CSA on board her ship, and only relented when Mander gave the approval to off-load the cargo. Polite security team members cleaned out the cargo in record time and retreated to their positions at the doors.

"They also have been more helpful in giving us supplies and equipment," said Eddey, slipping on his data goggles and grimacing at the readout. "I think you sufficiently convinced the commanding officer that we are not raiders ourselves."

"Did you Voice her?" asked Reen.

"'Voice' her?" replied Mander, looking perplexed.

"You know. *Voice* her. Jedi Hoodoo. Mind tricks." She made a theatrical wave of her hand. "Tell her *You want to let us land on the planet* or something like that. And then she agrees and we go off."

"Did Toro tell you we can do that?" asked Mander.

"I saw it in the holofilms," said Reen.

"She watches too many of those," Eddey put in.

"It doesn't work quite like that," said Mander.

"So it's a myth," said Reen. "Jedi can't do that."

"It is no myth," said Mander with a sigh. "But it is not as easy as you portray it."

"So you can't change people's minds," Reen pressed.

"We can," said Mander patiently, "but there are consequences. A person's mind will be changed, and their immediate actions will be influenced, but it has a long-term effect as well. If it is as simple as getting past a guard or encouraging someone to share information, the damage is minimal. The guard will probably not think about the situation again, or will blame it on a lapse of attention or judgment. We use it to avoid fights or gain information. But when you try to move someone to do something they don't honestly want to do, they rebel."

"And they won't do it," said Reen.

"Worse," said Mander, "*they will*. And then the effect will spiral further, as they unconsciously seek to justify those actions to themselves. And that is hard on a lot of people's minds. It is like an avalanche started from small stones. Your very presence bothers them, since something went wrong when you last saw them. Sometimes using it again against a target will remind them they have been subject to the effect previously, with unpleasant consequences. The Jedi seek not to do damage, so we use the 'mind tricks'—as you call them—only sparingly, and usually on individuals we don't think we're going to encounter again. We don't know how long we're going to be here, so no, I did not 'Voice' her."

"Does it feel like anything?" pressed Reen. "Would the person know if it had happened?"

"If you're asking if I have used it on you, the answer is again no, for all the reasons I previously mentioned," said Mander. "Free will, for all its problems, is easier to work with. When it is attempted—and yes, Jedi are trained to resist this sort of thing—it feels like a pressure against your mind, like a wave passing over you. An impulse, a strong desire, a random thought. And if you are subject to it, when the wave passes, you have little knowledge that it struck in the first place."

Reen looked at him long and hard and said, "So what you're saying is that you didn't Voice her."

Mander let out a deep sigh. "And on that note, you are invited to the commander's table for dinner." He gave her a smile.

Reen did not return it. "No."

Mander blinked. "No? Any reason?"

"I don't like the Corporates," she said.

"You didn't like the Hutts, either," Mander said, "but it did not stop you from meeting with Popara."

"That's different," said Reen. "The Hutts are treacherous, but you can count on them to be treacherous. The Corporate Sector is completely by the book, and when they feel they are right, according to that book, there is no stopping them. One of the reasons I was keeping them off the ship was to give Eddey a chance to pull the navigation unit offline. I didn't want their slicers getting the coordinates for the Indrexu Spiral."

"Before we get a chance to sell them," added the Bothan.

"But you managed that, and they are none the wiser," Mander said. "So you should come to dinner with our gracious hosts."

Reen shook her head. "We need to get the ship back together and out of here."

Mander cocked his head a moment. "Something else is wrong."

"Nothing else is wrong," said Reen. "We're just busy. And I don't want to leave anyone alone in the ship."

"No, no, something is definitely wrong," said Mander. "And I don't need the Force to tell me that."

"Tell him," said Eddey, not looking up from his work.

"Nothing is wrong," said Reen, folding her arms over her chest.

"Something is wrong," said Mander.

"Tell him—or I will," said Eddey.

Reen scowled deeply. "I've had run-ins with the CSA."

"You've smuggled," said Mander succinctly.

"Some," Reen said, shrugging. "A little. Nothing bad, nothing major, nothing that a Jedi would blow a circuit about."

"Small package trade, really," said the Bothan calmly. "Personal items, artifacts of dubious provenance, objects of art. That sort of thing."

"Nothing bad or horrible," Reen added quickly. "Nothing like hard spice. Nothing like . . . Tempest."

Mander nodded and thought he understood. Reen and her partner were part and parcel of the shadowy world of spacers, the great majority of whom wouldn't think twice about bringing contraband through planetary customs if there was a bonus in it. But it was that same evasion of authority that made the spice trade possible, and the same avenues may have been used to bring in the Tempest that killed her brother.

She knows how smugglers think because she has been one herself.

He said, "The Jedi are not religious leaders. We don't provide absolution or forgiveness. The best we can do is help others come to terms with what they have done, and help them make amends. But that does not explain why you wouldn't want to meet with a CSA lieutenant commander who doesn't even know you."

"Ah," said Eddey. "There's the rub."

"The original *Ambition*," started Reen.

"The one probably being sold for scrap on Keyorin to pay for the docking fees," clarified Eddey.

"The *Ambition* was," Reen continued, "for lack of a better word, damaged as result of escaping a CSA corvette, conveniently parked behind a moon near a rendezvous point." Her cheeks flushed dark again.

"Ah." Mander mimicked Eddey. "I understand. And even though it is unlikely that anyone will make the connection, you aren't sure if you are in a database somewhere, the information just waiting to leap onto Lieutenant Lockerbee's datapad and surprise you."

"That sums it up," said Reen, but she didn't look up at the Jedi. The Bothan let out a small cry of triumph as he pulled away a particularly stubborn gasket, now reduced to a tattered black mass.

"Very well—I will be dining with Lieutenant Commander Angela Krin," said Mander. "And if your name comes up, I will take note. In the meantime, though, I intend to avail myself of the hospitality her command offers, and try to persuade her that she should trust us enough to let us go planetside. Three days. I think three days should do it, one way or another."

"We can get things operating in three days," said Eddey. "If we can get the parts. Tender our regrets to the good commander," he added to Mander, "and both of you can leave me to my work in peace."

"Indeed," said Mander Zuma. "I think it is time to renew my research in CSA standard operating procedures."

Three days passed with a glacial slowness. Most of the planetary transceivers were in Tel Bollin, and as far as Mander could tell most of their operators were stricken by the plague or just laying low until the pestilence had passed over. From what little Mander could gather, general society—always a rough-and-tumble affair on mining planets—had collapsed entirely in the wake of the disease. Looting and fires were common; what civil authority was left had its hands full surviving on its own, and therefore had precious few resources to help offworlders. One of the few full holoconversations Mander managed took place with a tired, exhausted officer with white crusts at the corners of her eyes and mouth, her hair an unruly tangle. She didn't know anything about Hutts onplanet, but said that any exomorphs should have gone to ground, since the survivors were looking for something to blame and nonhumans fit that bill. Then the officer terminated the call in the middle of a prolonged coughing jag.

Once further attempts to contact anyone on the ground proved equally problematic, the Jedi turned to the ship's library. It was a smart little operation consisting of a set of military histories and CSA law, the former well thumbed while the latter apparently pristine since the ship was first launched. He mixed the two, in particular checking out the regulations and specifications of the Corporate Sector Authority's navy.

Each evening, Mander would present himself, in clean and formal robes, to the Commander's Galley. The first night was with senior officers, and Mander got the standard array of questions directed at the Jedi in the wake of the fall of the Empire: *Is the Order starting again? What are your intentions? Will you rule from Coruscant? How have things changed?* He deflected them as politely as he could, and got the officers talking about their own experiences in space instead. The nature of the Force was forgotten in stories of running down raiders and recovering contraband.

After that first evening, Lieutenant Commander Angela Krin met privately with Mander, and the Jedi soon came to understand her position. She had the responsibility to maintain the quarantine but could not deal with matters onplanet, Endregaad not being an official world of the Corporate Sector. So they were in orbit as people suffered and died below, charged by a distant bureaucracy with keeping others away. What help they could provide was advisory only, and any personnel were under the control of a now-collapsed government.

"The spice you brought was both welcome help and a can of worms," she said, over dinner. "On the one hand, we desperately needed the medicines, but on the other I don't have specific permission to use them."

"Surely even the CSA can see the wisdom that such an opportunity presents—having the medicine, if from an unexpected source," said Mander.

"You would think so," said Angela Krin, moving her meat around in its gravy idly. "But in reality, the wheels of bureaucracy spin slowly but fine. The supply officer tasked with delivering the CSA-authorized medicine from Duroon blew a gasket when I sent him word that yours had arrived. He had been assuring me that there was not enough medicinal spice at hand to cover a planetary emergency, and he needed approvals to access the surplus stock." She shook her head. "And this was while one in ten people on Endregaad were dying."

"I hope that our contribution can have some effect," said Mander.

Krin popped a morsel into her mouth, "It already does, though not the way you'd expect. As a result of your shipment, suddenly the floodgates have swung wide and sufficient amounts of medicine should be arriving by week's end. In military terms, you gave them a good hard kick in the pants."

"Have you distributed the spice we brought?" asked Mander.

Angela Krin's face darkened slightly. "They are still checking it over. It is a standard issue, broadband soporific with strong antibacterial and antivirus properties. But it is very high-grade. Any idea where it came from originally?"

"You would have to ask Popara," said Mander.

"I don't think we're his favorite people," said Krin.

"This part of space is filled with species and factions that have been competing for millennia," said Mander. "Trust is a hard coin to find."

"There's that," said Krin, "but there's also the fact that the Hutts were not particularly supportive and encouraging before you came along. The missives we got were as high-handed as you would expect from a Hutt, filled with demands and insults. And then, when we didn't produce immediate results, they got nastier."

"Popara sent these? Or did you talk to a green female named Vago?"

"Neither," said the lieutenant commander. "It was a big lumpish blue one. Zonnos, I think his name was."

"That would be Mika's brother," said Mander. "I've met him. A soft touch is not what he is noted for. That's one reason they brought in a Jedi."

Later, in the *New Ambition,* Mander related the events of the dinner to the others over a mug of Karlini tea. The Bothan was checking over the parts list against the schematic, while Reen debugged the latest software install.

"Do you think Zonnos is just an oaf, or is he trying to get his brother killed?" asked the Bothan.

"I don't know," Mander said. "It could be both. He certainly gave me a wink and a nod that Mika's safety was not a priority for him. And if his younger sibling doesn't come home, then that leaves more of the family business for him."

"What I find curious," said Reen, swiveling in her chair away from her station, "is the amount of time you spend with this commander. Doesn't she have a planet to protect?"

"She does, and it is obvious that it troubles her," said Mander. "She's by-the-book, I'll give you that. But she's also smart enough to see that the book doesn't cover every situation, even though she keeps trying to make it do so. The CSA is a large bureaucracy, and it takes a long time to turn large things and head them in the right direction."

"Are you talking about the CSA or Popara the Hutt?" asked the Bothan.

"Both, perhaps," said Mander, staring into his mug at the dregs of his tea. "I don't need the Force to feel her frustration. But all the same, I want to be off from here as soon as possible. How are the repairs?"

The Bothan smiled broadly. "Every time you have dinner, we get a delivery of more supplies that they just 'happened' to find. I think we'll be ready by tomorrow. Local midnight or so."

"Good," said Mander. "I hope that I can convince her to let us land."

"It is out of the question," said Krin the next evening. She was in dress uniform, and her hair was in a tighter bun than normal, not a hair out of place. Mander for a moment thought it was for him, but he soon discovered that she'd been on the transceiver, reporting to her superiors about the quarantine, and in particular dealing with the complaints of a local bureaucrat from Duroon. Her eyes were a little haggard, but her jaw was firm and set as she shook her head.

"You will have to distribute the medicine soon," said Mander. "Even the CSA bureaucracy can't hold it up that long. Let me volunteer the ship as a shuttle for supplies and medical personnel."

"I'd like to, but no," said the commander. "We have sufficient shuttles—or will when the remaining supplies get here. It is one thing to redirect scrap durasteel for a private freighter that did me a favor. It is another to countermand direct orders. And that's what I have: a direct order to chase down anyone who tries to break quarantine, going in or coming out."

"With what support you have," said Mander.

"With what support I have," she said, handing him a glass of emerald wine and offering a toast with hers. "May you have a safe and uneventful return home."

"May we all have safe and uneventful trips," replied Mander.

When Mander Zuma returned to the *New Ambition,* Eddey had already finished the preflight check and Reen had reinstalled the navicomputer. The Bothan looked up and said, "Did you work that Jedi charm? Are we going down to look for the Huttling?"

"Take us out. Here's the flight plan," said Mander, handing over a datapad.

Eddey looked almost crestfallen, "We're leaving, then."

"You see it there, clear as day," Mander replied, sighing. "Apparently our lieutenant commander spent most of the day dealing with very officious types, and was not in the mood to waive a few rules. Head over the pole of Endregaad, and make for the sector where we met the Bomu raiders."

Eddey growled and closed the hatches, securing the last piece of equipment as the deck officers cleared and evacuated the bay. Reen fell into one of the crash chairs while Mander settled himself in. "I'm sorry," she said. "But I *did* tell you these CSA types were stiff-necked." Mander said nothing, just leaned forward in his seat, lacing his fingers.

The force shield holding back space flickered out and the *New Ambition* left the *Resolute,* banking slightly to take the polar route Mander had plotted and filed. The planet cast the Dreadnought in deep shadow, and beneath the *Resolute* the city of Tel Bollin was a muddle of indistinct lights. As they rose over the white-tan polar deserts of the world, a false dawn of the system's sun greeted them.

They had passed over the polar terminator when

Mander finally took a deep breath and said, "Right—we're going in. We're making landfall."

Eddey almost jumped in his seat, then allowed himself a toothy smile and started reconfiguring the thrusters. Reen looked surprised and said, "Should I get to the turbocannons?"

"Not yet," said Mander. "For the moment, keep an eye on the sensors. I'm sure Lieutenant Commander Krin isn't foolish enough to pull off her patrols just on my declaration that we were going away."

"You lied," said Reen. "I didn't know Jedi did that."

"I'd prefer to think of it as dissembling, or shading, or at most mangling the truth," said Mander. "But yes, when push comes to shove, Jedi are allowed to lie. Don't tell anyone. It would just ruin our reputations." And he allowed himself a smile almost as wide as the Bothan's.

They fell into the sunlit side of the world, and the fire-wisps of reentry curled around the cockpit.

"They're on to us," said Reen as a pair of blips appeared at the corner of the scanner. "Two IRDs, matching course. Contact in about ten minutes."

"Faster than I thought. She's good, I'll give her that," said Eddey Be'ray.

"Textbook approach," said Mander. "Standard operating procedure. Bring the ship down shallow, and bank her to the left. We want to come back around the planet to Tel Bollin before the sun rises there."

"Steeper would have a better chance to lose them," said the Bothan.

"I know, but we don't want to lose them just yet," said Mander.

Visual contact came nine minutes later—a pair of IRDs similar to the ones that had blown up the Bomu raider. The transceiver crackled, and a voice that sounded very much like Flight Officer Lockerbee snarled, "Attention, *New Ambition*. You are in violation of interdicted space. Pull up and return to the *Resolute,* or we will be forced to open fire."

Reen pulled the microphone toward her, but Mander pulled it out of her hands. "Attention IRDs. We are experiencing difficulties. Our repairs did not hold. We are losing altitude and will have to ditch. Systems are fail—" He stopped midword, and returned the transceiver to the cradle. "If they call back, don't answer."

"You're doing horrible things to your Jedi reputation," said the Bothan.

A pair of ionic blasts bracketed the craft.

"That's one," said Mander. "Regulations say they have to try twice more, since we are apparently in distress." They were deep inside the atmosphere now, and the Jedi scanned the horizon, looking for one particular feature. "There," he said, pounding Eddey on the shoulder and pointing to the east.

"Dust storm," said Reen. "Pull up to get over it."

"No—" said Mander, "head into it."

"It will play hobs with the navigation," said the Bothan. "And I just cleaned everything out."

"Exactly," said Mander, and another pair of blaster bolts streaked past the cockpit. "That's two. They won't wait as long to fire the third . . . and then all bets are off."

Mander held his breath as the wall of sand and dirt, visible from orbit—carried from one side of the world to the other—approached and then towered over them. It filled the observation scanners, panning across them. There was a third blast of ionic fire now, but Mander didn't even pay attention to it. Another couple of seconds and—

They were inside the cloud, the dust screeching against the hull. Eddey cursed, more for the damage done to the finish than any real effect on the ship's structure. Around them the storm licked at the engines and coated the flight surfaces. The sky lightened and a string of bolts laced around them, but none of them hit.

"They're on instruments now," said Mander. "Can you manage?"

"I've got my own scanners up, but we're awfully low," said the Bothan.

A dark shadow passed by the ship, then another, and a third. "Those are rock formations!" shouted Reen. "We're too low. Pull us up!"

"Not for another minute," said Mander. The Bothan did not reply, though he clutched the steering yoke in a death grip.

Another set of bolts, but these were wide and faint. Then the sand started to diminish, and they were clear of the leading edge of the storm.

And there was a mesa wall dead ahead of them.

Cursing, Eddey pulled back on the stick, pitching the ship almost perpendicular. They cleared, but as they topped the rise, the IRDs caught sight of them again. They closed, their forward-facing guns blazing. One of the IRDs smoked along the side as a concussion missile fired.

"They're going to catch us," said Eddey. "Sorry."

"Ten more seconds," said Mander. "Gun it."

The *New Ambition* screamed as it lunged forward. The concussion missile was fast, but the chunky Suwan-tek's engines were more powerful, and it fell away behind them. The two IRDs could have redoubled their own speed, but instead they pulled up almost vertically, heading for space.

The three in the cockpit let out a long sigh, and Eddey tried to bank the sand-clogged engines. "What happened?" asked Reen.

"Standard operating procedure," said Mander. "The IRDs have air-breathing capacities, but maintenance rules say they can only spend so long in a planetary envelope. Failure to do so would result in a notation on their personal record."

Reen looked at the Jedi and said, "You said you were reading their manuals . . . you knew that was there."

"I knew *something* was there that we could use," said Mander. "Even so, I think we'll need to keep a low profile once we get to Tel Bollin. Eddey, if you can find some dry wash close enough to the city that we can reach it by cargo skiff, but beyond their normal scanners, I would be much obliged."

"Done," said the Bothan. "And let me be the first to welcome you to scenic Endregaad. After this landing, everything else that happens will be smooth sailing."

TEL BOLLIN

They left the *New Ambition* a short distance from Tel Bollin. Mander set some security monitors along the perimeter of the camp while Reen and the Bothan unfurled long strands of red-tan camouflage netting and draped the ship in it. It wouldn't stop a determined searcher, but the odd passerby or aerial patrol would not give it a second look. Then the pair readied the Ubrikkian Bantha III from the cargo hold. The Bantha III was a lightweight repulsorlift skiff that could carry them and a young Hutt, if need be. It had the smooth lines common to most of the Ubrikkian pleasure craft products, and it did not surprise Mander that Popara had put one in the ship's hold.

Mander watched the Bothan and Pantoran working together quickly and efficiently. There was a minimum of words between them, yet one would have a tool ready when the other needed it. They seemed to fit naturally into the world, as if assembling a cargo skiff on a plague-ridden planet while hiding from the Corporate Sector Authority were the stuff of everyday life.

It was never like that with Toro, Mander thought. From the start the young Pantoran was hidden from him—not particularly secretive, but not open, either. The young man was so intent on becoming a Jedi—so driven to live up to the image from the holofilms and the legends—that he found the older archivist, with his magnaspecs and dusty old records, to be a bit of a disappointment. He said nothing at the time, but to Mander the young man was clearly crestfallen when they first met, expecting something more heroic.

And the disappointment remained even after their first sparring session, when the youth rushed at him and Mander dispatched him easily. The older Jedi sidestepped every charge, blocked every attack, and met the young Pantoran's passionate fury with a calm response. But it did little to remove that doubt. Now in the young student's eyes Mander Zuma was a mystery to be solved, a puzzle to be unlocked. The older man held secrets that belied his unassuming appearance, and Toro wanted to learn them. Indeed, how could an unassuming person such as Mander Zuma defeat a dedicated opponent, if not by Jedi magic?

For his part, that first mock duel was equally troubling to Mander. Yes, he had beaten the youth calmly and handily, but wasn't that what was expected of a Master? And even then he could feel the Force within the youth, impatient though he seemed. It was clear that with the proper training, Toro Irana could be a powerful Jedi.

The proper training. Mander shook his head. Perhaps that was Mander's ultimate failure. He had calmed the fury of the youth, but had never taught him to master it. Toro was always challenging, both in training and in philosophy. He was always questioning, always pushing, always looking for a weak spot. The ability to see a weakness in a plan or an opponent was invaluable as a Jedi, yet Toro would always go for that weak spot immediately, often ignoring caution.

Was that what led his former student to Tempest? Perhaps he was looking for something even more powerful to master than the philosophies of his teacher. He wanted to prove himself better. He wanted one more advantage on others. It was a common enough road to destruction, and Mander had read enough tales in the Archives to know that it was a tempting trap.

Mander set the last of the perimeter monitors and watched the sky, a dusty inverted bowl lightening only slightly with the dawn, the ruddy brown stain of the sky darkening with pollution in the direction of Tel Bollin. The cloud cover would keep them safe from most observers above the atmosphere, but a determined scan would punch through the clouds and find their ship with little problem. The question, he thought, was how determined any search would be. The lieutenant commander was headstrong enough to pursue them, even if it meant breaking a few directives of the CSA—directives that Mander had found in his own research. And while her obvious intelligence made Mander feel that she was aware of those directives, he hoped that her dedication would keep her from violating them too blatantly.

While he was in thought, Reen had come up with a bundle of cloth. "Here," she said. "Put this on."

Mander unraveled a poncho-like cloak. "It's a zerape," she explained. "Local coloring out here in the Outer Rim worlds. Even if Krin is too busy to scan for us, she probably has told people what to look out for."

"We are a Jedi, a Bothan, and a Pantoran," said Mander. "I don't think we're going to be able to blend in with the local population too much." Still, he took the garment and shed his outer robe. The zerape was little more than a blanket with a neck-hole, but it fit well enough, and left his arms free.

"I don't know—it's not like you're what I expected from a Jedi," said Reen.

Mander started. Her words mirrored his own dark thoughts. "You've met other Jedi?" he asked. "Other than your brother, I mean."

"No," said Reen, "And I didn't see Toro after he left

to join your Order. But the holofilms. The old epics and the news reports from the war. The Jedi were always moving, always attacking, always taking risks. Heroic. You seem too . . ."

"Insufficient?" suggested Mander, and the dream rose in the back of his mind.

"Ordinary," Reen suggested, but the word gave Mander little solace. "Normal. You were more willing to talk than fight me when we first met. You were polite to Popara and his people. And you surrendered the medicine to the CSA."

"They *will* be better at distributing it than we would," noted Mander.

"Fine. But I still expected you to brandish your lightsaber, or throw someone across the room, or use your mind control powers to make them dance," Reen said.

"What makes you think I can't do any of that?" said Mander, smiling—and hoping that the smile would turn aside further questions.

It did not. "What do you do as a Jedi?" she asked.

"Different Jedi have different roles," suggested Mander.

"But what is yours?" Reen insisted.

"I was Toro's Master," said Mander. "I taught him in the ways of the Force."

"Yes, I know," said Reen. "And when he mentioned you in his messages, he spoke well of you. Is that all you do, teach young Jedi?"

Mander gnawed his upper lip. "There are few teachers and many who need instruction," he said. "But no, I do have other tasks."

"Such as?"

Mander let out a deep sigh. "I go where I am sent by the Order. Currently, I am overseeing the Jedi Archives on Yavin Four. One of my tasks is to track down texts and holos throughout that region of the galaxy and compare them against those in the Jedi library on Coruscant. During the Galactic Civil War, many of the vital records were corrupted—"

Reen interrupted, "You're a librarian."

"Archivist, if you please," said Mander.

"Librarian," said Reen, with a small laugh.

Mander felt himself redden with embarrassment. "I served as an apprentice to the great Jedi historian Tionne Solusar. She has been trying to restore the Archives in the old Jedi Temple, and my work has been vital in identifying and confirming lost texts."

Reen beamed a wide smile, and Mander would have called it a playful and winning smile if the woman weren't being completely insufferable. "A librarian!" she laughed. "My brother never told me that. But I should have guessed. He complained you were always sending him to this text or that volume for some quote from an old Jedi philosopher who was dead long before the Republic was created!"

The Jedi wanted to respond, to point out the fallacies in her argument, but Eddey hollered from outside the ship. The Bothan had closed up the cargo bay and was already at the control pedestal in the floater's stern. Reen moved at his call, and was down the hillside and clambering onto the skiff.

Mander let out a frustrated sigh and wondered why he let her get under his skin. Probably because she was very much like her brother. The Jedi pressed the last security code into the monitors and followed her.

The skiff was open-topped, in the Ubrikkian style, and Eddey skated along the dry wash at a good rate of speed, such that any conversation of less than a shout was lost in the swirling dust they kicked up. They passed between a pair of sentinel rocks and were out of the wash and into the open bottomland that held Tel Bollin.

Mander turned to confirm where they had come from. The dust in their wake shifted from red and tan to a lighter shade, and the Jedi realized that the city was built on an evaporated lakebed, probably the remnant of when the planet last saw rainfall millennia ago.

The town itself was a dirty smudge on the horizon that did not look much better close up. Like most miner worlds, the place had a temporary look about it, the walls made of precast concrete dropped in from orbit and supplemented by mud bricks. Nothing was more than two stories tall, and all the edges were worn away into soft curves. Were the city to be abandoned, it would disappear into the lakebed within a generation.

It seemed to be well on its way already. Most of the outlying buildings were empty, open doors and windows staring blankly out at the world. Some were scorched around the entrances from fire. Some were marked with a crimson skull and a number underneath. Plague houses, indicating the number of bodies found inside. There was no movement on the streets, and if there were inhabitants, they were watching weakly from the shade.

Eddey slowed the skiff and Mander said, "Find a place to set this down, and we'll go farther into the city on foot. We'll stand out on this skiff. After all," he added for Reen's benefit, "we want to blend in."

Eddey chose a location that was either an abandoned scrap yard or a multivehicle pileup. The scrap yard's office, if it had been the former, had been gutted by flames, and smoky stains marked the walls. Mander made sure no one was about while Eddey secured the skiff. Reen adjusted her blaster, setting it to ride low on her right hip.

From eye level, the city did not improve in the least. As they moved deeper into Tel Bollin, there were finally people—dust-covered wretches moving through the morning light. It would normally be the time when people would be abroad, before it got too hot, but the inhabitants were few and far between. Small beads rattling in a much bigger box. One of them staggered by—a miner, by his look—and Mander hailed him, asking where he might find the Skydove Freight offices. That was Popara's business, and that was where they should start.

The man looked up suddenly, as if Mander had manifested himself out of the desert air. His eyes were red and rheumy, and thick deposits of white crust hung from the corners of his eyes and mustache. For the first time, Mander wondered about the efficacy of Popara's proposed vaccinations. The miner's mouth worked a few moments but nothing came out. Instead he pointed in a general direction, to the right of one of the metal towers in the center of the town. Mander thanked him and pressed a few credits into his hand. When he looked back at the end of the block, the miner was still standing there, looking at the credits in his hand as if Mander had given him beetles.

"Try using Huttese money next time," suggested Reen. "A couple of wupiupi will do."

Mander nodded and said, "Sixteen wupiupi to a trugut, and four truguts to a peggat, which is worth forty standard credits. So a wupiupi would be worth about two-thirds of a credit." Reen made an exasperated noise, and Mander regretted immediately sharing the information. He had learned the conversion rates back on Yavin 4, when he had first known he would be dealing with Hutts, but what truguts and wupiupi he had brought were unused in his pocket.

There was a whine of engines behind them, and the few people on the street quickly sought the safety of nearby doorways. The trio was on a low sidewalk beneath a veranda, so they turned to look.

Half a dozen swoop bikes—low, lean machines—

screamed up the city street. Unlike their surroundings, they were brightly colored and well maintained, their riders deeply tattooed and grinning as they carved up furrows of dust in the empty street. They didn't wear any unified colors or uniforms Mander could notice, but clearly shared a love of the noise and the effect it had on the natives.

Mander folded his hands in front of him to watch them pass, and realized that Reen and Eddey had melted back into one of the doorways. As the repulsor bikes flared past, kicking up dust, one of the riders flung a bottle in the Jedi's general direction.

It did not seem intentional, and the throw was wide in any event. Mander did not flinch as it struck the wall a few feet to his right. Then the swoop gang was gone, swallowed again by the city, and the natives emerged, moving around as if nothing had happened.

"We're trying to keep a low profile," said Reen. "You should have stayed in the shadows with us."

"I didn't realize you were gone until it was too late," said Mander. "Besides, the one with the bottle had terrible aim." Still, the Jedi pulled at his zerape to shake the dust loose.

They were encountering shops now, run by merchants who looked like they were uninfected or survivors of the plague. Still, they were haggard and worn, and had little more than information to sell. They got better directions to Skydove Freight, though, as well as a warning to stay clear of the center of town. The CSA was rounding people up, an old woman selling discolored fruits said. Mander dropped a couple of wupiupi into her hand. She nodded but shot Eddey a sharp, nasty glance before retreating to the back of her shop.

Two blocks later a landcruiser bearing CSA markings rattled around the corner. This time Mander followed the local customs and pulled far enough off the street

not to attract attention. The craft looked a little battered, and its forward weapon was obviously plugged
and nonfunctional. The pilot behind the wheel was in a
CSA uniform, but Mander noted that he was wearing a
full breathing rig. Obviously the CSA had concerns
about the usefulness of their own vaccine stores.

A landcruiser of this type could carry a squad of
troops, but this one had been kitted out with a loud-
hailer, which blared in Basic, Huttese, and a few other
languages. Medicine was available, barked the loud-
hailer. It would be distributed at the slingball pitch to
the south of the city center. Only those with CSA-
provided identity tags would receive vaccinations. All
citizens should have tags. Those without tags would be
violating the law and given tags. Please proceed in an
orderly fashion. Be sure to bring your tags. The landcruiser shifted to another language and continued to
lumber on, ignoring the people on the streets. For their
part, the citizens seemed to be in no rush to take the
CSA up on their offer.

"The distribution has begun," said Mander. "That
should help us. More people on the street."

"And it may be that we'll find the Skydove offices to
be empty," Reen said, "because they're all out getting
the medicine we could have brought them."

The office of Skydove Freight *was* empty, but it seemed
unlikely that the workers were out for a vaccination
break. The front door was caved in, the barred windows
smashed into jagged shards. Inside, the place was a
mess—overturned desks, their electronics hanging out
of them, rendering them inert and useless. Smashed datapads and crystals crunched underfoot. Interior closets
were vandalized and chairs reduced to kindling. What
might have been a safe was now a large hole in the floor,
with drag marks leading to the door.

And across one wall, written in dark paint, were words in Huttese script.

Mander read the glyphs aloud. "'The Fallen Warrior.' Is that a reference to Mika? A testament to his protectors?"

"I don't think of Hutts as warriors," said Reen. "Probably a brag from the people who did this. Maybe a group of them, like the swoop gang we saw."

"Odd name for a group," said Mander. "You two look about. See if any of the datapads survived. I'm going to ask the neighbors."

There were no neighbors—just another handful of empty offices. Some were vandalized, but others were left untouched. He did find a young man sulking in one of the doorways.

"Spice, spice," the young man said as Mander approached, low and indistinct.

"You have spice?" asked Mander.

"I have medicine," said the man. "Fell off the back of a loader this morning. CSA is swimming with it, not that they want to share it without all their red tape."

"Let's see it," said Mander, and the youth produced a grimy vial filled with yellowish crystals. It looked like the medicinal spice they had brought the same way that Mander looked like the Jedi of Reen's imagination.

"Good quality," lied Mander, "but what I really need is information. The Fallen Warrior." He tilted his voice with just a bit of the Force, enough to keep the young man talking.

He hissed. "You don't want to go there."

"So it is a place," said Mander, keeping the Force in his voice. "Tell me why I don't want to go there."

"It's a cantina for nonhumans," said the youth. "Nonhumans brought the plague, some say. They weren't getting sick. The Hutts, the Toydarians, all of them. Early on, when things got bad, people drove them away."

That was why Eddey was getting strange looks. When society was under pressure, they blamed people who were different. Aliens. Outlanders. He recalled the holo-conversation he'd had on the *Resolute* with the young officer stationed planetside. "They drove a Hutt away?" asked Mander.

The youth paused, and Mander wondered if he was trying to answer correctly or fighting the Force-powered command in the Jedi's voice. At last he shook his head and shrugged. "I don't know. There was a Hutt here. Didn't see him later. Could be dead. Could be at the Warrior. There was a Nikto that came in before things got bad. He was here after they looted the place. Lousy aliens."

Mander found the youth irritating. "Where's this place I shouldn't go?"

The young man told him, then blinked at him and said, "You want that spice?"

"That's not spice," said Mander, scowling now, throwing the Force fully into his voice.

The youth took a step back, then shrugged. "It's not really spice."

"What you should do is get vaccinated." He brought the Force up hard with the command, and the youth almost staggered back a step.

"I really should get vaccinated."

"And tell others to do so as well."

The youth nodded, his eyes vacant now. "I should tell the others." And with that he turned away and disappeared down the street, his feet slowly carrying him away as his brain tried to figure out what had happened.

Mander frowned. He hadn't needed to do that, but after being needled by Reen, the urge to demonstrate a little Jedi mind power was too strong—even if she didn't see him do it. A momentary weakness, he realized, like a child kicking over an anthill. And just as mature, especially since he had already gotten what he needed.

He returned to the office to find the others making a desultory search. "They were thorough," said Reen. "There are not enough functioning chips here to light up a droid's eye sensors."

"I found out that the Fallen Warrior is a cantina about ten blocks from here," Mander said, "and that the locals are blaming nonhumans for the plague. So we should be careful." The others said nothing, but, as they stepped back into the sunlight, both the Pantoran and the Bothan were looking up and down the street for potential trouble.

The Fallen Warrior was built like a bunker, and Mander realized that it would be a good sanctuary if the mobs were looting nonhuman businesses. Its walls were the original permacrete of the colony, built up with additional layers of mud. Low stairs led up into the building itself, which was set apart from the other structures by broad alleys and a large plaza. There were a couple of obvious side exits as well.

Mander also noticed, parked beneath a huge but bare-leafed tree, a collection of brightly colored swoop bikes.

The gang was inside, claiming half of the bar and driving the alien clientele to booths along the sides. A stern-looking, statuesque, white-haired woman was behind the bar itself, and gave them a nod that, in one motion, welcomed them, demanded to know their business, and instructed them that the business had better involve drinking.

Mander and the others scanned the rooms, blinking as their eyes adapted to the darkness. A bleary-eyed Ithorian sprawled forward over one table. A couple of Neimoidians were talking to a Duros cousin in another booth. No Rodians, which made Mander offer thanks for small favors. Some Chiss who pulled back a beaded curtain of their booth to give the new arrivals a once-over, then returned to their plotting.

And one Nikto: an Esral'sa'Nikto, also called the Mountain People among their species. This one had the traditional flat features common to all Niktos, but bore a set of facial fins that dominated his pale gray features. The Nikto was at the far end of the bar, asleep or drunk or both, his back against where the bar met the rear wall.

The tattooed swoop gang had made the Nikto a target for their game. In turn, each would slide a half-filled mug down the length of the bar, toward the inert alien. The idea was apparently to get as close to the Nikto as possible without dropping the drink in his lap. Of course, eventually they would.

"That's probably our Nikto," said Mander. "We should stop this."

"What are you going to do," said Reen, "talk them to death?" Mander ignored her and motioned for the pair to stay by the door.

One of the swoop gang, a big thug in a broad-brimmed hat, gave his mug too hard a push. It slid down the length of the bar, sloshing a pungent, frothy liquid as it spun. It caromed off another glass and right toward the Nikto's lap.

And Mander was there to pick it up, settling himself on the stool next to the Nikto, raising the mug in a toast to the swoopers, and then setting it down on the bar. "Sorry to interrupt the game," he said, "but I need to talk to this one. I'll let you get back to your fun in a moment." He turned to the Nikto and shook the alien by the shoulder. "Wake up. I am looking for Mika the Hutt."

"Hey!" shouted a voice behind him, and the swooper who had flung the most recent glass stormed down to their end of the bar. Mander turned and realized that he had made a mistake. The swoopers were not tattooed. Instead the dark lines on their faces were veins. Dark veins, standing up from the flesh.

Tempest, he thought. But what Mander said was "Leave us in peace for a moment," throwing as much of the Force as he could quickly muster behind his request.

The thug should have stopped in his tracks and spat something about leaving them in peace. Instead, he raised a massive fist and smashed Mander across the jaw.

Surprised, Mander dropped to one knee, the room swimming in his vision. When he looked up, the other swoopers had descended on Reen and Eddey, three thugs apiece. No weapons had been drawn, but Reen had already knocked out one opponent, while Eddey was fending off his trio with a chair.

The big one standing over Mander had a chair as well, raised above his head to bring it down on the Jedi. Mander's head cleared in an instant, and he reached across his body to pull his lightsaber, only to get it tangled in the folds of his zerape. He rolled out of the way as the thug brought the chair down on the space where he had been, the Jedi pulling himself fully upright.

Mander brought the lightsaber out, but had it backward. He could have easily flipped it in his hands, but instead he drove the butt-end of the device into his attacker's belly. The air rushed out of his opponent's lungs, and Mander, not stopping, brought the metal hilt of his blade straight up, connecting with the swooper's jaw. Now it was the big thug's turn to fall backward from the force of the blow.

Mander looked up at the others. Reen had downed a second one, and Eddey had lost his chair, but one of the swoop gang was collapsed at his feet. Still, there were more swoopers than allies.

The big one was struggling to his feet, the veins rich

and dark on his face, a purplish crust at the corners of his eyes. Now Mander spun the lightsaber around in his hand, igniting it as he did so. It crackled to life like caged lightning. The bully brought himself up centimeters from the tip of the blade. The others, alerted by the noise, stopped fighting immediately. Everyone stared at the lightsaber glowing like a beacon in the darkened cantina.

Fear drained the face of the lead swooper. He suddenly looked very pale in the light of the weapon.

"I think you should go," said Mander. He did not need to put the Force into his voice to make his point. "Now."

The lead swooper took a step back, then a second, and a third. Then he turned and bolted for the door, his still-conscious allies following him. There came the satisfying sound of swoop bike engines engaging, then fading into the distance.

Reen motioned the barkeep over to discuss damages and what to do with the unconscious gang members. Eddey picked up the big swooper's wide-brimmed hat and tried it on. It fit passably enough. Mander turned back to the Nikto, who was now awake and plastered in fear against the back wall.

"Mika the Hutt," said Mander softly. "We're looking for him. I've been sent by his father."

The Nikto stammered something in Huttese, then gulped a deep breath of air and said in Basic, "Yes, yes. I will take you to him. He's to the north, in Temple Valley." He rose unsteadily to his feet and almost pitched forward.

Mander helped the Nikto out of the cantina, and saw that three of the bikes had been left beneath the dead tree. He made for them, Reen and Eddey behind him. He set the Nikto behind him on one of the bikes while

Eddey broke open the security system on the ignition systems.

"That went well," said Reen. "You know, I didn't expect you to really try to talk him to death."

"I know," said Mander, covering his own discomfort. "But you saw the dark blood vessels. The rage."

"I saw it after the fight started. Tempest."

"Well, apparently it interfered with my Jedi mind tricks." Mander looked at Eddey, who bypassed the security on the last swoop bike and fired it up. The engine revved satisfactorily and the Bothan gave him a thumbs-up.

"It interfered with your abilities. That's a bad thing," said Reen.

"That's a very bad thing," agreed Mander. "Let's get back to the cargo skiff. We can leave the bikes there for their original owners to find and take the skiff to Temple Valley."

By the time they had gotten back to the skiff, the Nikto had recovered enough to apologize to all of them for abandoning his post and being found drunk. He had been entrusted to watch over the office when Brave Young Mika chose to abandon the city. That was early on, when the deaths were rampant and people were blaming the outlanders. He had been living in the office after Mika left, until a mob broke in one night. He had escaped, but the place was ruined. So he had left a note as to where he could be found. Now that help had arrived, he would take them to Temple Valley.

Temple Valley was one of the more pleasant locations on Endregaad, more rolling hills than sharp-walled arroyos. Still, great rock formations had erupted from the landscape like partially buried cathedrals, giving the region its name. The Nikto's directions were exact, and they topped the last rise to see an unexpected sight.

It was a crashed spaceship, its engines ripped from

their mounts by the force of the impact. A shallow trench and debris field stretched from the ruins about a kilometer to the west, with large fragments dotting the landscape like metal altars to a forgotten god. The main body of the ship was cracked almost in half lengthwise, and the port side had plowed into the hillock.

Beneath the starboard wing a small collection of tents had been set up against the heat, using the ruined ship and a parked luxury skiff as supports. As they approached, Niktos stirred from the shade of the ship— Red, Green, and Mountain subfamilies, all descended from a common stock. All of them were armed, but when they saw the Nikto with Mander, they set up a cheer.

Eddey settled their skiff and they debarked, the Mountain Nikto explaining in rapid Huttese to the others what had happened. He was going too fast for Mander to make out everything, but the phrases "Wise Popara" and "*Jeedai*" were used a great deal.

Mander looked over at the camp beneath the ship's wing, and another large shape moved into the sunlight. This was a Hutt, smaller than the others he had seen, his flesh a pale yellow-green with a lighter underbelly. It was wearing an incongruous zerape made out of a large blanket, and had a broad-brimmed hat shielding its eyes. Mander stepped up to the Hutt, meeting it halfway.

"I am Mander Zuma," Mander said in Huttese. "If you are Mika the Hutt, I should tell you that your father is concerned."

"I am Mika Anjiliac," said the young Hutt in educated, precise Basic. "My father has every right to have been concerned. Welcome to ground zero for the Endregaad plague."

MIKA THE HUTT

"When the plague came, we had no chance to get off the planet," said Mika. "And to be frank, I had no desire to. I had been negotiating with the miners over a particularly rich substratum of geodes, and was shocked by how quickly they succumbed to the disease. We did what we could, but had precious little medicine with us. Even my Niktos were infected, though the survivors developed an immunity."

They were gathered beneath the wing of the ruined craft. The Nikto bodyguards had rigged up thick fabric tarps around them that kept most of the dust at bay, and appointed the quarters in comfort for their Hutt master. Brocaded cushions were strewn about on carpeting that may have come from the ship itself. Reen and Mander sat on the cushions, while Eddey, still wearing his broad-brimmed hat, wandered around the ship's exterior, poking at the damage. Two Nikto guards followed him at a discreet distance.

Another Nikto brought Mika a steaming bowl, and the Hutt poised his face over the rim, letting the hot vapor rise. Despite such ministrations, the Hutt's skin was dry and cracking in numerous places. Other servants brought Reen and Mander thin glass flutes of scentwine. Even hiding in the wilderness, Mander thought, the Hutts still liked their luxury.

Mika breathed deeply and continued. "Things quickly

went from bad to worse in Tel Bollin. Effective civil authority collapsed, and the existing stocks of medicine were exhausted. Entire blocks would be infected overnight. Then the stories began to circulate that outworlders, traders, and aliens were responsible for the plague. Houses and buildings were burned."

Mika sighed. "It turns out that those blaming the outworlders were right, though not the way they thought. I tracked the spread of the disease through the region and discovered that it appeared first in the Temple Valley. When things became too uncomfortable in the city, I decamped with my entourage and came looking. I left Orgamon, here, back at the Skydove offices and charged him with getting word out, and waiting for help." He looked at the now-sober Nikto, who was chatting quietly with his companions. "It sounds like he failed in the first case, but succeeded admirably in the second."

The Hutt turned back to the others, regarding them with wide, expressive eyes. "I confirmed that the first and most virulent cases came from this area, and once we arrived, we searched the region until I found this ship." He looked up at the blackened and twisted metal. "From the weathering and exposure, this wreck is recent. I would guess two or three weeks before the epidemic hit Tel Bollin, at most."

"And whose ship is this?" asked Mander.

"That is the thing of it," said Mika. "I do not know."

"It is a YV-100," said Reen. "Corellian Engineering Corporation model, but even from the remains it looks heavily modified. That's not unusual for this type of ship."

"We know the make of it, but have no record of the owner," Mika clarified. "Nothing on our registry or that of the Miners' Guild in Tel Bollin matches it, and none of the onboard records survived the impact. We found the bodies of the crew—Corellians, by the way—and we burned the remains as best we could in accord with their customs."

"You could pull the inspection numbers off the engines," suggested Reen. "They have customized serial numbers."

The Hutt paused for a moment, and then nodded at one of his guards. The Nikto immediately went over to one of the cast-off engines with a datapad. Meanwhile, Mika pointed to the west. "I assume they were smugglers—geode smuggling is fairly common here. Otherwise they would have landed at Tel Bollin. Nearly as I can reconstruct it, the ship came in at a very shallow angle from the west. I think it clipped one of the sentinel stones in that direction. Perhaps it was at night, or in a bad storm. Had the pilot been more capable, she would have been able to land the craft. Perhaps they were already affected by the disease."

"What was the ship carrying?" asked Reen.

The Hutt shrugged, a full-body ripple that radiated down his back. "It was empty when my people found it. It could have been making a dead-head run. Traveling empty. Perhaps coming to pick something or someone up."

"Or someone else got to the wreck before you did," said Eddey. Mander hadn't realized that the Bothan had returned and had been standing there, listening to their discussion. Eddey crossed over to Mander and held out a cupped hand. "I found this near the remains of the cargo bay." He carefully poured the contents into Mander's palm.

Eddey had given Mander a handful of sand. Mander looked closer, and saw that among the sand were bright crystals of purple.

"Tempest," said Reen, who was leaning in as well.

"There's not a lot of it, and it's mixed in with the dirt and sand, but I think it came from the ship," said Eddey.

"Tempest?" said Mika, his eyes wide with curiosity.

"A hard spice, very addictive," said Mander, offering the tainted sand to the Hutt. Mika shrank back but waved for one of his Nikto servants to take it. A proper container was provided, and the Hutt stared at it, as if trying to divine its mysteries with his large, bright eyes.

"There were some other purple splotches in the sand when we arrived," said Mika at last. "I had thought it to be merely some lubricants that leaked out of the ship after the crash. It is a spice, then. But not one I have seen before."

"We've seen it before, and its effects," said Reen. "It promotes sudden rage and discolored veins near the surface of the skin." She raised her voice slightly at the end, obviously fishing.

Mika frowned. "I think I saw some humans with those effects in town. My family does deal in spice on occasion, but not the harder varieties. My father would not hear of it. But it does help make sense of it all. If the ship was carrying a dangerous drug, they would have been making a rendezvous with a local contact out here. Something goes wrong and the ship crashes, and the contact finds the ship first."

"And brings the spice into town for resale, bringing the plague with him," Reen finished.

The Hutt nodded at the idea and added, "And if he hired local geode miners to help move it, that would be why they were infected first."

"I found the drug in Makem Te," said Mander, "and crossed blades with some members of the Bomu clan—Rodians who were selling it. Then, when we hyperjumped into the system, we were immediately attacked by a raider that identified itself as Bomu as well."

Mika leaned forward, intrigued. "So if these Rodians

were involved in selling the spice, this ship may have been one of theirs. Or perhaps the raiders knew about the spice shipment and engaged the smugglers' ship, and that is why it crashed in the first place."

"Possibly both the Rodians and the Corellians you found dead here work for the same operation," said Mander.

Mika leaned back and stroked what could have been, beneath the rolls of fat, his chin. "Your raider would have been in space because they couldn't get to the surface and the shipment of Tempest."

"Or they had nothing to do with this shipment at all, and were just in space waiting for us," said Reen. At that the Hutt's wide eyes turned on her with a quizzical look.

Mander said, "Rodians take vengeance very seriously, and we gave them good enough cause. And they may have been involved in the death of a . . . companion of ours."

The Hutt looked at Reen and recognition dawned. "You are a Pantoran, like the other Jedi. Toro, his name was?"

"His name was," said Reen, frowning. "He was killed."

The Hutt's face fell in on itself. "I am sorry," he said, and sounded like he meant it. "I met him only a few times, when he was negotiating with the family. He seemed very brave and honest."

"It's one of the things we are looking into," said Mander, and the Hutt turned back to him. "The Bomus may be after us because of the Tempest, or they may be after us because of the coordinates of the Indrexu Spiral."

"Ah," said the young Hutt. "That deal went through, then? And that was how you got here. Yes, I've used the route myself."

"Was there anyone else interested in those coordinates?" asked Mander. "Or more important, was there anyone who would *not* want other people to have those coordinates?"

"No," said Mika, after a moment's thought. "We . . . *acquired* . . . that hyperjump path about six standard months ago, and used it to speed our deliveries. But we also found it was a route better for light freighters than big ships. My father always said, *Jopando ki fofon*—information is like fruit. It is perishable, and can quickly go bad. As soon as you discover something, the chance that someone else discovers the same thing—or discovers that you have discovered it—goes up exponentially. The Bothans know this very well." He nodded to Eddey when he said this, who touched the tip of his hat in recognition.

Mika returned to the subject, saying "We put out word about the existence of the route, and were surprised when the most reasonable response came from the new Jedi Order. We figure it was a good sale, in that you would then distribute that information with less of an immediate profit, and we would benefit most from the situation. You can check with my father, but there were no other serious bidders that I knew of."

"That doesn't mean that someone else wasn't using the Indrexu Spiral, and hoping to keep others away," said Mander.

The Hutt thought about it for a moment, then nodded. "Especially if they were using the Spiral for smuggling this hard spice, this Tempest," said Mika. "They might be properly motivated to stop anyone who threatens to give away their secrets."

"Including the Anjiliacs—" Mander began, but he was interrupted from pursuing this tack further by sudden shouts from the Nikto guards. They were pointing up the hillside that led back to Tel Bollin.

Mander rose and walked to the edge of the shade provided by the ruined wing to get a better look. The ridge was occupied by about two dozen humans, all mounted on colorful swoop bikes. The Jedi noticed that the three bikes they had liberated earlier and later abandoned were among their number.

"Our friends are back," said Mander.

"Friends?" said Mika.

"Swoop gang," shouted Reen, pulling her blaster. "Tempest addicts." Eddey had pulled his blaster as well, and was alongside her. Mander noted that his was a small, discreet weapon, and realized he had not seen him use it previously. The Jedi ignited his lightsaber, the blade coming alive with a harsh crackle.

Behind them a handful of Nikto closed over Mika, hustling him back to his larger skiff. The others were scrambling with their blaster carbines to find cover.

The leader of the swoop gang—the large one without the hat—raised a hand and let out a war whoop. The wave of swoops surged down from the crest, their forward blasters firing.

The opening volley caught a few of the Niktos in the open, cutting them down, but now about three others had taken up positions among the wreckage and were returning fire. A couple of the swoop riders fell, but the entire wave came on.

One bike in particular, festooned with a gundark skull on the leading edge, bore down on Mander, weapons blazing. The Jedi deflected the blasterfire, then, as the bike was almost on top of him, he leapt upward.

It was a good leap, and he cleared the gundark skull and the forward repulsor. He tumbled over the bike, dragging his blade beneath him as he spun. The rider tried to fall out of his seat, but moved too slowly, and his head and right arm struck the dirt separately. The unmanned swoop continued forward and caught an outcropping, toppling end-over-end into the crashed and ruined starship.

Mander landed and winced at a sudden pain in his ankle. By that time, the first wave of the swoops had passed through the camp, and was now regrouping at the far side for another strafing run. Only about four had fallen, leaving more than a dozen. The leader gave another wave, and with a shout they surged back into the camp.

Mander looked around quickly. There was no sign of Mika and his defenders. Eddey and Reen had hunkered down behind some crates and were returning fire, shot for shot. On closer inspection, Mander could see that most of the original Nikto defenders were down. The attackers had mobility and firepower, he realized. The best he could do to even the odds was to take out the chain of command.

The Jedi ran into the open, toward the swoop gang leader. The gang leader had produced a long, curved blade and was piloting the swoop one-handed, intent on cutting Mander down before everyone.

Mander felt the pain of a twisted ankle radiating with every step, and favored the leg as he ran forward. The swoop leader saw the limp and screamed again, his face twisted in a spasm of Tempest-induced rage. Mander waited for the last second, then brought his blade up to match that of the leader.

The lightsaber cut through the blade effortlessly, but the blade was not Mander's target. Instead he followed through to dig into the leader's torso—and the seat itself—cutting through the couplings and thrusters. The swoop let out a shriek and pitched sideways, dragging its dead rider across the sand before impacting into the side of a ruined starship engine.

Blaster bolts cut around him, and Mander deflected what he could, but limped toward Reen and Eddey's position as they lent him cover. The attackers were down to less than a dozen, but only a couple of Nikto body-guards were still standing. The surviving swoops spun around for yet another pass. Removing the leader had done little to shake their resolve.

Then Mika's own skiff rose from behind the wreckage of the freighter, the small Hutt manning a forward-mounted gun. The weapon swung in a smooth, prac-ticed arc, shots falling among the swoop bikes. Two of them went up in flames, and the concussions flipped an-other pair of swoops. The survivors turned tail at that, fleeing up the hill, Eddey and Reen firing a few shots at their retreating backs.

Mander turned toward the Hutt's skiff. The small Hutt saluted the Jedi, but as he did so a last swoop bike rose behind the skiff, its wounded rider training twin guns at the Hutt's back. Mander tried to shout but the blasters erupted too quickly . . .

And the Hutt ducked. It happened in an instant, too fast for even Mander to realize. The Hutt slumped and threw himself to one side, so that the blaster shots ripped through the forward housing of his skiff and one of his guardian Niktos, but left the Hutt unscathed. In a mo-ment shots from Eddey, Reen, and the surviving Niktos cut the biker down.

As soon as it had started it was over, the battlefield nothing more than corpses and smoking blaster scoring. Mander checked out the Niktos, to find only one or two still alive. Of the swoop riders, none survived the en-counter. Their dead faces were twisted in rigid snarls, mapped by the tracery of Tempest-swelled blood vessels.

Eddey and Reen came up to him, and Mander shook his head. "No survivors."

"I didn't know you wanted to question them," said the Bothan.

Reen shook her head. "Maybe you should have kept

one alive yourself. Of course, your lightsaber doesn't have a stun setting."

Mika slithered out from the shade of the shelter, two Niktos trailing behind him.

"Thank you," Mander said to the Hutt.

"Your excellent service will be rewarded," replied the Hutt. "You weakened them sufficiently for me to act. If I had brought the skiff out too early in the battle, it would have just drawn all the fire. You know who they were?"

"The Tempest addicts we ran into earlier," said Mander. "They probably followed us."

"Probably," said the youthful Hutt, but he did not seemed convinced. "What happens now?"

Mander looked around at the debris. "If you have nothing else going on here, I'd like to head back to our ship. Quietly."

"We can load our wounded on one of the skiffs, and I can go with you on the other," said the Hutt. "Do we leave then?"

"We will send word to your father once we reach our ship," said Mander. "But if we don't have any more trouble, we should stay a few more days. The CSA is distributing the spice your father gave us to the infected populace. It would be easier to wait until the quarantine is lifted."

"Hang on," said the Hutt, looking skyward. "I think there is going to be a change of plans." Eddey growled as well, hearing something above human recognition.

Reen looked up at the dust-filled sky. "What? I don't hear anything."

Mander scanned the horizon. "You're right. More visitors are incoming." He had just managed to get the words out of his mouth when the IRDs came screaming across the sky. They were three of them. One of them banked toward Tel Bollin while the other two circled over the campsite, looking for a place to touch down.

"The cavalry arrives," muttered Reen. "Once all the fighting is over, of course."

"More likely the fighting is what drew them in the first place," said Mander.

"Do you have a recommendation for our next action?" said Mika, looking sidewise at the Jedi.

"Let's play nice," said Mander, and Reen growled at the concept. "After all," he continued, "your father *did* ask the CSA to find you, and now they have, after their own fashion."

Flight Officer Lockerbee was in his cleanly pressed uniform, though more cautious and officious than Mander had previously thought possible. He stood farther away from the Jedi and the others as he spat out orders: Everyone will remain in the campsite. A shuttle will be dispatched from the *Resolute* for them and their wounded. The other IRD is tracking the fleeing swoops. No, they will not be allowed to return to the *New Ambition*, at least not until Lieutenant Commander Krin has had a chance to speak with all of them. And one more thing: she wishes to speak with Mander Zuma immediately.

REPERCUSSIONS

By saying that she "wished to speak" with Mander Zuma, Lieutenant Commander Angela Krin apparently meant to say she "wished to lock him up and throw away the key."

For the next two days Mander was provided with comfortable but secure quarters aboard the Dreadnought *Resolute*. It was a pleasant set of rooms, which would qualify as a suite on many worlds, with a separate bedroom and bath. These wonderful accommodations were only marred by the carbine-wielding CSA troopers posted outside his door, visible only when food was provided. He was not allowed visitors or contact with others. He was also denied any access to communications or to the ship's library.

He was left alone with his thoughts, which at first blush seemed to be punishment enough.

He meditated and slept between meals, and if there were any spycams in walls—which he assumed likely— it would show for most of the time the Jedi engaged in eating, sleeping, and resting in a state that *looked* like sleeping. In reality, Mander was reviewing what he knew and what they had learned from Endregaad.

The plague was tied to the Tempest trade, which meant that it might show up on other, more populous worlds. Perhaps it already had broken out on other planets and would most likely disappear among other, more virulent diseases or be handled by medicines that were regularly prescribed in more urban areas against a host of ills. No, an isolated outpost on an otherwise lightly populated planet was a perfect place to come down with a new disease.

So had this ship of unknown provenance and origin berthed previously on the disease's original homeworld, or did the Tempest itself come from a plagueworld? Mander reminded himself to ask the lieutenant commander if she could check the spice and the disease to determine an origin point. That is, if he ever saw her again.

Of course they would let them go, eventually. It was too much trouble to keep a Hutt incarcerated, particularly one whose family was interested in his release. And once Mika was returned to his family, the news that Mander was a guest of the CSA would likely spread— the Anjiliacs would sell that information, if nothing else—and the Order would ask for his release. And he would refuse to go unless Reen and Eddey Be'ray were released as well.

Patience, then, was the best medicine. Though he wished he could get a message to the two of them, Reen in particular. He could not imagine her taking this confinement to quarters in good spirits.

He thought about her and Eddey, and wondered if the pair had anything in their permanent records that might make the CSA bring other charges against them. He decided that it was unlikely. Reen was reticent to admit she and the Bothan had previously engaged in smuggling, so the Jedi assumed that it was a relatively rare matter, and the fact they got burned on it and lost their ship indicated that they probably had not been doing it as a full-time profession. More than likely it was something the Pantoran had agreed to on an impulse, or had decided that the reward was high enough to make it worth it.

Reen reminded him much of her brother Toro in that degree. Impulsive. Emotional. Ready to take the big risk without considering the outcome. With that impulsiveness came an ability to think beyond the standard responses, which was an advantage. But by the same token, that ability had often led the younger man into the trouble that required that kind of thinking in the first place.

Mander Zuma thought of their last duel together, as Master and apprentice, at the praxeum on Yavin 4. What had begun as training exercises had blossomed into a friendly and weekly rivalry, in which Toro would try out new tactics and moves that he had been developing. Mander found himself spending more time in practice, researching old holotexts on fighting styles and understanding their underpinning. Usually one of Toro's new moves had been discovered, exploited, and countered centuries before by some Jedi. Still, the young Pantoran was eager and enthusiastic, and showed no regret that a previous Jedi had walked that path long before he did.

Apprentice Toro Irana had brought his own lightsaber as well that day. He had crafted it by hand, with crystals that he himself had harvested, as Mander had done before him. His blade had a blue-white purity to it that reflected off his deep blue flesh. The handle was shorter than Mander's, but he wielded it with a fluidity where the blade led and the body followed effortlessly. Mander noted with regret that Toro would soon leave the Praxeum and act as a Jedi Knight on his own. He had not realized at the time how soon that would be.

The pair saluted and began to spar, their blades sliding off each other as they touched. Both were holding their blows, Toro waiting for the moment to unleash his latest supposed discovery, Mander waiting for his student to try something. Toro pressed, Mander retreated a few steps and turned aside the attack, riposted, and forced Toro back as well.

Then Toro saw something that Mander never did in the heat of combat—some weakness in Mander's responses that opened the older Jedi to an attack on one side. Suddenly Toro seized the opportunity, pressing with a series of wide swings. Mander knew his peril in a moment, and quickly parried the blade, but Toro had already pulled back and unleashed another onslaught, this one culminating with a double-handed overhand smash.

Mander recognized the series from a set of old holos in the archives—it was used two hundred years previously, primarily for its flashy nature. This was an assault that played to the crowds, but had several counters, the most effective being a steering block.

Mander brought his blade up and the two lightsabers crackled as he caught the descending blade squarely with his own. The force of the blow staggered him slightly, but Mander gave with the knees and resisted the blow. Despite being beneath his opponent's blade, Mander now had the advantage. He could steer the attacking opponent, who was overextended and could not keep the pressure up beyond the initial blow. Mander could move him easily to the right or left, breaking the contact and putting Toro at a disadvantage.

Instead Mander held the blades for a long moment. Through their clashed lightsabers, he could feel the pressure of Toro's blade shift first to one side, then the other, trying to slide past the block. Always Mander countered these attempts, keeping Toro in the blocked position. The apprentice was trapped. His only choice was to release the pressure and fall back, surrendering the momentum, and perhaps the match, to Mander.

Toro knew all that, Mander realized. Using the steering

block to trap your opponent's blade was a basic maneuver, and no Jedi would hold it once it became clear that his opponent had that level of control. What was he planning?

"Master," said Toro, the Force flowing into his voice, "you want to drop your weapon."

A wave of the Force swept over Mander, and it felt like his mind was a ship, riding up that wave. For an instant he thought this was a reasonable request, and he reduced his pressure on his student's upper blade. Toro grinned and pressed his assault.

Then suddenly the boat of his mind crested the wave and Mander knew what Toro had tried: he was using the Force to weaken him—a simple mind trick. Mander's own resolve rose within him, and he pulled back farther, causing Toro to overbalance now and fall toward him, losing the control that his mind trick had temporarily given him. Mander guided his opponent's lightsaber to the right and stepped away, executing his own push at the last moment and sending his student sprawling. Mander finished his disengage with a twist of his wrist, and Toro's short-hafted lightsaber flew from his fingers.

Toro rolled to one side and tried to rise, his hand reaching out to pull his lightsaber to him. He stopped when he realized that Mander was standing over him, lightsaber pointed at his apprentice's chest.

Toro raised both hands in surrender. The match was over.

Mander, however, did not move. He fought the sense of anger within him.

"That was incredibly foolish," he said, trying to make his words sound less furious and more instructive. He failed utterly. "Do not use the Force like that on me!"

Toro's eyes went wide, and for the first moment Mander saw something that he had not seen before in his student—fear. Slowly, Mander Zuma raised his lightsaber and shrank the blade back into its hilt. He reached down and offered Toro his hand. Toro hesitated for a moment, half a second at most, then grasped his Master's hand and got to his feet.

"I am sorry, Master Zuma," said Toro Irana. "I did not mean to anger you."

"You didn't," said Mander, and knew it was a lie as soon as the words left his mouth. "You *did* surprise me, which I assume was your intent."

"It was," said Toro, looking for forgiveness in Mander's face. "I didn't know it had been tried before."

"It has," said Mander, his voice softening as he moved from upbraiding to instructing. "And that's why you don't use it. When you attempt to use the Force to manipulate the mind of another of similar ability, that attempt is clear to your target, and will probably be met with extreme resistance and retribution. And that includes them using the Force to manipulate you as well."

"Then," Toro said—and Mander could see that the young Pantoran was digesting what he had said, looking for a way around it, "I could use it as a tactic against opponents who were not strong in the Force."

"If you could," said Mander, "you probably would not need to draw your lightsaber in the first place. 'The Force can have a strong influence on the weak-minded.'"

"That was a quote," noted Toro.

"Yes," said Mander. "From my Master's Master's Master. And an apprentice's mind tricks should not work on the one who taught them to him. Should you find yourself in a situation where someone uses the Force on you in this way, try the Meditation of Emptiness. It clears your mind, and with it the influence of others."

"I will remember that, Master," said Toro, smiling now, sure he had been forgiven.

Mander managed to smile back at his student, though his mind was neither empty nor clear on the matter. "Come," he said. "Let me tell you of the dangers of using the Force in that way. We can spar again later."

But they never did spar again, and Mander knew that would be the case. Even without his attempt to use the Force, Toro was more than capable of taking Mander's full measure and the older Jedi knew it. So when the opportunity appeared for Toro Irana to leave the Praxeum on Yavin 4, he took it, and his travels thereafter never took him back. The next time Mander saw him, the young Pantoran was dead, lying still in a Swokes Swokes mortuary, his body ravaged by the effect of the Tempest and a fall from a great height.

Was it his fault? Mander wondered. If he had not reacted in such anger, humiliated the young man, would he have stayed? Would he have been a better Jedi with more training? Or if someone else had trained him? Or did he let the young man pass into the greater universe without sufficient training, because he himself lacked anything else to teach him?

Or, Mander thought, was the fact that Toro took Tempest simply the young Jedi's own doing? Was he looking for that edge? If Tempest increased the resistance to the Force, then was he looking for something that wouldn't let others manipulate him as he could manipulate others?

There was a knock and the hatch slid open, shaking Mander from these musings. Lieutenant Lockerbee appeared with two guards. "The commander wishes to see you at your earliest convenience," he stated. He and his companions did not move from the entrance, indicating that they would wait for that time to arrive.

Mander let out a sigh and pulled himself to his feet, reaching for his formal outer robe. "I was having trouble meditating anyway," he said, following Lockerbee as the two guards fell in behind them.

As they approached the command conference deck, the door hissed open and another lieutenant, escorting Reen Irana, emerged, followed by two more guards. There was a brief moment as the two groups sought to move past each other in the hallway without breaking protocol.

"It seems she wants to talk to all of us," said Reen as she passed near Mander.

"What did she ask you about?" said Mander.

Reen made a face and said, "What do two women always talk about?" Seeing the confusion on his face, she answered her own question: "Men." And then the changing of the guards was complete and she was gone, back to her own private, guarded suite. Mander was issued into the lieutenant commander's presence.

The command conference deck was as spartan as Mander remembered it. Only one chair was before the large desk console. Mander noted that the holo-chess game was paused in mid-game to one side. Behind Lieutenant Commander Angela Krin, Endregaad spun slowly on the viewscreen, unchanged from the time when the plague held that world in its grip.

Angela Krin did not look particularly pleased to see Mander, despite the passage of two days.

"It goes without saying that your actions reflect badly on my judgment," said the lieutenant commander.

"I don't think it was bad judgment at all," said Mander calmly.

"You were my personal guests when you first arrived. For three days," Krin said. "Three days. At the end of that time, you did not proceed out of the system as instructed, but rather immediately attempted to break the medical blockade, landing on a quarantine world."

"In all fairness," Mander said calmly, "the blockade

should have been in place to keep people from leaving, thereby spreading the infection. Breaking *into* a plague house pretty much carries its own penalty."

"You then violate CSA law," she said, ignoring his comment, "get into a brawl with local thugs, and finally engage in a firefight with those thugs at the site of a previously unreported crash site—which may have been the cause of the plague in the first place." Angela Krin shook her head and asked, "What do you have to say for yourself?"

"You're welcome."

Before the lieutenant commander could recover, Mander added quickly, "We delivered medicinal spice to you before your own government could, making it easier to restore the rule of law on Endregaad. We took it upon ourselves to locate a missing Hutt, whose recovery both reflects well on you diplomatically and reduces the number of irritating holomessages you would receive from his concerned family. We took out a swoop gang that was terrorizing the disease-weakened populace, and in addition discovered that a deadly hard spice called Tempest was being smuggled onto the planet. All of which you could do on your own—and commendably well, I may add—were it not for the fact that you were trying to hold everything else together and maintaining a one-ship blockade. By retroactively delegating a few choice decisions in your report back to the CSA, you might even be commended for you initiative and problem-solving abilities."

Lieutenant Commander Angela Krin looked at Mander long and hard. Surprisingly, she allowed herself a laugh and said, "You are not what I expected from a Jedi."

"Oddly, you're not the first person to tell me that," said Mander.

The CSA officer settled herself into her chair. "The

CSA medicines did arrive, by the way, and are being distributed. The plague is, for all intents and purposes, curtailed."

"As I said, you had matters well in hand," said Mander. "We only helped enable your efforts."

"And this Tempest you found . . . ," said Angela Krin.

"You know of it?" asked Mander.

"Not directly," she said, tapping her datapad. "There are reports of this addiction all along this spiral arm. It is coming into the Corporate Worlds from outside, in particular those that have a lot of trade connections. And the increase in the drug's usage is coupled with an increase in violence. Enough to reduce planetary efficiency numbers."

"Which makes it a problem the CSA cannot ignore," said Mander.

The lieutenant commander set down the 'pad and rubbed her face. "So I solve one problem to find a greater one. That Hutt you rescued, he's not what I expected, either."

"I've noticed," said Mander.

"He speaks in Basic, and seems almost . . ." She thought for the word she needed, then settled on ". . . helpful. He gave a full reporting of his situation, and your contribution. He provided the engine numbers so we can track down the craft. He also provided some samples of this Tempest spice for my people to analyze. He has proved easier to work with than you were."

"He also plays holo-chess," said Mander, tilting his head toward the half-completed game.

"He plays very well," said Angela Krin, "and he was almost complimentary about the CSA's work against the plague. He said our efforts were sufficient."

"That is Hutt-speak for 'thank you,'" said Mander. "But where does that leave us?"

Krin smiled now, and it was a conspiratorial smile.

"This strange young Hutt and I had some discussions, and he made clear that he thinks well of you and yours, and would like to see matters resolved positively. I suppose with some careful language in my reports and a commendation for Flight Officer Lockerbee, you would be cleared of charges and released under your own recognizance. As such, you and yours are free to go, with the general and blanket stern warning never to do this again."

"I will attempt to keep myself off plague-ridden planets with Hutts in the near future," said Mander, grinning back.

The lieutenant commander touched a few buttons on her desk, and rose. "I do have a message for you. I took the liberty of contacting the Hutts after your return, and sending them a full report. This came in response." She touched a glyph and the head of one of Vago's H-3PO units crackled into view, bleached to a white ghost by the transceiver.

The droid burbled, "Popara, may his tongue always be tipped with sweet oils, extends greetings to the *Jeedai* Mander Zuma and his most capable associates in regard to the recovery of his youngest son, Mika, and hopes that you have found the agreement made to your liking. He wishes you to escort his beloved spawn Mika back to Nar Shaddaa, where Popara will be waiting to further reward you for your efforts, as well as speak of additional matters of mutual benefit." The message cut off without asking for a response.

"I don't have to warn you," Angela Krin said gently, "how dangerous it is to deal with Hutts. Even helpful ones." She looked at her datapad. "I will check out Mika's information on the spice smuggling. In the meantime, fly careful, Mander Zuma."

Mander rose and said, "Fly careful, Lieutenant Commander."

Outside the briefing deck, Mander encountered Eddey Be'ray, flanked not by guards but by a pair of shuttle pilots. "They're letting me go down and bring back the *New Ambition*. They offered to fetch it themselves, but Reen would not let them know where it is. She's possessive that way."

"I understand," said the Jedi. "Did you have a chance to talk with the lieutenant commander over the past few days?"

Eddey Be'ray shook his head. "Not I. Reen did the talking for the two of us."

"Reen said they were talking about men," said Mander.

The Bothan's mouth spread into a lupine grin, "She's pulling your chain," he said. "The CSA was talking with us about a job."

Mander blinked. The idea that Reen and the Bothan would leave never occurred to him. "A job? What kind of job? Are you taking it?"

Eddey held his palms up and shrugged, and Mander was suddenly aware that they were surrounded by four officers of the CSA. "Let me put it this way," Mander said, pushing his other questions to the back of his mind. "Are you available for a short haul?"

Again the lupine grin. "I think we can do that, but you'll have to talk to Reen."

"Good enough," said Mander. "When you get back with the ship, we will fit it out for a trip to Nar Shaddaa. Popara wishes us to bring his wayward child home to him, and I think we should oblige."

Eddey made an indeterminate noise. "All right. I have to admit, though, it's hard for a Bothan to trust a Hutt. Professional rivalry and all that. But beyond that, there is more going on here than meets the eye."

"These Hutts have been very helpful. Even you must admit that," said Mander.

Eddey nodded. "But like Reen says, at their heart, they're still Hutts. We should be careful with their gifts. You know that saying Mika quoted, 'Information is like fruit'?"

"Yes?"

"It's a Bothan saying," Eddey said. "They stole it."

A NIGHT ON NAR SHADDAA

"Once upon a time," Reen said, "the Hutts did not live on Nal Hutta, or on its moon Nar Shaddaa. They lived on planet called Varl, and it was a terrible place, perfect for the Hutts. The world orbited two stars, Evona and Ardos, whom the Hutts said were gods and lovers. Evona was consumed by darkness, and Ardos, in rage, exploded, destroying all the other worlds of their system and blasting the very atmosphere from Varl itself." She tweaked the descent controls, and the traffic relays glowed green on her console for their final approach. The bow of the *New Ambition* dipped toward their destination.

"Evona was consumed by a black hole," said Mander. "Ardos went nova and is now a white dwarf."

Reen ignored him. "The Hutts fled before the devastation and came to the Y'Toub system, and found the world Evocar, which they called Nal Hutta—'Glorious Jewel' in their language. But Nal Hutta was occupied by another species, the Evocii, who welcomed them and thought to share their lands. The Hutts did not like the idea of sharing, and drove the Evocii from their world, resettling them on the largest of its moons, now called Nar Shaddaa. And then the Hutts took over Nar Shaddaa, the Smugglers' Moon, and killed all the Evocii anyway."

"I am well aware of the stories and the histories," said

Mander. "I've read them myself in the archives. You have a point?"

"The point," said the Pantoran, "is that the Hutts have survived the deaths of their gods, and think of themselves as suitable replacements for those deities. They consider everyone and everything else expendable."

They had spent an inordinate amount of time in a holding pattern beyond the orbit of the Smugglers' Moon, waiting for permission to land. Mander thought that while Popara was a powerful force in the Indrexu sector, his was not one of the Clans of the Ancients, the true ruling families of this world. He was ultimately a small fish in this wider and more deadly sea.

Now, coming in low among the tall spires of Nar Shaddaa, Mander could think of nothing else but a mudwasp nest—always buzzing, always active, but with precious little planning. Nar Shaddaa was known as both the Smugglers' Moon and as Little Coruscant, and though it had the sprawling urbanism of the former Imperial capital, it had nothing of that planet's grace and organization. The towering spires of Nar Shaddaa were thrown up without concern for their effects on one another, and as such contended for airspace among boiling rivers of aircars and floater vehicles. These traveled in only the barest semblance of the ordered airlanes of the original Coruscant, and small craft weaved and dodged among larger vehicles like the *New Ambition* in a twisted confusion of air skimmers, speeders, swoops, flitters, repulsorlifts, and the occasional rotorcraft. Reen muttered a curse as a glidezep hove into their path, and Eddey's knuckles were white beneath his fur as he clenched the control yoke. They were among the top spires of the towers, and the ground was still kilometers below them.

"I will see to our guest," said Mander, and left the

pilots to the perils of navigating Nar Shaddaa's airspace at rush hour.

He found Mika in the galley with Orgamon and another Nikto, the other survivors left behind to salvage what they could from the Skydove warehouse and claim salvage rights on the crashed freighter. Mika had swapped his oversized zerape blanket for an equally large vest, brocaded in gold stitching. The two Niktos were sponging the Hutt with a concoction that smelled like rotting flowers.

"We will be landing in a few minutes," Mander said. "The air traffic is difficult."

Mika nodded. "The air traffic is always bad. Hutts take it as a good sign when no one has time to obey traffic laws." He waved off his two supplicants with an instruction in Huttese to gather his belongings. Mander remained.

"Your companion, the Pantoran," said the Hutt.

"Reen Irana," said Mander.

"She is the sister of a Jedi, no?" asked Mika. "Does she have the power within her as well?"

"She is Toro Irana's sister," said Mander. "And while the Force can be strong in family lines, she does not have either the aptitude or the training of her brother."

"Yes, the aptitude," Mika said. Then, "The brother—he is truly dead?"

"Yes," Mander said quietly.

"And these Bomu, these Rodians—they killed him?" said the Hutt.

"I think so. Toro was . . ." Mander thought for a moment on how much he should tell the Hutt, then said, "Poisoned. Drugged with Tempest. He fell from a great height."

"I am sorry," said Mika, and lowered his eyes, almost in respect. "That would explain much, then."

"Much?" asked Mander.

"The young female," said Mika. "She was very curious about the cargo of the plague ship. She asked the CSA lieutenant commander much about it, and about what the Corporate Sector knew about the Tempest spice. Angela Krin in turn asked me and I provided what information I could. But I find it interesting."

"How so?" said Mander.

The Hutt let out a nervous hiccup. "The man you sent to negotiate with my father is killed with this Tempest spice. And the plague ship I find was carrying this spice as well. Surely there has to be a connection. The galaxy is too large for such a coincidence, such a twist of fate."

"Hence the questions about the Bomu clan," said Mander.

Mika the Hutt gnawed on his lower lip. "I will check this out, once I talk to my father. I don't know if we use the Bomu clan in our dealings or not. Something is going on, though, and if we are not aware of what it is, we are at a disadvantage. I don't like it."

"Neither do I," said Mander. "If there is anything you can do to find out who is ultimately responsible, I would be most appreciative." Mika nodded in agreement, but the Jedi did not make to leave the room.

Mika looked at him. "There is something else?"

Mander frowned, wondering how to best approach the subject. "Back on Endregaad, when we were attacked by the swoop gang."

"An experience I hope never to relive," put in Mika, though he smiled as he said it.

"Your help was . . . greatly appreciated," said Mander. "But at the end, that last swooper had you dead in his sights . . ."

"Yes?"

"He missed you."

"You shouted out a warning," noted Mika.

"Not in time," said Mander. "Besides, you were ducking before I got a chance to shout."

"I was . . . most fortunate, then," said Mika. "I guess sometimes there just *is* a twist of fate."

And with that, Mika the Hutt closed his eyes—a sign of dismissal. Mander would have pressed, but a string of Bothan curses erupted from the cockpit, and he went forward to lend what moral support he could to the pilots. He did note that Mika called his Order the "Jedi," and not the Huttese *Jeedai*. As Lieutenant Commander Krin had noted, Mika was a very odd Hutt.

After what seemed like a small eternity, the bulk of the *New Ambition* nosed its way through the traffic and settled at last on a landing pad thrown out from one of the lower spires. The durasteel supports groaned under the ship's weight, and a stricken look crossed Reen's face at the idea that the pad could collapse, casting them into the Hutt-made canyons below. The supports held, though, and Eddey began deactivating systems and setting controls to standby. Both spacers slung their blasters at their belts.

"Landing pad X-1256 AEB," said Eddey. "Remember the number if we get lost and split up."

Mander let Mika lead the way down the landing ramp—the Jedi, Pantoran, and Bothan following, and the two Niktos bringing up the rear. They were greeted by another pair of Niktos, these armed with blaster carbines, each flanking a green protocol droid, one of Vago's H-3POs.

"*Young master Mika!*" said the droid, followed by a cascade of Huttese that Mander followed along as best he could. The gist of it was how valiant young Mika had been in adverse situations, how fortunate it had been for those on Endregaad that he had been present, and how wise mighty Popara had been to enlist the aid of such competent employees as the others that now followed in his illustrious wake.

Then the droid turned to Mander and the others. "A feast has been prepared in your honor, to celebrate Mika's return. You will accompany me and I will bring you to Popara's tower."

As he was about to accept the invitation, Mander caught a gleam of something on the catwalks over the entrance. He had been too slow, before, on Endregaad. This time he *did* manage to shout a warning before the sniper squeezed off a series of shots.

Mander dropped to a crouch, lightsaber up, and alongside him both Reen and Eddey had their blasters in hand. The Niktos converged on Mika, who fell back a few steps behind their protection.

The H-3PO unit had no such protection, and as it turned to look, it took a blaster bolt to the head. The cranial housing shattered under the force of the shot, and the now-headless droid staggered a few paces before collapsing.

Both Reen and Eddey returned fire, but there was nothing after the initial shots. Mika motioned the bodyguards forward, and Orgamon and the others stalked to the entrance. They looked back and shook their heads. Mika returned to the *New Ambition* while the Niktos chattered on comms.

Mika frowned and looked at the jade remains of the droid. "Not the homecoming I expected."

Reinforcements arrived in the form of an entire squad of Nikto family retainers, along with another H-3PO unit. Mander recognized this one from the dent in its temple, and wondered if the Anjiliac household had gotten a deal on buying the droids in bulk or merely taken over the factory producing them. This H-3PO unit remained behind to oversee the cleanup of its brother protocol unit with half the squad. The other half closed ranks about Mika and the others and marched through twisted passages and over bridges crossing steep permacrete canyons. At each new juncture, the Niktos sent in advance scouts to make sure the area and its inhabitants were not hostile. Mander noticed that despite the blaster carbines being waved about, few of the other inhabitants of the towers even paid attention to their presence, and those who did reacted by simply getting out of the way. Apparently such activities were common on the Smugglers' Moon, in particular when the Hutts were involved.

"Did you get a good look at the shooter?" asked Reen during one of the frequent stops as the Niktos were clearing the way.

"Not a good one," said Mander. "I saw a thin, narrow head. I think our attacker was a Cerean, but other than that, nothing."

"So why take a shot at Mika?" asked Reen. "You think that someone is worried about what he found out on Endregaad?"

"Possible," said Mander. "Or someone wants to send a message to Mika—or perhaps even to Popara."

"A high-energy message."

"A message nonetheless," Mander continued, realizing as he did that he was scanning the surrounding arcades as well, expecting another attack. "Why else hire a bad assassin on the Smugglers' Moon?"

Reen thought about it. "You're right—you wouldn't. Hire a bad assassin, that is. This place is overflowing with capable opportunists who would not hesitate to take a contract."

"Exactly," said Mander. "Yet we were fired upon by a sniper who literally missed the broad side of a Hutt. A small Hutt, but a Hutt nonetheless."

Reen thought for a moment, then added, "But said

sniper then nails a protocol droid in the temple. Heck of a bad shot. Unless Mika wasn't the target."

"I think someone wants us to think he was," said Mander, "but I don't think he was one they were paid to shoot. Like I said, they are sending a message."

The trio was brought up several more turbolifts into one of the larger nearby towers. As they rose higher into Popara's home territory, the surroundings became more opulent. The rugs took on a deeper plush, the fittings became gaudier, and the light fixtures changed from simple domes to crystalline forms that cast Hutt-shaped shadows on the walls. Finally they reach the last doors, huge vault-like monstrosities of heavy wood and metal, emblazoned with Popara's beneficent face. Only then did Mika turn to address them.

"I must meet with my father," he said. "I had forwarded a report earlier, but he may have further questions. And he will want to know about the most recent incident. We will meet again, at the fete. We will be serving in the penthouse, at sunset." And with that, the Hutt took his leave, swallowed by the opulent doors to his father's chambers.

The three travelers were shown to a small suite of rooms to freshen up. A tailor droid was made available, and both Reen and Eddey availed themselves of its services. Mander had brought his formal robes with him, and while the other two were talking about fabrics and color swatches, he stepped out onto a wide balcony.

The best parts of Nar Shaddaa were dingier than the worst parts of Coruscant. Despite himself, Mander tried to find some order among the madness of the towers, each one equipped with balconies, galleries, bridges, overlooks, awnings, verandas, and decks of various levels of functionality and form. Some seemed to be landing pads, while others looked like they had no other purpose than to cast the floors beneath them in shadow.

Mander looked down but wasn't sure he could even see the ground—rather, the towers themselves expanded out until they became a second skin to the moon. Welling up from those depths and dancing around the towers were a plethora of vehicles, again ranging from the nondescript repulsor vans to gaudy signblimps offering every vice and service known to sentient life.

And above it all, hanging corpulent and visible even in the late-afternoon sun was Nal Hutta itself, a rotten fruit that was now home to the Hutts. Few outworlders were welcome to the steaming swamp estates of the Hutt overlords, though Mander did not doubt that the Anjiliac clan had their own dacha somewhere on the planet above him.

A day on Nar Shaddaa was eighty-seven standard hours long, so they planned on a nap and a light meal, though the meal was light only in terms that a Hutt could appreciate. It was in effect a portable buffet consisting of a large platter of sliced bantha rump roasted with tigmary, stewed kebroot, flatbread, spiceloaf of various intensities, and inert piles of mounder potato rice. For Eddey, a bland-looking fish called salar was presented, and the Bothan declared it better prepared than most. At the center of the display was a spice-jelly cast in a mold that resembled Popara's beneficent form. The effrikim worms were served with both heads still attached and went untouched by all.

Over the meal Mander said, "I understand that the lieutenant commander offered you a job."

Reen looked up from the bowl of thick soup she had been eating and shot a glance at Eddey. "See," she said, "he *did* think we were talking about him."

To Mander she said, "She seemed interested in the trade in Tempest spice, particularly after she talked with the Huttling."

"Had she spent a lot of time speaking with Mika?" asked Mander.

"Don't be jealous," said Reen. "The lieutenant commander spent a lot of time talking to you and you didn't see me get all offended."

"You told me you didn't want to talk . . ." Mander bit the inside of his cheek to keep from sounding foolish. "So," he started again, "I understand that the lieutenant commander offered you a job."

Reen nodded. "Mika apparently got her very interested in the Tempest. She wanted to know if we were interested in helping investigate."

"Are you?" asked Mander.

Reen help up a finger and swallowed a particularly large lump of something in the soup. "Absolutely. We find the source of the Tempest, and we find Toro's killer. Not that I don't want to help you as well. But two approaches maybe are better than one. And the CSA has greater resources. But . . ."

"Here it comes," said Eddey, eyeing another piece of salar.

"I don't know if I trust her," said Reen.

"And you trust me," noted Mander.

"Enough to accept the coordinates of the Indrexu Spiral in exchange for a little risking of one's life?" she asked. "Of course. Besides, people are supposed to trust you. You're a Jedi."

"So people keep telling me," said Mander. "Though I'm not the Jedi they apparently expect."

"True but beside the point," said Reen. "The point *is* that Krin laid out her offer in very precise terms. It all felt very cut and dried. Very calculated. Very . . ."

"*Bloodless* was the word you used," said Eddey, tucking into another piece of the fish.

"I know I don't trust her much," said Reen. "But not trusting her wouldn't keep me from accepting a job."

Mander nodded. It seemed clear to him that Reen was leaving, but had not fully realized it herself. And she was right about one thing: there would be more resources available with the CSA than with a single Jedi. Still, he could not see her fitting in neatly with the by-the-book, "bloodless" nature of the Corporate Sector.

"You'd work for them even if it didn't get you closer to your goal," said Mander.

Reen shrugged. "Look at how I feel about the Hutts. It doesn't stop me from eating their food." And with that conversation drifted off to other matters, and left the ultimate decision, like the effrikim worms, unfinished.

Deep in the bowels of Nar Shaddaa, a beeper chimed at Koax's belt. The one-eyed Klatooinian moved back to her sleeping pod and activated the privacy filters—standard-issue models, but easily modded to actually provide the privacy they claimed. The small room secure, she pulled out the portable holoreceiver from beneath her bunk and toggled it on.

Her lord's image appeared on the central display. As always, the Spice Lord's hulking form was lit from behind, facial features invisible. Any who might observe their conversation would only be able to tell that Koax was speaking with a Hutt, its pointed triangular head rising from a heavy, neckless body.

"*Ma Lorda,*" said Koax, nodding her head slightly and closing her one organic eye in respect. "It has been too long."

"Your work has been sufficient," said the Hutt in a voice filtered to a tinny hum by the device. "And you have not needed any correction. Tell me of our most recent matters."

"Market penetration of the Corporate Sector Authority proceeds apace," said Koax. "The Tempest is extremely popular, and there is sufficient corruption in the bureaucracy to allow us to establish a foothold. Several small-time dealers have tried to sell lesser spices dyed to look like Tempest, but those same corrupt authorities have cracked down on them."

"Good." The shadowed form nodded and for a moment Koax felt reassured. She had pleased the Spice Lord. "How is the expanded spice production proceeding?" the Hutt said.

"Recovering nicely after the loss of the ship on Endregaad," said the Klatooinian. "With the Corellians vulnerable, we subcontracted out to several smaller, lighter firms. And we are breaking up the supply chain, such that the same ships that bring in the raw spice are not the ones that take out the finished product."

"More ships, more chances of mischance," said the darkened Hutt, and it sounded as if the Spice Lord was quoting older wisdom.

"The ships that are carrying the spice out are highly vetted before we give them the coordinates for our secret path," said Koax. "And those coming in system are running empty cargo bays, and as such are not breaking any laws."

"Our secret path is secret no longer," said the Spice Lord, "but unless they know where to look, we should be secure enough. And our security in the manufacturer's system?"

"The requisite bribes have been issued," said Koax, toggling a small chip along the side of the receiver. A blue-white spreadsheet appeared in the air between her and the Hutt's image. "As you can see, they are well within our budgetary expectations, with marginal impact on our bottom line."

"Do not teach your superiors how to suck geejaw eggs," said the Hutt churlishly. "I was determining the profit-and-loss statements before you made your first kill."

"Of course, *Ma Lorda*," said the Klatooinian, regretting almost instantaneously the implication that the Hutt did not understand economics. Seeking to put herself back into the Spice Lord's good graces, she added, "The weapons that were discovered near the manufacturing ship . . ."

"Yes?"

"We cannibalized about half the parts to get the other half operational," said the Klatooinian. "They were in amazing condition for being so old."

"Excellent," said the silhouetted form. The Spice Lord was pleased again, and that brought a warmth to the Klatooinian's heart. "On to other matters, then. What of the Nuiri sector?"

"There was a split in the organization we were dealing with—our longtime distributor and one of her daughters. I evaluated the offers from both sides and found the daughter's offer to be better for us. Her mother and her mother's supporters have been eliminated and operations consolidated under the daughter, and I have rerouted the drug owed to Makem Te to our new ally as a reward."

"I would expect no less," said the Spice Lord. "And speaking of that unpleasant planet, what of Makem Te?"

"They are on subsistence drops for the moment," said Koax. "Their bungling brought the attention of the *Jeedai* down upon us."

"A minor inconvenience, which we can handle," said the backlit image. "You are here on Nar Shaddaa?"

"As per your orders. I have also made contacts with the Bomu matriarch, and she has sent support as well."

"Excellent," said the Hutt. "Gather them, then, and wait for me to contact you. And you have the . . . item?"

Despite herself, Koax's hand went to the oversized hip pouch on her belt. The lightsaber weighed heavy against her side. Even in the shadowed profile, she was sure the Hutt caught her motion, and was amused by it. "Shall I bring it to you?" she asked.

"No," said the Spice Lord quickly. "Things are going to become extremely unsettled very quickly. Be ready, and keep a strong watch on the doings of the Anjiliac clan. They are hosting the *Jeedai* and his allies. The *Jeedai* is about to learn the dangers of meddling in Hutt politics. Be prepared to move—and move quickly—when my call comes."

Again Koax bowed. "As you wish."

"As I wish," said the Hutt, and broke the link.

Koax collapsed on the bunk of the sleeping pod. She could have said that the Bomu were getting particularly hard to deal with, that their matriarch proposed increasingly direct and dangerous methods of vengeance, but that was something her lord did not need to know. All the Spice Lord needed to be informed of was that the requested support was in position. The control of that support was her problem.

Koax had riled up the Bomu clan and now, upon the Spice Lord's command, was going to unleash them on the *Jeedai*. Maybe it would be enough to end this particular threat. And who knew, perhaps each would wipe out the other and solve all of their problems. If the Bomu happened to be particularly enthusiastic in their work, who was she to fault them?

The one-eyed Klatooinian reached into her hip pouch and pulled out the Spice Lord's prize. The metal hilt of the dead *Jeedai*'s lightsaber glittered in the weak light of the sleeping pod. She thought about turning it on, feeling the power that radiated through it, but demurred. There was little enough room in the sleeping pod for herself and the hololink, and she would likely achieve nothing more than shredding the surrounding walls.

And that might attract undue attention.

She had met the Spice Lord but once in the flesh, and when they met, the Hutt had said simply, "Protect me." Since that day she labored to keep her master's empire intact—despite long periods without contact—and to be ready, at a moment's notice, to carry out the Spice Lord's will.

And if the Spice Lord desired a Jedi lightsaber, who was she to argue?

She replaced the Spice Lord's trophy, packed up the holoreceiver, returned the security screens to their factory-issued insufficiency, and left the pod. She had to rally the Spice Lord's hounds in the hope that they would remove one more problem from her list.

The dream returned to Mander, but this time with a difference. He was in the great library on Coruscant again, and this time he was not alone. There were voices around him now, unseen among the dimly lit records on the shelves. He looked down one corridor of the stacks, then another, but there was nothing there. The voices sounded like a celebration. The voices sounded like a discussion. The voices sounded like a heated argument.

In the distance, a low bell pealed, as always, and turning around he could see the lights go out, a darkness claiming the shelves, one at a time. Yet this time he could see in the distance a single light shining in the darkness. It was the blaze of a lightsaber, blue-white in the darkness.

Mander started for the light, moving in that dream speed where his mind was running but the world around him moved slowly. The darkened shelves were now mere ghosts, reflecting their own pale illumination, and Mander noticed they were empty.

The light receded and bobbed, and he could hear footsteps ahead, retreating, fleeing him. He was closing now, and nearing that moment of recognition when he knew this was a dream—and a familiar one. But that did not stop him from pursuing the bobbing light.

This is a dream, thought Mander. *This is a dream and I can affect it. I can catch up with my opponent. I can make him slow down.*

The thin line of the lightsaber's blade paused up ahead, and for just a second Mander could see that it reflected a blue face, looking at him, frustrated and angry. Then his prey moved off to one side, down one of the long rows of the now-darkened stacks. Mander realized the voices were gone, along with the tolling bell and the sound of footsteps.

Mander reached for his own blade, and it came up in his hand—not a serpent this time, but a hard, cold hilt that chilled him as he ran a thumb over the raised switch and ignited it. He spun around the corner, and there was a crate in the middle of the aisle, a typical crate like the ones found in the Bomu warehouse. The top was open, and there, swaddled in a blanket, was a small Hutt child, its flesh a pale blue.

The Hutt opened its eyes, and Mander had a moment of disorientation.

"Hello," said Mika Anjiliac in flawless Basic.

Mander bolted awake, startled from the dream. Despite the drawn shades, the light of the westering sun still carved thin lines on the opposing wall, and even with the supposed soundproofing, the dull rumble of the air traffic outside seeped through the permacrete and into his bones.

He rolled out of the bed, shook his head, and pinched the bridge of his nose, trying both to shake the fogginess from his brain while at the same time retaining what had happened in the dream.

Part of it was obvious—Toro had been running away from him. Despite his teachings, he had rejected him. Once he had attained his own Knighthood, Toro had sought to carve his own path, a path that led to his own destruction. But Mander had put the details of his former student's death aside to finish Toro's assigned task for the Order. He had hoped that gaining the coordinates would give him some sense of closure, and that by completing his student's task he could lay Toro's spirit to rest.

But it was not to be. Too many loose ends strayed out of this particular tangle, not the least of them being that Tempest was more widespread than the Jedi had first thought. This was no failing of a single Jedi, or a single Jedi's training, but a plague in its own right, sprawling out in the galactic arm unnoticed until now.

Then there was a matter of Mika. The strange Hutt was a part of his unease. There was more to Mika than he'd first thought. And the fact that there was Tempest on the plague ship where he was found . . . another mystery, tempting him. The Hutt's involvement could be part of the greater picture, or just another distraction.

He wondered how the discussion would go between Mika and his father about the Tempest. Would Popara see the rise in Tempest use as a threat, or as an opportunity? Reen's words about not trusting Hutts came back to him. Would Popara be willing to help the Jedi track down and eradicate this scourge?

Then there was the matter of the CSA and Angela Krin. They seemed very interested in the Tempest as well. Again, Mika seemed invaluable in having spurred that interest. Mander wondered if he should encourage Reen to work with them. It would free up the Jedi to conduct his own work. Or allow him to simply return to the Archives, if matters were truly in capable hands.

Mander Zuma shook his head again and padded out

to join the others for a light—for Hutts—snack before the main meal.

In his absence, the tailor droids had arrived with new outfits. Reen had chosen a practical outfit of deep violet spacer's slacks with matching vest, both highlighted by white piping. A silver-gray shirt of Dramassian shimmersilk blended well with her azure skin, and she had touched up her facial tattoos with ocher powder. She still had her holster, but apparently had left the blaster on her ship. Eddey, on the other hand, had chosen a bulky, open-fronted tunic with padded shoulders, worn over a ruffled white shirt. Just as the sun—blood crimson from pollutants—touched the horizon, the dented H-3PO unit came to escort them to the party.

The droid buzzed with something that resembled excitement. "Generous Popara, may his name always be praised by his clients, has a number of guests this evening, and will be holding audiences throughout the meal. Many of the guests would like to meet you as well, as word of your exploits has spread. Would you be opposed to sitting at different tables?"

Mander started to respond, but Eddey put in quickly, "We would prefer it that way. We have seen enough of one another while crammed into our ship, and would enjoy new company." Mander looked at the Bothan, and nodded. If they were talking to different guests, they could gain more information. The assassination attempt was a message—perhaps the one who sent that message would be present.

The penthouse was not quite at the tip of the tower's spire, but occupied an entire floor close to it. A turbolift deposited them at one end of a large room ringed with windows overlooking the city. On one side, the setting sun was being overtaken by the girth of Nal Hutta. Out the other set of windows, the city-moon was already in shadow, alive with its own brilliances of signs and lights.

Across the far side of the room a translucent white wall reached from side to side, with two great sliding screens. Against the screens, they could see the shadows of Popara, Mika, and a third Hutt with a narrow, triangular head moving about in animated discussion.

The room itself was an assemblage of guests and bodyguards. Each of the crescent-shaped tables was dominated by a Hutt. Mander noted Cereans, Bimms, and a pair of male Twi'leks. Reen pointed out a table with several Rodians with a subtle nod of her head. Popara's Niktos lined the wall behind Mander and the others.

Zonnos was there with his Wookiees, and to Mander's eyes he had already dipped deep into the Kashyyyk ale with his furry companions. The eyes of Popara the Hutt's eldest son widened when they came in, then reduced back to slits. The hulking Hutt muttered something to one of the Wookiees and turned back to his drink.

The spread was, if anything, more indulgent than the catered meal delivered to their quarters earlier. Platters of Hutt delicacies littered the tables, include braised fork tarts, sand gizzars, and strained kebaddas. Small bowls of crunchbugs peeped softly in the center of the table. Live tuskettes were kept in cages on hand near each of the Hutt guests as a palate cleanser. Effrikim worms were served, heads on, and consumed in one gulp—though only by the Hutts. Mander was unsure if several dishes were intended as food, utensils, or table decorations. Each table was dominated by a larger spice-jelly crafted to look like Popara, Zonnos, and Mika together. One happy family captured in suspended gelatin. In addition to the Kashyyyk ale, there were heavy pitchers of boga noga and gardulla, next to fluted crystal ewers of what looked like clear, fresh water.

The back wall slid open and the three Hutts emerged. Vago came first, heading directly to the turbolift, one of her ubiquitous jade-green droids in tow, apparently too busy for the festivities. Then Mika, who went to the empty table where a clutch of Rodians gathered. Finally, Popara came forth, resplendent on a liftpad, flanked by his three female Twi'leks.

"*Gijee bo mabonna matah,*" said the elder Hutt, welcoming the collected species. "*Chowbaso padunky.*" Reen looked expectantly at Mander.

"Gentlebeings and fellow sentients," translated Mander softly for the others, "Welcome to my home."

"*Jeema mojja nanyar kodowin Mander Zuma keeja Jeedai, Reen Irana, bo Eddey Be'ray, lomarin geejo mokyin Endregaadi. Gon kodowin pumba mallin.*"

"He said—" Mander began, but Reen interrupted, "I caught our names. Did he say 'thank you'?"

"As much as a Hutt ever does," said Mander. "He said our efforts were more than sufficient."

The Pantoran sniffed and scanned the tables. "Dibs on the Rodians," she said. "I want to see if I can shake something loose about the Bomus."

Mander nodded and let himself be guided to the table with the Cereans and a large female Hutt with a diamond insignia in her forehead. Eddey was seated with the Twi'leks and Bimms. None of them sat at Zonnos's table.

A tall Cerean introduced the Hutt at Mander's table as Lungru Nokko, an old business associate of the Anjiliac clan. The tall Cerean himself was named Kir Sesad, and was Lungru's chief adviser. There were a trio of Quarren at the table, but only one spoke Basic, and that one with a sibilant lisp. When this Quarren translated the table conversation to the other two, her native language sounded much more delightful.

Lungru, of course, only spoke in Huttese, and Mander could follow well enough, though Sesad would step in when Lungru slurred a colloquialism or Mander had difficulty making a point. The female Hutt was particularly interested in their adventures on Endregaad, and more than once referred to Mander as Mika's savior. "Such a child needs protectors," said the Hutt.

"Popara's youngest son seems more than brave and capable enough," said Mander. "We had an incident earlier today. Came under sniper fire. He did not flinch in the face of that."

Lungru's eyes widened in surprise, and Mander added, "I believe our shooter was Cerean."

Lungru made a chortling noise and burbled in Huttese, "A Cerean? Do you recognize him at the table? Perhaps Kir Sesad here slipped away from my entourage to take a shot at Popara's favorite!" The Cerean adviser gave Mander a look as cold as deep space, but the Hutt continued, amused at her own joke. "Perhaps you snuck away when I was not looking, eh, Kir Sesad?"

Kir Sesad replied stonily, "I would never do anything without your orders, *Lorda* Lungru," but the Cerean's stare never left Mander.

Lungru proceeded to say that she would never do anything so crass as to assassinate a rival *before* a dinner party, and noted that Mika being a target was not the young Hutt's fault, after all. "Popara babies him. It happens to older Hutts. We get soft, sentimental. We miss opportunities. We don't take advantage. The Popara I remember was much stronger, more cruel. Now he is just old, like me."

At that point one of the Twi'lek handmaidens arrived and informed Lungru that Popara would see her. The female Hutt pushed herself away from the table, and the other Cereans followed the handmaiden up to the sliding doors. Kir Sesad brought up the rear. Popara's liftpad drifted back into the inner chamber, and the translucent walls slid into place.

Popara was mixing business with pleasure, Mander

realized, turning a celebratory feast into little more than a well-fed waiting room. The Quarren were having their own discussion, which did not include him. He looked around, and Reen caught his eye and excused herself from Mika's table. She half collapsed into Kir Sesad's chair.

"I need to trade seats," she said.

"How are your Rodians?" asked Mander.

"They are *accountants*," said Reen, throwing as much venom as she could into the word. "They belong to the Kemu clan, and they are as dry as a desert world. I have never been as deeply bored in my life."

Mander managed a smile. "Poor Mika."

Reen let out a frustrated snort. "Poor Mika? He apparently loves this sort of thing. They've been discussing the revised strictures on post-Imperial import levies among the Core Worlds for the past half hour."

"So no luck, then."

Reen shook her head. "They know of the Bomu clan, but consider them clowns and incompetents. I couldn't really disagree about that, given their track record. They think smugglers go into the business because they can't handle the paperwork."

"You should get back," said Mander. "Here comes my table."

The wall-sized panels slid open and Lungru slithered out, her entourage in tow. She looked like she hadn't had a good meeting, and on her way back to the table snagged a hokuum pipe from a serving tray and took a long hard pull on it. The Cereans sat stone-faced as their mistress drew the smoke deep into her lungs; even the Quarren were quiet.

Lungru looked at Mander at length, then let out a torrent of Huttese that Mander had trouble following. The Jedi looked at Kir Sesad for a translation. The serious

Cerean merely said, "You know about the Tempest spice."

Mander slowly nodded. "We encountered it. On Endregaad. It seems to be spreading through the galactic arm."

"It is an opportunity," said the Cerean, and Lungru let out a snort that sounded like a mud bubble popping. "An opportunity that Popara is passing up."

"Gah ja boftah," said the Hutt, which translated as "He is getting soft."

"It is a dangerous spice," said Mander.

"All things are dangerous," said the Cerean, in a way that sounded like he included himself in that estimation. "It is here, on the Smugglers' Moon. The spice. We have seen it. And if anyone happens to know where it came from, how to manufacture it, who to talk to—well, that would be valuable information." Kir Sesad managed a toothy smile and leaned forward. "Very valuable."

"Agreed," said Mander, leaning forward. "I would be interested myself in knowing those things. Keep me in mind." To Lungru he said, in butchered Huttese, "I *will* find out." And he made it sound like a threat.

Mander pushed himself back from the table, leaving Lungru sputtering and the Quarren giggling in his wake. The Rodian accountants had had a brief meeting with Popara, and the other Hutt, Parella, was now ushered in. Rather than go rescue Reen from further discussions of Republic-era precious metal policy, he stopped at Eddey's table, where the Bothan was conversing with the Bimm.

"It is good to see someone is having a pleasant time," said Mander.

Eddey smiled. "The Bimm here were rescued by one of Popara's ships, and have been negotiating to pay off the debt for that rescue. Since the food is pretty good here, they are in no hurry." The Bimm nodded and held up some sod creepers roasted in their own shells.

"And the Hutt at your table?" asked Mander.

"Strange one," said Eddey. "His name is Parella, and he likes to hunt."

"Hunt?" said Mander.

"Most Hutts are, well, slugs," said Eddey. "Inert invertebrates. This one likes the thrill of bringing down his own kills. Has been going on at length about knocking whirlbats out of the sky on his estate on Nal Hutta. He likes weapons of all sorts. Oh, and he's probably going to corner you about your blade."

"My lightsaber?" said Mander, the deactivated hilt feeling heavy at his side. "Why?"

"New weapon for him," said Eddey. "He'll want to try it out."

"A lightsaber can be dangerous in the wrong hands," Mander replied. "Jedi study for years to master its nuances. Without the Force, it is dangerous to its user as well as to its opponent."

"I told him something like that," said the Bothan. "Needless to say, a Hutt hears nothing he doesn't want to. Have you noticed Zonnos?"

Despite himself, Mander turned to look at Popara's elder son, locking eyes with him across the room.

"He's been staring at you for most of the evening," said Eddey. "His Wookiees were irritated by me last time we met the Hutts, but now, nothing. They've been staring at you. And every time you do anything, Zonnos just gets angrier. You're doing something to get his ponderous back up."

The Hutt's eyes narrowed and one of the Wookiees said something, earning a cuff across the back of the head from the Hutt. Zonnos looked, if anything, angrier and more dangerous than earlier. His thick bluish hide seems to radiate rage and irritation. Mander turned back to Eddey. The Bothan said, "He probably doesn't know if you said anything to his father about the little chat you two had before we went to find Mika. Or what you *will* say."

"Meaning?" said Mander.

"Meaning we could theorize that the target of this afternoon's assassination attempt was someone other than Mika," said Eddey. Mander thought about it for a moment, then nodded.

The panels to the back room opened and Parella the Hunter emerged, a smile across his broad face. Did he get what he wanted, Mander wondered, or did he simply not want that much in the first place?

Reen manifested at the Jedi's side, one of Popara's Twi'leks visible behind her shoulder. "We're up next," she said, and the Twi'lek motioned for the doors.

They walked through the doorway and Mander felt a tingling along his flesh, as if he had passed through a bubble made of static electricity. A force field, he realized, arranged to allow slower-moving bodies to pass through while deflecting energy weapons and probably high-caliber bullets.

Popara was no fool, and was making sure just in case an assassin decided to send him a message in a more direct fashion.

The Hutt was still stretched out on his repulsorlift, his Twi'lek servants ministering to his needs. One held the stem of an ornate hokuum to his lips. A second stood to one side with a datapad. A third carried a large bowl with what looked like pale, wriggling worms.

"Bet he doesn't say thank you this time, either," said Reen softly, and Mander shushed her.

Popara Anjiliac took a long, slow pull on the water pipe, nodding at its Twi'lek bearer. She backed away and the Hutt exhaled the smoke from his narrow nostrils. Then the Hutt unleashed a long torrent of Huttese—

Popara was getting down to business at once. Mander caught the gist of it, but the Twi'lek confirmed his thoughts in translation.

"Mighty Popara bids you serve his family," said the Twi'lek, as Popara grabbed a fistful of pale white worms and stuffed them enthusiastically into his maw. "His youngest son, Mika, has uncovered that the plague that trapped him on Endredgaad was tied into a new form of spice. A hard spice that thickens the mind and inflames the passion. Mighty Popara would never condone trade in such a spice, despite the urgings of others." Here Popara swallowed his mouth full of worms and continued with another torrent of Huttese, hooting with each statement.

"The Tempest spice is throughout Hutt space and the galactic arm, and is a bane to us all. Mighty Popara believes that young Mika found out enough to call attention to his actions and those involved in the smuggling targeted him for elimination." Popara at this point levied a long series of curses, many of which Mander knew but several of which sounded extremely innovative. The Twi'lek chose to edit those out of her translation.

"Popara will not have his family threatened. He has crushed his foes and left clan homes empty among those who have challenged him. For this reason, he wants to find out who is responsible for this new addiction on the worlds, so he may destroy them." Popara patted his belly, let out a belch, and motioned for more worms. After downing another handful, he took a long drink from a crystal ewer, and continued.

"You are of similar mind, Mighty Popara thinks, as he is. The Jedi do not care for shackles, either on the body or on the mind."

"Mighty Popara is correct in his assumption," said Mander, in the best Huttese he could manage. Popara chuckled, and for a moment a pained look crossed his face. He motioned for the ewer, downed a healthy portion, then burbled another long speech.

The Twi'lek followed her master's words and translated. "Fatherly Popara does not wish his youngest son, so recently returned, to put himself at risk. Similarly, Vago is most competent, but Vago is like a daughter to him and should not be endangered, either. Zonnos is the eldest and one does not imperil the family heir. You will investigate this matter on our behalf." The Twi'lek with the datapad stepped forward and handed it to Mander. "This is a list of local tapcafs at which Vago determined that this Tempest was sold," the second Twi'lek said. "Perhaps you will be able to trace the source, or find our would-be assassin."

Mander slipped the datapad inside his robes and said simply, "It would be our honor to be of service." Reen started to say something, but Eddey nudged her with an elbow and she thought better of it.

Popara started to say something, then stopped, repeated himself, and let out an indecorous belch that took the Twi'leks aback. He started to say something else, but stopped again, even as he seemed to sway for a moment on his repulsorlift. Then his eyes widened in pain and horror.

Eddey said, "What's going on?"

Mander didn't know, and crossed toward the great Hutt. It would normally be a transgression to approach him, but Popara was clearly in pain now. Popara's belly started to swell, and the great Hutt patron started to croak like an injured frog. The Twi'leks were clearly frightened, and one of them pushed Mander back, away from their master. Still the Hutt's massive form expanded, his eyes wide with panic. His skin was stretched taut, like a balloon about to pop.

Reen shouted, "I'll get help," and turned back to the doors. They slid easily apart, and Mander realized what it would look like to the assembled party—Popara in obvious pain, the Twi'lek shouting in fear, and the rest of them standing right in front of the Hutt's distended form.

"Reen, don't!" Mander said, but Eddey grabbed him and pulled him to one side. Popara was almost ovoid in shape now, and screaming in a low, throaty roar.

And then the flesh gave way in half a dozen places and Popara exploded, his organs rupturing in all directions around the room. The Twi'leks screamed, diving for cover, and Reen was flung forward by the power of the explosion and bounced off the force field, along with the former Hutt patriarch's interior organs. Both the Pantoran and the Hutt's digestive system were moving too fast to allow the screen to let them pass.

There was silence for a moment, and Mander looked out at the assembled guests—Hutt and Quarren, Bimm and Rodian, Wookiee and Cerean. All of them looked at the gory tableau beyond the open doors in shock. It was only for a moment, but Mander felt his heart hammer from the certain knowledge of what was to come.

Then Zonnos shouted in a drunken bellow, "They killed my father! Death to the *Jeedai* and his allies!"

PURSUIT IN THE DEPTHS

Mander, Reen, and Eddey were fortunate, in that the first impulse of the guests and bodyguards was to pull whatever weapons they had, concealed or otherwise, and unleash a volley at the three accused killers. Fortunate in that the energy screen held and their initial high-caliber energy shots splayed helplessly against the invisible barrier.

Mander scanned the room. There was no obvious way out, other than the lift at the far side of the chamber—and on the wrong side of the now-howling mob. Popara probably had a hidden turbolift somewhere in his office, but locating and activating it would take time. Time they did not have.

"You have a plan?" asked Eddey. His small blaster had manifested from beneath his voluminous tunic.

"Get Reen and follow me," said Mander.

Reen, her back splattered with blood, was already up. Two of the green-skinned Twi'leks were in shock, moaning over the remains of their Hutt master. The third descended on Reen in an enraged fury, head-tails lashing and sharpened nails curled to rend the Pantoran. Reen ducked inside the blow and brought her elbow up hard against the Twi'lek's chin. The handmaiden went down with a whimper.

Mander ignored the battle and ran to the back of the audience room, to the grand window that displayed the expanse of Nar Shaddaa beyond. It seemed like he was looking out at an inverted sky, Nal Hutta solid, dark, and gravid above them, the lights of the city-moon cluttered constellations below. Aircars and signblimps moved like comets in these overturned heavens. Mander pulled his lightsaber and thumbed the switch. The blade erupted with a satisfying hiss. The Jedi drove the blade against the transparent wall.

The window did not break, and only grudgingly melted, which gave Mander hope. He strained and forced the blade through like an oarsman struggling against a flowing river. In a matter of moments he had carved a humanoid-sized circle in the back wall.

Mander looked over his shoulder as the first blaster bolts fell among them. The Niktos, Wookiees, and Cereans were using the doorway for cover, their carbine barrels jutting into the room beyond the screen. Apparently Eddey had hidden Reen's blaster under his tunic as well, and the pair of them were returning covering fire over the cooling remains of Popara and the now-shrieking Twi'leks.

Mander kicked the molten oval outward, and it disappeared into the darkness, glittering in the reflected light of the surrounding buildings. "Onto the ledge!" he shouted, and stepped out into the void himself.

The ledge was ornamental, but ornamental in a Hutt style, which meant that it was narrow but not impossible for a normal-sized humanoid to navigate. He slipped out to the right, and Reen and Eddey followed him. The winds at this altitude curled around the buildings and threatened to pluck them from the ledge and send all three of them screaming to their deaths below. He flattened against the wall behind him and moved toward the corner.

Behind him, the window shuddered with blasterfire. Eddey flinched at the impacts.

"It is made of transparisteel," said the Jedi. "They'll be able to break through it, but it will take time. We have to get off this side of the building."

The shots tracked them as they reached the corner, and now a pair of Niktos had made it to the egress the Jedi had cut and were firing along the side of the building behind them. Reen, pulling up the rear, used the corner for cover and returned fire. This wall was also made of transparisteel, and the Wookiees were concentrating their fire ahead of their path, hoping to break the window before the escapees got to that point. They were trapped.

"Good plan," Reen shouted over the gusts. "Now how do we get off this crazy thing?"

"Shush," said Eddey. "He's working on it."

Mander leaned back against the shuddering transparisteel and cleared his mind. Ahead of him one of the signblimps was sagging its way slowly across the sky. He reached out, mentally, and pulled it toward them. The lighter-than-air vehicle bobbled in their direction, but the droid driver revved its engines to let it clear the building.

"Size matters not," Mander muttered. "Inertia, however, is a pain in the butt."

He shifted his attention away from the signblimp and to the air between him and the vehicle. The air gusted away effortlessly, and pulled the blimp, with its surprised and cursing droid pilot, right up against the side of the building. There was a crinkling impact as the thin heglum gas envelope crumpled slightly.

"Jump on!" shouted Mander, but Eddey was already scrambling over the airship's diode-laced sides, his boots knocking light emitters loose and scrambling the signblimp's message. Reen took a pair of final shots and joined him.

Mander leapt and the transparisteel wall behind him

shattered. Bolts laced among them, and a couple struck the signblimp, leaving jagged tears in the outer skin and puncturing some of the flotation cells as well.

The signblimp fell away from the building, losing altitude steadily.

"We're falling!" shouted Reen. Beneath them, the droid sputtered a mixture of orders and obscenities in Huttese. Behind them, the blasterfire was already dropping off.

Mander pointed to one of the gallery bridges between skyscrapers and bellowed in Huttese, "Aim for the bridge!" He threw in a few Huttese curses as well. Whether the instructions, the curses, or the winds were the cause, the signblimp lunged to port and mated in an ungainly fashion with the span. The impact burst the bulk of the flotation cells and the bridge groaned as the entire weight settled upon it. The three escapees clambered onto the bridge and into the wide atriums of an adjoining skybridge.

"What happened back there?" said Reen.

"Our patron, Popara the Hutt, blew up," said Mander.

"I caught that part," said the Pantoran. "How?"

"Binary bioexplosive, most likely," said Eddey. "One component administered by one vector, the other administered by another. Neither traceable as dangerous by itself."

"Something in the smoke, something in the worms," said Mander, "and maybe a trigger as well to go off at a certain time or in a particular place. We'd have to search the penthouse."

"Unlikely they would let us do that. Zonnos has already determined we're responsible," Eddey said.

"He was quick with the accusation," said Reen. "And he was giving you the hard eyes the entire meal. Think he was expecting it?" Her implication was clear: *Do you think he did it?*

"Perhaps," said Mander. "Or maybe Lungru or Parella or someone we don't know about."

"Or perhaps the Bomu clan is not as incompetent as we thought," Reen added. "The Hutts do not lack for enemies and schemes."

Mander thought about it. "Adding the attempt on Mika's life this morning, it is most likely an effort to thin the ranks of Hutts interested in where the Tempest comes from." He looked around. "Either of you know where we are?"

"No," said Eddey. "We could probably find our way back to the *New Ambition,* but it is likely that Zonnos and his Wookiees will get there first. No, make that definitely."

"We just got that ship!" said Reen. "We can't abandon it!"

"It wouldn't be the first time," Eddey said. Reen scowled at the Bothan.

"We have the datapad of tapcafs selling Tempest," said Mander, producing the pad from beneath his robes. "If Popara's death is connected with the spice, we can track our suspects through it."

"And maybe find a ship to get us offplanet," added Eddey. "There should be a surplus of shady spacers on the Smugglers' Moon."

"Regardless, I'm going to need a new outfit," said Reen. "I reek of dead Hutt lord."

The vendor-droid they came across was supremely disinterested in Reen's bloodstained gear, and suitable replacements were gathered, along with hooded robes for both Eddey and Mander. The vendor-droid wasn't the only one incurious about the trio. The bulk of Nar Shaddaa's population seemed singularly unaware of Popara's sudden and explosive passing, or that there was any pursuit of his accused assassins.

"It is the nature of the Hutts," Eddey said. "They try to solve things inside the family. Let's hope it stays that way. What is our first opportunity?"

Kuzbar's Cantina was an upscale tapcaf on level 42, not far from Popara's skytower. A Rodian chanteuse warbled in the corner in Huttese, accompanied by a Bimm on a Kloo horn. The barkeep, a member of a humanoid species that Mander could not immediately place, took a few credits from them and directed them to a particularly corpulent Sullustan named Min Gost, who had occupied a corner booth like his own personal fiefdom.

"I understand you're looking for information," said the Sullustan, lacing his fingers before him on the table in an expectant pose.

"We need travel offplanet," said Mander. "Can you arrange it?"

"Easy for me, expensive for you," said Min, his lips curling up in an amused expression.

"Set it up," said Mander. "Payment on delivery." The Sullustan shrugged.

"What do you know about Tempest?" Reen asked suddenly. Mander frowned. In his desire to get everyone away, he had forgotten why he had the list of tapcafs in the first place.

The Sullustan's eyebrows twitched. "Others have been asking about Tempest. Those others smell of military, and I have told them nothing."

"Do we smell of military?" asked Reen, and the Sullustan laughed. Mander put several Huttese truguts and a few of his remaining credits on the table. Reen smiled back and pressed, "So what do you know about Tempest?"

"I know many things about this Tempest," said Min. "It is new. It is profitable. It is very, very hard. Tends to kill your customers. Bad for repeat business. You want some, I can find some for you."

"Do you know where it comes from?" asked Reen.

Min shrugged again. "No one knows. We had a dealer here, Rinnix. Nice Trandoshan male. Did good business. No one has seen him for a while."

"You know where he got his supply?" asked Reen, and Mander moved to put a few more coins from his depleted supply on the table, but the Sullustan waved him back. "If I knew, I would not be selling information. I would be selling Tempest."

"Who did this Rinnix sell it to?" asked Eddey, and the fat Sullustan blinked, as if noticing the Bothan for the first time.

The Sullustan paused, rolling the flavor of his information on his tongue before letting it loose. "A select few. Mostly upscale. Popara's boy, Zonnos, was a buyer."

Reen sat upright and looked around the room. "Zonnos comes here?"

Again the Sullustan laughed, "A Hutt lord's son here? No. He sends his Wookiees. He thinks he is being subtle, but who else employs Wookiees?" He laughed again.

A squat droid with a holoprojector mounting on its bulbous head lumbered into the tapcaf, taking up a position in the center of the room. It let out a soft clanging noise to draw attention. Mander felt the hairs on the back of his head bristle as the face of Zonnos the Hutt manifested in the holobeam. Mander realized now that he could see the veins at the sides of Zonnos's head throb with anger.

"*Wundara Nar Shaddaa seetazz!*" boomed Zonnos in Huttese, a melodious female voice translating in Basic simultaneously. "Attention citizens of Nar Shaddaa! Popara Anjiliac the mighty has been assassinated, cruelly slain by these creatures!" The screen changed to pictures of Reen, Eddey, and Mander, taken in one of the turbo-lifts before the party. "I will pay one hundred thousand peggats for their arrest and/or destruction!" The holo-beam winked off and the droid turned to leave.

Mander fought the urge to scan the other patrons to see if they had noticed them. Reen flipped up the hood of her new jacket. Eddey leaned back into the deep plush of the booth. "I don't think it is being kept in the family anymore," he muttered.

Min Gost laced his chubby fingers in front of him again and smiled at the three fugitives. "So, it seems I have a question for you: how much of my silence are you willing to pay for?"

"How long do you think we have?" said Reen as they left the tapcaf.

Mander was scanning the area outside for immediate threats. It was a maze of archways and bridges. He considered the remainder of his funds provided to the Sullustan, translated it into time, and divided by two. "Twenty minutes before he tells someone we were here. If we're lucky."

They were not lucky, and the Sullustan was greedier than they thought. It turned out they had only ten. They had descended one of the larger interior ramps and were making for one of the more fragile suspension connectors when there was a hideous screeching of metal behind them, and a thunderous, mechanical voice shouted out: "*Hagwa doopee!*" Don't move!

Turning, Mander saw a strange form emerge from the shadows of an archway beyond the bridge. It looked like a Hutt wrapped in metal, its semi-fluid body covered with overlapping plates. Its neckless head was enshrouded in a dome of durasteel, with narrow windows cut for the eyes and ringed with sensors. The entity carried a stun baton in its metal-shod hands. The armored Hutt barked again, and this time a translation vocoder squawked in Basic.

"Flee, you cowards!" said the translator. "Make this a good sport! For you are the prey of Parella the Hunter!"

"You have *got* to be kidding me," said Reen, and opened up with her blaster. Eddey joined her. Their bolts ricocheted off the metallic hide and into the space between the buildings.

"Flee!" shouted the translator. "Do not make it too easy for me!" Parella the Iron Hutt lumbered onto the bridge. Its supporting wires hummed at the additional weight, and the bridge itself sagged slightly.

"Can we outrun it?" asked Reen, still firing.

"Possible," said Eddey. Small wheels appeared at the edges of the battlesuit. "Make that unlikely."

"I will handle this," Mander said. "You go on, find a place to hide, and wait for me." He unleashed his lightsaber. "Five minutes, then go on without me. Check the other tapcafs on the list, and if they don't pan out find a ship off this moon."

Eddey and Reen fell back, firing at the Hutt's eye-slits as they did so, only to discover that the windows were as heavily reinforced as the rest of the suit. For his part, Mander strode back onto the bridge, lightsaber in hand.

"Oho, a challenge!" said the Hutt, and raised its one-handed stun baton in a salute.

Mander returned the salute and leapt forward in a sweeping overhand attack, his blade catching the stun baton. The lightsaber should have sliced through the baton, but instead it slid along the haft, leaving the weapon unscathed.

"Mandalorian iron," belched the vocoder. Parella brought the baton around, its surface humming with accumulated discharge. Mander somersaulted backward, landed on his feet, and launched himself at his assailant.

Mander ran forward and the Hutt swung low, hoping to chop out his legs beneath him. The Jedi jumped at the last moment, clearing the blade and pushing off from the armored Hutt's gauntlets. He landed on the helmeted head and drove his blade downward, between its eyes.

Or rather, he attempted to do so. The blade slid off the helmet as effortlessly as it did the weapon. Mander was surprised, and his surprise became literal shock as electricity raged through his body. He fell backward, holding on to his lightsaber but landing in a sprawl on the bridge, its support cables straining from the weight.

The armored Parella could have pressed the advantage, but instead let out a throaty laugh, its vocoder keeping up with it. "You cannot cut my weapon. You cannot cut my armor. Your allies have all fled. What now, little *Jeedai*?"

What now, indeed, wondered Mander. He picked himself up and saluted the Hutt once more. The Hutt returned the salute and Mander charged again, exactly as before. The Hutt brought up his stun baton to block, but this time Mander took the parrying blow and slashed to his right, slicing through the bridge's support cable on that side. Then he rolled to the left and, coming up, cut through the cables on the other side.

The armored Hutt spun on its wheels to face him, raising its baton to smash him off the bridge. That was when, even through his sensors, Parella could hear the sound of the bridge's cables begin to separate, the metal peeling back as the strands gave way one at a time.

Parella the Hunter had time to let out a surprised curse as the remaining support cables separated with sharp twangs, and the bridge surface cracked apart beneath the heavy Hutt. Mander leapt for one of the hanging cables. Parella lunged forward as well, hoping to take the Jedi with him, but the Hutt's gauntlets closed on empty air and the great metallic slug fell, tumbling end-over-end into the canyon between the buildings.

Mander, hanging from one of the remaining cables, sheathed his lightsaber, then swung himself overhand toward the remaining stump of the bridge. Once he landed, he looked down, but all he saw were the swirling pollutants of the lower levels.

Reen and Eddey were waiting for him around the next turn. "What happened?" said Eddey, relieved to see the Jedi alive.

"We had a falling-out," said Mander, no hint of a smile on his face. "We need to be more careful. Zonnos has decided to make this more than a clan matter, and we should see other pursuers soon."

They made their way carefully now, their hoods up, through the lower areas. The opulence of the upper levels was far behind, and the walls were stained with blood, oil, and other fluids. The walkways were crazed with cracks, and those inhabitants they could see watched them with suspicion from doorways and storefronts.

The Dark Melody was on level 35, and most of the inhabitants were aliens, brought here to Nar Shaddaa years before for one reason or another, and who upon arrival never developed the ability or the reason to leave. Attempts to secure passage offplanet at the Melody were met with derision, and when Mander asked about Tempest, they were directed to a Trandoshan corpse propped by the front door.

"I think we found Zonnos's connection," said Eddey.

"Hmmm," said Mander. "He has the pronounced dark veins of a Tempest user, but no signs of violence."

"So?" asked Reen.

"So," said Mander, "he probably didn't fall victim to the rage we've seen elsewhere." To the ponytailed barkeep he asked, "How did this one die?"

The barkeep shrugged his tattooed shoulders and said, "He was alive, then he was dead. That was it."

"What are you thinking?" Eddey said to Mander.

"If we had the chance to check out the corpse," said Mander, "I think we'd find that he was poisoned. By something he *thought* was Tempest."

"How do you figure?" asked Reen.

"No one knows how Tempest is made, or by whom," said Mander. "Let's assume that the individuals responsible are advanced biochemists, since no one seems to be able to synthesize it."

"And such a biochemist would be able to create a binary bioexplosive that could slide through a Hutt lord's security," said Eddey.

"And would be able to poison our friend here," said Mander. "Someone is cleaning up his tracks. Whoever is behind this knows someone is looking for him. We have one more place on our list. Let's go."

The lights grew more infrequent, the corners and alleys darker. There was no sky above now, only a jagged ceiling made up of taller structures. It was impossible to determine if they were in any particular building, or if the towers of Nar Shaddaa had all broadened into one great moon-girding sprawl. The passages were little more than tunnels, broadening into larger courtyards bereft of plants or fountains. Inhabitants were now fewer, but Mander sensed they were watching, waiting for something to happen. Ahead of them was a dip in the tunnel, once perhaps part of an underpass now buried deep in the heart of the arcology that swallowed it.

It was a perfect spot for an ambush, Mander realized, just before the first blaster bolts erupted around them.

There were two attackers, hunkered down behind some trash compactors at the far end of the tunnel, their green trumpet-like antennae visible only when they popped up and shot. Bomu Rodians, laying down quick, random bursts, not risking their safety by poking their heads too far into view.

Mander pulled his lightsaber out, but too slowly, and the stresscrete around them fractured and chipped from the blaster shot. He had the blade up soon enough, though, and deflected the most accurate of the shots. Reen and Eddey had their blasters out now as well.

"Back up!" shouted Eddey. "We can try another route."

Mander started to shout that this would be impossible, that the Rodians ahead were not trying to kill them, but rather to herd them. But then the barrage came from behind them as the larger force of Bomus set up more withering, accurate fire and his observation was rendered moot.

Reen and Eddey both returned fire on the more exposed pursuers, but Mander found himself torn in two directions, trying to deflect charged energy bolts from the front and rear, protecting the others while not getting in their way. Following the course of the bolts by mere feeling as opposed to careful thought, he felt his control slipping, and one bolt passed deadly close to the side of his head.

"We go forward!" shouted Mander. "Take the two at the compactors and use them as cover!"

The Jedi now backed away from the more numerous pursuers, deflecting the beams as Reen and Eddey laid down a steady set of blasts forward, stitching carbonized scars across the front of the compactors. The Bomu ahead of them were now popping up, trying to make accurate shots. Mander, dealing with an avalanche of fire from behind, could feel the sweat trickling down the back of his neck from the strain, and could feel his concentration fray against the onslaught. Each shot seemed to live in its own particular moment, and he had to strike at them all lest any hit the Pantoran and the Bothan in the back.

Reen let out a shout as one of her shots potted a Bomu just as the raider stood up to lay down fire. The other kept up a steady barrage. "We've one left," shouted Eddey.

"Rush him!" shouted Mander, and turned to urge the pair forward into the random fire. He spun as he ran, deflecting bolts as best he could, but was now counting on Rodian timidity in combat more than his own abilities.

Eddey and Reen dived over the first compactor, spun about, and started firing back at their pursuers from cover. Mander jumped over the second. As the Rodian raised his blaster rifle, Mander cut through the barrel, intending to cut down his attacker with the backhand recovery. This Rodian did not fall back, however, but rather lunged forward, driving the melted barrel of his weapon into Mander's belly.

The blow caught Mander by surprise, and he rolled to one side, the breath driven from his body. His lightsaber dropped from his hand and went spinning down the alleyway. He managed to twist, and landed on his back on the side of the compactor away from the rest of the fire. But now the Rodian was straddled over him, wielding his rifle like a club. Mander tried to squirm out of the path of the blow, but the heavy rifle stock caught him in the side of the head. The Rodian raised his weapon again to deliver a deathblow.

And then there came a staccato of blasterfire, and the Rodian pitched over, his head a smoking ruin. Mander thought it was Reen or Eddey who had saved him, but no, the blasts had come from the wrong direction. Mander's head was spinning from the blow, and the outside world was reduced to a narrow tunnel. He could hear himself struggling to draw breath, and the distant blast-erfire, and Reen and Eddey shouting.

Someone was kneeling next to him. Someone with red hair and corporate sector civvies, who now crouched over him and joined the others in repelling the Bomu attackers.

"I swear," said Angela Krin, "you are not like any Jedi I have ever met."

BENEATH THE SMUGGLERS' MOON

"I am officially on detached duty," said Lieutenant Commander Angela Krin. "While you were my guests on the *Resolute*, I started investigating the Tempest trade, and convinced my superiors that the trail led to Nar Shaddaa."

The Bomu ambushers had fallen back once Angela had joined them—not outnumbered, but now facing three blasters operating from behind cover. Angela half led, half carried Mander to a nearby courtyard with a defensible entrance. Reen had recovered Mander's now-deactivated lightsaber and handed it to him. Mander looked at it hard and long before he took it back. He had made an apprentice's mistake, thinking the Rodian who had cut him down would just fall back in the face of the lightsaber's power.

"You followed us," said Reen to the CSA agent.

"I followed the *trail*," said Angela frostily. "A trail you happened to already be on. I found you at the Dark Melody." To Mander she said, "I have a contact nearby. We should go, if you're ready."

Mander let out a deep breath. He should have been aware that they had been followed. His side hurt, and he wondered if he had cracked a rib. The ringing in his ears had subsided to a great degree. "I'm good," he said, standing up slowly. "Let's press on."

The surroundings decayed further now, the very pretense of civilization washed away. Here was the place that the trash and waste of the upper levels ended up. Piles of discarded packing and abandoned tools now littered the hallways, along with deactivated and repeatedly scavenged droids. There were humanoid bodies as well. Some of them had been partially eaten.

"Vrblthers," said Angela Krin, and Reen shot a questioning look at her. She explained, "They are or were a native life-form, scavengers that hunt in packs. They've adapted terribly well to life in a Hutt city."

"One more thing to worry about," muttered Reen, now paying particular attention to the shadows.

"You said the trail led to Nar Shaddaa," said Mander. "How did you come to that conclusion?"

"Remember the crashed ship, the one that brought the plague?" Angela said. "We managed to track it by the engine numbers."

"And what did you find?" Eddey asked. "Who owns it?"

"It was a Skydove ship," Angela said, her face betraying no emotion. She was watching the Bothan for any reaction on his part.

Eddey did not disappoint, a wave of surprise spreading across his face. "Skydove Freight? It was an Anjiliac ship carrying the drugs?"

Angela Krin nodded. Reen snarled, "So Popara lied when he said that he didn't deal in hard spice."

"I don't know about that," said Angela. "My contact was sure that Popara was unaware. That someone else in the organization was responsible."

"And we can talk to this contact?" asked Mander.

"He is waiting for us at the Headache Bar," said Angela. "Always start with the last place on your list. And yes, my contact knows about your list. If you hadn't gotten pinned down back there, you would have met him already."

Ahead a sign flickered erratically. The Headache Bar, the three syllables of its name on different timers, long since fallen out of sync. Inside the place was unsurprisingly empty, a single spotlight over the central bar and deep shadows in a plethora of corners.

One of those shadows moved.

"My contact," said Angela.

Mika the Hutt slid out of the darkness and beckoned the others to join him. He was wearing the same style of vest he'd sported at the party, but this one was set in greenish flamewire and small red gems. With a small bag slung over one shoulder, he looked like nothing so much as a Hutt running away from home.

Eddey flinched at the sight of him, and Reen reached for her blaster. Mander put a hand on the Pantoran's shoulder. He said to Angela Krin, "That's how you found out it was a Skydove ship, isn't it? Mika told you."

"The CSA would have discovered it eventually," said the small Hutt. "The registration was buried behind a couple of false-front companies, but not so well that a dedicated investigator would have missed it. Smuggling, as you know, often depends on people looking the wrong way, either by accident or design. I myself was unaware that one of the family's ships was being used for the trade until I personally tracked the engine numbers that your Pantoran provided."

Reen ignored the idea that she was anyone's Pantoran, and instead said, "So your father was responsible for the Tempest?"

Mika blinked in what would pass for a shake of his neckless head. "No. When I came back, I checked through my family's records. The Endregaad ship was reported as lost in a comet storm two years ago. Someone took it out of service and repurposed it. I think they did it without my father's knowledge. He would have been shamed and angry if he knew." Mika let out a deep sigh, and Mander wondered if it was from grief for his parent or that the Hutt was embarrassed to reveal a weakness in the family.

The Jedi said softly, "We think that Zonnos may have been taking Tempest as well."

Mika's eyes flew open, obviously surprised by the idea. But, catching himself, he quickly returned them to slits. "Yes," said the small Hutt. "That makes a sort of sense. But surely even my brother would not seek Popara's death!"

Mander shook his head. "Not directly. There is more intelligence in play here than Zonnos has displayed so far."

Mika let out a snort. "If you are saying that my brother is not smart enough to blow up my late father, you may be right. He must have had help, then."

Mander asked, "What is the situation in your tower?"

"Uncomfortable," said Mika. "And if it is true Zonnos is an addict, I can see much of that now in his behavior. He has put a bounty on your heads, regardless of your innocence. Zonnos is looking for someone to be blamed for this, so he can establish himself as the full heir to the Anjiliac clan. A change in leadership often leads to problems for the lesser siblings. I fled here soon after the . . . incident . . . with my father, to meet with my CSA contact." He waved a stubby-fingered arm at Angela Krin.

"Can you get us offplanet?" Reen asked the woman.

"I can," said Angela.

"My own resources are limited," added Mika. "All the more so if my brother is truly under the influence of spice and involved in the smuggling. But I have enough sway to make sure you have a safe ship and a trustworthy pilot. Zonnos is not the only one with a couple of ships that exist off the official books."

"The CSA maintains a safehouse near here," said Angela, and Mika was startled at the news. Both things made sense, Mander thought. The CSA should have resources on the Smugglers' Moon. And Mika would not think that they were there. She continued, not noticing Mika's reaction, "We can hide there until you make arrangements."

With that the group quit the Headache Bar. They had to avoid what passed for public transportation on the planet, and to reach the safehouse plunged still deeper beneath the concrete skin of the world. Even Mika seemed nervous now, clearly in unfamiliar terrain. If Angela was equally unfamiliar with the territory, she betrayed no sign, instead quietly pointing out the new direction at each crossing.

Up ahead, they could hear low growls.

Angela froze for a moment, and then said, "Vrblthers. We can loop back and find another way."

Then there came a high-pitched, all-too-human screech, and Mander was suddenly moving toward it. Toward the growls.

A pack of lizard-like bipeds had surrounded a pile of trash long since brought down from the towers, scavenged, and then abandoned. The vrblthers had leathery hides the color of overly ripe fruit, and short, curled horns perched above underslung, fanged jaws. Their prey, a humanoid child, was scrabbling backward up the slope of loose trash. The vrblthers stalked forward on thick-knuckled claws.

Mander cut through two of the beasts from behind before they even knew he was there. He moved up the loose hillside of trash to the child and spun about, facing the rest of the pack. The loss of two of their members did nothing to deter the vrblthers, and they closed in on their new target.

Mander brought his blade up hard beneath the chin of the leading attacker, bisecting it from its chest to the top of its sloped forehead. The beast dropped without time to howl from the damage, but it was replaced immediately by two more. A sweeping, lateral blow caught both of these in their slavering jaws, and the Jedi could feel the trash beneath his feet give way. Rather than try to stop it, he rode the small avalanche of detritus down, taking three more of the beasts out in the process. Vrblther parts joined the other discards on the pile.

Now blasterfire sizzled the air around him as Reen, Angela, and Eddey caught up with him, a weaponless Mika alongside them. The newcomers peppered the flanks of the surviving pack. These wheeled on their new assailants, but to no good end. One broke from the rest of the pack and hurled itself at Mika. The small Hutt brought his hands up before him in what Mander thought was a feeble attempt to ward off the blow. Instead the creature yelped as it was flung backward, away from the Hutt, as if it had struck an invisible wall. The Hutt fell back behind the protection of the others, and Mander spun around and decapitated a beast that was trying to drag off the child while its fellows were otherwise occupied.

With another volley from the group's blasters, the entire pack was dead. Mander deactivated his lightsaber and climbed back up the trash pile, where the would-be prey was curled and weeping.

It was a child, definitely, but the species was unknown to him. Its skin was the pale yellow of guinchin fruit, and a ring of small protrusions, proto-horns, formed a lopsided ring along one side of its head. It was dressed in rags that at one time long before may have had a color.

"Come on," said Mander, "I won't hurt you." He held out his hand.

The child looked up, its luminous eyes weeping pale green tears, and reached out a slender hand to take

Mander's. The pair climbed down the trash heap. The child looked up at the others in wonder, but visibly shrank away from the Hutt.

"Amazing," said the Hutt. "I thought they were all dead."

"What is he?" asked Angela.

"Evocii," said the Hutt. "They once lived on Nal Hutta, and were exported to Nar Shaddaa to help build the Smugglers' Moon. They were never very hardy. I thought they had proved nonviable."

Reen gave Mander a hard look, but before she could say anything, Eddey said, "He's not alone."

At the other entrance there were more of the Evocii, older and taller but still similar to the child. They were dressed in a tattered collection of rags and battle armor, and carried what Mander hoped were inoperative blasters.

Mander raised both hands to show that he bore no weapons or ill will, but the child burst loose from them and ran to the adults. He buried his head in the robes of one of the females and unleashed a torrent of what Mander could only identify as a creole of Huttese and Basic.

The lead Evocii strode forward, shot a withering glance at the Hutt, but bowed to Mander. The Jedi returned his bow, but when he straightened, all but the leader had vanished back into the darkness of the tunnels. The leader nodded·at him, and then retreated as well.

Mika's satchel made the sound of a baby chick in distress. The Hutt fumbled at the satchel and pulled out a holographic comlink. He frowned at the winking telltale light of an incoming message.

"I should take this," he said. "The rest of you might not want to be seen."

Reen and the others took a few steps back, allowing

the darkness of their surroundings to cloak them. Mander took a step back as well, but stayed close enough to see the hololink clearly.

The head and shoulders of the dented H-3PO unit appeared in the radiance of the beam. "Kindly Mika, I hope that you are safe," said the droid. "Zonnos has called for your return, and the destruction of all who stand with you. Crafty Vago has blunted the worst of his rage, but your brother has become more and more irrational with each passing hour. Vago thinks that it may be to your advantage to be somewhere else for a while. A shuttle to the family estates on Nal Hutta is waiting at dock Q2214 on level twenty-two. The pilot is expecting you." There was some disturbance behind the droid. It turned and the connection was abruptly severed.

Mika's face drew in on itself, the Hutt biting his lower lip. Mander stepped back into the light.

"My brother seems intent on confirming his control of the clan," said Mika. "That control does not seem to include me."

"So it appears," said Mander.

"Vago wants me to hide out in our estate until Zonnos calms down." Mika did not seem to like the idea.

"But what if Vago is working with Zonnos?" said Mander.

"That has occurred to me as well," said the small Hutt. "It is a very distressing thought. My family dynamics have been always . . . strained."

Mander looked around. Reen and Eddey were checking ahead for any ambushes, and Angela Krin had fallen behind to see if they had been followed from the Headache Bar. The Jedi said, "Anything you can tell me may help us."

"We are a family, but we are an organization as well," he said. "Popara was both our father and the patron of all those in his employ. Some Hutt leaders treat this as if they were invested royalty, but Popara, may his spirit rest quietly, took the concerns of his workers very seriously. If you were in my father's employ, he demanded much, but he rewarded good service as well."

"There were only the two of you as his heirs," said Mander.

"The only two still living," said Mika, and was quiet for a moment. Then he added, "I never knew most of my siblings. Hutts live a very long time, but the nature of their lives makes death by natural causes an unlikely occurrence. And given our biology—you know about that, as scholar?"

"You can be of either gender," said Mander.

"That is putting it succinctly," said Mika. "But yes, and part of it is that our fertility rate is very low. Perhaps damage from when we lost our first world, Varl. So descendants are normally a problem, and my father favored me, as the baby of the family."

"And you think that might create problems with Zonnos?" asked Mander.

Mika puffed the air out of his cheeks in desperation. "Perhaps. Zonnos is the heir, and he's a Hutt's Hutt. The other families, the Council of Elders, would approve of him. He's not the sharpest vibroblade in the armory, as you've noted, but he has that *something* that others respect in our political circles."

Mander watched the little Hutt and felt sympathy, even pity for the creature. He was not a typical Hutt, and was afraid of being punished for it. The Jedi looked around, but things were still quiet. It was a peace that was sure not to last. "What can you tell me about Vago?" he asked.

Mika shook his head. "She's dedicated to my father. She makes things work. She's always been more dedicated to the family shipping business than Zonnos ever was. And she has always been very kind to me, teaching me about the business and encouraging me to explore on my own. Trips like the one to Endregaad were with her urging. I think that she feels that if something happened to Zonnos, I should know enough to handle myself in negotiations. I'd hate to think that Vago is wrapped up with this."

Angela Krin joined them at this point. "Nothing behind us. We can still hide at the CSA safehouse. Find our own way offplanet. We can protect you, Mika."

Mika looked at Angela, and Mander imagined he could see the wheels spin in the young Hutt's mind. Accepting the CSA's aid would be a safer choice, but carry with it additional obligations. Plus, not responding to Vago's offer to help might cost him an ally. If Vago *was* truly an ally at this point.

"You want to go to Vago," said the Jedi, trying to form the words as a question but failing. He added, "You should not go alone."

The Hutt nodded. "Yes," he said, "we should contact Vago. But we should be careful. The rendezvous spot is only a couple of levels above us."

Angela Krin looked like she would disagree for a moment, but then furrowed her brow and nodded. Mika said, "Should I disappear, don't let Vago get away with this." Again, she nodded, but this time more slowly. Mander wondered what that promise would entail.

The group set out again, and the young Hutt proved more than capable in keeping up with others. As they ascended, more citizens of the depths appeared in the courtyards and arcades, and if they thought it odd to see a Hutt traveling with his retinue so deep beneath the spires, none said anything about it. There was still no open sky above them, but as they climbed, Mander felt a weight being lifted from his shoulders.

The shuttle pad was set along the length of a shaft bored through the towers and slums of the Smugglers'

Moon, with landing pads jutting out at different levels. Beneath them, the shaft continued down to the blast pits. Far above them a retractable dome had been pulled back, and Mander imagined he could see open sky at the very top. Catwalks and cross-supports turned the passage into a twisted maze for any pilot.

Cradled on the pad was a squat shuttle of SoroSuub make. A Quarren leaned against one of the support struts, sucking on a death stick. He caught sight of the five of them, waved, and entered the shuttle to make final preparations. The dented H-3PO unit emerged and waddled toward them.

Mander and the others walked out onto the narrow bridge to the landing pad as the droid approached. Mander realized he had been holding his breath and let out a relieved sigh. Eddey and Reen seemed to relax as well.

The droid came up, and in a conversational voice said, "Zonnos made me lie to you. You should run now."

A squad of Wookiees tumbled out of shuttle, bellowing and brandishing blaster rifles and stun net projectors. Reen cursed and brought up her carbine, while Eddey spun around and shouted, "Pull back!"

The two forward Wookiees each dropped to one knee and aimed their stun nets. Microfilament netting blossomed from the barrels like greedy flowers ringed with electrified weights. Mander moved one aside easily with the Force, but the other found its mark and draped over the surprised Mika. With a ragged growl of pain the young Hutt slumped, small bolts of lightning sparking his light green flesh from the microfilaments.

They were halfway back to the blast doors when a group of Rodians boiled out from around the corner, armed with blaster pistols and stun batons. They cut off the retreat, laying down a withering pattern of fire. Mander leapt in front of the others, lightsaber drawn, and batted away the charged pulses of ionic energy as best he could. Behind him, Eddey and Angela Krin returned fire, dropping a Rodian with every other shot.

"Think they're working together?" shouted the CSA agent.

"I doubt it!" the Bothan shouted back. "I think the Wookiees want to take us alive. The Bomus do not seem to be as discerning."

Mander shot a glance over his shoulder and realized that Reen was still back along the platform, closer to the shuttle. She had taken up a position behind the stunned form of Mika, and was blasting the charging Wookiees.

She dropped two of them in quick succession, but the third was on top of her, and brought the butt of his blaster hard across her face. The Pantoran dropped like a rock.

"Reen!" Mander shouted.

"Look out!" bellowed Eddey. "They have a detonator!"

Mander looked back as the depleted Rodian force rolled a small thermal device toward them. He reached out with the Force and tried to shove it off the landing pad, out into the empty space of the launch tube itself.

He almost succeeded.

The detonator spun under his direction, teetering at the very edge of the pad. Then it exploded.

The thermal detonator became a brilliant red-white star for a moment, and half the pad disappeared. The stress rocked the rest of the landing structure, and the Wookiees behind them fell down. In the shuttle itself, Mander could see the Quarren pilot fighting with the controls, and the side thrusters came to life along the sides of the hull. The shuttle took a sharp lurch off its cradle and began to tip into the abyss beneath them.

Then the ground fell away beneath Mander's feet.

Without thinking, he leapt for the shadowy catwalks above. But they were too far and he realized that he would miss them.

A narrow, pale yellow arm, clad in rags, reached out of the darkness and grabbed Mander's outstretched arm. Looking up, Mander saw the face of the Evocii leader.

"Sometimes you fight, sometimes you run," said the leader in broken Basic. "This time you run if you want to fight later."

Mander looked around and saw that Eddey and Angela Krin were in the hands of other Evocii, being pulled to safety at upper ledges. Behind and below them, the pilot was trying to save his craft from the crumbling landing pad, firing his landing thrusters to stay stable. He was failing.

Two of the Wookiees were protecting the fallen forms of Mika and Reen, while the others now bunched along one side of the shuttle, pushing it off the side of the platform. Unless the pad was lightened, it would collapse into the blast pits.

The Quarren at the controls panicked now and the main engines flickered for a moment. If they fired up, the entire pad would be incinerated, killing them all. The Wookiees let out a howl and pushed with all their might. The shuttle pitched over the edge of its cradle and for one brief moment Mander thought the pilot could regain control. Then it fell like a stone from heaven, spinning as its thrusters failed along the far side, spiraling into the depths.

His Evocii rescuer shoved him through the safety of a blast door as he heard the distant thunder of the crash. He wondered if the debris and flames would channel this far up the shuttle tube. Then the blast door safety engaged and the durasteel doors shut behind him with a final clang.

CHAPTER TWELVE

TRIAL AND TERROR

"It is not your fault," said Eddey.

"I could have gotten rid of the thermal detonator," said Mander. "I could have saved them both."

They were standing on the balcony of the CSA safe-house. It was surprisingly accommodating for a surreptitious hiding hole, situated halfway up one of the skytowers of the Nar Shaddaa arcology. From this viewpoint, they could look out over a wide swath of lower construction and ruins, and see the bulk of the Anjiliac tower, nestled against the structures of other powerful Hutt clans.

Which may have been a reason why the CSA maintained this apartment in the first place, Mander realized. To keep an eye on the Hutt clans. The long night of Nar Shaddaa had passed, replaced with the gray, polluted day.

The Evocii had brought them here, under Angela Krin's orders. Now half a dozen of the warriors were camped out in the main room, some noticeably afraid of being this far above their normal haunts, the others raiding the larder and putting food aside to take to their families down below.

Angela came out to join the others on the balcony, apparently unconcerned that so much of the CSA resources were going to the refugees. Mander had an errant thought and wondered what her expense account would look like after this.

"I've found a way offplanet," she said. When she noticed the questioning look on Mander's face, she explained further. "I called in a couple of corporate favors. We can leave before local nightfall—which is only forty hours away."

"We have to rescue Reen," said Eddey. Mander hesitated for a moment, and then nodded.

"That would be your choice," said Angela Krin, looking at Mander. She already knew better than to argue with the Bothan. "But you are more likely to find out about the Tempest spice if you're alive. Which you will not be if Zonnos finds you."

"We have to rescue Reen," said the Bothan again.

Angela Krin shook her head. "Losses happen, even in well-planned operations."

Which this was not, Mander thought. He looked out over the sprawling multilevel traffic of the lunar city.

"Besides," continued the lieutenant commander, "we don't even know if she's still alive." Her eyes lost focus for a moment, lost in thought, "Or if Mika is alive, either."

"She's alive," said Mander, pointing at a signblimp.

The face of Zonnos the Hutt sprawled along the lightpips of the signblimp, and the bass voice of the Hutt thundered over the din of the traffic. "The assassin of my father has been captured!" translated the droid pilot, as the picture changed to that of Reen, battered but alive. "She will be executed at forenoon, in two hours' time. The trial and execution will be broadcast on these blimps. Watch the worthy demise of the murderer of my father, and see the firm justice of the Anjiliac clan!"

"He is solidifying his power," said Angela Krin. "Telling the other Hutts he is fit to lead. It is theater, nothing more."

"Theater that will kill Reen," said Mander. "No mention of Mika, though."

"He's probably a prisoner in the skytower," said Angela Krin. "Were he dead, that charge would have been added to the accusations against Reen as well. But if anything happens to him, I swore that Vago would pay for it."

Mander looked at Angela, and saw emotions cross her face in quick succession—fear, anger, and frustration—before it smoothed out again into the calm demeanor of a CSA officer. *She was willing to see Reen die, but swears vengeance on Mika's behalf.*

"We have to rescue her," said the Bothan again.

Angela blinked, then looked at Eddey, then at Mander. At last she said: "All right, we have to rescue her. How?"

"Do you have an aircar among your corporate resources?" Mander asked.

Angela thought a moment, then nodded.

To Eddey, Mander said, "Can you fly it?"

"I can fly anything," said the Bothan.

"You have a plan?" asked Angela.

"I do," said Mander, "but I need one of your blaster carbines."

The master assassin, the slayer of the beloved Popara Anjiliac, accused and all but convicted of her crime, stood apart from the assembled court, chained on a lit platform. She was on display, to be holorecorded and transcripted until the inevitable judgment was passed upon her.

Reen Irana occupied the center of attention of this media circus, and she was not happy about it.

The holocam droids swung on their pivot gimbals, their tricloptean lenses capturing the infrared and ultraviolet spectrums for those aliens who preferred their media in those ranges. At the broadcast booths, labels, news crawls, tickers, chyrons, logos, and commentary would be added in a variety of languages for personal consumption. The bulk of the live broadcast would be in Huttese, of course.

The penthouse had been reformatted as a court of Huttese law. Screens had been dropped over most of the panoramic windows, and those panels that had been damaged by the earlier blasterfire had been replaced with temporary sheets of lightweight durasteel. The barrier between Popara's private study and the feast hall had been removed, along with its protective force field. A holoprojector in the corner displayed the resplendent image of the victim, Popara Anjiliac, looking wise and venerable and completely unexploded.

In the center of the room stood the accused, chained by thick links of plasteel. Her face was bruised from injuries supposedly sustained during the thrilling capture, where, according to the press release, she was kept from killing Mika the Hutt only through the personal efforts of Zonnos's own heroic Wookiee guards. Even so, she destroyed a shuttle and crippled a vital set of shuttle tubes. No charges were brought against her for these crimes, as they paled beside the charge of Hutticide. And of that crime she was already found guilty. All that remained was holding the trial and carrying out the sentence, as determined by Zonnos Anjiliac.

The lift tube doors opened and Zonnos entered with his retinue. Mika was not there, nor Vago, but Popara's robed Twi'lek handmaidens now moved demurely behind their new master. The Wookiees came next, throwing their heads back and roaring for the holocams, marching to the far side of the room and standing guard behind the prisoner. Last came the household Niktos, their reputation diminished in that they had failed not only to protect their former master, but also to capture the designated assassin. These unfortunate bodyguards lined up behind Zonnos and the Twi'leks.

Zonnos was dressed in a cape of gold scales, though Reen did not know if this was a symbol of mourning or power among the Hutts. His blue-tinged face was a maze of engorged blood vessels, darkened to a violet shade by Tempest use. The veins seemed to throb as she watched, and violet pus collected at the corners of the Hutt's wide eyes. He was deep in the throes of a Tempest binge, Reen realized, striving hard to maintain the façade of calmness. He oozed his way up a short platform to a dais that allowed him to tower over the Pantoran.

The left side of Reen's face was swollen, but her eyes blazed with anger at the Hutt. She refused to be intimidated, even at this point. Above her a swirling constellation of disintegrators hovered, installed specifically to carry out instantaneously the will of Mighty Zonnos.

A toady she had not seen before—a huge-headed, multi-eyed Vuvrian—strode forward with a massive two-handed club in its insectile claws. For a moment Reen wondered if she would have to fight this minion one-on-one, but the being slammed the base of the club against the floor and let out a stream of enthusiastic Huttese. The Vuvrian could be a lawyer for the prosecution, stating the charges against her, or some courtier extolling the virtues of the late Popara—or just sucking up to Zonnos. Whatever his role, he was taking his time about it, and threatening to pull all the oxygen from the room.

Reen wondered if that was a method of Hutt execution: boring the accused to death. Despite her battered state, she smiled at the idea. Mander would like the concept. Zonnos caught the smile and glowered at her, interrupting the Vuvrian and bellowing something incomprehensible at her. Oily spittle dripped from his lips as he flung insults and accusations at her.

Reen looked the Hutt square in the eye and recited the only Huttese that she knew. It was short and obscene and made scandalous reference to both Zonnos's bathroom and his dining habits, equating the two.

Zonnos blanched at the curse; then the purplish stain on his face deepened, and he grabbed the club from the Vuvrian and swung it above his head. Reen thought she could twist at the last moment, bring up the chains, and maybe use the brute's own rage to break them.

If she couldn't, she would be dead, and at least she would be spared any more of the Hutt's legal proceedings.

She tensed herself for the leap, and that was when the wall exploded behind her.

All eyes in the penthouse-turned-courtroom, living and mechanical, had been trained on her as she verbally and publicly assaulted Zonnos. As a result, no one saw the aircar that peeled away from traffic, and therefore no one had the opportunity to think it odd that such a vehicle would try to form its own lane. They would be surprised, though, when the aircar took a sharp left and picked up speed, aiming at the penthouse itself.

It blasted through the durasteel panels that had so recently been installed over the shattered windows. The panels themselves held, but the temporary fasteners were not so resistant to impact, and huge plates popped inward, into the room. The Wookiee guard, strung along that wall in a place of honor, was completely bowled over by the force of the blast, and many were crushed beneath the multi-ton plates.

The canopy of the aircar shattered and a lightsaber beam was clear in the smoke. Mander Zuma strode out of the wreckage. Angela Krin and Eddey Be'ray flanked him, their blasters drawn.

The Niktos were caught gaping at the sight, and Eddey and Angela mowed down the bulk of them. Two of the

Twi'lek handmaidens fled back to the lift, shrieking. The third, calmer than her sisters, retreated behind them in good order. The Vuvrian toady dived for cover among the holocam droids.

"Let her go," shouted Mander, sounding more angry than commanding.

Zonnos seethed with rage, but was still a Hutt in his heart. He picked up one of the blaster carbines and grabbed Reen, pulling her as tight to him as her chains allowed.

"Kickeeyuna je killyo," said Zonnos. Reen didn't know what the Hutt said, but she got his meaning: Mander could surrender or watch her die in a spasm of blasterfire.

Mander stopped, and for one cold moment Reen was sure that the Jedi would surrender, would offer himself in trade for her. And Zonnos would accept and then kill them all.

Then Mander reached into his robes with his free hand. He came up with a blaster.

And before Zonnos could move—before he could cower behind his hostage—Mander Zuma shot Reen Irana once, dead center, in the chest.

Reen slumped in her chains, falling through Zonnos's arms and collapsing on the floor. The powerful young Hutt, deprived of his hostage, let out an enraged bellow, and charged Mander, wielding the blaster as a club. His eyes were feral now, and all trace of cunning or guile was replaced with an overwhelming rage.

He got halfway to Mander and stopped short. A lightsaber had blossomed in his chest, its blade driven deep into his soft flesh.

Mander recovered from the throw and somersaulted forward. He grasped the handle of his blade and tore upward, through the tough flesh of the creature. Zonnos the Hutt, master of the Anjiliac clan for less than one day on Nar Shaddaa, collapsed at his feet.

The surviving Wookiees and Niktos had regrouped, taking cover among the destroyed chairs and droids, and now had their weapons leveled on Mander and the others. But a pall had descended on the ersatz court-room. No one fired.

"What now?" asked Eddey, flanking Mander.

"They aren't sure," said Angela Krin. "They don't know if they have a master or not. There is no one to give them an order."

The turbolift doors slid open and Mika the Hutt slid out, flanked by Niktos. He looked out of breath. To Mander it seemed that he had been pulled from what-ever room he was being held prisoner in here and rushed to the scene as soon as Zonnos's death was broadcast.

"*Ap-xmasi keepun!*" Mika barked, and the Niktos put up their weapons immediately, trained from birth to jump at the word of a Hutt. The Wookiees hesitated a moment, then did the same.

To Mander he said in a commanding voice, "*Reloj ba preesen!*" Free the prisoner. The Hutt's voice had a note of command and power, and despite his small size Mika seemed to dominate the room. Mander knelt next to Reen's fallen form and cut through the chains. Eddey hoisted her body. Angela Krin stood guard over all of them.

Mika shouted at the pair of them as they worked. "*Jee gah plogoon du bunky dunko.*" You are a plague on my house. Mander was stunned for a moment by Mika's anger and the power in his voice—then realized that the holocam droids were still operating. They were broad-casting Mika's words to an audience of Hutts, all of them weighing those words and whether this youngest member of the house deserved to run the clan. He was playing to the cams.

Mika spoke in Huttese, now, slowly enough that Mander could understand him. "I have discovered that it was Zonnos who was responsible for my father's death. You are mere pawns in his plans. Come with me. You will darken my father's halls no longer!" He beckoned for Mander and the others to follow. Eddey carried Reen, and Angela Krin kept her weapon drawn and ready in case any of the Wookiees decided to curry favor with their new master by trying something.

Once beyond the cams, in the safety of the lift, Mika allowed himself to deflate slightly. "I hope I was convincing," he said, smiling weakly, speaking Basic once more for the benefit of the CSA agent and the Bothan.

"I was thoroughly convinced you were a Hutt," said Angela Krin. "What did you say?"

Mika shrugged. "The truth. Or at least the truth as I understand it. It always served my father very well. I told them that Zonnos was responsible for my father's death, and that you were nothing but a distraction. An irritating distraction that I would now throw out of my house with great show and fanfare."

Mander said, "We will try to look appropriately abashed."

"Your services will be rewarded," said Mika. The door shushed open to reveal a nondescript hoverbus with blackened windows. "This will take you back to your ship. It is fully prepped and ready to go." Angela went in first, and helped Eddey bring Reen's unconscious form onboard.

"Thank you," said Mander. "There is one thing, though," he added, looking to make sure that the others could not hear them. "When we fought the vrblther, you seemed to . . ."

". . . use a special talent," finished the Hutt.

Mander nodded. "A talent that many of my brethren share."

Mika's face darkened in embarrassment. "I am thought of as an unusual son of an unusual Hutt to begin with," he said. "Can you imagine how the other families would react if they knew that I had . . ."

". . . a special talent?" said Mander.

"It is a tool that I would prefer others not to know about," said Mika. "My father knew. And your apprentice found out, and helped me understand part of it. But so much of your teaching is alien. I cannot wrap my mind about it, no matter how hard I try."

"Not everyone who feels the Force can be a Jedi," said Mander.

"I know," said Mika, and seemed to fall in on himself, seeming smaller than he was before. "I can work children's tricks, no more. I would prefer that no one else knows this, either among the Hutts or the Jedi."

The small Hutt's brow furrowed and he shook his flat head. "I will have my hands full. Vago is missing. I don't know if Zonnos had her killed, or if she has fled. I don't even know how much she was responsible for what happened. I will have much work to repair my family's reputation as it is. This is a secret I would prefer to be kept."

"I understand," said Mander. "And I want you to know that if you need help, you can trust this Jedi to keep your secret."

Mika smiled weakly, "Your efforts will be rewarded," he said with a shrug.

Mander said, "For our part, we will continue to pursue the Tempest trade."

Mika shook his head sadly. "Of all the things, that particular drug has damaged my family the most. Perhaps with Zonnos's death it will finally abate. Please keep me informed about your progress in this matter, and for my part I will tell you if Vago turns up."

"Of course," said the Jedi.

"Now hurry," said the Hutt, "before the cam droids figure out where your ship is."

Mander boarded the hoverbus and it pulled away. Through the darkened windows, he looked back to see the lone, small Hutt standing on the platform, lacking family, lacking support. A singularly unique Hutt trapped in a life he had not planned.

And then the hoverbus lifted into the clutter of air traffic, and he was gone.

CALCULATIONS

Koax the one-eyed Klatooinian stood her ground as waves of abuse in Huttese spilled out over the holoreceiver. Spittle showed up as snowy static as the Spice Lord dressed her down. In her sleeping pod, she was glad she had set up the privacy shields to maximum. No one wanted to hear an angry Hutt through the walls.

"An amateur operation!" snarled the faceless silhouette hovering above the receiver platform. "Your Rodians could not handle the simplest of tasks, covering their own tracks on Makem Te. Why should I expect them not to make an akk dog's breakfast of something like this? Why should I not put you and them out on the street!"

Koax visibly blanched at the thought. "With respect, *Ma Lorda,* Rodians are by their nature creatures of violence and vengeance, and the Bomu clan more so than most."

The Spice Lord was unimpressed with her line of argument. "And you thought not to inform me that once you unleashed them, they would surge through the undercity like a plague, shooting everything that moved and blowing up the foundations of our very towers?"

Koax stammered for a moment, and the light in her red eyes seemed to flicker from nervousness. For Klatooinians—indeed, for most of the client races under control of the Hutts—disappointing their lords was a cardinal sin.

And yet inwardly she seethed—this was not her problem. The Spice Lord had gotten what the Spice Lord had wanted. "I apologize for their . . . enthusiasm. They were meant to merely herd the group into Zonnos's trap instead of trying to blow it up."

The Hutt made a growling noise that could have been laughter or indignation. "Zonnos. That was the price paid for their 'enthusiasm.' He should have gotten his trial and meted out his punishment to all three of them, taken Popara's place, and proved to be a useful tool for us. Instead we have *Jeedai* and CSA agents sniffing at the hems of our robes."

Koax's gem-like eye gleamed in mischief. "Should I cut ties with the Bomu clan?"

"Yes," said the Hutt, then considered a moment. "On second thought, let us do the opposite. Provide the Bomu clan with more opportunities to serve. Stretch them thin. Send them in a number of different directions, far away from the *Jeedai* and their hunters. Do not give them time to pursue their vengeance, while we recover and strengthen our own forces. When the time is right, we will sacrifice them."

The Hutt laughed at the thought, and Koax cautiously joined the Spice Lord. "You are a good servant, Koax," said the Hutt, "and your failings can be forgiven when compared with the gifts you bring."

The Hutt raised a thick-fingered hand and produced the trophy, the weapon that had been in Koax's possession until so very recently. Looking at it, Koax felt another pain—one of jealousy. There had been no question of her failing to turn over the lightsaber to the Spice Lord, but still, she missed its familiar weight from when she'd kept it safe.

The Hutt ran a thumb over the activator plate and the blade sprang to life, illuminating the Spice Lord fully to the Klatooinian. For the first time in their conversations over the holoreceiver, Koax saw her master's face.

She fought the urge to step away, to quail in the Spice Lord's presence. Instead she said, "I am glad that you received it. I am glad you find me worthy to continue my service to you."

"A good craftsman keeps good tools," said the Hutt, and toggled off the transmission.

Koax stared at the blank holoreceiver, and realized that she was shaking. She had seen the face of the Spice Lord, and the expression on that face: cold, cruel, and calculating. Despite the encouragement, Koax knew the Spice Lord would leave her for dead at the merest suspicion of incompetence or failure.

She could not let that happen.

She would have to redouble her efforts, keeping the Bomus busy, taking care of the hundred and one things that needed doing that the Spice Lord was too busy for. Because for a Klatooinian, failing a Hutt is the worst failure of all.

"You shot me," said Reen.

"A lightsaber does not have a stun setting," said Mander. "You said that yourself."

"You *shot* me."

"Only to keep you alive," he said, but the words sounded weak.

They were in the belly of the *Resolute* again, moving slowly through Corporate Sector space. Angela Krin had requested they redirect to her ship after leaving Nar Shaddaa. Now, in the medlab, a medical droid was prodding the blistered skin of the Pantoran, applying balms and ointments to her chest. She had her shirt off, and her anger allowed her to ignore the potential embarrassment of it. For his part, Mander found the far wall of great interest, and concentrated his attention there.

The medical droid, a B1E unit, clattered with approval and rolled backward on its tripod wheels. Reen shrugged her shirt back on and Mander felt more comfortable with the conversation immediately.

"And I missed out on all the fun," she added, buttoning herself up.

"It was hardly fun," said Mander, turning back from the wall. "I had to kill Zonnos."

"It would have been fun for me," she said. "And I don't think the Tempest ends with him."

"I agree," said Mander. "He wasn't smart enough to pull off such a trade himself."

"And he would have been sampling his own stock," said Reen.

"That is a mistake in the spice trade, I'll admit," noted Mander.

Reen shook her head. "No—he had someone buying the drug in Nar Shaddaa. One of his Wookiees, remember?"

"So?"

"Would you send someone out to pay street prices when you had a ready and steady flow yourself?" Reen asked.

Mander opened his mouth, and then stopped. She was right. "Vago hasn't been seen since Popara's death," he managed to say.

Reen regarded him coolly. "And Vago *is* smart enough to pull this off."

Eddey manifested at the medlab door. "Good to see you up and around," he said to Reen. "The lieutenant commander wants to see us in her office."

"After you," said Reen, dropping off the examination table.

"Go ahead," said Mander.

"Are you kidding?" said the Pantoran. "I'm not turning my back on you. You *shot* me." Mander looked at her for a trace of amusement in her face. He saw none. Troubled, he left the medical bay ahead of the Pantoran.

The commander's office was as bare and utilitarian as always. The holo-chess set was in idle mode once more. This time the viewscreen showed simply deep space, the distant stars drifting only slightly. Lieutenant Commander Angela Krin stood facing those stars as the three were ushered in, dressed once more in her full uniform. She waited for them to be alone. Then she turned to her desk and punched a few buttons.

"While we were in Hutt space, I had the Corporate Sector medtechs examine both the Tempest spice and Endregaad disease. Here is the disease." She toggled the screen, and a spiral of chemical markers danced above the tabletop. Along one side of the image, lines radiated from points of interest in the molecular chain, zooming in on particular connections.

Mander and the others nodded. The lieutenant commander's fingers stroked open another file from the desktop. It displayed next to it a bulkier, more geometric image. This one was built not on a double helix, but on a three-dimensional hex grid. Again, lines radiated from particular items the medtechs thought interesting.

Mander leaned forward, but shook his head. The two drawings seemed as widely different as a puppy and a droid.

Eddey, though, pointed at a swooping line in both drawings. "Those parts are similar."

Angela nodded. "My techs caught it as well. They both have a similar organic structure along those root splines. There's a link between the two."

"The plague on Endregaad was caused by the spice?" asked Mander.

"No," said Angela, "the spice is a mutated form of a normal spice. At its heart, it is a spice—or several spices—common to a dozen worlds, but it has undergone a modification in its treatment and manufacture that brings out its lethal nature. Wherever the spice is refined gives it its exceptional properties. We believe it to be harvested from elsewhere and then treated, and that treatment location is where this disease originally appeared."

"All right," said Mander, "where did this disease originally appear?"

Eddey squinted at the spinning spiral diagram of the disease. "Is that hard-radiation scarring in those molecules?"

Angela smiled. "Exactly. Hard radiation in a very narrow type of wavelengths, found among white dwarves. We knew the disease came from a highly irradiated world. Now we know what type of system our origin point is in."

"There are hundreds of thousands of white dwarf worlds in the galaxy," said Mander.

"But only tens of thousands within easy transport distance of Endregaad and the Corporate Sector," said the lieutenant commander. "I can break free some resources for a methodical search for traders operating in dead systems, strange comings and goings, and other telltales."

"Still," said Mander, "that would mean finding a needle in a slightly smaller haystack."

"That's where our experienced consultants come in," said Angela Krin.

Reen, who had been silent to this point, suddenly brought her head up. She had apparently been thinking about other things. "Us? What do you need from us?" Apparently, thought Mander, she had not decided about the CSA's job offer quite yet.

"Information," said Angela calmly, though Mander

could hear stress in her voice. "You know the ins and outs of spacers better than anyone under my command. Where would they hang out? If they were making a transfer of contraband, where would it be? What systems are considered the softest for smuggling operations? Who are their contacts?"

"We don't smuggle," said Reen, her face darkening with embarrassment.

"Of course you don't," said Angela Krin. "No one here is saying that you do. What I am saying is that my own resources in the Corporate Sector Authority are limited, and if we can use your knowledge, perhaps even smugglers that you know among the trading community, we can save ourselves a lot of trouble."

Reen paused for a moment, and yes, her face turned a deeper shade of blue. Mander had seen it before in Toro. Not embarrassment. Anger.

"No," she said simply.

"No?" said Angela Krin. She seemed shocked, an officer not used to insubordination on her own command deck.

"No," said Reen. "Sorry." She took a deep breath. "You offered your help to find Toro's killer, but I'm not sharing every spacer secret with you just so you can go looking."

"I don't think it is like that—" Mander started, but the lieutenant commander cut him off. "You don't seem to understand how serious the situation is. This is larger than just the death of your brother."

"And so I have to trust you," said Reen.

"Yes," said the CSA commander.

"No," said the Pantoran.

"We can discuss this," said Mander. At the same moment Angela said, "We can pay you well for your services." Mander wished the commander would quit making matters worse.

Reen shook her head. "You don't get it," she said to Angela. "You have more than enough people in the CSA to pull this off. People you can trust. People you can order around. You don't know us at all. You don't have to take these risks. *We* don't have to take this risk." She moved to the door. "I'm going to head down to the *New Ambition* and, with your kind permission, sweep her from stem to stern to see if the Hutts put any bugs into the system while we were on Nar Shaddaa. Then Eddey and I are going our own way." She turned to go.

"Captain Irana," Angela Krin said, raising her voice to Reen's back; the Pantoran halted before the door. "Mander Zuma did the right thing in shooting you. You would have been used as a tool against us. As a hostage. He had to take you off the board."

Reen spun around and opened her mouth to speak, then spun back and left the conference room in a fury. Mander looked at Eddey.

"What just happened here?" asked the Jedi.

"I think we just quit before we were hired," said Eddey. To Angela Krin he composed himself and said, "Sorry about that. The science here seems pretty interesting." He looked at the schematics of the Endregaad plague spinning slowly over the lieutenant commander's desk. He did not move to the door.

"Aren't you going down to help Reen?" asked the Jedi.

"I could," said Eddey, "but I don't think I'm the one who has to talk to her. Besides, I'd rather stay here and talk with the lieutenant commander about her medtechs. Is it possible to download this on a datastick?" he asked, addressing Angela. "I've got some 'spacer resources' of my own that I'd like to check it against." Angela Krin said nothing, but nodded, her mouth a noncommittal line. To Mander it seemed that she was trying to pin down the exact moment when she'd totally lost control of the situation.

Mander left them behind and descended to the docking bay where the *New Ambition* was moored. Climbing the ship's boarding ramp, he could hear Reen clattering around inside. She had already pulled off one of the forward avionics sections and was on her back, her head buried among the wiring.

"Make yourself useful, Eddey," she shouted. "Hand me the reflek sculptor. I swear there are some welds that weren't here when we got the ship."

Mander sat down in the copilot's seat and looked at the open toolbox. He rooted around and handed her a likely-looking suspect, a long beeping device with multiple heads. She dropped it like a live snake, and shouted "*Reflek* sculptor, Eddey. Don't clown around with me."

"Eddey's still up talking to the lieutenant commander," said Mander. "How can I help?"

Reen pulled herself out of the avionics section and scowled at Mander. "I thought I was clear on this. We're not interested in another kriffing adventure."

"That part was clear," said Mander. "I'm just not sure on the *why*. I mean, I guess after what happened on Nar Shaddaa, anyone would be rattled . . ."

She looked at him with an expression that reminded him of her brother. "You shot me."

"I *stunned* you," said Mander. "And it seems to bother you more than it should. You've surely been shot at before. I know. I was there."

"You don't understand," she said, trying to hide her irritation. Again, so much like her brother.

"Try to make me understand," he said, remembering old conversations he had with Toro. He had been younger than Reen when Mander had taken him on as an apprentice, but no less stubborn.

"You shot me," she said, "And I didn't *expect* it."

Mander leaned back in the copilot's chair and let out a deep breath. "So you're angry that I *surprised* you?"

Reen leaned back against one of the consoles, trying not to look at the Jedi. "I thought I had figured out how you thought. I mean, you're a *librarian*."

"Archivist," corrected Mander, but she ignored him.

"You've been the one to recommend talking things over first," she said. "Careful planning. Knowing your opponent. Waiting for someone else to make their move."

"I think we knew Zonnos pretty well by that point," Mander noted. "And I thought we planned pretty well for the situation."

"And your solution was to ram an aircar into the building and shoot me?" Her voice climbed as she spoke.

"We were pressed for time," Mander said, "and shooting you was only an option if Zonnos took you hostage. Which he did."

"You were just . . ." Her voice trailed off.

"Acting more like a Jedi?" suggested Mander Zuma.

"Yes!" she said, slapping her knee.

Mander was silent for a moment. Finally he said, "Sometimes adventure leaps onto us. It is not like we had a choice in the matter."

Reen started to protest, but Mander shushed her, continuing. "I think I know what you mean. Part of a Jedi is the ability to process all manner of threats and situations, analyze them, choose the best option, and then act. It is supposed to happen very quickly for us. We inherently know the best action. It is part of being connected with the Force, and our training enhances it."

He let out a deep sigh. "I've always been good at processing and analyzing a situation. I've never been so good at acting on what I learn. Acting instinctively and immediately. Until that fight in the depths of Nar

Shaddaa, with the vrblthers. Suddenly I knew what had to be done and I did it. And when I had to deal with Zonnos, I had the same feeling." He looked at Reen and added, "Sorry to have surprised you."

The two of them sat in silence on the flight deck of the *New Ambition*.

"So where do we go from here?" said Mander Zuma.

It was Reen's turn to sigh. "You're still my best lead. Particularly since I upset the lord high commander up in her briefing room by not ratting out my fellow spacers."

"All right then," Mander said, and thought for a moment. "Bomu clan."

"They've been hunting us throughout this," said Reen.

"On someone else's orders," said Mander. "You said it yourself—they are basically small-time. But if we shake them up enough, maybe they can tell us who they are working for."

"Some other small fry," said Reen, frustrated.

"Who is working for someone else who is working for someone else," said Mander. "And eventually we get to the one who *isn't* working for anyone else, and he, or she, is the one we're looking for."

Reen thought about it a moment, then said, "It sounds like more fun than spilling what I know about smuggling to a CSA agent."

"Or searching a thousand dead systems filled with hard radiation," noted Mander.

"And it's not like the Bomu clan is going to be any *less* angry at us," said Reen with a smile. It was an easy smile. The storm had passed.

"I am sorry I had to shoot you," said Mander. "But it was the right thing to do at the time."

"Warn me next time," said Reen, then paused for a moment. "Why are *you* still here?" she asked. "You've gotten the coordinates and finished Toro's last mission, rescued your traveling companion, and killed a Hutt and lived. I know why I need to go forward, and even Angela's reasoning. Why are you still here?"

"I want to find the origin point of the Tempest," said Mander. "I want to put an end to it."

"For Toro?" asked Reen.

"In part," said Mander. "And for you." *And for Mika,* he added to himself. For an odd little Hutt who lost his family because of the Tempest trade.

"And for yourself?" asked Reen. "Are you sure that you're not dealing with your own personal Tempest? Is the excitement, the chance of playing the hero, clouding your better judgment?"

"I don't know," Mander Zuma said. "Do you want to come along and make sure my judgment doesn't get clouded?"

Reen made a noise and disappeared back under the avionics console. "Sure. Regardless, I still have to check out everything on this boat. Go tell Eddey it's safe to come down here and help."

Mander said, "Of course," and stood up. Reen popped her head out one last time. "And Mander?"

"Yes?"

"Tell the commander we are not game pieces," said Reen. "We're not to be taken off the board, or used as pawns. I hate that."

"That was a poor choice of words on the lieutenant commander's part," said Mander. "But I will keep that in mind as well." But Reen was already back under the console, muttering at the welds and trying to figure out if they had been there before Nar Shaddaa.

THE TRAIL OF THE TEMPEST

Rolan was the last member of the Bomu clan on Makem Te, and it felt to him like he was the last Rodian in the galaxy. Pushing his way through the mortuary bazaar, flanked on all sides by the heavy Swokes Swokes, Rolan felt trapped. When he was outside he was afraid of being spotted, and when he hid it felt like he was just waiting for his fate to catch up with him.

So he moved, not staying in the same place any one evening. He crashed in alleyways and in the shadows of the great tombs. He stole where he could, ran when he had to. He stood out in this population of flabby, neckless monstrosities, and could not rest for a moment.

There was no way for him to get word out. With the disaster in the spice warehouse—with the arrival of the *Jeedai*—their best warriors had died. Dejarro, his contact with the Spice Lord's people, disappeared soon after that. The word was that the *Jeedai* had caught up with him, but Rolan thought that unlikely. It was more likely that Dejarro had bolted for space, and would not be heard from again.

Then matters got *worse*. The Tempest shipments dried up . . . then stopped entirely. Attempts to reestablish the supplies were met with apologies at first, then with indifference. Those of the Bomu clan who had survived the *Jeedai*'s attacks slipped out in ones and twos. Some were called away on clan business, sent to new opportunities. Some were around one day, gone the next, and no one knew where. Eventually, the only ones left were the low-level dealers who were unaware that everything had gone south. Low-level dealers who were unaware that their supplier and patron, this Spice Lord, had turned away from Makem Te.

Low-level dealers like Rolan.

It got worse when the spice stopped. Their customers felt the pain first, as withdrawal surged through their systems, heightening their rage. Even though the Swokes Swokes lacked pain receptors, their flesh was still prone to the anger the drug brought. And they knew it came from the Rodians.

And too late, Rolan realized the danger of having a clientele that was taking a spice that made them angry. A clientele that was near invulnerable in combat.

An angry, volatile, near-invulnerable clientele that knew what you looked like.

Rolan paused beside an open display of necrotic sugar candies cast in the shapes of various types of skulls—human, Cerean, Wookiee, and of course the Swokes Swokes. His stomach grumbled a protest and Rolan realized he had not eaten since the previous day. He looked at the clerk, who was at the other end of the counter helping a heavily bejeweled native.

Rolan glanced around. Was anyone watching? He didn't look at the candies directly, but rather snaked out a greenish hand to grasp a particularly nondescript example, one that didn't seem to represent any known species. Some mistake in the casting that wouldn't be missed. An overstock.

Then he froze—he was being watched.

She was across the aisle from him, a hooded figure at another booth. She should have been examining the muja fruit in her hand. But she wasn't looking at the fruit. She was looking at him.

With her free hand she pulled back the hood, and her flesh was blue, marked with yellow tattoos. Like the dead *Jeedai* that started all this.

Rolan froze for a moment, then bolted away from the booth. He had gotten three paces before the side of his head exploded from the impact of the muja fruit. The rind burst and the pulpy interior splattered along the side of his face, its juices stinging his large eyes.

Rolan staggered but did not drop, instead plunging into the crowd, the lumbering Swokes Swokes cursing as he pushed among them. Behind him he could hear the muja salesman braying a complaint, and wondered if that would delay his pursuit.

It did not matter. There was another outlander up ahead, bearing down on him. This one was robed, too, and glowing red spectacles pinched the bridge of his nose. Something heavy was slung from his belt. This one was definitely *Jeedai*.

Rolan made a sharp right-hand turn, jumping over a low stall of flower arrangements. The proprietor took a swing at him, but he slid underneath the blow and was out the other side of the booth in moments.

He had gained but seconds on his pursuers, and he needed a place to hide, quickly. The bazaar was fed by numerous alleyways and, not bothering to look behind him, the last of the Bomu clan on Makem Te plunged into the darkness.

Only when he was safely wrapped in the fetid darkness of the alley did he dare to look back. His pursuers, the woman and the *Jeedai,* were at the entrance, looking around. Rolan held his breath. They stayed there, their backs to him. He had lost them.

Slowly he turned to move through the darkness to the back of the alley and escape. That was when he noticed the blaster aimed at him.

It was a small blaster, but Rolan had no doubt about its power. It was in the furry paws of a Bothan, who smiled at the surprised Rodian with a toothy grin.

"Hello," said the Bothan in a surprisingly cultured voice. "My friends and I would like to talk to you about where you get your spice."

Threnda of the Bomu clan, inhabitant of Teg Kithri on the planet Budpock, considered herself a business-woman first and foremost. Not the cantina out front—that was more of a hobby, a place to do *real* business from. Truth be told, it was a loss leader. No, the long warehouse in back was where the real credits were made, where a trio of CLL-6 worker droids busied themselves with pallets and Mitt, her Trandoshan helper, worked on the opened chassis of a fourth. Everything was automatic, except for making the deals and count-ing the money.

So when the trio came into the warehouse area, she knew there was trouble. Human, Pantoran, and Bothan. The human and the Pantoran were in hooded robes too warm for the summer night, and Threnda considered hidden weapons immediately. The Bothan wore a zer-ape and a large, flat-brimmed hat.

"Cantina's out front," said Threnda, jerking her thumb toward the doorway. She shot a glance at Mitt, and the Trandoshan stood up quietly, a spanner still in its scaled hand.

"We're not here for drinks," said the human, casually. "We're here about some spice."

Threnda's eyes narrowed and she barked in Basic, "I don't do retail. Wholesale only. You represent some-one?"

The human parted his robes, and Threnda caught the gleam of a lightsaber hanging from his belt.

"Budpock is an open planet," said Threnda. "The Jedi don't have any influence here."

"True enough," said Mander Zuma. "And I expect that you've paid up your protection money to your family gangs so that ten minutes after you summon them—which I'm guessing you already have—they'll be here, ready to help. We will be gone in three."

Mitt had circled around them by this time, coming up from behind, still wielding the heavy spanner. The Bothan wheeled and leveled a small blaster, previously hidden beneath the folds of his zerape, at the lizard man.

Mitt took two steps back and put the spanner on the floor; the Bothan motioned him to stand next to Threnda. The third figure, the Pantoran, started moving down the aisles with a scanner, checking the codes on the various boxes. The brute-brained loadlifter droids ignored her until she rapped one on the leg, and it followed her in her search.

Threnda frowned but continued, "I trade in spice all the time. What is it to you?"

"We're looking for a particular kind of spice," said the human. "Tempest."

Keep him talking, thought Threnda. *The clanbrothers should be on their way.* "Never heard of it."

"It is a dangerous drug," said the Jedi.

"I don't deal in hard spice," said Threnda with a sneer.

"Found it," said the Pantoran, as a binary loadlifter placed a particular nondescript container on the open floor. She tapped the transportation code on the container's side as the droid backed away.

"Open it," said Mander, and the Bothan provided a pry bar from beneath his zerape. The sealed lid parted easily to reveal white trays set with thin layers of the deep purplish spice. The heady pungent odor filled the warehouse around them.

"First time I've ever seen that," said Threnda. "Must

be a mistaken shipment. Happens all the time. Like I said, I don't carry hard spice."

"Then you won't mind if we get rid of it for you," said the Jedi. "Eddey?"

The Bothan produced a small grenade and held it over the crate, putting his thumb on the arming toggle.

"Wait," said Threnda. "All right, what do you want? Information?"

"No thanks," said the Jedi.

Threnda goggled at him. "*No?* I can tell you where this came from, and you leave me alone."

"No," repeated the Jedi. "You got this shipment from the *Demoneye* out of Ventooine. It picked up the shipment from the Bosph system." He looked at Threnda's startled expression, "This isn't the first distribution point we've been to, and some of them have been positively chatty. Eddey?"

The Bothan thumbed the activation switch. A red light flashed at the top of the orb.

"Ten-second fuse," said the Jedi. "You should stand back."

Threnda and Mitt dropped back and fell to the ground as the grenade detonated. The resulting blast caused the container to bulge outward, and a pulse of violet fire to spring from the top of the case. Fragments of burning Tempest scattered around the warehouse, and some of the other crates smoldered in the flames. A thick purplish smoke oozed from the top of the box, surrounding them like a fog.

Threnda cursed and slammed Mitt on the shoulder. The Trandoshan ran for a fire extinguisher, pulling the heavy lifters away from the fire on the way.

The three visitors stood there, unaffected by the blast.

"It has been three minutes," said the Jedi. "We're going now."

"Why are you doing this?" yelled Threnda over the flames. Behind her Mitt was cursing and trying to operate the fire extinguisher with his thick reptilian fingers. "What do you want?"

The Jedi paused and turned back. "We want you to send a message to the rest of your clan, and to the Spice Lord you work for," he said. "We're going to stop the Tempest trade, and it doesn't matter how long it takes." And then he was gone in the swirling smoke.

"At least you still have the cantina," said the Bothan, and he was gone as well.

Ma Lorda," said Koax, her face in the holoreceiver a grim mask. "The *Jeedai* and his allies have proved most nettlesome."

"Report your status," burbled the Spice Lord. As usual, the Hutt chose to have a bright light shining from behind, cloaking the Spice Lord's cruel features. Koax was always careful when contacting her superior, but the Klatooinian had turned anxious and nervous of late, and had none of the proud declarations and good news that had been typical of her.

"The *Jeedai* has been striking against our distribution centers," said the worried Klatooinian. "In particular those tied with the Bomu clan. He and his allies have hampered our cash flow."

The Hutt made a dismissive noise, the sound of mud dropped from shoulder height. "There will be spot shortages, which will be good for the trade," said the Spice Lord. "Drive up the price, create some desire. I trust your ability to expedite the orders to the most critical areas." The Hutt leaned back and took a hokuum pipe from a nearby holder, making a show of unconcern.

"With respect, *Ma Lorda,*" said the Klatooinian, choosing her words carefully, "it is more than merely a tightness in the market. We are seeing a dramatic slow-down in sales as local governments are becoming aware of the Tempest spice. In the Corporate Sector alone, market penetration has halted completely, and we are in danger of losing our new prospects in the Nuiri sector. No one wants to deal in a spice that might promote a visit from the *Jeedai*. They strike and say they are send-ing a message—that they will end the Tempest trade."

The Spice Lord leaned forward. "What are you not telling me?"

Koax stammered for a moment, then cast her eyes down. "The Bomu clan," she started.

The Spice Lord let out a laugh that made the Klatoo-inian, far away at the other end of the connection, jump. "The Bomu clan! Have we not had them all killed or made them too busy to think about revenge?"

"They are resilient," said Koax, "and numerous as well. But the losses the clan has sustained at the hands of the *Jeedai* are sufficient to make them question their . . . loyalty. One of them has given up the name of Morga Bunna, the depot runner." She let the last word trickle out like an admission of a secret.

The Spice Lord wondered how long she had kept that information to herself. "Ah," said the Hutt, leaning backward. "And you fear that they will cut their losses. That they will decide that this *Jeedai* will be pleased if they simply tell it what they know and they can be done with it. That they will lead the *Jeedai* back to me."

"Not that you could not handle it," said the Klatooin-ian firmly, "or that the *Jeedai* and his allies would not fall to your obvious power. But it could affect our work further."

The Spice Lord chuckled. "Yes, I see. I do not fear them tracking the spice back to its origins—we have left a tangle of warehouses, drop points, and supply depots throughout the spiral arm. But I appreciate your concern. Set up a meeting with the Bomu clan matriarch. Tell her I am pleased with the achievements of her clan and concerned about this most recent threat, and will do whatever I can to help protect her. Go yourself. Make it clear to her that the protection of the Spice Lord is upon you. I will protect you as you seek to protect me."

Koax smiled, her gemmed eye glittering in the wash of the Spice Lord's image. "I will protect you," she said, reassured and at peace. "It is as you wish."

"It *is* as I wish," said the Spice Lord, and terminated the connection with a tap of a stubby finger against the side of the hokuum. Koax had served long and well, but she had clearly been rattled. And she had been concealing the worst of the news from her master. Her actions could be corrected, but the nervousness she now exuded could spread like a disease among those she dealt with, into the rank and file.

What Koax did not know was that not all of the spice shortages came from the *Jeedai*'s actions. More was being shuttled elsewhere, through other pipelines. The Bomu clan had been overexposed through their vendetta, raising their profile to the point that others were paying attention now. That was bad business. Better to close down this less profitable operation and move on.

And if Koax was one of the casualties of that change, it would be regretted, but it would not stop a good Hutt from making the decision.

The Spice Lord snapped thick fingers, and a jade-green droid moved out of the shadows. "I think," said the Hutt, "that it is time to deliver a message of our own."

DEALINGS

The outermost moon of Bosph was a moon only out of pity, a mere chunk of rock that was the remains of a larger chunk of rock that had been blasted apart in a forgotten war. It was far from the planet and far from the primary, and was as desolate a spot as one could wish for, far from the populated space lanes of the galaxy.

It was the perfect place for Morga Bunna, retired Bosph bounty hunter, to set up his supply depot.

The tides of trade were fickle, Morga knew. A seller might want to hold on to an item until he found the proper buyer. Unfortunately, such an item could be rather warm to hold on to, sometimes being as hot as the surface of a sun. And the seller may not want to meet directly with the buyer. And that was where Morga Bunna's depot came in useful. It served both as a cache point for particularly hot items, and as a trading post for individuals who did not want to deal face-to-face.

Over time, Morga had burrowed through the moonlet, carving out halls and passages and storage rooms, as well as building himself a translucent pleasure dome along one side. There were things that had been there for years, their original owners having forgotten about them or died. And there were other materials that moved smoothly as the tides favored their sale and they were shipped out.

Yet Morga Bunna did not become an old Bosph by being a fool, and he was prepared when a ship identifying itself as the *New Ambition* contacted him through a channel that only clients should have, requesting a meeting.

The *New Ambition* landed on one of the transport pads, little more than level spots on the moon, while droids maneuvered access tubes to the ship's air locks. Three individuals left the ship, as he had been warned— a Bothan, a Pantoran, and a Jedi. He met them beneath the transparisteel dome at the heart of his complex.

To the new arrivals, Morga looked like any prosperous and respected Bosph—his four arms inscribed with the star maps that recorded his travels, his slender horns tipped with gold, his compound eyes newly washed and gleaming, his robes of the finest quality. He stood calmly in the center of his small dome, surrounded by native plants of his homeworld, growing under radiation lights. The oppulent garden space was flanked by balconies leading off into other parts of his den.

Morga rocked back and forth as the three approached. "Welcome to my humble shop," he said. "Are you the Jedi called Mander Zuma?"

The human nodded, and motioned to the others. "These are my companions, Eddey Be'ray and Reen Irana. I must confess that I am surprised by your allowing us to land."

"Civilization reaches out even to the darkest corners of space," said Morga. "I would offer a libation, but I don't know your preferences, and to be honest I hope that this exchange will be brief."

"You know my name," said Mander. "Do you know why we're here?"

"I can guess," said Morga Bunn. "I know your name, and those of your companions, because you have been tearing through the space between Hutt Space and the

Corporate Sector, discomforting a lot of my normal clients. This has been both good and bad for me, as there have been those who have come to me to extract their supplies, and others who have sought to hide them here."

"We are here about Tempest spice," said the Pantoran.

The Bosph raised all four arms. "Fresh out," he said. "Oh yes, I had some in. Quite a bit of it. But when news began to spread of you destroying stocks of Tempest wherever you found them, well, I sent what I had on, and refused all new contracts." He proffered a data cube. "Here are the transaction notes, for what good it will do you."

Mander took the small cube as if it were a crystal of Tempest itself. "You realize, of course, we need to be able to confirm this."

"Yes," said the Bosph, "just as you realize that I must refuse. I have no problem giving you what I have to send you on your way, but if you stick your nostrils in the rest of my business, I am afraid I must draw a line."

"I think you want to tell me," said Mander.

Morga Bunna staggered back half a step, as if Mander threatened to strike him. He raised a tattooed hand to his forehead and shook his horned head. Then he let out a deep sigh. "There is no need to use your warlock ways, Jedi. There is nothing I can tell you. All of my deliveries, going in and going out, are by blind drops. And they change shipping schedules regularly. And within the last few weeks, shippers as well. You can fire your jets for years without getting any closer to touching the Spice Lord."

"We could take your computers and find out for ourselves," said Reen, clearly frustrated now.

"You could," said the Bosph, "but I would not recommend it." He snapped a set of fingers, and along the balconies now stood a squad of black-garbed mercenaries, their carbines drawn and aimed at the three newcomers.

"They arrived three days ago," said Morga Bunna. "They had been hired through one of those aforementioned blind drops, with orders to come here and offer whatever help they could muster. I welcomed them, of course, much like I welcome you. It gets lonely out here in space, and any company is welcome."

Mander frowned at Morga Bunna. "I think you should have them put down their weapons, and we will talk about your dealings with this Spice Lord." Strangely, his suggestion lacked even the slightest hint of the Force.

"There are only three of you," Morga Bunna scoffed. "You are outnumbered. I implore you to return to your ship before they get nervous and open fire."

"We haven't gotten what we came for," said Mander. His hand drifted to his lightsaber, but he shot a look at Reen. She shook her head, and he nodded.

"For that I am sorry, but you must go," said the Bosph. "This is too big for just three people."

"We know," said the Jedi.

"That's why we brought reinforcements."

There was an explosion and the entire moon seemed to list briefly to the right. Morga looked up and gasped, as the hulk of the CSA ship *Resolute* hung above them, like a hammer ready to strike. The great looming ship swarmed with IRDs, and even now shuttles were deploying to the surface.

The mercenaries looked around, and for a moment Morga was afraid that they would try to fire through the dome. Their weapons would not be able to punch through the reinforced transparisteel, but he had no doubts that the ship's turbolasers would have no such problems. He gave the order for the mercenaries to stand down; slowly, they obeyed.

"You have me at a disadvantage," said the Bosph. "But as I said, I have no information on the Spice Lord that can help you. The one you seek speaks to very few as I understand it, and the deliveries he stored here come from a variety of sources. I fear that I am a dead end."

"Perhaps not," said Reen. "Can you tell us where to find the leader of the Bomu clan?"

"Ah," said the Bosph, looking up at the towering shape of the *Resolute,* dwarfing his little moon. "There, I believe I can help you."

"The Bosph is telling the truth," said Angela Krin. "We did a scan on his data drives, and the bulk of his business is through blind drops. No identifier as to what ships stop here or who is paying the bills. There is simply no other data than pickups and deliveries."

The four of them were sitting in the commander's briefing room once more. Angela Krin punched a few more glyphs on her desk, and several items appeared in the holographic stream—jewelry, weapons, and even a small starship. "We did, however, find a number of items belonging to CSA citizens."

"I think you're within your rights repossessing those and returning them to their true owners," said Mander Zuma. "But you should let him go on the rest. He was straightforward with us."

"A true man of his word," said Angela Krin, sarcasm in her voice. "But yes, we are far outside of our patrol area, and a larger incident would raise questions back at headquarters. Still, I did get an interesting message when you were talking to the Bosph. Let me play it."

She shifted a few more toggles, and the full form of Mika Anjiliac appeared on the screen.

"To Lieutenant Commander Angela Krin, House Anjiliac bears greetings and hopes that you are in contact with Mander Zuma and his people. Our clan is rebuilding in the wake of the deaths of my father and brother. Much remains to be done. Vago is still missing, and I fear the worst. However, one of our traders found this droid in a spaceport."

Mika stood to one side, and an H-3PO unit shuffled into view. Even in the blue static of the holofield, it was clear that it was one of Vago's protocol droids.

"Very important," said the droid. "Very important, very important, very important. I must get back."

"It was badly damaged, and most of its memory units were scrambled," said Mika as a Twi'lek led the droid away. "But from what we can gather, Vago is meeting with the head of the Bomu clan. I cannot go myself, but I know that you will be interested.

"I hope this helps, Angela Krin," the Hutt concluded, "and I wish you the best of luck."

And with that the transmission returned to static.

"He sent us the coordinates where the droid was found," said the lieutenant commander. "Vago is apparently on . . ."

"Dennogra," said Reen, cutting the CSA officer off. "She is on Dennogra."

Angela Krin halted, her mouth open in surprise. Then she scowled and nodded. "How did . . . ?"

"Morga Bunna," said Mander. "We could not track where the Spice Lord is, but Reen thought to ask where someone who *might* know was."

"So we have two leads that take us to Dennogra," said Eddey. "Trap?"

"Likely," said Mander. "But the question is, for whom?"

"The droid was sent to Mika," said Angela Krin. "An opportunity to lead him into the krayt's den?"

Mander stroked his chin. "I don't know. But I do know one way to find out."

Reen nodded and rose. Angela Krin said, "Keep me

informed. I have to bring the *Resolute* back from this 'extended drill' and smooth a few ruffled Corporate feathers. Bringing back some lost treasures will help to a great degree."

Eddey stood up. "One more thing, Commander. Can you punch up that molecular map of the Tempest and the Endregaad plague for me?"

Krin ran her fingers over the desk, and the two images spun above its surface. "Here they are. We are still checking white dwarves, but haven't come up with any good candidates."

"That's okay," Eddey said. "What I am looking for is here." He pointed at another loop of molecules in the plague. "Can you compare it with similar chains, and figure out where it comes from?"

Angela Krin said, "I can get some lab techs working on it. It shouldn't be too hard."

"What are you thinking about?" Mander asked Eddey.

"A hunch," said the Bothan, shrugging. "In the meantime, we have a date on Dennogra."

THE RODIAN MATRIARCH

"The problem with your people," Hedu, matriarch of the Bomu clan, said in Huttese, "is that you think the Hutts are gods."

Koax bristled at the frail, ancient Rodian's words, but replied, "And by 'your people' you mean . . ."

"Klatooinians, Vodrans, all the various breeds of Niktos," snapped the matriarch. "All you faithful species that have sworn fealty to the Hutts."

They were in the main room of a manor complex on Dennogra, on the outskirts of Zio Snaffkin. The city itself was a mud-baked sprawl broken by larger piles of whitewashed complexes owned by the more powerful bandits, pirates, and scoundrels in the area. The Bomu clan's grandhouse was no different from half a hundred others within five kilometers.

The main room itself was dominated by an elevated dais, upon which sat a single chair, occupied by the wizened crone who had shackled so many of her own kin to the Spice Lord . . . and who had thrown so many away in foolish attempts at vengeance. Four of her clanchildren stood behind her, blaster carbines at the ready, and Koax could hear others moving around the house.

"With respect," Koax said, "your Rodians serve the Hutts as well."

"For better reasons!" hissed the matriarch. "We serve

for money, not because we follow after them like tamed dark wolves."

"And for vengeance," noted Koax, quietly.

"Vengeance!" hooted the Rodian, her trunk curling up in delight. "Kriffing right!"

Koax reflected that the Spice Lord was correct—the Bomus were explosives just waiting for a spark, and the best she could do was to point them in the right direction. She had wondered once if Matriarch Hedu was dipping into the Tempest herself. Now, in her presence, she knew the ancient Rodian had succumbed to the drug of power long ago.

Koax refused to be beaten down by the old woman's bombast. She drew herself up to her full height and regarded her with her baleful crystal eye. "*Ma Lorda* has expressed concern for your health, and that of your clan. *Ma Lorda* wishes it to be known that you are welcome to seek the Spice Lord's protection. *Ma Lorda* requests that you fall back, regroup, gather your forces, and move out of the spotlight cast by the *Jeedai*."

"*Ma Lorda*," mocked Hedu. "Why doesn't the Spice Lord just fit you with a collar and be done with it? We are Rodians, members of a proud clan. We do not 'fall back.' We do not run. We do not hide. The *Jeedai* preys on our businesses, businesses we set up for *your* Spice Lord, and we will strike back hard."

"Your history says otherwise," said the Klatooinian calmly. "I have been sent to offer you the Spice Lord's protection. I have not been instructed to argue if you are too foolish not to take it."

The older Rodian spat. "Tell your Spice Lord that we are legion, and we are well protected. They will never find us. We will find the *Jeedai* and we will have our vengeance."

In the distance there was the thunder of an explosion, and the chandeliers of the manor swayed slightly. The honor guard behind the matriarch looked at one another, puzzled.

"What's that?" snapped Hedu.

"Hubris," muttered Koax. "If you reject the kindness of the gods, you will be punished for it."

Another explosion, and the sound of running feet. Then shouts in Huttese and the staccato of blasterfire.

Hedu rose shakily from her throne and motioned her clanchildren before her. Once assembled, they ran toward the double doors at the far end of the room. Koax stepped up to the dais next to the matriarch.

"Do you have an escape route?" the Klatooinian started to ask, but she was interrupted as the doors sprung open and a surge of Rodians fell backward into the room, firing behind them as they retreated. There was a cascade of blasterfire coming from their weapons and an equally heavy cascade of return fire.

Then their attacker jumped into the room, and it was clear that the return fire was just the deflected shots of the Rodian defenders. It was the *Jeedai,* his two associates following behind and adding their blaster shots as well.

"Defend me!" shouted the matriarch, and her honor guard dropped to one knee and added their own shots to the onslaught. The *Jeedai,* who was spinning tornado-fast by now, moved even swifter, catching their bolts and throwing them back effortlessly. Rodians began to fall as the attackers cut a swath toward the dais.

The matriarch turned to Koax and said, "Protect me! I accept the Spice Lord's offer! We both know too much to be captured! Protect me!"

Protect me, said the Spice Lord, when Koax first met the Hutt. The Klatooinian knew what she had to do and pulled her own blaster pistol.

Leveling it against the Rodian matriarch's head, she pulled the trigger.

The sound of the shot was lost among the avalanche of sound, and none of the defenders—concentrating on the Jedi and his companions—noticed the old woman collapse to the floor. Koax spun around and ran for one of the doors at the back of the house, hoping that they would lead to a reasonable exit.

"She's running!" shouted the Bothan.

"I'm on it!" answered the Pantoran.

The Jedi shouted something, but it was lost in the din as the Pantoran leapt around the edges of the conflict, ignoring the Rodians and diving after the fleeing Klatooinian. By this point, the Jedi had fought his way into the front lines of the defending Rodians, and they had other things to worry about.

Koax ran swiftly down the back hall, hoping for a door to an outside courtyard. She would still have to get over the walls, but open space would give her more room to fight. Nothing in the hall, though, so she took the last door on the left.

A study. Clan trophies along the wall. Low divans and chairs. A small holo-chess table, used for storing knick-knacks. A skylight high in the ceiling. No windows, as it backed on the outside wall.

Koax cursed and backed into the hall, but a volley of blasterfire from the Pantoran drove her back into the room.

The Klatooinian looked around again. No exit presented itself. She kicked over one of the low divans, turning it into a barricade, and waited for the Pantoran to enter. A shadow appeared in the doorway, and she fired at it, but it dodged back before she could hit it.

There was a pause, and the Pantoran said in Basic, "You might as well give up now. Tell us what you know. Make it easy for yourself."

Koax watched the door, but the shadow did not move.

Why should it? The Klatooinian was bottled up, and soon the Jedi would come and tease all of her secrets out of her brain.

Protect me, the Spice Lord had said.

Koax pulled one of her tribal daggers from her belt, pressed the tip against her belly, and took a deep breath.

"That the last of them?" said Eddey.

Mander Zuma looked around at the carnage of the fallen Bomu warriors. "I think so. No sign of Vago, though."

"Can't say I'm surprised."

"Where's Reen?"

Eddey nodded toward one of the doors at the back of the room. "She lit off after the Klatooinian, the one who shot the matriarch."

Mander ran for the door, but Reen appeared. She looked a paler shade of blue.

"What happened?" asked Mander.

"She killed herself," said Reen. "I had her trapped in one of the rooms, and rather than fight, she . . ." The Pantoran shook her head.

Mander looked at Eddey, and the Bothan shrugged. The Jedi said, "Search for any tablets and data cubes you can find, but then we have to be off. Dennogra may be a viper's lair, but sometime soon people are going to come to see what all the noise was about."

Reen remained quiet most of the way to the jump point, letting Eddey do the piloting while she sat back in the galley and went over the looted datapads, datasticks, cubes, and crystals with a reader.

"How is it going?" asked Mander.

Reen made a face and waved a hand over the pile. "We'll know more once a slicer gets past security on some of these, but for the most part it is all here. Deliveries, clients, contacts, payoffs—every bit of the Tempest trade that the Bomu clan was involved with." She let out a sigh.

"Except?"

"Except where it came from," she said. "Except who this Spice Lord is."

"Not all the answers come on datasticks," said Mander.

"I know," she said. "I look at all of this and I say—is this enough?"

"Enough?" Mander raised an eyebrow.

"Toro," said Reen, and Mander nodded. "You thought that by finishing his mission it would be enough. I thought bringing down the people who gave him the spice would be enough."

"And yet here we are," said Mander.

They sat in the galley for a long moment, the deep rumble of the ship filling in the need for words. "I'm still mad at Toro," Reen said at last.

"Mad?"

"Angry," she said. "I think he did something horrible and foolish and I want him to be here so I can yell at him. I wonder if that goes away."

"I don't think so," said Mander. He sat quietly for a moment. "I want to ask him why."

"I don't think those answers are on datasticks, either," Reen said, shaking her head. "So, now what?"

"We turn over the information to Angela Krin," said Mander. "She gets it into the hands of the local authorities, and they take it from there. And we keep looking for who is responsible."

Reen let out a sigh and said, "Well, every girl needs a hobby."

The intercom beeped and Eddey's voice said, "We have an incoming message from the *Resolute*. You might want to be here."

"Speak of the demon," said Reen and pushed away from the table, following Mander to the bridge.

When they got to the bridge, Lieutenant Commander Angela Krin was saying ". . . congratulations on the successful mission. The surviving members of the Bomu clan will likely regroup under a new leader, but hopefully one who doesn't adhere so much to the idea of vendettas. I wish I had been there."

"No Vago, though," said Mander.

"So it was a trap," said the CSA officer.

"I don't think so," said Mander. "They didn't seem ready for us at all, and both the matriarch and the Klatooinian were surprised when we came in."

Eddey put in, "I think our Spice Lord leaked the information in the hope we would tie up a couple of loose ends."

Mander nodded. That made sense.

Angela Krin also nodded and moved on without batting an eye. "I checked out that chemical chain you asked about. It's very interesting."

"Interesting? How?" asked Mander.

"It's an odd organic loop. The sort of thing that shows up in oscillating high-gravity zones. Black-hole radiation."

Mander thought about it a moment, then said, "I'm guessing there aren't too many in this region of space near a black hole *and* a white dwarf."

"No," said Angela Krin. "Most planets do not survive their primary falling into itself and becoming a black hole in the first place."

"So we need a planet that survived a stellar collapse, that's scarred by radiation, and that's in close proximity to a black hole," said Mander.

"Varl," said Reen, who had been quiet up to this moment.

"Varl?" said Mander. "The original Hutt homeworld?"

"Remember the story I told you?" said Reen. "Evona fell to darkness, and Ardos exploded in rage. Ardos is our white dwarf. Varl is in orbit around Ardos."

"But Varl is a dead planet," said Mander. "The Jedi Archives were clear on that."

"Maybe not as dead as we thought," said Eddey.

"Didn't you check out Varl?" Mander asked Krin. "Even without knowing about the black hole, it still has a white dwarf and it's in the heart of Hutt space."

In the image, Angela Krin froze for a moment, though Mander thought it might just be spatial interference. Then she lurched forward, punching a few unseen buttons. "We should have. Ah. Here it is. On our list, but we had to get permission to follow up with the Hutt Elders. It is still their planet, even though they are gone. I should have followed up on that." Even through the distortion of the holoprojector, the lieutenant looked confused. "Funny, that."

"You've been monitoring ship traffic into the Ardos system?"

"Yes," said Angela Krin, punching a few more unseen buttons. "Nothing leaving the surface of Varl, of course. But here's something interesting: we have a couple of independent flight manifests that are listed as carrying spice. They pass through the Ardos system, but when they get to their destination, no spice is ultimately delivered. They come into Ardos with a load of spice, and leave empty."

"And I'll bet that those independents started running shortly after the plague broke out on Endregaad," said Eddey. "After the smugglers lost a Skydove Freight ship."

"And carrying it out using the Indrexu Spiral," Mander said. "And *those* jump coordinates were in the hands of the Anjiliacs. There may be others they were unwilling to share."

"Vago," said Eddey. "She had the coordinates, and she could make ships disappear from their rosters."

"And Vago has disappeared as well," said Mander. "Maybe to Varl." He looked at the lieutenant commander. "You have a plan?"

"I think so," said the image of Angela Krin, and Mander could have sworn he saw the ghost of a smile on her face. "We can't bring the *Resolute* into Hutt space without a major diplomatic incident, but there are other options. Rendezvous with us at these coordinates, and I think we can get you to Varl."

VOYAGE TO VARL

The *Barabi Run* came out of hyperspace above Rhilithan on what should have been a milk run, carrying a load of spice that was eventually bound for a dead world. The Hutt defense ships in the neighborhood of their ultimate destination knew they were coming, and to let them through. No blockades to run, no local picket ships to evade, no customs agents, and no serious questions.

Instead the *Barabi Run*'s captain found the *Resolute* and its sister ship, the *Vigilance*—two CSA cruisers far outside their normal patrols—lying in wait. His sensors were spammed white within moments of emerging from hyperspace, and his comlink crackled with the voice of a Lieutenant Commander Angela Krin. IRDs were alongside the *Barabi Run* before he even had the chance to deep-space his cargo.

The *Barabi Run* was guided into the huge docking bay and settled down next to a Suwantek TL-1200, a reconditioned model that was in pretty good shape, barring a few scorch marks along the hull. There a spit-and-polish CSA lieutenant made it clear that their ship was being requisitioned by the CSA, and that they were to be the guests of the *Resolute* until the CSA no longer needed use of the ship.

No, they could not leave.

Yes, the CSA would provide a receipt.

* * *

Reen spent most of the next day scanning the *Barabi Run* for bugs and tracers. She found a handful of tracking bugs, most of them different models and several of them long defunct, remnants of earlier owners and previous deals. There was also a self-destruct bot—an insect-sized device that had been crawling around the fuel manifold wiring. It had touched a bare wire and fried itself, its mission unknown and uncompleted. And there was some new hardware in the avionic core that she deactivated. She kept the transponder intact with the next set of jump coordinates and the approach to Varl.

Finally, the *Resolute* cast off the *Barabi Run,* and the commandeered transport resumed its normal course. Reen was in the pilot's chair and Angela Krin was co-pilot, now in civilian clothes again. Mander was with them, seated behind the command seats, while Eddey would shadow them in the *New Ambition,* in case they needed additional support.

Mander looked at Angela's sharp features as she and Reen ran down the checklist before hyperjump. He knew that she could have sent them on this mission by themselves, or assigned a subordinate like Lockerbee to oversee them. He wondered if the lieutenant commander herself had been bitten by the adventuring bug as well. Chasing Tempest smugglers was certainly more exciting than guard duty high above a planetary surface.

The ship shook as they entered hyperspace, and Mander gripped the side of his chair as it lurched to the left and the stars lengthened ahead of them. Reen let out a brief curse and toggled a few switches.

"Did you miss something?" Angela Krin asked. Her voice was calm, but Mander noted she was gripping her controls with white knuckles.

Reen shot her a look, then said, "Nothing out of the

ordinary. This ship is a rust bucket that has seen too many runs. I knew the warp space motivators were gummed up when I first checked it out, but nothing short of a full rebuild would fix them. It's going to be a bumpy ride." She pushed back from the controls. "Keep us steady up here, Commander. I'm going back to check the energy stacks." Without waiting to see if Angela Krin followed her order, she headed for the lift to the engine deck. Angela slid into the now-unoccupied pilot's chair and the pair of them watched the stars flick by on the forward screen.

"You did the right thing, you know," Angela said.

"What thing was that?" asked Mander. "Shooting her?"

"That," said Angela, "and manipulating her to come along. She and the Bothan are both very effective."

"You assume I manipulated her," said Mander.

"Isn't that what Jedi are good at?" Angela said, allowing a stern grin to blossom on her face. "Every time we talk, I check my recordings afterward to determine if you've used any mind tricks on me."

"And have I?" said Mander.

"Not that I can detect," she said. "So either you don't, or you are very good at it."

"The best weapons are those that never need to be used," said Mander. "But no. I only told her the truth. Though it may be a while before she can trust me fully."

"The important thing is that she trusts you enough."

The entire ship gave a shudder, and the shaking reduced from a gut-wrenching lurch to a deep-seated thrum. Reen appeared back on the flight deck, but motioned for the CSA officer to keep the pilot's chair.

"Loose interweave coupling," said the Pantoran. "Nothing much to worry about. How are things up here?"

"Going smoothly," said Angela.

The last jump put them in what at first appeared to be deep space, in the great emptiness between stars. Far in the distance, one star glimmered brighter than the rest. That would be Ardos, Varl's primary.

"Sensors are lighting up," said Angela Krin. "We've got a lot of company out here. Inert masses, though. Asteroids."

"That would be the remains of the other planets," said Reen. "Ardos's other children, blasted apart in the storm." She flicked a switch. "Eddey, are you there?"

The comlink crackled and the Bothan's voice resounded. "Just came in. Feels a little crowded here. I'm going to find a likely-looking chunk of rock to hide behind, but I'll be around if you need to get offplanet quickly."

Mander checked the screens and saw the dark shape of the *New Ambition* hovering nearby. As he watched, a trio of side thrusters fired and the ship drifted off into the surrounding murk.

"We're going to leave Eddey out here," said Reen, answering Mander's unspoken question. "In case Varl has its own protectors."

"A good idea," said Mander. "Despite what the Archives say about it being a dead planet, I find it unlikely that the Hutt Elders would leave their original homeworld unguarded."

They fell for nearly an hour toward the hot white dot that had once been a sun. Finally, the comlink crackled and a voice boomed out in Huttese. On the port side another shape heaved up; in the wan light of the primary Mander could see a blocky-looking patrol ship. Not a flashy vehicle, but likely one with heavy weapons mounted onboard.

"They're demanding the proper approach codes," said Mander, translating.

"Here goes nothing," said Reen, flicking a switch on the transponder unit.

"I'm surprised to find a Hutt this far out," said Angela Krin.

"The words are too clipped," said Mander. "None of the sibilant lip-smacking noises Hutts make. It could be one of the servant races, or even a droid on the other end."

"Or it could be a droid or a servant answering to a Hutt," said Reen, now nervous.

They paused for a long moment, waiting for confirmation. Mander noticed that Angela's hand drifted to the weapons console, hoping to get any jump they could should the patrol ship decide to open fire.

The comlink burped a short word, and the dimly lit shadow swung about and vanished back into the darkness of space.

Varl itself looked horrible, a mottled brown pebble creased by darker mountains that stuck up out of its depleted and smoky atmosphere. The ground itself, where visible, was the color of dead brown leaves, broken only by glowing pools of sickly green radiation.

"Is it safe?" asked Reen.

"You'll need a breather mask," said Angela Krin, "and probably all sorts of tests afterward. Also, the type of life that Hutts raise tends to be extremely hardy and opportunistic. It would have to be something on the order of a star falling in on itself to kill life on a Hutt planet and keep it dead."

"We shouldn't be staying long," said Mander.

They leveled off now, cutting through the thin remnants of atmosphere. The ancient devastation became clearer—the skeletal frames of entire cities were canted across the landscape, tilted testaments to a civilization that once ruled this world and its neighbors. Shattered piles of greenish stone loomed around them. They could have once been monuments to the Hutts or to their gods, or hardened eruptions of twisted magma—now eroded—that found their way to the surface in the planet's death throes. Mander spotted what might have been blasted brush beneath one such eruption, and thought he saw movement along one of the radiant green pools— something large and pale and painfully slow.

It was not a dead world, but it was close enough.

The transponder beeped as they rose above the dead horizon. "Our destination is just ahead," said Angela Krin.

It looked like it had once been a crater, though whether from a ground-based ion explosion or an asteroid impact even Mander could not tell. The upper walls jutted black out of the atmosphere itself, and the side facing the dawn had entirely fallen away. Cradled in the heart of the pit was a diseased green lake, throwing up its own malignant radiation on the walls of the crater. And on the shores of that lake sprawled a single long building, tapered at one end, solid and blocky at the other. Heavy struts supported the plant where the rough ground formed deep ravines carrying oozing creeks of green pollutants to the lake.

"I think we have found our manufacturing plant," said Angela.

Mander blinked and realized what he was seeing. "It's a ship. They landed a starship here and transformed it into a factory."

"That makes sense," Angela Krin said. "Who could build something of this size onplanet?"

Reen gently put the ship down onto a lit landing pad, the only piece of warm, yellow light in the entire crater. "It looks like they are expecting other guests as well, and soon."

Indeed, the sides of the building were already decorated in heavy netting, their color intended to blend with the dark stone of the crater. In addition, large spherical ion cannons had been mounted around the landing field, and the emplacements set for more to come.

"Another month, and they would have made themselves undetectable," said Krin, surveying the defenses. "And unbeatable as well."

The *Barabi Run* settled on the landing pad and Reen's fingers danced over the controls, shutting down the last of the boosters. She toggled the ramp and unlocked the cargo shells. "We have company."

Already asp droids, small and spindly, were waddling toward the unlocked cargo containers.

"What happens now?" asked Reen.

"According to our guests back on the *Resolute*," replied Angela Krin, "they would drop the cargo, and then take off again. Payment would show up in their accounts, routed through a number of shell companies. They never saw anything more than the loading droids. That's their standard operating procedure."

"So we're going to break the procedure," said Reen, strapping on her holster.

"Hang on," said Mander, looking at one of the side screens.

There, standing at the cargo doorway of the plant, was a jade-green protocol droid, checking over the shipment with a datapad in its hand.

Reen let out a low whistle. "One of Vago's droids. I think we've found our Spice Lord."

THE HEART OF THE TEMPEST

The three of them descended the landing ramp to the entrance. They determined that Angela Krin would lead, as she had never met Vago or her servants. Reen and Mander followed, their weapons ready beneath their cloaks, their hoods casting their faces into deep shadow. All three wore breather masks, and even though it was a matter of mere meters from the ship to the factory, Mander felt himself holding his breath, fearing the toxins and viruses that might leak around the seal.

The asps paid no attention to them as they strode to the entrance. The 3PO unit, on the other hand, was not so complacent.

"Is there a problem?" asked the droid.

"I need to see your boss," said the CSA officer. She was trying to sound tough, as opposed to merely official. To Mander's ears, it sounded false.

"This is unusual," said the H-3PO. "I don't know the proper protocol for this situation."

"Vago," Angela Krin pressed. "She's here, isn't she?"

The droid looked at Angela Krin, startled, then at the other two behind her. "You should return to your ship." Its digits flicked onto the pad, "Let me check . . ."

Reen's blaster was up at once, and the side of the droid's head exploded in a single shot. The droid slumped to the ground, its fingers still poised to check on its superiors.

The asps all froze in place, their conical faces twisting toward Reen and the others.

"Labor dispute," snarled Reen. "Get back to work!" She sounded much more convincing than Krin, Mander thought. The asps all resumed unloading the containers of spice, tumbling over themselves in compliance.

"So much for subtlety," snapped Angela Krin.

"They are going to find out we're here eventually," said Reen. "I just bought us a few more moments." She swept into the open plant entrance while the droids clattered about behind them.

Mander Zuma thought Reen correct, for as they passed into the plant itself, everything seemed quiet, save for the bustling asps with heavy containers of normal spice. He spotted a number of holocams in the hallway, and pointed them out to Reen and Angela. They shot them out. By now the Spice Lord might know they were there, but they would do what they could to keep the Hutt from knowing too much.

They followed the loader droids deeper into the ship.

After a long passage, a final cargo door opened onto a great balcony overlooking the heart of the ship. The central spine of the grounded starship had been cleared of its interior walls, and had been transformed into a huge factory. To their right, piles of ordinary spice had been heaped, dumped by the asp units from the *Barabi Run* and half a dozen other smuggler ships that had previously docked here. The spice, glittering in a rainbow of pale shades, was fed into long conveyor belts, which dumped them into great open vats.

The vats themselves were fed by a pale green mixture that sluiced through clear pipes. Mander realized that this was the runoff from the sides of the crater, gathered and fed into the ship itself. Where it first touched the spice, a venomous-looking cloud arose, yet eventually the spice—now dyed with a deep purple hue—floated to the top and was harvested by droid-operated skimmers. The skimmed spice then passed under great drying lamps, gaining its lustrous violet finish. The conveyors in turn led to a distant exit to the stern, near the engines, where the Tempest was likely broken up into smaller parcels for transport out. The pungent smell of ordinary spice and the distinctive aroma of Tempest hung heavy in the air.

Varl *created* the Tempest. Perhaps it was just this crater, but it was the blood of a dead world that made the deadly spice.

But where was the factory's master? Mander looked toward the turbolifts on the far side. The bridge, most likely.

Asp droids moved among the great vats, operating the skimmers, feeding the spice along the conveyors, and monitoring the quality control. Other, larger droids moved among them—huge, hulking metallic beasts, unlike any droid or robot Mander had ever seen. These were bipedal, and their upper torsos bristled with heavy armament. Their armored casings were scarred, and they lumbered among the more nimble asps in a jerky fashion, as if they had to double-check every step.

"What are those?" asked Reen.

"Ancient . . . Hutt war droids," said a feminine voice slowly behind them, and the three spun to see Vago standing there. She had arrived behind them from some side passage, and was flanked by two of the late Popara's handmaidens. The handmaidens were no longer dressed in light robes, but rather in heavy plates of padded armor, with only their long-tailed heads exposed. They wore shock gloves, but also carried blaster pistols, and these weapons were leveled on the three of them. Even so, they seemed to hang back, slightly behind the Hutt, as if using Popara's former adviser as a shield.

Perhaps they were wary because every time they encountered the Jedi and his allies, their current master died.

Mander also saw that the veins along the Twi'leks lekku were darkened with pulsing veins. These had already fallen prey to the power of the Tempest as well, making them doubly unreliable and dangerous. Vago was unarmed. She said, haltingly, "Talk first . . . There will be time to . . . fight and die . . . later."

Reen and Angela Krin looked at Mander, and he nodded. They lowered their weapons slightly. The Twi'leks dropped theirs not at all.

Vago talked slowly, and Mander wondered if the Hutt was also under the influence of Tempest. If so, there were no other visible symptoms.

Then the realization blossomed in Mander's mind: Vago was speaking in Basic. She knew Mander could understand Huttese, so why speak in Basic? And why were the armored Twi'leks not translating for her?

"These hulks . . . were found in an abandoned weapons cache . . . when this plant was founded," said Vago. "They date back to . . . to . . . to"—she slipped into Huttese here—"*tatammo nar shaggan.*"

"A time before you had servants," Mander translated for the others. Before the Hutts met with and dominated the Klatooinians, the Niktos, the Weequay, and others. Mander's hand drifted to his lightsaber, but one of the Twi'leks saw the motion and snapped out an order in Huttese.

From the surrounding shadows issued more security droids. These were not the stumbling hulks from below, but rather serpentine-bodied constructs with two arms on their upper torsos, one ending in a passable four-fingered hand, the other in a refurbished blaster carbine. Their crested, conical faces lacked obvious eyes, their sensors hidden beneath discolored armor plating.

"Yes," said Vago, still in Basic. "The droids have no . . . designation. Names? . . . But they serve well."

"This is over, Vago," said Mander.

"Perhaps . . . ," said the Hutt. "You served . . . mighty Popara well. Perhaps you can serve . . . us. A *Jeedai* would be . . . useful." The last phrase rolled off her lips like a poisoned candy.

"The Corporate Sector knows we came here," said Angela. "They will send someone else." Mander glanced at her, but could not catch her eye. He looked at Reen, but the Pantoran's eyes were locked on the Twi'leks, waiting for them to make a move. The Twi'leks' eyes were shifting, from Vago to the three of them and back. They were distracted by the conversation.

"That would be . . . difficult," said the Hutt, and Mander saw that pools of perspiration were forming along Vago's forehead. The Hutt was nervous, and more nervous than just the three of them accounted for. "If you would agree to . . . go back to your ship . . . and say you found nothing . . . you would be rewarded." Her chest worked like a bellows now, and she drew in vast hiccups of air as she spoke.

"Fat chance," said Reen.

"Then you will have to remain here . . . as guests," said Vago.

"As prisoners, you mean," said Angela Krin. Vago managed an uncomfortable, revealing shrug.

And suddenly it all made sense to Mander: The Hutt's nervousness. Speaking in a language she obviously hated. The bodyguards that seemed more interested in keeping an eye on their supposed employer than protecting her.

Vago wasn't their employer at all, and they were not her bodyguards.

"She's right. We would be captives," Mander said firmly. "Captives like you are, Vago Gejalli."

The Hutt's eyes flew open wide in surprise, and she unleashed a curse at Mander's accusation. More surprised, however, were the Twi'lek bodyguards. One brought up her blaster pistol, while the other barked an order and grasped Vago the Hutt firmly with her shock glove. Vago let out a cry as electrical arcs ringed her conical head and sparks danced in the depths of her wide, liquid eyes. The Hutt slumped to the floor.

But the Twi'leks were not as fast as they had hoped. The one who'd drawn first, fired wide. Reen had been waiting for the opportunity, and her blaster was up and her shot caught the former handmaiden square in the face. The Twi'lek fell backward without firing another shot.

The remaining Twi'lek, the one who'd shocked Vago, was now bellowing orders. The serpentine droids slid forward, blasters blazing. Mander pulled his lightsaber and swung it in a perfect pattern, deflecting each blaster bolt in turn back on the enemy. He could see the patterns in the blasts, able to determine which ones were wide to start with—and could therefore be ignored—and which were potentially dangerous to the three of them. These, he could analyze easily, knowing which among them were of the most immediate danger and the quickest reach, then curling the arc of his blade against them so the photonic energy caught on his blade and was bounced away. And even then, he could see where the now-deflected shot would land, and target it against one of the droids, avoiding both his allies and the fallen form of Vago.

Time slowed for him as he moved forward, staying out of the way of Reen and Angela Krin's own shots, making himself the target of the ancient droids, directing their fire to him, and allowing him to return each volley clearly and cleanly. Already four of them were toppling, their battle-scarred housings punctured with shots from their own upgraded weapons. For Mander, it didn't feel like a cold analysis progression of one shot, then the next shot, but rather like music, where each note logically followed the next. Where each motion smoothly dovetailed into the next, where each action was clear, and where thought itself was not necessary.

Then something drove hard into his stomach and time resumed, the real world in all its conflicting messiness descending on him. He had concentrated on the blaster-fire, and had paid insufficient attention to the surviving Twi'lek, who now had risen from behind the fallen Hutt and lunged at him, slamming the Jedi with her shoulder and driving him backward. He held on to his blade, but the handmaiden-turned-bodyguard had rolled him back and stepped onto his wrist with a heavily booted foot. She stabbed one hand under his chin, throttling him by the neck. The other, the one bearing the shock glove, she raised high about her head. Her sharpened teeth glittered in maniacal delight, and the Tempest-thick veins on her head-tail throbbed.

And just as quickly, the Twi'lek was gone, screaming, vanished into the midst of the surrounding battle. Mander pulled himself off the floor and saw that Reen had grabbed the handmaiden's lekku halfway up its length and pulled back sharply. The head-tails were particularly sensitive and the Twi'lek shrieked and clawed at the Pantoran, the shock glove trailing bolts of lightning as she lunged. Reen dodged beneath the clumsy assault and brought the heel of her pistol up hard across the handmaiden's face. The Twi'lek collapsed with a whimper.

Angela Krin, for her part, had laid down a withering rate of fire, blasting the remainder of the serpentine droids in quick succession. One, partially hidden by the bodies of its comrades, raised a head cautiously above the debris . . . only to have that head explode with a carefully aimed shot from the CSA officer's blaster.

Krin walked over to Vago's prostrate form and pressed the barrel of her blaster against the Hutt's head. Mander grabbed her by the wrist and turned the weapon away as the dazed Hutt muttered something that, in another universe, might be considered a phrase of gratitude.

Angela Krin stared at Mander. "We can't trust her. She's part of this. She killed Popara."

"She *didn't*," said Mander. "She was a prisoner, a hostage of the Twi'leks. She was acting under duress."

Angela shook free with her weapon. "It doesn't matter—she needs to die. She's a Hutt. She's a threat to Mika."

"All the more reason to keep her alive," said Mander. "Someone has to explain this to the Hutt Council of Elders when we're done."

"*Jeedai,*" muttered the groggy Hutt. "*Mika respoonda. Gosa o breej.*"

"I know," said Mander to the Hutt.

"You know what?" asked Angela.

"Who is really responsible for this," replied Mander. "The Tempest, the smuggling, Popara's death. All of it."

Reen came up, her blaster drawn and ready. "So what are we waiting for?"

Mander turned to the Pantoran. "You both need to take Vago back to the ship and take off. Call Eddey for help."

He looked at Angela, who was still staring at the prostrate form of the Hutt. Emotions played across her face. Anger, fear, and frustration, each in turn. Mander had seen it before. It was as if conflicting programs were all running at once in her mind.

"We need to protect him," said Angela Krin, and once again tried to bring her weapon to bear against the female Hutt.

And Mander realized what was going on in her mind.

To Angela he said sternly, "You need to protect Vago." He flexed his voice as he said it, fitting the words into the crenellations of her brain, backing up his words with the power of the Force. He moved his hand slightly as he said it.

Angela nodded and parroted his words, "I need to . . ." And then she stopped, a look of angry betrayal spreading across her face. "That's a mind trick! You were using the Force on me!"

"Yes," said Mander. "And it's not the first time it has happened to you, is it? Think about it. Back on your own ship, after we got back from Endregaad."

Angela's face fell with a sudden realization, and she looked at the Hutt and the blaster in her hand. And a cold look of anger settled finally onto her face.

"He did it to me, didn't he?" she said. "I was worried about you and *he* was the one."

"Yes," said Mander. "But you don't have time to be angry—you have to get Vago to safety. Can you do that?"

Angela Krin blinked for a moment, and said, "Yes, yes I can. But is that my decision, or yours?" She looked at Mander, a touch of fear in her eyes.

"The fact you asked the question gives you the answer," Mander said gently.

"What's going on?" asked Reen. She had been scanning the area for more of the ancient droids.

"Angela was mind-controlled by someone using the Force," said Mander. "I thought she was bit by the adventuring bug, and that she was acting oddly for that reason—sometimes calculating, sometimes emotional. But it was something much worse than I realized."

Angela Krin gave him a stern look. She was back in control once more. "I should go with you."

"There is precious little time," said Mander, "and I

need both of you to keep Vago alive." To Reen he said, "Angela may be confused for a little while. Can you handle both of them?"

Reen nodded and said, "Only if you insist. Where are you going?"

"To the bridge," said Mander. "That's where this will end."

"You'd better hurry," said Reen. "They've got more reinforcements on the way."

Already the metal ramps around them sounded with the heavy footfalls of the ancient war droids and the metal scrapings of the serpentine security droids.

"We're going to have to fight our way out," said Reen.

"Then you better start now," said Mander pressing a comlink into his ear. "Keep Vago alive. Call me on the comm when you're safe." And with that he was gone.

The turbolifts to the upper levels and the bridge were on the far side of the vats. Mander leapt up to one of the catwalks and dashed for the lifts.

Behind him, he could hear blasterfire. More droids had descended on Angela and Reen's position, and he hoped the two had found more cover than that provided by a stunned Hutt. Beneath him, the larger war droids on the factory floor were now opening up from a variety of torso-mounted weaponry. A staccato rainbow of ionic bolts laced through the catwalk.

Mander dodged them nimbly, but the onslaught of firepower took its toll on the catwalk wires. The elevated grating behind him separated and cascaded into the turbulent pits of Tempest below. Wires ahead of him, overloaded by the strain, gave way and snapped, and the catwalk fell out from beneath Mander's feet.

The Jedi leapt onto one of the clear pipes carrying the effluvia from the crater without losing a step. The war droids below did not let up their fire, and the pipes were pierced in numerous places from their blasts. Greenish liquid showered down on top of his attackers, its acids etching them deeply. The acid shower worked into their gyros and power packs as well, and Mander heard the rewarding sound of multiple explosions as the war droids beneath him blossomed into fireballs.

He had reached the far balcony when a particularly ancient hulk of a war droid lumbered out of the shadows. This one was twice the size of its comrades on the floor, though of the same design—spindly bipedal legs supporting a top-heavy torso bristling with firepower.

What had been the ancient Hutts' model for this, wondered Mander as he charged forward.

The war hulk unleashed a salvo that could have brought down a small starship, but Mander had already anticipated the attack, closing the last few meters in a single rolling cascade, curling as he flew forward, his lightsaber at a right angle to his body. He landed hard and spun horizontally across the floor, passing between the legs of the ancient war droid.

And then he was up on the far side. He turned, pausing for only a moment. The huge droid seemed initially unscathed, but as it tried to turn, its legs started to fall away from the body. The hulking overloaded torso slid forward along the seams cut by Mander's lightsaber, and the entire top half of the droid clashed to the ground. The legless torso tried to raise itself on its weapon-arms, but finally collapsed in cybernetic surrender.

The great plant had gone quiet, and Mander hoped that it was a good sign; that Reen and Angela Krin had gotten Vago back to the ship. Without waiting to check, he turned to the turbolifts and ascended. As he rocketed upward, Mander took a deep breath, trying to calm himself. Find his center. What had to be done would not be pretty, but it was necessary.

The lift chimed and Mander stepped out. The entire

bridge was lit with emergency lights, broken by blue-hued screens.

"I've come for the Spice Lord of Varl," said Mander.

"Ah," said Mika the Hutt, standing at the captain's console, "I see you've finally arrived. It has taken you long enough."

THE SPICE LORD OF VARL

Mika the Hutt was apparently alone in the red-hued darkness of the bridge. He wore a long vest-like coat, open in the front, but cut in the fashion of Mander's own formal robes. The Hutt's light yellow-green flesh glowed with the warmth of a hearth in the red light, highlighted by blue holoscreens.

The screens showed scenes in and around the factory-ship. There was the main floor, littered with wrecked droids and burst vats. There was another display, showing a near-identical picture, unscathed. Another manufacturing bay, perhaps to the aft. Hallways throughout the plant flickered in turn, and several holocams showed the *Barabi Run* on its landing pad, the spice unloaded, the headless body of the H-3PO unit still discarded by the entrance.

There was no sign of Reen or Angela Krin, though a large number of the screens were beset by gray-blue static, and Mander remembered that their passage into the ship had knocked out a number of cams.

But Mika had known they were coming from the onset.

"When did the wupiupi finally drop?" asked Mika, his face wide and open, his tone as congenial as when they had first met him. "When did you realize you had been played?"

"Only at the very end," said Mander, keeping his eyes

on the Hutt. "There was still a chance that Vago was responsible, or someone else in your household. Maybe even your father's Twi'leks. But after we met Vago as the Twi'lek's hostage, there was no one really left who could handle something this extensive."

"Yes," said Mika. "Pity about my brother. I had hoped that he would have been pleased enough just to take our father's place, and not ask too many questions. Business could continue and I would be hiding safely behind my image as the innocent and ineffective younger child. Imagine my surprise when he actually showed the wherewithal to capture me and gin up a show trial for your Pantoran. His plans were that I would quietly disappear after he solidified his hold on the business, and I couldn't have that. That was when I knew that he would not survive, but I still needed another decoy to take his place."

"Vago," said Mander. "She didn't know, did she?"

"Not at first, no," said Mika. "It is so easy to move things around when no one really suspects you. Vago never expected anyone else in the family to access the Anjiliac finances. Popara trusted her exclusively to carry out his will. Zonnos only cared for his own pleasures, whiling away the time until he finally controlled the family empire in name, but comfortable to let Vago continue to run the day-to-day. They were all expected to continue to play their parts. No one expected me. Or the Tempest."

"How did you find it?" asked Mander, slowly closing the gap between them. A step at a time. "The Tempest, I mean." He tried to keep his voice light and free of the Force. The Hutts were known for their resistance to Jedi mind tricks, and this one would be tougher than most.

Mika smiled, and it was clear that he saw through Mander's casual charade. He backed up a step, putting a control panel between him and the Jedi. "I was interested in our home planet. I found records of our most ancient times, speaking of its great cities and powerful families. And later, the reports of a blasted, almost airless world, exposed to the raw ravages of space. And after a time, those reports petered out. The Council of Elders still assigned patrols to the region, to keep others away, but the planet itself was considered so much dross, insufficiently profitable, a dying world spinning around a dying star."

"So you didn't come for the spice, then?" said Mander, and his eyes flicked to the various screens surrounding the Hutt. None of them showed his companions, or Vago.

"That was a happy accident," said Mika. "I was actually searching for the old droids that you found guarding the plant. I thought at the time that their designs might prove useful in the modern age. Then an employee who was an . . . aficionado . . . of a less damaging breed of spice brought his own supply here. That supply was in turn affected by the air and water of this world. He died, both the first recipient of the drug and the first victim of its effects. I had the body autopsied, of course, and in the process discovered the Tempest. After that, it was a simple matter to backtrack and confirm, then set up the plant. This was the ideal location, and the cache of ancient droids made perfect workers and protectors."

"Pity it is over now," said the Jedi.

Mika let out a deep sigh. "It does not have to be this way. You could become part of the organization. You and the others. The offer I made through Vago still stands."

"The refusal still stands," said Mander. "As does our warning. We have allies waiting for us."

"You want to help me," said Mika calmly, smiling. He passed his hand in front of him.

The emotional pressure upon Mander was immediate,

a bow wave of the Force striking him head-on, penetrating him utterly. For a moment he was taken by surprise, his own will washed away, replaced briefly with the desire to help this little Hutt—this small, strange, persecuted being, all alone in the greater universe. Despite himself, he staggered back. Part of his surprise was that he had felt the style of this mental attack before, and knew where the Hutt had learned the trick.

Mander Zuma took a deep breath and dropped into himself mentally. He embraced the Meditation of Emptiness and let the wave of outside desire pass through him.

"No," Mander said, and Mika's broad smile disappeared with the refusal. "An apprentice's mind tricks will not work on the one who taught them to him."

Mika let out a growl and said, "So you know that as well now?"

Mander nodded. "Toro Irana taught you that. He tried it on me, once, and it failed then as well."

"It was one of the few tricks I could learn," said the Hutt, and laughed. "There is a cosmic irony in being able to affect the minds of lesser beings, but then to be surrounded by servants who would jump to my very word in any event. And to then keep the company of Hutts, who are naturally resistant to its effects!"

"But Toro could not teach you much," said Mander. He made it sound like an insult.

Mika the Hutt chewed on his lower lip, and his face blanched. "Do you know what it is like? I could feel your Force. I could almost see it around me. Yes, I know that is basic to you *Jeedai,* and it is what you look for in your students. But I could not *utilize* it. I would attempt to and it would all slip away. It was like grabbing at water. I could close my fingers on it, but never hold it firmly."

"Not everyone who can use the Force is made to be a Jedi," said Mander. "There have been many disciplines in history."

Mika ignored his words. "I needed someone to train me, but I proved a poor student. I was a fish looking at animals on the dry land, or a mammal watching the birds fly. I could hear the voices of the party that I could never attend. You want to help me."

Again, he pushed hard with the Force, turning the casual request into an imperative command. Mander was ready for it this time, and batted it aside mentally, dismissing it as soon as he heard it. "And you killed Toro. You addicted him and then killed him."

"I thought he could be controlled," said the Hutt. "I know better than to try that again. For all your supposed talk of controlling your emotions, you Jedi are extremely passionate. You are an Order of believers. It became clear that Toro Irana was responding badly to my new spice, and rather than let him fall back into your hands and reveal my actions, I thought it best to take him off the board."

"You play holo-chess, then," said Mander, thinking of the board in Angela Krin's office—and her own words—all the while looking for an opening, for the Hutt to lower his guard.

Mika was silent for a moment, then said, "I dabble." He added, "I miss Toro Irana. He was a good teacher. I think that, in the end, he wanted to prove himself. To show he could have his own apprentice."

"He taught you to gather the Force to influence others," said Mander. "And to control minds."

"In a clumsy fashion," said Mika, trying to appear unthreatening. "At heart, I could not wrap my mind around your philosophy. I am afraid that a Hutt remains a Hutt."

"You used the Force on Angela Krin," said Mander.

"I was subtle," replied Mika. "Nothing major, a nudge here, a warning there. When we were talking in orbit over Endregaad, I made clear my concern about the Tempest, because I wanted to know how much the CSA would find out. After your Pantoran found the serial numbers, I knew it would be only a matter of time before they tracked it back to Skydove Freight and my family. I had to prepare. I asked her to protect me."

"Which is why she came to Nar Shaddaa, supposedly to track down the hard spice," said the Jedi. "You put the idea in her mind."

"That and more," Mika said, nodding. "I had her keep me apprised of what the CSA knew. I led her to understand what a danger I thought Vago was. Then I had planned to maneuver her into the same room with my father's counselor and let 'nature' take its course." He held his hands out in a plaintive fashion. "But you knew that."

"I am slow, but I get there eventually," said Mander. "It's why I came here by myself. There's no one else for you to manipulate. Now it is time to stand down, Mika. Your Hutt mind tricks don't work on me."

"Then I will have to try something else," said Mika. *"Killee du schoon!"*

Mander heard the sound of a lightsaber engaging and immediately thumbed the activation plate and brought his own weapon up. Even so, he was nearly bowled over by the force of the blow.

The third Twi'lek handmaiden, her skin as green as the irradiated pools outside, had leapt at him, igniting a blue-white blade as she jumped. Mander caught the weapon on his own blade. As the two blades ground against each other, the Twi'lek arched over his head, landing between the Jedi and the Hutt. She shook her Tempest-veined head-tails, and Mander noticed that they were shod in overlapping coppery plates—no vulnerability there.

She raised her blade to threaten Mander, and her eyes were a solid, deep violet from the Tempest spice. She was wielding Toro's short-hafted lightsaber. Mika's agents must have recovered it back on Makem Te, before Mander arrived.

"I could not learn to wield one of your blades," said Mika, "so I choose to employ others who can."

The Twi'lek hissed and leapt again, her blade cutting down on Mander.

Mander parried the blow, but now he was prepared, his blade steady as he brought it up. Their blades crashed with a crackling electrical static—Mander's lightsaber and Toro's cascading a series of nova bursts as they slid off each other. But Mander steered the lithe form of the Twi'lek to his right, and pushed her off as their blades parted. The Twi'lek was surprised by the move and landed badly, sliding across the bridge and into a control bank.

Such a move would have left an ordinary opponent dazed, but the handmaiden was fueled by anger and hard spice. She flipped up to her feet immediately and met Mander's own attack with a sharp strike toward the hilt, near the blade emitter. Despite himself, Mander pulled back, seeking to protect both his hand and the emitter. The Twi'lek seized that moment to press forward with a flurry of blows, Toro's former blade arching like ionized lightning in the red-hued light of the factory-ship's bridge. Mander was driven back, parrying blow after blow, but at last he caught and held his former apprentice's blade on his own. The Twi'lek tried to move past the blade, but Mander held her at bay, guiding her back to a neutral position. She would have to retreat—lessen the pressure—if she was to make another attack, and then he would have her.

"Too evenly matched," said Mika. "You have knowledge but she has rage. Perhaps I can rattle that monk-like calm that you Jedi love so much."

The Hutt pressed a couple of toggles on a console and the holoscreen changed. Instead of showing locations within the factory, they all showed the same display: the *Barabi Run*, perched on its landing cradle outside.

"Where are your friends, Jedi?" asked Mika. "You had them when you came in. Did you think to send them to safety while you tried to deal with matters by yourself?"

Mander let out a shout, but the Hutt's pudgy digits punched a button. From half a dozen directions, beams of ionic power laced through the poisoned atmosphere and struck the ship. It disappeared in a ball of flame.

Mander cried out at the sight, the image chilling him to his soul. The Twi'lek took advantage of his distraction. She jerked her head back, and then forward, arching the metal-shod tips of her head-tails above her and down onto the Jedi. One of the copper-colored tips carved a deep, hot crease along the side of Mander's face, and the pain blossomed across his cheek and ear.

He fell back from the Twi'lek, rolling as he did so and regaining his footing, buying himself time. But the Twi'lek did not pause from her assault, swinging wildly at him. He danced back, bringing his own blade up, but she beat it back, recovering in time to unleash another assault and not giving him a moment of peace. He could deflect the blows, but not return any of them, and with every assault she forced him farther back. Another two steps and she would have him against the wall, with nowhere to run.

The Twi'lek, sensing her victory, made a broad, slashing attack against Mander's stomach. He jumped back, against the wall itself, but smelled the burning of his robes as the blade passed too close to his flesh. His assailant was already recovering, bringing the crackling blade back along the same path.

Mander thought of Reen, fighting this Twi'lek earlier in the Popara's penthouse, and how easily she had dealt with her. Tempest or no, trained or not, this was the same woman with the same vulnerabilities. He ducked beneath the returning blade, and in doing so deactivated his own. He stepped into the arc of the Twi'lek's attack, after the blade had passed, and twisted the lightsaber hilt in his hand before bringing the pommel up sharply against the Twi'lek's chin.

The Twi'lek's violet eyes rolled up into her head from the shock and she pitched backward, losing her grip on the blade. The deactivated lightsaber followed the curve of her attack and flew, useless, across the room, spinning to a stop beneath one of the large holoscreens showing the burning wreckage of the *Barabi Run*.

Mander turned toward Mika, standing at the command chair of the bridge. His face stung from the Twi'lek's assault and, reaching up with his free hand, he felt something wet. His hand came away red with his own blood and fragments of plastoid. His comm had taken part of the blow, but jagged slivers of it were now piercing his flesh. He brushed the back of the bloody hand against his hair, shaking most of the splinters loose. His robes smelled of burned fabric, and his limbs ached from the fight.

Mander thumbed his lightsaber alive once more and pointed it at Mika. He stepped toward the Hutt, who did not respond, but instead smiled at the Jedi as he advanced.

"Surrender," said Mander Zuma, though in his heart he wished the Hutt would try something. Go for a weapon. Try to flee. Try to use the Force on him again. Something that would give him a reason to cut him down and avenge Toro and Reen and Angela Krin. For a brief moment he could feel an abyss of emotion and temptation yawn before him.

"It's over," he said simply.

"Not yet," said the Hutt, and his stubby hand reached down to the command console, slamming a cluster of buttons.

At once the massive engines flared to life, and the ship gave a violent jerk. Mander was unprepared as the entire cabin lurched forward, the factory-ship tearing loose of its moorings and straining upward. Outside, he could hear small explosions as final connections were jettisoned. He stumbled, dropping to one knee. Mika smiled and pressed another series of buttons on the console. The factory engaged its huge rear engines, and the ship almost cleared the lip of the crater, the rocky edge scraping along the lower fuselage as it passed.

Mander fell backward, his lightsaber flickering back to an inert state as he slammed heavily against the rear bulkhead. Dazed, the Jedi tried to bring the blade up, to reignite it and parry whatever assault the Hutt had planned, but he was too late.

Mander writhed in pain as something heavy smashed into the hand holding the lightsaber, and in his grip the Jedi could feel his weapon come apart, sharded into pieces by the weight of the blow. The hilt split beneath the impact, the emitter crystal fractured, and fragments scattered in all directions.

He had been bludgeoned by the blunt end of a heavy electrospear. Above him towered Mika the Hutt, a look of victory in his broad face.

"Now," said the Hutt. "*Now* it is over."

FALL OF THE HUTT

"I was surprised to discover how many materials in the galaxy can resist the power of a lightsaber," said Mika, leaning on the electrospear and driving its heavy hilt harder onto Mander's damaged hand. "Of course, there is a great inducement for people to discover them. This particular one is called phrik. It was rare before the war and is even rarer now. Still, there are surviving examples, which are available for a discerning collector."

Mika leaned forward, driving his weight down onto the Jedi's hand. Mander could feel cartilage grinding and bones cracking as his hand was pinned beneath the butt of the electrospear. The pieces of his lightsaber were scattered around him. Mander rolled toward the remains of his blade's housing and flung the pieces upward, hoping to catch the Hutt in his broad, taunting face.

His throw was close enough, and the weight lessened for just a moment as the Hutt pulled back in surprise. Mander pulled his injured hand out from beneath the electrospear and rolled in the other direction, away from the Hutt.

Beneath him the floor vibrated, the ancient ship now taking to the sky. The deck was tilted upward, away from him, and Mika was framed in the forward screen. Ahead of them Ardos burned with a vengeful and ineffective white fury, the other stars behind it clearly visible in its corona. The holoscreens were now all filled with static, and the bridge was a patchwork of red light broken by blue-gray bursts. The fallen form of the Twi'lek handmaiden was still slumped by one console.

Mander rose to his feet, cradling his shattered hand against his torso. He could feel the bones slide against one another, and was sure that at least three of them were broken. He wanted to concentrate, to use the Force to reach out and gather the wounded parts of himself together and assuage the pain, but there was no time.

"I really wanted you to be on my side," said Mika, stalking Mander across the bridge, slowly. "I wanted to have one of your Order working for me. It would have been an emblem of power, of control. A status symbol. I thought I had simply made a mistake with young Toro, that I had tried the wrong approach. Giving into his weaknesses, downplaying his strengths, making him need my Tempest. Need *me*. But now I see that I did as well as I could have expected. You *Jeedai*, you could never be . . ." He rolled his tongue around, searching for the right word. At last he settled on ". . . domesticated."

"We've found your base on Varl," said Mander. "Others will find it as well." He pushed the pain away and stood up straighter.

"You've inconvenienced me," said Mika. "Now I have to find another, newer methodology. Perhaps stripmining Varl's poisoned soil and setting up shop in some asteroid base, far from the normal space lanes. That would be another step in the process, and that means more people to hire and more pseudopods to grease. As I said, it is an inconvenience. Nothing more."

Mander looked around. His lightsaber was fragments and dust. The Hutt hefted the heavy-tipped electrospear and coiled up on himself, readying himself for action. Should Mander try for the exit, the Hutt would block him. Mika was preparing to charge him anyway, to rush him and overwhelm him with his bulk.

"You have been a good tool," said the Hutt. "But all tools break eventually and must be discarded." And with that the Hutt rushed him.

Mander reached out with his unwounded hand and let the Force surge through him. Ignoring the pain, ignoring Mika himself, he reached out to Toro's short-hafted lightsaber, lying sleeping and inert by the Twi'lek's collapsed form.

He pulled the hilt toward him.

It was in his hand in an instant, and the blade leapt from its emitter at the first touch. He caught Mika's phrik spear in his assault, and felt the energy blade try to bite into the silvery metal, to cleave it in two. But the electrospear was too resilient, and the best Mander could do was bat the weapon away, dancing from the momentum of Mika's bulk.

Mika staggered backward and again coiled on himself, his tail pulled under his body. "Good," said the Hutt. "I would have been disappointed if you had just let me kill you."

Across the room, Mander swayed on the shuddering deck. He felt odd and out of place here, far from his records on Yavin 4, bearing a strange weapon wielded in the wrong hand. He could not feel half of his face. He *could* feel his wounded hand all too well. Yet Mander cleared his mind and said simply, "As I said before, Mika, it is over."

Mander leapt forward himself now, with a fluid grace that caught Mika unaware. The Hutt brought up the electrospear to block his assault, but Mander beat his way past it, aiming a blow at the Hutt's triangular head. Mika dodged the blow, but only just; the lightsaber left a burning crease along one side of the Hutt's face, from the corner of his mouth to his small ear.

Mander landed to one side, his feet firmly planted, finally sure of himself. He circled the tip of his blade at the Hutt, daring him to charge.

Mika's eyes flashed with anger, but only for a moment, and Mander could see Toro's training in the Hutt. A burst of hot anger, then tamping it down, bringing his rage under control, planning for the next move.

The Hutt lunged, his full weight behind his assault, using the heavy shaft of the electrospear as a staff. Mander fell back in firm, careful steps, letting the Hutt's torrential assault pound with futile effect against a series of precise parries. As he fought, Mander felt the defenses with Toro's blade come to him more easily, and his deflections were now sure and steady. The shortened hilt made such parries easier than with his own blade.

And Mika's maneuvers were familiar. Mander had seen them before, on Yavin 4, training his apprentice.

Mika the Hutt was sweating, his skin glistening with a thin slime. He had sparred with Toro, yes, but Mander's apprentice had never taken the Hutt to his limits. Mander danced to one side, dodged a precise stab, and was up again. He feinted to the other side of the Hutt's face, and Mika brought up his weapon in a panicked countermove to avoid another scorching wound.

Mika made a heavy overhand smash with the electrospear and Mander caught it with a steering block, catching the blow with his own blade. Against a normal foe this would stalemate the fight, but the Hutt used his weight and size to his advantage, leaning forward and pressing Mander both backward and downward.

The Jedi felt his knees start to buckle, and knew he could not throw Mika back nor steer the blow aside. Instead he pulled backward on himself, retreating less than a step, a sudden break from the assault.

Mander was gambling that Toro had not taught Mika this trick, the one that Mander had used the final time they dueled. Mander was right. The Hutt tumbled forward with a surprised cry, and Mander had the blade up again, aiming for the soft knuckles on the Hutt's right hand, where Mika had gripped the electrospear.

The Hutt let out a shriek of pain as Toro's lightsaber bit deeply into his fingers, and he fell back, the phrik electrospear clattering to the floor. Mika held up his ruined hand, the dark blood already cauterized and crusted on the stumps of his fingers. Anger burned in the Hutt's eyes, an anger deeper than any Tempest-inspired rage.

Mika cursed and with his good hand funneled the Force, fueled by that sense of wounded rage, against Mander Zuma. The blow of energy caught the Jedi square in the midsection, and Mander sprawled backward. The unfamiliar lightsaber, wielded in the wrong hand, flew from his stunned grip . . .

. . . and into the hand of Mika the Hutt, retrieved by the Force. "I've been a fool," said the Hutt. "I should have *made* the Pantoran *Jeedai* teach me the ways of this weapon."

Mander rolled out of the way as the Hutt tried to use the lightsaber like a club—a heavy, unpracticed attack that did nothing but leave a deep gouge where the Jedi had been moments before. Mander jumped to his feet and lashed out a wicked kick against the Hutt's midsection. He did not remember enough Hutt biology to understand where it landed, but Mika howled in pain and brought Toro's blade around again.

And a blaster bolt caromed off the Hutt's rubbery hide.

Screaming, Mika wheeled, and Mander saw that Reen Irana was gripping the side of the canted control room doorway, a smoking blaster carbine in her hand.

"I knew I shouldn't have left you alone," she shouted, leveling another shot at the Hutt.

Mika was fast now, moving like a serpent, closing the

distance between him and the Pantoran, the lightsaber burning in his good hand like a torch. Reen fired a few wild shots at the Hutt, and then disappeared out the doorway. Mika wheeled again to take care of Mander before pursuing the smaller prey.

When the Hutt turned, he saw Mander with the electrospear, cradled against his wounded side, charging point-first. Mika did not have time to bring the lightsaber up as the Jedi slammed into him, driving the spear through the Hutt's body and into the bulkhead beyond it. The Hutt's eyes widened in fear and what Mander thought for a moment was indignation. The lightsaber died and dropped from the Hutt's nerveless fingers. Mika tried to speak, but the only thing in his mouth was blood.

Mander Zuma dropped to his knees next to the Hutt, pinned to the wall like an insect in a collection. Reen reappeared, kneeling beside him.

"You look horrible," she said, and touched the bloody scar along Mander's face.

"You should see the other guy," said Mander, and nodded at the Hutt. He tried to manage a laugh, but found he could not. All he could manage was a deep wheeze.

"We have to go," she said.

"We just need to get control of the ship," said Mander. "Put her in a steady orbit and contact the *New Ambition*. We should be all right."

"No," said Reen, putting a hand on his shoulder, "we have to go *now*. We couldn't fight our way out to the *Barabi Run,* so we retreated to the engineering deck. When the engines started, Angela and I threw the cutoff switches. We thought we could stop it from taking off, but we weren't quick enough. We did manage to sabotage the main drive, though, and here's the thing: we're not going to reach escape velocity."

Mander blinked, realizing that the deep rumble of the ship was missing now, and had disappeared sometime during the fight. He looked up at the main screen and saw that they were no longer pointed at Ardos and the stars. Instead Varl's bulk was rising in their path. The spice factory that was really a ship was not a ship at all anymore.

It was a projectile launched from the planet, now falling back to its point of origin.

"Vago knew about an escape pod. Can you make it?" asked Reen. She was already under Mander's shoulder, helping him up. Mander shook her off gently and cleared his mind. *Push down the pain. Push down the hurt. For just a little longer.* He swayed a bit as Reen separated from him and moved around the damaged bridge. Probably trying to figure out if something could be done on this end, Mander thought. Probably determining it was too late.

"I'm okay," he said after a few heartbeats. "Let's go."

"Jeedai," said Mika the Hutt, pinioned to the wall, his voice bubbling with blood.

Reen and Mander looked at each other. The Hutt was still alive.

"Take me with you," Mika said. "I will come quietly. You win."

Mander almost took a step toward the Hutt, but realized the familiar feeling in the base of his brain. A quiet, reassuring voice saying, *The Hutt is harmless, the Hutt is weak.*

Why be afraid of the small Hutt?

Even at the last, Mika was trying to use the Force to influence them.

Reen said, "We can't just leave him."

Mander shook his head. "You go into the hall," he said. "I will follow."

"But . . ."

"He's doing to you what he did to Angela Krin." Reen looked at him, surprised and shocked, and then fled the control room.

"I can be useful to you," said the Hutt, his eyes filmy and unfocused now. "A good craftsman keeps good tools."

Mander shook his head, dispelling the fantasies that Mika's voice put there. The Jedi leaned in close to the dying Hutt.

"That's where you went wrong in the first place," Mander said. "We aren't tools." And he, too, left the bridge, Varl now huge in the main viewscreen. Behind him Mander could hear Mika bellowing in pain and frustration.

Reen and the others had been busy earlier, while he had been on the bridge. The catwalks were blackened with blasterfire, and large rents had been furrowed into the bulkheads. Pipes of Varl fluid were shattered and spewing over decks, reducing them to slick pools. Droid chassis were scattered everywhere, and what asp droids were still functional were flailing about at the limitations of their programming, some trying to reactivate the ship's systems, others trying to contain the spills of semi-refined Tempest, and still others continuing to move containers from one place to another. Mander and Reen encountered one of the ancient war droids, now damaged and walking in a circle, one leg shattered and useless, its weapons depowered.

The pair arrived where the escape pod was supposed to be, but only found Angela Krin pulling herself off the deck. Of the escape pod or the adviser to the Anjiliac clan there was no sign.

"After you left," she said, "Vago slammed me into a wall and took the pod." She shook her head. "I'm an idiot."

"Yes," Reen said. "Yes you are. And I'd like to remind everyone about what I told them about trusting a Hutt."

Angela's eyes were slightly unfocused, and Mander realized that Vago had hit her hard. "We tried to raise you by the comm," she said, then her eyes tightened and she saw Mander's wounds. "What happened?"

"Bad things, but better now," said Reen, tapping on her own comm. "Time to go to plan B. Eddey, where are you?"

The handheld communications unit crackled and Eddey Be'ray's voice chirped through the static, "I had to duck a Hutt patrol ship or two. My ETA is about seven minutes."

"Make it three if you can," said Reen. "We're flying a rock right now, and it's going to crash very, very soon."

Four long minutes later Eddey positioned the *New Ambition* alongside the stricken ship-turned-factory and unspooled an umbilical between the two. Angela Krin went first, then Mander, and Reen brought up the rear, helping the Jedi when he stumbled. Varl loomed below them, the thin atmosphere already warming up the hull of the stricken ship.

"All on board," shouted Reen, sealing the door and jettisoning the umbilical bridge.

"Hold on to something," shouted Eddey. "We're already very low and very fast." Even with the warnings, the three had to grab their seats as the Bothan pulled the ship out of its steep dive. Varl, which was filling the forward viewport, moved slowly out of their way. A white streak against the dead world showed the path of Mika's ship—and the trajectory of the Hutt's ambition.

Mander slumped into a chair and surrendered to the darkness. As unconsciousness took him, he still thought he heard the screams of Mika the Hutt, burning in the thin atmosphere as his ancestors' home planet rushed up to embrace him.

NEW MANAGEMENT

"Mighty Vago, may her wisdom never ebb, will see you now," said the newly polished jade-green H-3PO unit at the doorway. If it recognized Mander Zuma from previous encounters, it gave no sign. The door irised open behind it.

They were aboard the *Imru Ootmian,* perched on the borders of Hutt space. Off the port bow hung the heavy presence of the *Resolute,* about as close to the Hutt worlds as it could be without creating a diplomatic incident. After the action over Varl, Mander was sure that Lieutenant Commander Angela Krin had every weapon aboard trained on Vago and the Hutt's luxury yacht.

Mander Zuma flexed his fingers as he followed the droid into the audience chamber. His wounded hand had mostly healed, but he still felt a dull pain when he made a fist. He resolved to avoid making a fist.

The room was as before, yet different. The three alcoves were still there, but only the central one was apparently in use. Nikto guards were present, but no Wookiees or Twi'lek servants now. The only other beings present were several other gleaming H-3POs, and they all looked like they had just been uncrated.

In the center of the room was a holographic projection of a burial shrine, probably on Nal Hutta. It showed a great vault cut into the mountainside, overshadowed by a hulking statue of Popara Anjiliac. In the fore-

ground, surrounded by Hutt mourners, were three ban-
daged ovoid forms readied for internment: one large,
one of medium size, and one that seemed too small for a
Hutt.

Mander knew that only the middle-sized form contained a real body, that of Zonnos. Of Popara there was
only enough to load into a burial effigy, and Mika's
ashes were haunting the poisoned atmosphere of Varl.

Vago said, *"Gon kodowin pumba mallin,"* and the
droid on her flank immediately translated it to "Your
efforts were sufficient." Vago knew that Mander understood her, but let the droid translate anyway.

"It is good to see that the Hutt patrol ships found
your escape pod," said Mander, keeping his tone light
and level. "We could not remain long to ascertain your
safety."

Vago the Hutt let out a rolling belch, and the droid
was not far behind with the translation into Basic:
"Mighty Vago has no regrets for her opportune depar-
ture. She states that it was imperative that one of our
group survive to report back. Your status was unknown,
and the others would not leave without you."

"The lieutenant commander wishes to convey that she
holds no harsh feelings for your actions," lied Mander,
but he followed it with a truth. "She is more concerned
with the status of the Tempest trade."

"The Tempest trade is no more," said Vago, through
the droid. "The Hutt Council of Elders has been informed only that unscrupulous individuals have been
landing on our blessed original homeworld. The council
has appreciated the notification and is reevaluating its
security measures, replacing certain officers, and redou-
bling its patrols."

Mander bowed slightly. "But the knowledge of Tempest manufacture still exists."

"Only a few know of the full matter," replied Vago.

"All others have been silenced, one way or another." She nodded at the droid, who blissfully translated without understanding that its own memory had been wiped. "A CSA officer, two spacers, and a *Jeedai*."

"And you," said Mander.

It was the Hutt's turn to bow slightly. "One who is indebted to Mighty Popara Anjiliac Diresto, and one who would not think of doing anything that would blacken his name or weaken his family's power."

Mander blinked at the mention of Popara's full name. Almost all carried that final personal name to the grave. A Hutt identified with three names was dead, or legendary. Popara was both.

"Still, the Tempest is out there," said the Jedi. "It exists on half a hundred worlds."

"In ever-diminishing amounts. The Spice Lord . . ." Vago paused here, and Mander saw that the Hutt—loyal to the Anjiliac clan to the last—could not use Mika's name with his crimes, even now. "The Spice Lord was already very effective in covering most of his tracks. His efforts were sufficient in that particular matter. Officially . . ." Here again she paused, such that the droid waited for her to resume, which she did after a beat. "In the family histories, it will be simply stated that Young Mika discovered and eradicated the founders of the Tempest trade, though at the cost of his own life."

"Which is true, so far as it goes," said Mander.

"Popara leaves a legacy of honesty," said Vago. "I intend to preserve that legacy."

"There will be a lot of Tempest addicts going into withdrawal," said Mander.

Vago gave a rippling shrug that cascaded the length of her body. "There may be other types of spice. Spice that is less pleasing, perhaps, but less damaging to the user and to the social fabric."

"Spice that the Anjiliac family would be willing to deal in," said Mander. He was greeted with another shrug.

"Mighty Popara, may his name ever be venerated, was happy to aid others," said Vago through her droid. "Wise Vago sees no point in deviating from this sage practice."

"Wise Vago faces a great challenge," observed Mander. "While the holdings of the Anjiliac clan are extensive, it has lost not just its leader, but that leader's two official heirs. The logical remaining choice to take control will have a tough road ahead of her, and the last thing such a leader would need would be others investigating a renewed trade in hard spice."

Vago was silent for a moment, then unleashed a passionate string of verbiage, translated again by the droid: "Wise Vago sees that your interests parallel with her own. There will be no resumption of the Tempest trade, and those who seek to do so will be rebuffed. In addition, as a show of kindness, the aid to the addicts will be made at cost. No profit will be taken."

"Our interests parallel each other," agreed Mander, and bowed slightly. "Unless the Tempest spice reappears, we have no reason for our paths to cross again."

"Agreed," said Vago and held up a hand to silence the droid. In Huttese she said, "Now if you will excuse me, I have a commercial empire to rebuild." And with that the audience was over, and the droid motioned for Mander to accompany it. The Jedi stepped out of the audience room, and had one last glimpse of Vago the Hutt. She was looking at the holo of the funeral of her adopted family, and Mander could not discern the emotions behind her dispassionate face. Then the droid irised the door shut and the Hutt was gone.

The shuttle returned Mander to the *Resolute* and he was escorted by Lieutenant Lockerbee to the landing bay where the *New Ambition* was being prepped for takeoff. Droids and support crew were detaching the last of the hoses. Eddey was visible in the ship's cockpit, going over a final checklist on his datapad. Reen came up to the Jedi.

"The lieutenant commander says we're supposed to drop you wherever you want," she said. "Where would that be?"

Mander looked around. "Yavin Four, I suppose," he said, though the prospect of returning to the Jedi Archives seemed to pale slightly.

"Thought as much," said Reen. "Course already laid in. We're just waiting for you."

"I'm surprised," said Mander, then looked at Reen and started again. "I thought that the lieutenant commander would be here to see us off."

"She's been busy ever since we got back," said Reen, a smirk on her face. "I think she saw herself as being in control, being the one pulling the strings. It came as a bit of a shock to discover that she was the puppet and not the master. I don't think she trusts Hutts that much anymore."

"Or Jedi," said Mander.

"Or Jedi," repeated Reen, and the two looked out over the sprawling shuttle bay. The last of the support droids pulled away from the ship.

Reen let out a deep sigh and said, "I salvaged something from Mika's factory-ship," she said, "when you were talking to him, at the end. I was thinking of keeping it myself, but I think you're going to have better use for it." She reached beneath her cloak and pulled out Toro's lightsaber. She held it out, pommel-first, to the Jedi.

Mander looked at it for a long heartbeat, and then reached out. His injured hand closed around the short-ened grip, and it felt like he was shaking hands with an old friend. He hefted it aloft, thumbed the activator switch, and the blade sprang from the emitter. He flicked it easily from side to side, and it was as if the blade were an extension of himself.

"How's it feel?" asked Reen. Up in the cockpit, Eddey impatiently motioned for them to come aboard.

Mander thought for a moment, then said, "Good. It feels very good."

Read on for an excerpt from
Star Wars™: X-Wing: Mercy Kill
by Aaron Allston
Coming soon from Arrow Books

Imperial Admiral Kosh Teradoc paused—irritated and self-conscious—just outside the entryway into the club. His garment, a tradesman's jumpsuit, was authentic, bought at a used-clothes stall in a poverty-stricken neighborhood. And the wig that covered his military-cut blond hair with a mop of lank, disarrayed brown hair was perfect. But his *posture*—he couldn't seem to shake off his upright military bearing, no matter how hard he tried. Loosening his shoulders, slumping, slouching . . . nothing worked for more than a few seconds.

"You're doing fine, Admiral." That was one of his bodyguards, whispering. "Try . . . try *smiling*."

Teradoc forced his mouth into a smile and held it that way. He took the final step up to the doors; they slid aside, emitting a wash of warmer air and the sounds of voices, music, clinking glasses.

He and his guards moved into the club's waiting area. Its dark walls were decorated with holos advertising various brands of drinks; the moving images promised romance, social success, and wealth to patrons wise enough to choose the correct beverage. And they promised these things to nonhumans as well as humans.

One of Teradoc's guards, taller and more fit than he

was, but dressed like him, kept close. The other three held back as though they constituted a different party of patrons.

The seater approached. A brown Chadra-Fan woman who stood only as tall as Teradoc's waist, she wore a gold hostess' gown, floor-length but exposing quite a lot of glossy fur.

Teradoc held up three fingers. He enunciated slowly so she would understand. "Another will be coming. Another man, joining us. You understand?"

Her mouth turned up in the faintest of smiles. "I do." Her voice was light, sweet, and perhaps just a touch mocking. "Are you the party joining Captain Hachat?"

"Um . . . yes."

"He's already here. This way, please." She turned and led them through broad, open double doors into the main room.

Teradoc followed. He felt heat in his cheeks. The little Chadra-Fan—had she actually *condescended* to him? He wondered if he should arrange an appropriate punishment for her.

The main room was cavernous, most of its innumerable tables occupied even at this late hour. As they worked their way across, everything became worse for Teradoc. The music and the din of conversation were louder. And the smells—less than a quarter of the patrons were human. Teradoc saw horned Devaronians, furry Bothans, diminutive Sullustans, enormous, green-skinned Gamorreans, and more, and he fancied he could smell every one of them. And their alcohol.

"You're upright again, sir. You might try slouching."

Teradoc growled at his guard but complied.

There was one last blast of music from the upraised stage, and then the band, most of them nonhuman, rose to the crowd's applause. They retreated behind the stage curtain.

Moments later, the noise of the audience, hundreds of voices, changed—lowered, became expectant in tone. A new act filed out onstage. Six Gamorrean men, dressed in nothing but loincloths, their skin oiled and gleaming, moved out and arrayed themselves in a chevron-shaped formation. Recorded dance music, heavy on drums and woodwinds, blasted out from the stage's sound system.

The Gamorreans began moving to the music. They flexed, shimmied, strutted in unison. A shrill cry of appreciation rose from Gamorrean women in the audience, and from others, as well.

Teradoc shuddered and vowed to sit with his back to the stage.

Then they were at their table, only a few meters from the stage. A human man sat there already. Of medium height and muscular, he was young, with waist-length red hair in a braid. Costume jewelry, polished copper inset with black stones, was woven into the braid. He wore a long-sleeved tunic decorated with blobs of color of every hue, mismatched and discordant; it clashed with his military-style black pants and boots. He stood as Teradoc and his guard arrived.

"Captain Hachat?"

"The one and only." Hachat sat again and indicated the guard. "Who's your friend? He looks like a hundred kilos of preserved meat."

The Chadra-Fan seater, satisfied that she had discharged her duty, offered a little bow. "Your server will be here in a few moments." She turned and headed back to her station.

Teradoc glared after her and seated himself, facing away from the stage. He waited until his guard was in a chair before continuing. "Your messenger hinted at names. I want to hear them now . . . and to see proof."

Hachat nodded. "Of course. But, first—would it help you to stop smiling? It looks like it's hurting your face."

"Um . . . yes." Teradoc relaxed, realized that his cheek muscles were indeed aching. He glanced around, noted the postures of many of the patrons around him, and slid down a little in his chair to match their slouches.

"Much better." Hachat sipped his drink, a poisonous-looking yellow concoction that glowed from within. There were two glasses, mostly empty but with a similar-looking residue at the bottom on the table. "All right. I run a private space naval operation specializing in covert operations, especially retrievals."

Teradoc suppressed a sigh. *Why can't they ever just say, "I'm a pirate, a smuggler, a low-life piece of scum with something to sell?" Honesty would be so refreshing.*

"We recently found a prize vessel . . . one whose value could enable us to retire in luxury."

Teradoc shrugged. "Go on."

"The Palace of Piethet Brighteyes."

"I *thought* that was what your messenger was hinting at. But it's preposterous. In the centuries since it disappeared, the Palace has never been sighted, never reported. It will never be found."

Hachat grinned at him. "But it has been. Abandoned, intact, unplundered, in an area of your sector well away from settlements or trade routes."

"If you'd found it, you'd be selling off its jewels, its furnishings, all those paintings. Through a fence. Yet you come to me. You're lying."

"Here's the truth, Admiral. The vessel's antipersonnel defenses are still active. I lost a dozen men just getting into a secondary vehicle bay, where I retrieved one artifact and some lesser gems. Oh, yes, I could fire missiles at the palace until it cracked . . . but I would prefer to lose half its contents to a worthwhile partner than to explosions and hard vacuum. At least I'd get a partner and some good will out of it."

Teradoc rubbed at his temple. The *boom-boom-boom*

from the sound system on stage behind him was giving him a headache. He returned his attention to Hachat. "Don't use my rank. Don't speak my name here."

"Whatever you want." Hachat took another sip of his drink. "You have access to Imperial Intelligence resources, the best slicers and intrusion experts in the galaxy. They could get past those defenses . . . and make us both rich."

"In your original message and tonight, you mentioned an artifact."

"I have it with me. A show of faith, just as you proposed."

"Show me."

"Tell your bruiser not to panic; I'm only reaching for a comlink."

Teradoc glanced at his guard, gave a slight nod.

Hachat pulled free a small device clipped to his shirt collar and pressed a button on the side. "All right. It's coming."

They didn't have to wait long. A meter-tall Sullustan male in the blue-and-cream livery of the club's servers approached, awkwardly carrying a gray flimsiplast box nearly as tall as himself and half as wide and deep. He set it on the table beside Hachat's empty glasses. Hachat tipped him with a credcoin and the Sullustan withdrew.

Teradoc glanced at his guard. The man stood, pulled open the box's top flaps, and reached in. He lifted out a glittering, gleaming, translucent statuette, nearly the full height of the box, and set it down in the center of the table. Hachat took the empty box and set it on the floor behind his chair.

The statuette was in the form of a human male standing atop a short pedestal. He was young, with aristocratic features, wearing a knee-length robe of classical design. And it was all made of gemstones cunningly fitted together like jigsaw puzzle pieces, the joins so artful that Teradoc could barely detect them.

All the color in the piece came from the stones used to make it. Cloudy diamond-like gems provided the white skin of the face, neck, arms, and legs. Ruby-like stones gave the eyes a red gleam. The robe was sapphire-blue, and the man's golden-yellow hair, unless Teradoc guessed incorrectly, was inlaid rows of multicolored crystals. The pedestal was the only portion not translucent; it was made up of glossy black stones.

The piece was exquisite. Teradoc felt his heart begin to race.

There were *oohs* and *aahs* from surrounding tables. Teradoc noted belatedly that he and Hachat were now the object of much attention from patrons around them.

Hachat grinned at the onlookers and raised his voice to be heard over the music. "I have a cargo bay full of these. They go on sale tomorrow in Statz Market. Twelve Imperial credits for a little one, thirty for a big one like this. Stop by tomorrow." Then he turned his attention back to Teradoc.

The admiral gave him a little smile, a real one. "Thus you convince them that this piece is valueless, so no one will attack us outside in an attempt to steal it."

"Thus I do. Now, are *you* convinced?"

"Almost." Teradoc reached up for his own comlink, activated it, and spoke into it. "Send Cheems."

Hachat frowned at him. "Who's Cheems?"

"Someone who can make this arrangement come true. Without him, there is no deal."

A moment later, two men approached. One was another of Teradoc's artificially scruffy guards. The other was human, his skin fair, his hair and beard dark with some signs of graying. He was lean, well-dressed in a suit. Despite the formality of his garments, the man seemed far more comfortable in this environment than Teradoc or the guards.

His duty done, the escort turned and moved to a distant table. At Teradoc's gesture, the man in the suit seated himself between the admiral and Hachat.

A server arrived. She was a dark-skinned human woman, dressed, like the Sullustan man had been, in a loose-fitting pantsuit of blue and cream. Her fitness and her broad smile were very much to Teradoc's taste.

She played that smile across each of them in turn. "Drinks, gentlemen?"

Hachat shook his head. The man in the suit and the guard did likewise. But Teradoc gave the server a smile in return. "A salty gaffer, please."

"You want a real bug in that or a candy bug?"

"Candy, please."

Once the server was gone, Hachat gave the new arrival a look. "Who is this?"

The man spoke, his voice dry and thin. "I am Mulus Cheems. I am a scientist specializing in crystalline materials . . . and a historian in the field of jewelry."

Teradoc cleared his throat. "Less talk, more action."

Cheems sighed. Then from a coat pocket, he retrieved a small device. It was a gray square, six centimeters on a side, one centimeter thick. He pressed a small button on one side.

A square lens popped out from within the device. A bright light shone from the base of the lens. Words began scrolling in red across a small black screen inset just above the button.

Cheems leaned over to peer at the statuette, holding the lens before his right eye. He spoke as if to an apprentice. "The jewels used to fabricate this piece are valuable but not unusual. These could have been acquired on a variety of worlds at any time in the last several centuries. But the technique . . . definitely Vilivian. His workshop, maybe his own hand."

Teradoc frowned. "Who?"

"Vilivian. A Hapan gemwright whose intricately fitted

gems enjoyed a brief but influential vogue a few centuries back. His financial records indicated several sales to Piethet Brighteyes." Cheems moved the lens up from the statuette's chest to his face. "Interesting. Adegan crystals for the red eyes. And the coating that maintains the piece's structural integrity . . . not a polymer. Microfused diamond dust. No longer employed because of costs compared to polymers. Beautiful, absolutely beautiful." He sat back and, with a press of the button, snapped the lens back into its casing.

Teradoc felt a flash of impatience. "Well?"

"Well? Oh—is it authentic? Yes. Absolutely. I believe it's the piece titled *Light and Dark*. Worth a Moff's ransom."

Teradoc sat back and stared at the statuette. The Palace of Piethet Brighteyes—with that fortune in hand, he could resign his commission, buy an entire planetary system, and settle into a life of luxury, far away from the struggles between the Empire and the New Republic. A warmth began to suffuse his body, a realization that his future had just become very, very pleasant.

The dark-skinned server returned and set Teradoc's drink before him. He smiled at her and paid with a credcoin worth twenty times the cost of the drink. He could afford to be generous. "Keep it."

"Thank you, sir." She swept the coin away to some unknown pocket and withdrew—but not too far. It was clear to Teradoc that she was hovering in case he needed special attention.

Teradoc glanced back at Hachat. "I'm convinced."

"Excellent." Hachat extended a hand. "Partners."

"Well . . . we need to negotiate our percentages. I was thinking that I'd take a hundred percent."

Hachat withdrew his hand. Far from looking surprised or offended, he smiled. "Do you Imperial officer types study the same 'How to Backstab' manual? You are definitely doing it by the book."

"Captain, you're going to experience quite a lot of enhanced interrogation in the near future. You'll endure a lot of pain before cracking and telling me where the palace is. If you choose to antagonize me, I might just double that pain."

"What I don't get . . ." Hatchat said, shaking his head wonderingly, ". . . is this whole Grand Admiral Thrawn thing. Every hopped-up junior naval officer tries to be like him. Elegant, inscrutable . . . and an art lover. Being an art lover doesn't make you a genius, you know."

"That's an extra week of torture right there."

"Plus, unlike Thrawn, you're about as impressive as a Gungan with his underwear full of stinging insects."

"Three weeks. And at this moment, my guard has a blaster leveled at your gut under the table."

"Oh, my." Hachat glanced at the guard. He raised his hands to either side of his face, indicating surrender. "*Pleeeeease* don't shoot me, foul-smelling man. Please, oh please, oh pleasepleaseplease."

Teradoc stared at him, perplexed.

On stage, the porcine Gamorrean dancers moved through a new rotation, which brought the slenderest of them up to the forward position. He was slender only by Gamorrean standards, weighing in at a touch under 150 kilos, but he moved well and there were good muscles to be glimpsed under his body fat.

With the rest of the troupe, he executed a half-turn, which left them facing the rear of the stage, and followed up with a series of fanny shakes, each accompanied by a lateral hop. Then they began a slow turn back toward the crowd, the movement accentuated by a series of belly rolls that had the Gamorrean women in the crowd yelling.

As, with a final belly roll, he once again faced forward, the slenderest dancer could see Hachat's table . . . and Hachat with his hands up.

He felt a touch of lightheadedness as adrenaline hit his system. Things were a go.

Near Hachat's table, the dark-skinned server moved unobtrusively toward Teradoc.

The Gamorrean dancer, whose name was Piggy, stopped his dance, threw back his head, and shrilled a few words in the Gamorrean tongue: "It's a raid! Run!"

From elsewhere in the room, the cry was repeated in Basic and other languages. Piggy noted approvingly that the fidelity of those shouts was so good that few people, if any, would realize they were recordings.

Alarm rippled in an instant through the crowd, through the dancers.

Suddenly all the Gamorreans in the place were heaving themselves to their feet, sometimes knocking their table over in panicky haste, and the non-Gamorrean patrons followed suit. Confused, Teradoc took his attention from Hachat for a moment and turned to look across the sea of tables.

There were *booms* from the room's two side exits. Both doors blew in, blasted off their rails by what had to have been shaped charges. Tall men in Imperial Navy special forces armor charged in through those doors.

A flash of motion to Teradoc's right drew his attention. He saw the dark-skinned server approach and lash out in a perfectly executed side kick. Her sandaled foot snaked in just beneath the tabletop. Even over the tumult in the room, Teradoc heard the *crack* that had to be his guard's hand or wrist breaking. The guard's blaster pistol flew from his hand, thumped into Teradoc's side, and fell to the floor.

The server stayed balanced on her planted foot, cocked her kicking leg again, and lashed out once more, this time connecting with the guard's jaw as he turned to look at her. The guard wobbled and slid from his chair.

Then the server dived in the opposite direction, rolling as she hit the floor, vanishing out of Teradoc's sight under the next table.

Teradoc grabbed for the blaster on the floor. He got it in his hand.

Hachat hadn't lost his smile. He turned to face the glasses on the table and shouted directly at them: "Boom boy!"

One of the drink glasses, mostly empty, erupted in thick yellow smoke. Teradoc, as he straightened and brought the blaster up, found himself engulfed in a haze that smelled of alcohol and more bitter chemicals. It stung his eyes. Now he could not see as far as the other side of the table.

He stood and warily circled the table . . . and, by touch, found only empty chairs. Hachat was gone. Cheems was gone.

The statuette was still there. Teradoc grabbed it, then stumbled away from the table, out from within the choking smoke.

While the dancers and patrons ran, Piggy stood motionless on stage and narrated. He subvocalized into his throat implant, which rendered his squealy, grunty Gamorrean pronunciation into comprehensible Basic. The implant also transmitted his words over a specific comm frequency. "Guards at tables twelve and forty maintaining discipline and scanning for targets. But they've got none. Shalla, stay low, table forty's looking in your direction."

Small voices buzzed in the tiny comm receiver in his ear. "Heard that, Piggy." "Got twelve, twelve is down." "Forty's in my sights."

Now the guard who had brought Cheems to Teradoc approached that table once more. This time he had a blaster pistol in one hand. With his free hand, he shoved patrons out of his way. He reached the verge of the yellow smoke, then began circling around it, looking for targets.

He found some. His head snapped over to the right. Piggy glanced in that direction and saw Hachat and Cheems almost at the ruined doorway in the wall. The guard raised his pistol, waiting for a clear shot.

Well, it was time to go anyway. Piggy ran the three steps to the stage's edge and hurled himself forward. He cleared the nearest table and came down on Teradoc's guard, smashing him to the floor, breaking the man's bones. The guard's blaster skidded across the floor and was lost, masked by yellow smoke and patrons' fast-moving legs.

Piggy stood. He'd felt the impact, too, but had been prepared for it; and he was well padded by muscle and fat. Nothing in him had broken. He looked at the guard and was satisfied that the unconscious man posed no more danger.

Now he heard Hachat's voice across the comm. "We have the package. Extract. Call in when you get to the exit."

Most of the bar patrons, those who weren't running in blind panic, were surging toward and through the bar's main entrance, which inexplicably had no Imperial Navy troopers near it. Piggy turned toward the exit Hachat and Cheems had used. That doorway did have a forbidding-looking Imperial trooper standing beside it. Heedless of the danger posed by the soldier, Piggy shoved his way through toppled furniture and scrambling patrons. He made it to the door.

The armored trooper merely nodded at him. "Nice moves, Dancer Boy."

Piggy growled at him, then passed through the door, which still smoked from the charge that had breached it.

Once in the dimly lit service corridor beyond, Piggy headed toward the building's rear service exit. "Piggy exiting." He reached the door at the end of the corridor. It slid open for him and he stepped outside into cooler night air.

"Freeze or I'll shoot!" The bellow came from just beside his right ear. It was deep, male, ferocious.

Piggy winced, held up his hands. Unarmed and nearly naked, his eyes not yet adjusted to the nighttime darkness, he didn't stand a chance.

Then his assailant chuckled. "Got you again."

Piggy turned, glaring.

Situated by the door, armed not with a blaster but with a bandolier of grenades, stood a humanoid, tall as but not nearly as hairy as a Wookiee. The individual was lean for his two-meters-plus height, brown-furred, his face long, his big square teeth bared in a triumphant smile. He wore a black traveler's robe; it gapped to show the brown jumpsuit and bandolier beneath.

Piggy reached up to grab and tug at the speaker's whiskers. "Not funny, Runt."

"Plenty funny."

"I'll get you for that."

"You keep saying that. It never happens."

Piggy sighed and released his friend. His eyes were now more adjusted. In the gloom, decorated with distant lights like a continuation of the starfield above, he could make out the start of the marina's dock, the glow-rods outlining old-fashioned watercraft in their berths, not far away.

Much nearer was the team's extraction vehicle, an old airspeeder—a flat-bed model with oversized repulsors and motivators. It was active, floating a meter above the ground on motivator thrust. Signs on the sides of its cab proclaimed it to be a tug, the sort sent out to rescue the watercraft of the rich and hapless when their own moti-

vators conked out. There were sturdy winches affixed in
the bed.

In the cab, a Devaronian man sat at the pilot's controls. He turned his horned head and flashed Piggy a
sharp-toothed smile through the rear viewport. Cheems
and Hachat were already situated in the cab beside him.

Piggy moved up to the speeder and clambered into the
cargo bed. The vehicle rocked a little under his weight.
He looked around for the bundle that should have been
waiting for him, but it was nowhere to be seen. He
sighed and sat facing the rear, his back to the cab. Then
he stared at the club's back door, at Runt situated beside
it. "Come on, come on."

The door slid open long enough to admit the dark-
skinned server. Unmolested by Runt, she ran to the airspeeder, vaulted into the bed, and settled down beside
Piggy. "Shalla exited." She glanced at Piggy. "Weren't
you supposed to have a robe here?"

He knew his reply sounded long-suffering. "Yes. And
who took it? Who decided to leave me almost naked
here as I wait? I'm betting I'll never know."

Shalla nodded, clearly used to the ways of her comrades. "You made yourself a lot of fans tonight. Those
Gamorrean ladies were screaming their brains out. And
not just the Gamorreans. You could have had so much
action this evening."

Piggy rolled his eyes. As far as he was concerned,
those Gamorrean women had no brains to scream out.
Augmented by biological experiments when he was a
child, Piggy was the only genius of his kind. And unlike
some, he could not bear the thought of pairing up with
someone whose intelligence was far, far below his.

So he was alone.

Hachat turned to glare back through the cab's rear
viewport. "Kell . . ."

Piggy heard the man's response in his ear. "Busy, Boss."

"Kell, do I have to come in there after you?"

"Busy." Then the door slid open for Kell, the armored trooper who had let Piggy pass. He fell through the doorway, slamming to the ground on his back, one of Teradoc's guards on top of him.

Runt reached down, grabbed the guard by the shoulder and neck, and pulled, peeling the man off as though he were the unresisting rind of a fruit. Hent shook the guard, and kept shaking him as Kell rose and trotted to the speeder.

By the time Kell was settling in beside Shalla, the guard was completely limp. Runt dropped him and regarded him quizzically for a second. Then he pulled two grenades free from his bandolier. He twisted a dial on each, then stepped over to stand in front of the door. When it slid open for him, he lobbed them through the doorway. He waited there as they detonated, making little noise but filling the corridor entirely with thick black smoke. Then he joined the others, settling in at the rear of the speeder bed, facing Piggy. "Runt exited. Team One complete."

Cheems expected them to blast their way as far as possible from the Imperial Navy base and the city that surrounded it. But they flew only a few hundred meters along the marina boundary. Then they abandoned their speeder in a dark, grassy field just outside the marina gates and hurried on foot along old-fashioned wooden docks. Soon afterward, they boarded a long, elegant water yacht in gleaming Imperial-style white.

Within a few minutes, they had backed the yacht out of its berth, maneuvered it into the broad waters of the bay, and set a course for the open sea beyond.

Eight in all, they assembled on the stern deck, which was decorated with comfortable, weather-resistant furnishings, a bar, and a grill. Cheems sat on a puffy chair and watched, bewildered, as his rescuers continued their high-energy preparations.

The Devaronian, whom the others called Elassar, broke top-grade bantha steaks out of a cold locker and began arraying them on the grill. Piggy the Gamorrean located and donned a white robe, then began mixing drinks. Kell shed his armor, dumping it and his Imperial weapons over the side. Hachat disappeared below decks for two minutes and reemerged, his hair now short and brown, his clothes innocuous. Runt shed his traveler's robe and set up a small but expensive-looking portable computer array on an end table. A yellow-skinned human man who had not been on the speeder joined Kell and stripped off his own Imperial armor, throwing it overboard. Shalla merely stretched out on a lounge chair and smiled as she watched the men work.

Cheems finally worked up the courage to speak. "Um . . . excuse me . . . not that I'm complaining . . . but could I get some sort of summary on what just happened?"

Hachat grinned and settled onto a couch beside Cheems's chair. "My name isn't Hachat. It's Garik Loran. Captain Loran, New Republic Intelligence. Runt, do you have the tracker signal yet?"

"Working on it."

"Put it up on the main monitor, superimpose the local map."

No less confused, Cheems interrupted. "Garik Loran? *Face* Loran, the boy actor?"

Face did not quite suppress a wince. "That was a long time ago. But yes."

"I love *The Life Day Murders*. I have a copy on my datapad."

"Yeah . . . Anyway, what do you think this was all about?"

"Getting me out of the Admiral's hands, I suppose." Cheems frowned, reconstructing the sequence of events in his mind. "Two days ago, as I was being led from my laboratory to my prison quarters, I felt a nasty sting in my back. I assume you shot me with some sort of communications device. Little buzzy voices vibrating in my shoulder blade."

Face nodded. He gestured toward the man with yellow skin. "That's Bettin. He's our sniper and exotic-weapons expert. He tagged you from a distance of nearly a kilometer, which was as close as we could get to you."

Bettin waved, cheerful. "Damned hard shot, too. Cross-wind, low-mass package. Piggy was my spotter. I had to rely pretty heavily on his skills at calculation."

"Yes, yes." Face sounded impatient. "So, anyway, that was step one. Getting in contact with you."

Cheems considered. "And step two was telling me that I was going to be called on to authenticate an artifact, and that I absolutely had to do that, regardless of what I was looking at."

Face nodded.

"What *was* I looking at? The material had a crystalline structure, definitely, but it wasn't diamond or any other precious stone. In fact, it looked a bit like crystallized anthracite."

Kell, standing at the bar, grinned at Cheems. No longer concealed by his helmet, his features were fair, very handsome. His blond hair was worn in a buzz cut, retreating from a widow's peak. "Very good. It's a modified form of anthracite in a crystallized form."

"So I was within centimeters of ten kilos of high explosive?" Cheems thought he could feel the blood draining from his head.

"Nearer fifteen. Plus a transceiver, power unit, and some control chips in the base." Kell shrugged, accepted a drink from Piggy.

Cheems shook his head. "And I was passing it off as a work of art!"

Kell stared at him, clearly miffed. "It *was* a work of art."

Face caught Cheems's attention again. "Teradoc's habits and methods are well known to Intelligence. We had to have bait that required a gem expert to authenticate; we had to have a sneaky profit motive so Teradoc would bring you off-base to do the authentication; and we had to have the bait be very valuable so when trouble erupted he'd grab it and run."

"Back to his base." Cheems felt a chill grip him. "Back to his most secure area, where his treasures are stored. His personal vault."

Face gave him a now-you-get-it smile. "Which is where, exactly?"

"Directly beneath his secure research-and-development laboratories."

"Where, if Intelligence is right, his people are experimenting with plague viruses, self-replicating nonbiological toxins, and the project for which Teradoc kidnapped *you,* Doctor Cheems."

"A sonic device. The idea was that sound waves pitched and cycling correctly could resonate with lightsaber crystals, shattering them."

For once, Face looked concerned. "Could it actually work?"

Cheems shook his head. "Not in a practical way. Against exposed crystals, yes. But lightsaber hilts insulate the crystals too effectively. I couldn't tell the admiral that, though. To tell him 'This can't work' would basically be to say, 'Kill me now, please, I'm of no more use to you.'" Belatedly Cheems realized that he'd said too much. If this miracle rescue was itself a scam, if he was currently surrounded by *Imperial* Intelligence operatives, he'd just signed his own execution order. He gulped.

Runt turned to Face. "I have it." He repositioned the main monitor at his table so others could see.

The monitor showed an overhead map view of the planet's capital city, its Imperial Navy base, the huge bay that bordered both to the east. A blinking yellow light was stationary deep within the base. Then, as they watched, the light faded to nothingness.

Cheems glanced at Face. "Did your device just fail?"

Face shook his head. "No. It was taken into a secure area where comm signals can't penetrate. Its internal circuitry, some of which is a planetary positioning system, knows where it is—the research-and-development labs. Atmospheric pressure meters are telling it how deep in the ground it is. At the depth of Teradoc's personal vault, well . . ."

There was a distant rumble from the west, not even a *boom*. Everyone looked in that direction. There was nothing to see other than the city lights for a moment, then spotlights sprang to life all across the naval base, sweeping across the nighttime sky.

Faraway alarms began to howl.

Face settled back into the couch, comfortable. "Right now, the lower portions of the labs have been vaporized. Pathogen vaults and viral reactors have been breached. Sensors are detecting dangerous pathogens escaping into the air. Vents are slamming shut and sealing, automated decontamination measures are activating. Before the decontamination safety measures are done, everything in that site will be burned to ash and chemically sterilized. Sadly, I suspect Teradoc isn't experiencing any of that, as he was doubtless admiring his new prize when it went off. But we owe him a debt of gratitude. He saved us months' worth of work by smuggling our bomb past his own base security all by himself."

Cheems looked at Piggy. "I could use something very tall and very potent to drink."

Piggy flashed his tusks in a Gamorrean smile. "Coming up."

Face turned to Piggy. "I'll have a salty gaffer. In Teradoc's honor. Candy bug, please." He returned his attention to Cheems. "We'd like you to do one more thing before we get you off-world and into New Republic space. I'd appreciate it if you'd go below and appraise any gemstone items you find. We'll be turning this yacht and everything on it over to a resistance cell; I'd like to be able to point them at the more valuable items."

Cheems frowned. "This isn't your yacht?"

"Oh, no. It's Teradoc's. We stole it."